Prepare for a visit to Ponca City, Oklahoma. This comfortable, interesting, and growing community in the north central region of the state, known for its Native American heritage and prominent role in the history of petroleum production, is disturbed by a report that one of its citizens, an aircraft mechanic, allegedly has been abducted by space aliens. Is this a fact or is it a flight of this old man's imagination, fueled by a helping of his favorite bourbon? This incident, ordinarily one that would quickly fade into the category of a quaint urban legend, becomes an unexpected source of fear and tension for the senior residents of this quiet city, evolving into a national crisis that demands personal involvement and action by the President of the United States. In response to demands by a frightened population, the Department of Homeland Security calls upon one of America's foremost aerospace companies to design and construct a vehicle that can track and identify an extraterrestrial spaceship known to only one man. This vehicle must also be capable of counteracting any insidious intrusion. This is the story of how the executives and engineers of this premier supplier of propulsion systems meet the challenge. Working with limited configuration and performance information about this interplanetary threat on which to base a design, the company builds and prepares to launch a rocket-propelled airship that will fulfill the mission to save America and the world. But do the aliens really exist and, if so, what are their intentions?

THE
INTERCEPTOR
PROGRAM

Also by William Vietinghoff

This Island Santa Susana

The Moon by June

THE INTERCEPTOR PROGRAM

The Motion Picture That Reveals America's Aerospace Industry at Its Finest

Written, Produced and Directed
By
William Vietinghoff

A Verigood FILMS Production

Writers Annex™
Thousand Oaks, California

For information contact the publisher at
willvee@writersannex.com

ISBN-13: 978-0692294420
ISBN-10: 0692294422

Library of Congress Control Number: 2014955439

Book design by Writers Annex™
Cover design by Writers Annex™

First Edition 2014

10 9 8 7 6 5 4 3 2 1 Liftoff

To Willa, who understands these things

To Gladys, who said "Keep on working."

Acknowledgements

The adventures depicted in this book, although fanciful, relate to the encounters and labors of hundreds of real people, many in the aerospace profession. Of those that played a part there are too many to remember and too many have passed on. Some who have traveled this road, who pick up this book, may see themselves. The events all grew from a pinch of reality; but if the re-telling has taken too many liberties, please attribute those deviations to age, faulty memory, and a little impishness.

The author wishes it be known that many people provided the assistance, information, knowledge, resources, or inspiration that made possible the preparation of this book. Some assisted in the mechanics of getting ink on paper. The gift of others may have been simply an off-hand remark, the expression of an attitude, or the recounting of a memory from their days on the job in the rocket business. Some listed might consider their contribution small, and some may be totally unaware that they had any part in the success of this project, but thanks must be paid to all including: Larry Belfer, Cy Bruno, John Costello, Glenn Dickinson, Vonnie Douglas, Anita Gallardo, Mary Gonzales, Bill Haigler, Tom Handler, Ed Klodt, John Marzec, Charlie McKeon, Ken Choromanski, George Morgan, Donna Myers, Mike Plato, Al Porter, Kim Rener, Al Rolland, Kamara Sams, Aaron Shephard, Steve Spencer, Tim Taylor, Mary Ellen Vetter, and C. W. Wooster.

THE SCREENPLAY

The film opens to black. Ever so dimly, points of light appear: stars. These grow in number and intensity. The screen is soon filled with them, and the audience is confronted with a breath-taking view of a starry firmament* and the vastness of space. Following the credits, and overlaid on the image of the universe appear words in large, yellow block letters:

PROJECT "BLUE BOOK," THE LAST PHASE
OF A 21-YEAR STUDY OF UFO REPORTS BY
THE UNITED STATES AIR FORCE,
WAS TERMINATED ON DECEMBER 17, 1969

THE AIR FORCE REACHED THE CONCLUSION THAT
NO UFO INVESTIGATED IN THIS STUDY
REPRESENTED AN ADVANCED TECHNOLOGY,
PROVIDED EVIDENCE OF EXTRATERRESTRIAL ORIGINS,
OR THREATENED NATIONAL SECURITY

EXTERIOR. OKLAHOMA RURAL AREA. MORNING

A small, light-colored van speeds down an otherwise deserted two-lane road that cuts through flat countryside. Ahead, reflecting the bright sun, are the hangars of a small aircraft landing strip. Small private planes sit on the aprons in front of the hangars; one rolls along the ground in the process of taking off. A sign appears reading EAGLES' REST AIRPORT. The van makes a sharp right turn onto the unpaved entry road leading to the airstrip, throwing dust and gravel about.

*Producer's note: See if there is some cheap starry firmament footage left over from old Superman movies we can get our hands on.

The vehicle is a mobile television unit. On its roof a large, dusty, yellowing dish antenna wobbles as the van bounces about. Painted on the side is the identification: KPUT – CHANNEL 5 – PONCA CITY'S MOST POWERFUL. WE BRING YOU THE NEWS AND THE NEWEST.

CUT TO: CAB OF VAN

LEANNE FLAMBEAU, news reporter, sits in the van's cab on the passenger side next to DURWOOD PYLE, her camera operator. Leanne is the newsperson assigned to this event.

She is diminutive; her brunette hair is long in back with bangs in front. She is wearing a much-tailored outfit consisting of a white blouse tied at the neck with a bright burgundy bow, a black jacket and skirt of black fabric too heavy for the warm autumn. Leanne is job-focused, but always on the lookout for opportunities for advancement.

Durwood is dressed very casually. His short-sleeve khaki shirt matches his cargo pants. His gray hair hangs a little over his ears, and is very long in back. Except for a modest goatee, his face is clean-shaven. He thinks about his work in very practical terms. He is more experienced than Leanne, but lets her have her way.

> LEANNE (*looking about anxiously*): Keep your eyes peeled, Woody. I want to get to this guy before anyone else does.

> DURWOOD (*keeping his eyes on the road*): Who would want to? What other channel would send a crew thirty-five miles to interview some nut who claims he was abducted by aliens? I thought we didn't do those anymore?

> LEANNE (*excitedly*): Look! That must be him – that guy in the coveralls standing by the table just outside the green hangar.

CUT TO: HANGER 3 AREA

The van brakes briskly next to hangar 3. Leanne jumps from the cab, and trots in her high-heeled shoes over to ORVILLE PRESSFIT, aircraft mechanic, who is bending over a workbench, studying a piece of engine hardware. He is wearing loose-fitting, dark blue coveralls. Orville is sixty-two, but has a young, plump face. He is amiable, mechanically-minded, and fascinated by aircraft devices.

> LEANNE: Excuse me, sir. Are you mister Pressfit?

> ORVILLE: That's *me*. And you must be the lady I talked to at the TV station.

> LEANNE: Yes, I'm Leanne Flambeau, and I'm here to get the story about your adventure. Have you talked to anyone else about what happened?

> ORVILLE: *Nope*. No one seems interested.

Leanne nods in satisfaction and walks around the table peering at the miscellaneous aircraft engine parts spread around. She discovers an empty pint whiskey bottle standing next to a shot glass. She picks up the bottle, sniffs it, and replaces it with an expression of distaste.

Durwood, during this time, has opened the van and is removing equipment. He lugs his camera, an armload of cable, and a microphone over to Orville and Leanne by the table. Durwood holds his video camera up to his eye and hands Leanne the microphone. Leanne looks down at it in horror.

> LEANNE: The station letters! The station letters!

Durwood reaches into his pants pocket and hands Leanne the mic flag, a plastic, boxy part that has KPUT printed on four sides. She slides it onto the microphone. She smoothes her hair, adjusts her skirt, pulls slightly at her jacket, and holds the microphone up like a chalice raised for a toast.

> LEANNE: How do I look?

Durwood gives her a thumbs-up.

> LEANNE: Woody, notify the station we're here, all set up, and ready to go live.

Durwood punches some numbers on his cellular phone. There is a pause and he begins talking. There is a longer pause and he raises his camera to his eye, listening at the same time to his cell phone.

> DURWOOD: Looks good. Go!

INTERIOR. DEPT. STORE/TELEVISION SALES. MORNING

ANNA and HAROLD VERSERY stand before a bank of fifty television sets of various makes. The sets, arranged like blocks in a massive wall, are all tuned to the same news channel, KPUT.

Harold, who is seventy-two, is wearing shorts, a gray jacket, and a gray bucket hat to cover his small bald spot. He has an activist personality and is stirred up by current issues. If he were twenty years younger, he would run for mayor of Ponca City. He takes his eyeglasses from the breast pocket of his jacket and slides them on.

Anna, seventy-one, has on one of the better dresses she saves for shopping. A white sweater is thrown over her shoulders. She is impressionable, sympathetic, easily frightened, and loves to watch television.

The couple looks up and down and from side to side at the splash of images, comparing picture quality.

RAY KATHODE, one of the department's more aggressive sales associates, makes tiny steps toward the elderly couple. He is smartly dressed and has a diamond stickpin in his necktie. He is middle-aged and constantly jaded by his job, but he wants to set a sales record, so he practices radiating enthusiasm.

> RAY (*with warmth*): May I point out for you folks some of the features on the new sets we just got in?

ANNA: We're looking for something that has a picture in a picture.

RAY (*more warmth*): We have a new set for this year that just arrived. It has nine tuners, and you can get nine channels simultaneously. Can I turn it on for you?

Ray's sales pitch is interrupted by the image of Leanne Flambeau on the fifty TV sets that tower over him, Harold, and Anna. Leanne's WORDS BOOM out over the department. Everyone stops talking and shopping to watch and listen.

CLOSE ON TV SCREEN

The screen shows Leanne standing next to Orville. She is looking at the camera with a very sober expression.

LEANNE: I am here with Orville Pressfit, an aircraft mechanic at the Eagle's Nest airport. Mister Pressfit reported to our station – exclusively – that he had been abducted by space aliens last night. Please describe for our viewers, mister Pressfit, exactly what happened.

Leanne turns and faces Orville. She holds the microphone near his mouth.

ORVILLE: I was working here late when the alien ship came over. It was about nine p.m. and the landing strip was officially closed. I was finishing up replacing some spark plugs in that Cessna over there when this huge round dome – I guess you'd call it that – landed. Right there!

The TV camera moves away from Orville to show the area on the apron to which he is pointing. There is nothing to see.

ORVILLE (*off-screen*): A hatch opened, and three aliens came out and walked up to me. They watched what I was doing for a few minutes, looked into some kind of book, and said a couple of words. It sounded like English, but I couldn't understand. One grabbed my shoulder, pointed at the open hatch in the dome, and pulled me toward it.

The TV camera pans back to Leanne and Orville.

LEANNE: Would you describe these creatures as small, with bulbous heads, and large, dark, ovoid eyes? You know – the appearance we've heard described by previous abductees.

ORVILLE: Shoot! I wouldn't call them creatures. And no, they didn't have bulbs for heads, and they didn't have dark avoiding eyes. They looked straight at me. They were just guys! They looked like you and me. Well, not like you.

BACK TO SCENE

Anna, Harold, Ray, and dozens of other shoppers in the department store stare up at the bank of television sets, aghast.

ANNA: Oh, my God, Harold! We've got aliens right here in Ponca City.

HAROLD: I'm not surprised. I've heard other stories about strange goings-on in this area. Remember how missus Tipple called you about the lights over her shed last week? The police and the Feds keep saying they're either all hoaxes or airliners. Well, I think its just part of a national conspiracy to hide the truth.

CLOSE ON TV SCREEN

Leanne's expression on the TV screen turns even grimmer.

LEANNE: I realize this next question may be difficult for you to answer, mister Pressfit. As you know, victims like yourself have reported terrible treatment at the hands of these invaders from other planets. You stated the aliens had you as their prisoner in their spacecraft for many hours. You were probably injected with some mind-fogging drug. Do you recall them putting you through any intense anatomical examinations, subjecting you to weird medical experiments, and (*she looks down, hesitates, and speaks haltingly*) perhaps abusing you in some other way?

ORVILLE: Miss Flambeau, I can truthfully say they didn't inject me with anything. As a matter of fact, they gave me a rum and cola drink. I'll be darned where they got it. They spent all the time I was up there flying around trying to get me to understand some of their words and showing me schematic drawings and pieces of their equipment.

Leanne shuts her eyes and moves her head slowly side-to-side as a show of distress.

LEANNE: That was an inappropriate question for me to ask at this time. We appreciate that the trauma that this encounter of the third kind has induced in you makes recalling those moments of torture very painful. But we thank you, mister Pressfit, for allowing us to talk to you, and we, in Ponca City, hope these gruesome memories will soon fade. This is Leanne Flambeau, Channel Five, reporting to you live from Eagle's Nest Landing Strip, returning you to our main studios.

BACK TO SCENE

The scene on the television screens above the hypnotized audience in the department store has changed to an insurance commercial, but there remains an uneasy silence. Anna raises her hand to her forehead.

ANNA: Oh, my God. That poor man!

HAROLD (*angrily*): When is the government going to do something to protect us from these aliens? I'm going to write my Congressman, or the newspaper, or somebody!

RAY: Wait. We don't know if this guy is on the up and up. I heard on the radio this morning that he likes to take a nip now and then. The garbage truck probably came by when he was plastered, and the driver offered him a ride home.

That's what happened. Didn't you see the empty whiskey bottle on the table in that shot showing his tools?

Anna and Harold walk away, shaking their heads, ignoring Ray.

EXT. EAGLES' REST AIRPORT. MORNING

Durwood Pyle is coiling up his cable and stowing his camera in the back of the van. Leanne removes her jacket, places it on a clothes hangar, and carefully puts it on a hook in the cab. Durwood walks up to Leanne and leans against the van.

DURWOOD: When you signed off just now, you referred to this landing strip as the "Eagle's Nest." The correct name is "Eagles' Rest." "Eagle's Nest," Leanne, was the name of Hitler's mountaintop chalet in Berchtesgaden.

LEANNE (*standing stock still, placing hand on forehead*): Well, the News Director is probably out playing golf and didn't see it. With my luck his wife was watching me and will call him later. I don't think he likes me, Woody. Why else would he give me these stupid assignments?

DURWOOD: We've had some good ones. And remember, he hand-picked you to work the KPUT booth at the Century of Oil Exploration festival.

LEANNE: It doesn't matter. I'm not comfortable in this job. Did I tell you I received an offer from another station?

DURWOOD: Are you going to take it? Where is it?

LEANNE: KPOW . . . Channel three in Las Cruces. I'm thinking hard about taking them up on it. They offered me a fifteen per cent salary increase. What's more, I'll be far away from these idiots and their UFO nonsense. Did you know I have to work overtime this evening to host a panel discussing whether aliens really exist? And then tomorrow I'm supposed to cover some kind of a UFO protest rally at City Hall. The senior citizen groups in Ponca City, including the one this guy Pressfit belongs to, are up in arms. I've had it!

Leanne and Durwood climb into the cab. The van rumbles back onto the highway and disappears in the distance.

INT. PONCA CITY. TELEVISION STATION KPUT. EVENING

Four people are seated in cheaply upholstered chairs along a small oval coffee table of simulated marble in front of a simulated fireplace facing the camera in the interview set at the television station. Leanne Flambeau sits at the table's extreme right. At her right is SAMUEL BIGSTAFF, Mayor of Ponca City. Seated in the middle is JUSTIN CASE, Ponca City Police Chief. At the extreme left is DR. CLARENCE PEER, college professor.

Durwood Pyle stands behind the camera, his eyes fixed on the image of the group in the viewfinder; his hand turns a crank on the camera dolly.

Justin runs his hand down the front of his uniform, smoothing the fabric. Clarence adjusts his necktie.

> LEANNE: I want to thank you all for coming. We'll be on air in a couple of minutes, but relax for now. You'll know you're being seen when I announce the show, and the little red tally light over the lens goes on. See, over there.

Leanne points to the camera. She taps Samuel on the arm to get his attention.

Samuel is fifty; He has a squat face with fleshy cheeks and chin and heavy eyebrows. He is wearing a suit, but he has taken his tie off. He looks from side to side, evaluating the panelists. He is practical-minded and a mature thinker. He has devoted his interests to civic matters. He wants Ponca City to be attractive to tourists.

> SAMUEL: I've watched this show many times at home, Leanne. I never thought I'd be sitting here.

LEANNE: Well, this is a very serious matter, as you know, Mayor Bigstaff. The people of this city are looking to you to "clear the air" about this so-called space alien crisis.

SAMUEL: Don't you usually serve coffee to guests?

LEANNE: Woody! Do we have any coffee in the back?

Durwood slides off his headset; he hangs it over a handle on the dolly and exits the studio.

LEANNE (*waving a sheaf of papers at the guests*): Right after you were called with the invitation to speak today, we emailed you this set of questions I will be asking. I hope you each had time to prepare your comments.

Leanne notices that Justin has removed a sheet of paper from his inside pocket and is studying it.

Justin is fifty-five and is wearing his police uniform. He sits quiet, expressionless. Chief Case has a reputation as a no-nonsense, dedicated public servant. He runs a tight ship and does not look for notoriety. He only seeks recognition that the people in his department are doing a good job.

JUSTIN: Will this broadcast be seen nationwide?

LEANNE: I'm told that many stations in the large cities will be picking up our feed. So, whatever you say will be heard by people in New York, Chicago, and Los Angeles – not just Ponca City.

CLARENCE (*fiddling with notes*): Oh, good!

Durwood returns with a tray with four steaming coffee cups and a bowl with sugar and creamer packets. He sets it down on the table in front of the guests. He takes up his position at the camera and waves at Leanne.

ANGLE ON LEANNE

> LEANNE (*looking at the camera sprightly*): Good evening to our viewers in Ponca City and across the country. Welcome to KPUT and Night News. Sitting with us tonight is a special group of prominent members of our community who will provide some insight into the reality of a report about aliens from space, a story that that is growing as it spreads, and, I might add, (*with raised eyebrows*) creating a bit of hysteria along the way.

Leanne gestures toward the people at the table. The television camera targets Leanne and moves from person to person, capturing the smiling face of each guest as she announces them.

> LEANNE: This evening we have with us the Mayor of Ponca City, Sam Bigstaff; Police Chief, Justin Case; and Doctor Clarence Peer, Professor of Cosmology in the Homer L. Dodge Department of Physics and Astronomy at the University of Oklahoma. Fortunately, Doctor Peer was vacationing and visiting his mother in Ponca City when all this excitement occurred – which allows him to be here for this interview. I understand that at this very moment his mother, Paula, is sitting in front of a television set in the Entertainment Room at the Ponca Pines Retirement Village, watching this program.

BACK TO SCENE

Leanne gestures toward Clarence.

> LEANNE: I'm going to start my questioning with Doctor Peer. Is it probable or even possible, Doctor Peer, that there is life in other parts of the universe, life similar to humans, like us? If so, where could these "persons" be from, and how could they get here?

Clarence is a thin, balding man. He is wearing a light tan jacket with elbow pads, a gift he received on his forty-ninth birthday last week. His thoughts and his words reflect a fascination with the mysteries of the universe that began in childhood. From time to time he looks down, furrows his brow, and purses his lips. Clarence waves at the camera. His lips form the words "Hello, mother."

CLARENCE: Well, Leanne, you've posed several and, I might say, difficult questions. First you asked, "Is life possible in other places in the universe?" Well, first of all, the universe is very big and we can't see all of it. But we do know that NASA scientists reported in two thousand ten that their mission to Mars revealed the likely presence there of a form of pond scum.

LEANNE: Pond scum?

CLARENCE: Yes, freshwater algae – the building block of life.

LEANNE: I was asking if there might be big organisms, with arms and legs – you know – that look like people.

CLARENCE: No, they didn't see anything like that on Mars.

LEANNE (*looking down at notes*): What about people on some of the other planets?

CLARENCE: Well, the other planets in our solar system wouldn't be very livable for anyone like us. (*holds up his stack of note papers*) I can give you the surface temperatures of the other planets so you can understand how unlikely it would be to find anyone surviving there.

LEANNE: Please don't, Doctor Peer. I'll take your word for it.

CLARENCE: Now I suppose you're going to ask me if there might be habitable planets in other star systems in our own galaxy, the Milky Way.

LEANNE: Actually, I wasn't.

CLARENCE (*persisting*): I'm sure your viewers would like to know *this* fact. Within the Milky Way the nearest star to earth is Alpha Centauri. And even though I use the word "nearest" I have to add that it's still four point thirty-seven light-years away.

LEANNE: I take it that means it's a lot of miles from here.

CLARENCE: Oh, lots of miles! Even if the alleged intruders had a craft that traveled at the speed of light, it would still take them almost four and a half years to get here.

LEANNE: Maybe they're not in any great rush.

CLARENCE: I said that we only know about a *neighboring* star. Computer simulations indicate a planet that orbits Alpha Centauri is possible, but we've never seen one.

LEANNE: I recently heard about the discovery of something called "exoplanets." What are they?

CLARENCE: Oh, you must have read my recent article in the Astronomy and Astrophysics Journal.

LEANNE: I don't get that one. I read about these planets in some magazine at the salon where I get my nails done.

Clarence searches through his attaché case.

CLARENCE: I fortunately happen to have a copy of the Journal with me. I can read my article for your viewers.

LEANNE: I think our viewers would rather hear a short summary.

CLARENCE: The Kepler mission has sent data that indicates there are more than a thousand possible candidates for planets outside our solar system.

LEANNE: What does mister Kepler think about that?

CLARENCE: Oh, he's long gone. The name refers to the Kepler telescope that is circling the sun, looking at stars far away. About fifty-four of the planets are in the Goldilocks range.

LEANNE: You mean near a planet called "Goldilocks"?

CLARENCE: No, that means the fifty-four planets are just the right distance from a star – not too cold, not too hot. They could have life, but we don't have any proof. Besides, they're all five hundred to three thousand light-years away.

LEANNE: Could people come here from another galaxy?

CLARENCE: The next closest galaxy is Andromeda, but it is two and a half million light-years away.

LEANNE: What if they had a really, really fast spaceship?

CLARENCE: I don't think anyone there could make a trip of that distance to earth. They would have to have a really, really advanced technology. Think about this: we are barely able to have a functioning unmanned vehicle leave our own solar system.

LEANNE: Well, Doctor Peer, what you're saying sounds like you don't think anyone from another planet came here to abduct mister Pressfit.

CLARENCE: That's right, Leanne. I don't see how that would be possible.

Leanne turns to Justin Case.

LEANNE: Captain Case, what have you found out that might indicate this reported visit* by aliens really happened?

*Director's note: Shouldn't this word be "visitation"? It sounds more ominous.

JUSTIN (*holding up folder*): I have with me a report by two of my patrolmen based on their questioning of the man who allegedly was abducted, Oral Freshpit.

LEANNE: You mean Orville Pressfit?

JUSTIN: Excuse me. Yes, Pressfit.

LEANNE: What does the report say?

JUSTIN: We received a phone call about eleven p.m. from the airport. It was mister Pressfit. Our dispatcher said he seemed quite upset. We sent out two patrolmen. When they arrived, they found him sitting outside a hangar on a stool. They noticed he had the strong odor of rum on his breath. They didn't administer a Breathalyzer test however. (*chuckling*) He wasn't driving. However, I've directed my men to do that if this happens again.

LEANNE: What else did mister Pressfit tell the officers?

JUSTIN: He told them he had been carried off by some men in their spaceship. The officers noted that he seemed disoriented.

LEANNE: Disoriented?

JUSTIN: He rambled on a lot about how the men – or whatever they were – questioned him, but he was so incoherent that the officers weren't able to transcribe a complete story.

LEANNE: Could the persons that mister Pressfit claims accosted him have been burglars who came to pilfer aircraft parts, burglars who were surprised by his presence that late at night? Could they have locked him in their car while they robbed the place? Maybe he just *thought* he was in a spaceship.

Justin looks down at the papers in his hands.

JUSTIN: The report says that there was no evidence of theft; no vandalism, and, I might add, there were no traces or marks in the surrounding area to indicate a craft with rocket engines had landed there, if that's what the aliens came in. Everyone else at the airfield had gone home for the night, so there was no one to corroborate his story – or, for that matter, to state that there *wasn't* a landing.

LEANNE: When I interviewed mister Pressfit at the airfield for our morning news show, I saw an empty whiskey bottle on his workbench. The report you quote states there was the odor of rum. Could that be an error?

JUSTIN: I'll stick with the report. I'm sure my officers have enough personal experience with alcoholic beverages not to mistake whiskey for rum. (*acting flustered*) Perhaps I phrased that wrong. You know what I mean.

LEANNE: What is your opinion, then, about this event, Chief Case?

JUSTIN: We'll never know how mister Pressfit spent the hours before my men arrived or his frame of mind. He could very well have had a few relaxing swigs after the day's work, took a little nap, and drifted off into a very vivid dream. (*pauses and tilts head in questioning movement*) Based on the report and the circumstances I don't think we have to worry about any alien threat. (*smiles*)

LEANNE: In the future will your department be more on the alert for similar sightings and be more prepared to deal with them? For example, would it be expedient to establish and assign a special police unit to visit the airport area on a routine basis?

JUSTIN: Yes, it would, Leanne, as long as there is a question of public safety here. But unfortunately, as you know and the citizens of Ponca City know, our Mayor, Sam Bigstaff, has repeatedly ignored my requests for additional budget to fill positions for officers we lack.

LEANNE: Well that is an important but touchy issue that we should not attempt to resolve this evening, Chief Case. Perhaps we can address that topic in a future broadcast.

Leanne gestures toward Samuel.

LEANNE: Mayor Bigstaff, what is your take on this whole "creatures from another planet" gossip?

ANGLE ON SAMUEL AND LEANNE

The mayor frowns and shakes his head in disbelief.

SAMUEL: I'm troubled by the way this story of an invasion from space is being circulated, causing undue fear, before the full evaluation of what you've heard this evening has been issued. By the way, I must say this in response to Chief Case's earlier statement that the Mayor's office is purposely withholding funds. I simply don't think there is a need for an increase in the number of officers we have out on the streets watching over our community. The crime report for this year proves Chief Case's department is doing a satisfactory job with his current complement of officers. Besides, a single, unverified sighting does not justify putting more patrol cars on the road.

LEANNE: What then is *your* evaluation, Mayor Bigstaff? What is your message to the people of Ponca City and to America?

The mayor points to Clarence, who nods and smiles.

SAMUEL: Consider the information we've just heard, Leanne. Doctor Peer explained why there is no place in the universe we know of where people like us could live, a place close enough for them to make the trip here.

The mayor then points at Justin.

SAMUEL: Chief Case explained that his officers found mister Pressfit to be slightly, shall we say, under the influence, but otherwise safe and sound. The conclusion is obvious, Leanne. Ponca City has not been visited by extraterrestrial astronauts!

Leanne displays a relaxed smile.

LEANNE: Thank you for setting the record straight, Mayor Sam. That concludes our program for this evening. Remember you heard it first on Night News.

BACK TO SCENE

The panelists turn to each other and shake hands, bidding each other a "good evening."

INT. SOONER STATE SENIOR CENTER. MORNING

Dozens of elderly people, mostly women, are seated at long rows of tables, chatting, sipping coffee, and picking at plates of scrambled eggs with their forks.

Harold Versery stands before the front table, holding the opened front page of a newspaper over his head, displaying it to the members of the Sunrise Seniors Club who are attending a breakfast meeting.

CLOSE ON FRONT PAGE OF PONCA POST

The banner reads: MAYOR DECLARES NO ALIEN THREAT.
CUT TO: HAROLD AND DINERS AT TABLE

Harold turns from left to right so that all may see the large letters that stretch across the page he is holding. His expression is one of concern; the muscles of his face are tight.

HAROLD: Most of you have heard or seen the reports on the kidnapping by the aliens on Monday evening. Well, this is our city's response: do nothing!

One of the diners, OCTAVIA GENARIAN, puts her coffee cup down, takes the paper from Harold, and studies the front page.

Octavia has never told anyone her age, but the consensus at the Seniors Club is that she is eighty-one. She is sensible and good-natured, but longs for excitement. Her usual smile has changed to a frown. She runs her thin fingers through bluish-white locks that protrude from a cap she wears.

The woman to her right is EVITA AÑEJO. Evita is a little more bent over than Octavia, but her dark hair and large black rimmed glasses disguise her eighty years. Evita is fun-loving and always seeks companionship.

Evita punches Octavia's shoulder.

> EVITA (*in a whisper*): Go ahead. Ask him!
>
> OCTAVIA: Harold, how serious a threat do you think this is?
>
> HAROLD: Very serious! We haven't the slightest idea as to how many of those alien spacecraft are out there, and we know even less about how many of these creatures have possibly infiltrated our community.
>
> OCTAVIA: This is the first time anything like this has happened here in northern Oklahoma. Why don't we wait and see if there are future problems? I'm surprised they could find Ponca City.

Her voice breaks up with laughter. She turns to look at Evita who begins laughing and covering her mouth with her hands.

> HAROLD: You won't be laughing if you wake up in the middle of the night to see a little green man bending over you.
>
> OCTAVIA: Maybe so. I was hoping for one of the tall, tan ones.

Octavia and Evita begin laughing again, even more hysterically.

OCTAVIA (*excitedly*): On the subject of tall, tan creatures isn't this is the day Raul, our podiatrist, is coming to trim our toe nails?

EVITA (*holding her temples*): Oh, Chihuahua! You're right.

OCTAVIA: He's really handsome.

EVITA: And gentle.

OCTAVIA (*looking down*): This blouse has food stains. Let's go change.

Octavia and Evita push back from the table, pull themselves up clumsily, and hurry from the dining room.

EXT. PONCA CITY. CITY HALL. DAY

A crowd of about fifty people, mostly elderly women, has formed in the Centennial Plaza in front of the city hall. Some of the women are waving placards on flat sticks; some are resting their placards on the walk and are leaning on them.

The placards read: "SEND THE ALIENS HOME," "KEEP OUR SKIES SAFE," "OKLAHOMA FOR OKLAHOMANS," and "WHERE WILL THEY STRIKE NEXT?" The only man with a placard is raising and lowering it to gain attention.

A single police officer stands in front of the crowd with his arms outstretched, pushing them back. One of the women is shaking her fist at the officer.

INT. PONCA CITY. MAYOR'S OFFICE. DAY

WENDELL REAM, the City Manager for Ponca City, stands before the window that looks upon the Centennial Plaza. He pushes aside the blinds that obscure his view. He is a big man, forty-eight years old, with smooth features. He is orderly, business-like, and discharges the responsibilities of his job as City Manager with intensity. He is annoyed by activists of any kind.

The Mayor, Samuel Bigstaff, sits quietly at his desk, staring ahead, his hands clasped.

> SAMUEL: What do you see, Wendell?

> WENDELL: It's an angry and restless mob. I don't think that lone cop is going to keep these agitators away from the entrance to the building much longer.

> SAMUEL: Call Chief Case and tell him we need a team of his men, *now*, to deal with this possible intrusion into my office.

> WENDELL: I did. He told me to remind you that *you* stated we have sufficient uniforms on the street. He said if you want any more police assistance, loosen up the purse strings.

> SAMUEL: What will it take to quiet these people down?

> WENDELL: I recommend you issue a statement or take *some* action, Sam.

> SAMUEL (*shaking his head*): I don't understand all this anguish over a possible imaginary assault on a guy who works at an airstrip thirty-five miles away. The place is way outside the city limits.

> WENDELL: He just happens to live in Ponca City, and he just happens to be a member of the Senior Citizens Pinochle Club. (*stops talking abruptly and backs away from the window with a start*) Oh, oh.

> SAMUEL: What do you see?

> WENDELL: One of the women is swinging her purse at Officer O'Neil; you might have to call Chief Case yourself.

Samuel reaches for the telephone on his desk.

> WENDELL: Wait. Some items fell out of her purse. She stopped to pick them up. Officer O'Neil is helping her.

Samuel hangs up the phone, takes a pad of paper out of his desk, and begins writing.

> SAMUEL: Wendell, have this typed up. I want to issue some kind of position paper on this uproar. We'll need a committee to draw one up. You're in charge.

Wendell takes the paper and looks at it as he exits the office. Samuel sits silent with his head in his hands. The CHANTING of the CROWD grows louder.

INT. PONCA CITY. COMMISSIONERS CAUCUS ROOM. DAY

Four members of the Ponca City Board of Commissioners and Wendell Ream occupy chairs spread widely around a long, oval conference table. The members present are GEORGE KING, DAYAN KNIGHT, RENE ROOK, and ELIZABETH QUEEN. Wendell passes out pencils and writing pads.

> WENDELL: In the note sent to each of you, Mayor Bigstaff explained the purpose for this meeting today. He has designated you four as those most capable of carrying out his assignment and asked that you serve as the Resolution Committee. I appreciate your attendance. I'm here to serve as your facilitator.

Rene pulls a folded letter from an envelope, opens it, and peers at it through her bifocals. Rene is thirty-eight, about five feet, six inches tall, and somewhat rotund. She likes to wear scarves. She is well educated, sensible, and practical.

> RENE: Hmm. It says here, Wendell, that we're supposed to prepare a resolution. I haven't written any that I can recall. I wonder why I was picked. Where shall we start?

George opens a large brown envelope and pulls out a sheaf of papers. George is forty and small enough to pass as a jockey. An idea-man, he is efficient but dictatorial. He envisions himself as uniquely creative.

GEORGE: I felt we could learn from a good example of a resolution. I was able to obtain a copy of a one passed recently by the Kay County Board of County Commissioners. I have their resolution here on increasing tourism in Oklahoma.

George passes out copies of the Kay County resolution to each of the group.

Dayan reads the sample resolution George hands him. Dayan is a tall fifty-five-year-old black man with prominent bones in his face. He has an infectious positive attitude. He is very idealistic about city government.

DAYAN: This looks really okay. We can just copy this format. Apparently, we need a couple of "Whereas" statements.

RENE: Tell me again. What are we resolving?

WENDELL: Well, all of you saw the ugly demonstration in front of the city hall yesterday. The public is frightened. The public wants a retraction by the mayor of his statement on television that he sees nothing credible in the reports of extraterrestrial beings in this area. In fact, the protesters want some show of action; they want to see some steps by the city to confront and deal with these intruders.

Elizabeth tosses her copy of the resolution aside. A look of irritation crosses her face. Elizabeth is forty-one, always stands erect, and wears mostly black dresses with white lace collars. A former school teacher, she strives to represent the thoughts of the people of Ponca City.

ELIZABETH: Wendell, do you or the mayor secretly think there *might* be UFOs and aliens visiting us? Maybe he pooh-poohed the possibility to avoid a panic.

WENDELL: We don't. Neither Sam nor I believe this alien report has any merit, but the public outcry forces us to call for some action.

GEORGE: I'll volunteer to write the whole resolution – with everybody's inputs, of course – if you all don't mind.

DAYAN, RENE, and ELIZABETH (*in unison*): We don't mind.

GEORGE: How is this for starters? (*reading from his notes)* "Whereas the Board of Commissioners of Ponca City seeks to provide for the common defense and promote the general welfare of the community."

George pauses, staring fixedly at his pad.

RENE: Don't leave us hanging. What's next?

GEORGE: I'm thinking.

DAYAN (*nodding vigorously*): You're doing great, George. Keep going!

ELIZABETH: Write something that says we *do* take these creatures seriously. Let's force the mayor's hand.

George scribbles energetically across his pad.

GEORGE (*reading*): "Whereas there are reports of creatures of unknown origin that have taken captive one of our citizens and transported him into space against his will."

George pauses, deep in thought.

DAYAN (*nodding again*): That really says it all!

WENDELL: What you've written there sets the stage, George. Those ideas should be what the protesters are looking for. Now we've got to get some words in there that transition into starting some sort of anti-alien activity – you know, some sort of defense effort. I was thinking we could propose something like an interplanetary SWAT team that could swing into action if any aliens landed. They could be an extension of the police department.

Rene waves her hands with great animation.

> RENE: Hold on a minute! If you gentlemen will recall, we covered expansion of the police department during this year's budget debate, and we concluded we couldn't add any officers at this time.

> WENDELL: Rene! I'm not talking *expansion*. A few in the department would simply be given a *title*. This is an easy option. There aren't any *aliens*! The cops we assign would never really do *anything*! They would respond to infrequent calls reporting saucer landings. They do that now! We can assign a few to a special team, buy them black sweatshirts with the letters SETI on the back. You know, "Search for Extraterrestrial Invaders."

> DAYAN: The "I" stands for "Intelligence," Wendell.

> RENE (*shaking her head*): I still think it's going to cost us some money. There probably will have to be reports and more file space, or another damn computer program. And suppose there really *are* some aliens with ray guns? I was reading about that in Popular Science. We'd have to buy some special lead-lined vests.

> GEORGE (*gesturing at Rene*): You're right. We have to elevate the responsibility. Ponca City isn't equipped to handle a threat at this level. Listen to this: "Whereas we depend upon the Federal Government to defend its citizens against all enemies, foreign and domestic."

Dayan pats George on the back.

> DAYAN: That was well put, George. God! You have a way with words.

> ELIZABETH: Wendell, you mentioned something earlier about a defense effort. I think the government should have those aerospace guys build something that could go after the aliens. Didn't I hear the high school principal, mister Bleak,

say at the graduation ceremony that if we're smart enough to put men on the moon, we should be smart enough to catch UFOs?

WENDELL: I don't think it was in that context.

GEORGE: Elizabeth has a point; I'm going to add that we resolve that as a show of physical evidence of intent, the Federal Government shall have an aerial device designed and built that can track these UFOs and prove they exist.

Rene grabs George's arm.

RENE: George, one more issue. I was looking at this Kay County resolution you gave me. Shouldn't we put in some statement in ours about the detrimental effect of aliens on tourism? Don't you think it would strengthen it to add one more "Whereas"?

WENDELL: That's a sensitive topic. You don't even want to whisper the words "tourism" and "aliens" in the same breath. The mayor has a joint meeting scheduled this month at the Ponca City Chamber of Commerce with the promoters for the week-long festival later next month, the "Century of Oil Exploration." Believe me, aliens would not be welcome at that gathering.

George tosses his pad and pencil on the table and rests on his elbows.

GEORGE: I think this takes care of everything. Here's the clincher. "Therefore, be it resolved that the Ponca City Board of Commissioners demand that our nation's President initiate a program to pursue, identify, and combat any spacecraft and their operators that threaten our population."

Rene, Dayan, and Elizabeth applaud enthusiastically.

GEORGE (*smiling*): Thanks for your support. I'll use the idea in those words for the title. Let's see, we can name it the

"Resolution Demanding a Federal Space-Based Deterrent to Alien Invaders."

RENE: I don't mean to be critical, George, but what does that mean? *That could be anything*!

DAYAN: Yes, that's exactly why George used those words, Rene. We don't want to put limits on what the government can come up with.

GEORGE: At the bottom I'll add "Submitted by the Ponca City Board of Commissioners" and list all the board members' names with a place for their signatures – and the mayor's signature, of course.

WENDELL: When you're done, George, leave it on my desk. I'll have it done up on the word processor tomorrow and ready for Tuesday's board meeting for a vote of approval.

DAYAN: I'm looking at your sample, Wendell, don't forget to put all the "Whereas" and "Be it resolved" in bold and all caps.

WENDELL: I'll also prepare the cover letter to the White House for Mayor Bigstaff's signature.

RENE: Now we'll see some action!

The four gather up the pencils and papers, give them back to Wendell, and hurry out of the Caucus Room.

INT. WHITE HOUSE. OVAL OFFICE. DAY

THELMA GRAYFIELD, first woman President of the United States, picks up a meeting schedule from her desk and starts reading, jotting little notes in the margin.

She is wearing her usual dark gray suit. Her face is attractive and youthful, but a closer look betrays small wrinkles gathered from thirty years in the political arena. Her short, combed-back salt- and-pepper hair frames her face. Thelma is occasionally disorganized, but she is admired for being trusting, extroverted, and forthright in her opinions.

HAZEL LAZER, the President's personal secretary, enters the office carrying a large, white envelope which she holds out to Thelma.

Hazel is half-way to pudgy. She is wearing her favorite gray short-sleeved jacket. She is eligible for retirement, but has been urged to stay on because she knows her way around the White House. Her philosophy is to keep every task simple and don't put things off until tomorrow.

> HAZEL: Here's a piece of mail for you, Madam President. It was sent express. It looks important. As you instructed for all high priority mail, I gave it to mister Ferret for his review. He said he wants to discuss it with you as soon as possible.

> THELMA: Okay. Put it on the pile. Tell Lamar I'm available now. (*looking down at schedule*) I see there is an intelligence briefing I have to attend in half an hour.

> HAZEL: Mister Ferret said that because of that briefing, it is critical that he speak with you first to prepare you.

> THELMA: Okay. Send him in.

Hazel exits the oval office through the northeast door to her office, leaving the door ajar. Hazel's voice is heard repeating Thelma's words on her telephone.

A few moments later LAMAR FERRET, the White House Chief of Staff, steps through the doorway and pauses. Lamar is sixty. His face is heavily lined. His dark hair is cropped short. His gestures are nervous and quick. His career in government service has left him cynical; his decisions are always politic and sometimes Machiavellian.

> LAMAR: Did you see that last piece of mail?

> THELMA: I assume it is another one complaining about short post-office hours. I've had five this week so far. I'll do the mail after the briefing.

Lamar picks up the large white envelope from Thelma's IN tray.

>LAMAR: I strongly suggest you let me bring you up to date on a new issue.

>THELMA: Let me guess. Have there been any terrorist attacks?

>LAMAR: Worse.

>THELMA: Worse? Why am I hearing about this now?

>LAMAR: We're dealing with reports of incursions by visitors from outer space. You're going to hear more about it in the briefing.

>THELMA: Who's saying that? I thought I told those people in the Office of Presidential Correspondence that I didn't want to see any more letters on flying saucers.

>LAMAR: This is more than just letters.

She stiffens momentarily then looks at the envelope Lamar is holding.

>THELMA: Hold on! Have you been reading those tabloids you subscribe to? Is this some more of that Area fifty-one sensationalism? (*she looks directly at Lamar and glares*) Wait a minute! You're talking about that incident in Oklahoma, right?

Lamar holds up the white envelope.

>LAMAR: Yes, it's all here – a resolution from the City Board of Commissioners of Ponca City, Oklahoma. They're demanding that the Federal Government do something about this alien threat.

>THELMA: What's the nature of this threat? Did they supply any specifics?

>LAMAR: It's not clearly stated in the resolution, but I know from the articles in the press out there that they believe

the space aliens are targeting the senior citizens. They want you personally to alert our security agencies and to initiate some kind of program to go after the aliens.

THELMA: I was told two days ago that the police who investigated the case reported that the victim, the old man, had rum on his breath when they arrived. Are you suggesting that I modify national policy based on the remarks of an inebriate?

LAMAR: That odor was later believed to be from a parts dip he uses. It's rum-scented. He may very well have been completely sober.

THELMA: Lamar, this is all going to blow away — just like that scare we had about people from another planet getting jobs as counter personnel in the fast-food chains.

LAMAR: That's only because the Department of Justice cancelled the investigation. The possibility of their existence hasn't been disproved. Believe me, Madam President, this uproar is real and is with us *now*!

THELMA: But we don't know that all these events actually took place. I discussed these reports with the Commander of the Air Force Space Command. He reminded me that these reports are just a replay of the whipped-up hysteria back in the sixties, and that these claims and concerns were shown to be groundless and put to bed.

LAMAR: If anyone were to hear you say that, you'd have entire retirement villages screaming, "Smokescreen!"

THELMA: I'll read the resolution, but how do we know it isn't something a couple of people in the Ponca City Chamber of Commerce dreamed up to harvest a little national publicity?

LAMAR: The cover letter that came with the resolution is signed by the Mayor of Ponca City.

THELMA: You mean to say that the city officials are going along with this foolishness?

LAMAR: I called the Mayor, Sam Bigstaff. I couldn't get a reading on what he *really* believes, but he quoted me some statements from the senior groups in the area threatening more visible protests in addition to the crowds that have been pounding the doors at the city offices. He apparently is listening to their demands and he said the City Board of Commissioners is serious about getting a response from you.

THELMA: I don't want to brush them off. I carried Oklahoma in the election. I suggest you send a polite reply mentioning that the Air Force conducted an extensive investigation into UFOs way back and decided that they didn't exist. Didn't they call that Project Blue Book or something?

LAMAR: That was a long time ago; nobody in Oklahoma has ever heard of it or would remember it. Even if I could lay my hands on a copy of the report and send it to them, the City Board of Commissioners would tell me that the crisis they are facing proves it's outdated.

THELMA: Look, send them a letter anyway, with my signature. Tell them the usual — say I'm personally investigating this shocking occurrence. In the meantime, I'll get hold of a contact or two I have in the space business and ask them what they know about mysterious things that fly around.

Thelma waves Lamar off with the back of her hand. She opens a journal on her desk and runs her finger down the page.

INT. REPULSIVE TECHNOLOGY, INC. OFFICE AREA. DAY

Two men and three women sit at desks in individual cubicles in a large, well-lit office area. Some are bent close to their computer monitors, studying the screen; some are on the telephone. On an adjacent wall is a framed photograph of a rocket-propelled spacecraft leaving the launch pad, riding a shaft of brilliant orange-red flame. Next to the photograph a large sign reads RTI CUSTOMER AND PUBLIC RELATIONS.

One of the women, JOYCE PLAISANT, Public Relations Specialist, is sipping coffee. Joyce started at Repulsive Technology at twenty-two, straight out of college, and spent the next fifteen years working her way up the ladder. She dresses very formally every work day. For the last five years she kept her blonde hair short. Joyce exudes confidence and is very persuasive. She thinks quickly and can deliver a message clearly and pointedly with the written and spoken word. Her coworkers are always amazed at her ability to understand the variety of people that contact RTI.

She places her coffee mug on her desk and picks up a telephone that has begun ringing.

CLOSE ON JOYCE

> JOYCE: Repulsive Technology, Incorporated, Public Relations, Joyce Plaisant speaking.

Joyce listens to the caller, begins writing on a large pad.

> JOYCE: Did you say your name was Burrows? Mister Burrows, Repulsive Technology is currently not involved in any research on anti-gravity.

She continues to listen. Frown lines form on her forehead. Her hand moves faster across the pad.

> JOYCE: No, the company has not purchased any anti-gravity patents. No, we are not suppressing the use of any such patents. Where did you hear that? Would you hold for a moment?

She stops writing, rises from her chair, places her hand over the mouthpiece of the handset which she waves at the senior member of the department who is walking by: EDWARD CONFIRME, Customer Relations Manager.

Edward is in his late forties, is considered handsome, and is wearing a sport shirt with a loud pattern. His jacket, which he never wears, is on a hanger in his office. Edward keeps thinking he could do better in another career, but is not sure which.

Edward walks over to where Joyce is standing.

> EDWARD (*whispering*): Who is it?

> JOYCE (*speaking into the phone again*): Mister Burrows, are you there? I have a gentleman here in our department who can perhaps answer your questions.

Joyce presses the handset to her ear and shakes her head.

> JOYCE: He hung up.

> EDWARD: Why did you call me over?

> JOYCE: Didn't you get a call last week from someone asking about anti-gravity devices? This guy I spoke with just now thinks we're studying them.

> EDWARD: Yeah. That's a rumor that's been going around and pops back up occasionally. A few strange people out there are claiming that the company bought somebody's plans for a workable anti-gravity device and that we're suppressing that information.

> JOYCE: Sounds wonderful. If we could do that, why would we want to keep it a secret?

> EDWARD: They say it makes sense because an anti-gravity machine would cut into our rocket business.

Edward throws up his arms and walks back to his office. He stops, turns to look at Joyce.

> EDWARD: It's like that urban legend circulating fifty years ago that some petroleum refiner was suppressing the plans for the hundred mile-per-gallon carburetor because it would reduce the sale of gasoline.

    JOYCE: Why do I get all the weird calls?

Joyce's phone rings again. She ignores Edward, and picks up the handset.

    JOYCE: Repulsive Technology, Public Relations, Joyce Plaisant speaking.

Joyce leans on her desk. She listens briefly to the caller. Something she hears startles her. She stands upright.

    JOYCE: Are you sure you have the right number? You've reached Repulsive Technology.

Joyce waves again frantically to Edward who is standing in his office doorway.

    JOYCE: I'm going to put you on the speaker phone.

As Edward re-enters Joyce's cubicle, she pushes the speaker button on the phone base and replaces the handset.

    JOYCE: Would you repeat that please.

    VOICE (*on speaker*): This is Hazel Lazer calling from the White House. President Grayfield would like to speak to the President of your company, mister Masterly.

    EDWARD (*whispering*): Sounds phony. Stall. Get a number to call back.

    JOYCE: Mister Masterly is probably in a meeting. May I call you back with the best time to reach him?

    VOICE: Certainly. The White House switchboard number is area code two-zero-two, four-five-six, one-four-one-four. Ask for Hazel Lazer, the Personal Secretary.

A CLICK is heard. Joyce turns off the speaker phone.

    JOYCE: Do you think that could be the real thing or another wierdo?

EDWARD: In case it's legit, you'd better inform Masterly's office.

Joyce picks up the handset and punches in four digits on the keypad.

JOYCE: Angelique, this is Joyce in Relations. Is Walter there? I have an urgent message.

There is a long pause. Joyce taps her fingers nervously on her mouse pad. She recognizes the voice.

JOYCE: Walter. We seem to have received a call from the White House – from the President's Secretary or whoever. Is that possible?

Joyce listens and nods knowingly. She hangs up.

JOYCE (*to Edward*): Walter says he met President Grayfield once at a business conference. But he can't imagine why she would be calling him. I got the "okay" though.

EDWARD: Call the White House and ask for that Hazel somebody. If she confirms it was her, give her Masterly's direct line and his schedule. Wanna bet it's a prank?

Joyce raises her eyebrows and shivers a little as she places her hand on the telephone.

INT. RTI. PRESIDENT'S OFFICE. RECEPTION AREA. DAY

At a large desk in front of the doorway to the office of the President of RTI, the Administrative Assistant, ANGELIQUE DEL MUNDO, picks up a framed document and studies it. Angelique is thirty, has beautiful dark hair, and wears dresses that fit tightly. At work she is respected for her very reserved, personable phone manner. Her social friends would describe her as an outgoing party person.

CLOSE ON FRAMED DOCUMENT

The document in the frame reads CERTIFICATE OF RECOGNITION FOR CONTRIBUTIONS TO AMERICA'S ACHIEVEMENTS IN SPACE. AWARDED TO ANGELIQUE DEL MUNDO.
BACK TO SCENE

The telephone on Angelique's desk rings. She raises the handset unhurriedly to her ear.

> ANGELIQUE (*slowly and distinctly*):   Repulsive Technology. Walter Masterly's office. Angelique speaking.

She listens for a moment.

> ANGELIQUE: The White House? I'll put you through immediately to mister Masterly.

She presses a button on the intercom.

> ANGELIQUE: It's the President, Walter.

INT. OVAL OFFICE/ INT. MASTERLY'S OFFICE. SPLIT SCREEN. DAY

The images of the two leaders appear side by side. Thelma leans back in the Presidential swivel office chair, tapping a pencil on a tablet on the Presidential desk, cradling the Presidential telephone handset on her shoulder.

WALTER MASTERLY, President of Repulsive Technology, Incorporated, sits upright at his desk; his chair is turned slightly so he can look out the office window as he listens. He recently reached seventy-two. His hair is white. He has a strong resemblance to Anthony Hopkins*.

He is a good leader, conservative in his business dealings, avoiding risk wherever possible. But certain projects will excite his passions. The collar of his dress shirt is open. He rubs the handset against his ear.

---

*Producer's note: Perhaps this description should be changed or even eliminated. We may have no chance of getting Hopkins for this role.

THELMA: Walter, I knew the day would come when I would have reason to speak to you. How are you?

WALTER: I'm at the top of my game, Madam President. I'm honored by this call. Are you about to tell me you're cutting the aerospace budget?

THELMA: Nothing like that. When I met you way back, I found you to be among the most intelligent and honest people in the rocket business.

WALTER: I appreciate the flattery, but I will still have to send you a bill if you want an official document with any information you are looking for.

THELMA: I'm sincere about my regard for you, Walter. But what makes you think I need some kind of report?

WALTER: We had a request only last month from NASA for a report on the scope of our rocket engine test operations. NASA was being hounded with rumors that we were launching vehicles at our static test facility. We don't have the capability to launch *anything*.

THELMA: As a matter of fact, I thought you could give me a definitive opinion from your field of expertise. Have you heard that crazy story about the alien abduction in Oklahoma?

WALTER: I do recall a brief segment on TV showing a small airfield and some artist's rendition of a flying saucer. Who was abducted?

THELMA: I'm not sure, but that doesn't matter. What is important to me and my office is that it was an *older* person. For reasons I'll never understand, many senior citizens seem to be concerned that they are being targeted.

WALTER: Madam President, what do you need from me?

THELMA: I know you consider this foolish, but I'd like your company's opinion on what steps we might take to combat or mitigate these possible flyovers by aliens.

WALTER: Mitigate flyovers?

THELMA: Walter, I don't want you to think I take all this stuff seriously, but my Press Secretary is being hounded for a statement as to our position. I want to be able to say that we have the best minds working on solutions for dealing with this threat. Don't laugh, but just supposing that ships from another planet *were* visiting, and that they *were* swooping down and grabbing old people, is there anything in the way of a space vehicle that we have today, or one that we could design and fly soon, that could chase after these UFOs to get a closer look, and maybe scare them off?

WALTER: Do you want my honest opinion?

THELMA: I know your opinion. What I need is a paper — something official – something that shows we are on top of this. I want the paper to suggest how we might get a closer look at these aircraft, whatever they are.

WALTER: When do you have to have it?

THELMA: I want to take it with me to a press conference scheduled for eight days from now.

WALTER: I'll have a paper delivered to you within the week. Am I expected to act on the basis of this phone call?

THELMA: I'm holding a copy of an approved study contract that is already in the mail to you. (*laughs*) I was assuming you *would* go along with this request. The contract outlines and orders the issuance of the paper I just described. Sign it and mail it back with the report.

WALTER: In that case I had better end this call and get to work.

Walter stares at his handset, grimacing, shaking his head; He firmly places the handset down in the base.

Thelma carefully returns the handset of her phone to the cradle. She smiles and places her palms together beneath her chin.

INT. RTI. CHIEF ENGINEER'S OFFICE. DAY

We see a pair of hands holding an open copy of a magazine titled AEROSPACE PROGRESS. The view moves left to a blue cup half full of coffee. The lettering on the cup reads REPULSIVE TECHNOLOGY - PROMINENT IN SPACE. The view pulls back to encompass first the figure of JOHN FULBRANE, Chief Engineer of RTI, who is reading the magazine, then his desk, then the entire office.

John is sixty, keeps his hair cropped close, wears a stern look, and possesses a military demeanor, all probably left over from his service in the Army. He is technically sharp, focused, and extremely cooperative. Behind John are bookcases with aging textbooks from his college days.

The figure of Walter Masterly appears as he enters the office to stand in front of John. John looks up from the magazine at Walter.

> WALTER: John, do you have a moment?

John looks first at the clock on the wall and then smiles at Walter.

> JOHN: Do I? How often do I receive a visit from my President before nine in the morning? I have all the time in the world. Are you here to talk about the feature article in Aerospace Progress — the one about NASA's cut-back in heavy-lift engine research?

> WALTER: What do you know about UFOs?

> JOHN: Only what I read in the newspapers.

> WALTER: There is apparently a resurgence of sightings of strange unidentified aerial vehicles, this time over Oklahoma. We have been asked to chime in with our take

on the feasibility of such craft and to suggest methods for investigating them.

JOHN: Well, I hadn't heard that. Is this another one of those crank calls Joyce Plaisant and Ed Confirme get? Joyce keeps asking me to talk to these people on the phone – personally. Yesterday I talked to some guy who said he had read that rocket engine combustion could be thought of as "a continuous explosion." I said that was correct. But then I had to explain to him why trinitrotoluene, which he suggested, would not work as a rocket fuel.

WALTER: This was not a crank call. This request was made of me by the President of the United States.

JOHN: Some *person* in the White House or *the* President*?*

WALTER: *The* President.

JOHN (*whistles softly*): I don't suppose you told her that topic is not our field of expertise.

WALTER: I told her we would study the information and give her an answer.

JOHN: What information and when?

WALTER: I said we would have a report in her hands by this time next week. Can I count on you to pull something together that at least talks to the question?

JOHN (*holding his palms to his forehead*): I don't even know where to start.

WALTER: Joyce Plaisant has done some ground work for this. Call her. She has the names and phone numbers of people at the Ponca Post and at TV station KPUT in Oklahoma where the sightings occurred. They can tell you what happened; they have the contact information for some guy who says he was carried off by the aliens.

JOHN: Unreal! I assume that Thelma Grayfield *does* know that what we do is make rocket engines and vehicle stages. Doesn't the Air Force have the kind of information she wants? Wasn't there a Project Blue Book or something that looked into that?

WALTER: This doesn't have to be original research. Assign a couple guys to look up what's known about UFOs; have them write a few respectable looking pages; put them in a fancy binder, and we'll have it delivered overnight.

JOHN (*reaching for a pencil and his daily planner*): Okay. I have two guys that would be perfect for this: Corey Layt and Roy Cordu. Right now, they're working on a report requested by the Department of Defense – a list of critical materials we get from foreign suppliers, but that can wait a week or so.

Walter turns and walks out the office door. John swings in his chair toward the phone on his desk, presses the speaker button, and keys in a number.

COREY's VOICE (*on speaker*): Layt here.

JOHN: Corey, this is your best friend, John. Find Roy and meet me in Conference Room five, the one next to my office, in about fifteen minutes.

COREY'S VOICE (*on speaker)*: John, (*big sigh*), in five minutes I'm supposed to meet with someone in Purchasing to discuss the limited availability of rare earth alloy elements, it's for that report you requested. I can't believe we use that much iridium. Listen to this: we've been getting it from a country that may go on a "no-trade" list. This is hot.

JOHN (*nods*): I know, I know, but this is hotter.

John hangs up and leans back.

INT. RTI. CONFERENCE ROOM 5. DAY

John Fulbrane is seated at one side of a conference table, flipping pages in his planner. Across from him are seated COREY LAYT, engineering specialist in the Electro-Mechanical Devices Unit, and ROY CORDU, valve designer.

Corey is thirty-five, and always wears sharply pressed long-sleeve dress shirts, cuff links shaped like little rocket engines. He sips from a coffee cup. Corey has a curious nature and likes to find out what is going on in other programs at RTI. He is also creative.

Roy is making notes on a large pad. He is thirty-two, and keeps his hair long in back. He is wearing a long-sleeve, plaid, casual shirt. Roy is very experienced and methodical, but sometimes plodding.

> JOHN (*looking up at Corey*): Corey, didn't you once tell me you spent a lot of time collecting stories about UFOs?

> COREY: Well, that was a long time ago. The stories got to be repetitious after awhile, and I haven't heard anything new. I have no idea what's going around.

> JOHN: Roy, do *you* know anything about flying saucers?

> ROY: Only a couple of jokes. Did you hear about the blonde who reported seeing a "cigar-shaped" flying saucer?

> JOHN: Well, I would like you both to become experts for the next few days. More specifically, I want you to work up a concept paper. The subject is the configuration for a pursuit craft that could intercept a UFO, study it, photograph it, characterize it, and maybe even chase one off if it acted hostile.

> ROY: Who are we doing this for?

> JOHN: I'm not at liberty to say.

COREY: Did I hear you say a pursuit craft? I would have to have an estimate of what speed these UFOs can attain. What is the altitude we're operating at?

ROY (*waving his arm in circles*): Does this hypothetical pursuit ship fly around all day looking for strange vehicles or does it sit on the launch pad waiting for phone calls from little old ladies who think they see something weird over their house?

JOHN: I need you to tell me all that.

COREY: How much time should we spend on this?

JOHN: Spend as much time as necessary to make it hang together, but I want a full report on my desk in five days. I'll need a day to give it a once over, then it goes out.

COREY: It could turn out costing more than the government is willing to pay for something we might never use. And I can envision some technology development being required. For example, the tank design is going to have to accommodate a lot of propellant sloshing.

JOHN: You guys are engineers; at least that's what I'm paying you for. Give me a concept for some kind of bird that uses components we know about. Don't worry about the cost or whether we might have to develop a new alloy. It's not as though we would ever actually *have* to design and build this thing.

ROY: What do we charge this to?

JOHN: I'll have an Engineering planner bring you a charge number before the end of the day. (*closing notebook and rising from chair*) That's it.

Corey and Roy leave their chairs and walk to the conference room door.

JOHN: By the way, guys, don't tell anybody what you're
   working on.

*The two men pause and look back at John. Corey places his index
finger on his lips to indicate secrecy. Roy swings his hand in the air to
imitate a maneuvering aircraft.*

INT. RTI. CAFETERIA. DAY

*Corey Layt, Roy Cordu, and STEFAN ESPACAMORE, a young, new
engineering hire, enter the RTI cafeteria, pull the chairs out from a
small table, and sit down. There is no one else in the cafeteria except a
few employees in aprons filling the salad bar and preparing food for
the steam table.*

*Stefan is twenty-three years old, and wears the same sports jacket he
bought to go on job interviews. He is very good at mathematics, but
hasn't yet been asked to use any. He doesn't feel comfortable speaking
in public.*

ROY: Corey, why did you have us meet in the cafeteria? This
   isn't very private.

COREY: All the conference rooms were booked.

ROY: Have you told Stefan here anything about the UFO data
   search?

*A tall, thin man, one of the cafeteria workers, clutching a white dish
towel quickly moves toward the three engineers and begins wiping
table tops near them. Corey notices that he has turned his head
toward them, as if listening.*

COREY (*quietly*): Keep your voices down.

STEFAN (*whispering*): Is this meeting about some classified
   project? I don't have any clearance yet.

*The cafeteria worker drops the damp towel on the table where the
three are talking and starts wiping. Corey looks up at him sternly.*

COREY: Could you possibly come back later to do this table? It's clean enough for us. Okay?

The man smiles briefly at Corey. He picks up his towel, nervously arranges the salt and pepper shakers, and then walks to the swinging doors leading to the kitchen.

ROY: Did you notice how that guy's ears picked up when I said "UFO data search"? That looked suspicious.

COREY (*turning to Stefan and speaking softly*): The topic I'm going to bring up is not about any project we have in-house, so I don't know what security level might be assigned. All I can tell you is do not discuss whatever is said here after we break up.

ROY: We have a special assignment for you, Stefan.

STEFAN (*leaning forward on the table*): I want to get involved as much as possible.

COREY: Stefan, I was looking at your résumé. I believe it states that you had won a special award for an essay you wrote in your senior year at Northwestern in the course Engineering Contributions to Social Progress. The essay was titled "Maintaining Awareness of Extraterrestrials."

STEFAN: Yeah. The point of my essay was that although there was a lot of misinformation and a lot of hype circulating about extraterrestrials – you know, in the tabloids – there are some legitimate data that should be examined more carefully. Yeah, I spent a lot of time researching the literature on the subject.

ROY: Did you come across any report of valid evidence of alien life forms?

STEFAN: No, I found no valid reports of alien beings, or creatures, if that's what you mean. All of the evidence is related to sightings of unidentified aircraft.

The men stop talking as an attractive, young female cafeteria worker walks past them carrying boxes of paper napkins. She waves at Stefan who smiles and waves back*. Corey watches her until she leaves the area.

COREY: Do you still have any of the source material you used for your essay?

STEFAN: A few books and old magazines. But they're stored away in my parent's home.

COREY: Hmm.

ROY: Do you recall if any of your sources mentioned things like the observed velocity of these craft or a rate of acceleration?

STEFAN: No, but I could check for that if I had my books now – which I don't.

ROY: Can you get the books from your parents?

STEFAN: No, they're in Illinois.

COREY: Stefan, here's what we want you to do. Spend tomorrow, all day if necessary, in the company library looking for books on UFOs. See what information you can find on their configuration and flight characteristics.

STEFAN: Sure. Fortunately, I was given a tour of the company library and heard a lecture on library services by the Chief Librarian, Lydia Quigley. That was part of the New Hire Orientation Program. I had a chance to walk through the

stacks. I was looking for books on extraterrestrial phenomena 'cause that's my thing, but I didn't see any. However, I got to be good friends with Lydia. She may know of some reports that are packed away.

*Producer's note: This story doesn't have any love interest. Maybe we can develop something here.

ROY (*hurriedly*): No, no, don't tell Lydia what you're there for. She may start asking questions – or spread stories around.

STEFAN: I can also go to the public library. I *do* know they have more volumes on the subject of alien air vehicles.

COREY: Okay. But don't talk to anyone at the reference desk. Just use their computer search program. And be sure you're not wearing your company badge.

ROY: And don't check the books out. That could be a giveaway. Just copy the information.

STEFAN: When do you want me to turn my notes over to you?

COREY: Plan to meet tomorrow afternoon at this time. I'll make sure we have a room. I'll email you both the meeting notice.

The three men pull their chairs out from the table and walk toward the cafeteria exit. Roy stops to buy a doughnut on the way out.

INT. RTI. ENGINEERING BUILDING EXECUTIVE AREA. DAY

Corey Layt, Roy Cordu, and Stefan Espacamore walk through the double glass doors of the expansive Executive Hall and stop in front of the desk of ANITA GUARDLEY, administrative assistant to John Fulbrane.

Anita is forty, has brown hair, wears glasses, and has on a blue top of soft fabric and a black skirt. Anita is leaning forward, squinting at her computer screen. She is extremely goal-oriented, and continually expresses her concern to John that he must meet all of his commitments.

Corey carries a large, grey, wrinkled internal mail envelope under his arm. He speaks to her.

COREY: Anita, we're supposed to meet with John. Is he free?

ANITA: Yes, he's expecting you. He told me to hold all calls. This must be really important. What's going on? Am I missing something?

COREY (*smiling*): You'll find out in good time.

The three men walk past Anita and through the doorway of John's office. Anita slides her chair close to the doorway and cocks her head to listen.

INT. RTI. JOHN FULBRANE'S OFFICE. DAY

Corey, Roy, and Stefan slide into small chairs next to a small round table at the side of John's desk. John places a book he has been reading into his bookcase, walks to the door of his office to close it, and takes the fourth seat at the small table. Corey drops the gray internal mailing envelope in front of John.

COREY: Here's your report, Boss, the Interceptor White Paper. This is RTI's countermeasure for any alien airborne machine. It's ready to go to whoever is waiting for it, and that person will be impressed.

John lifts up the envelope to let a thick, bound document slide out. He raises the cover of the document, looks at the first page, and then closes the cover.

JOHN: What does it say? I'm going to read it later, of course, but warn me now if it's just a lot of arm-waving.

COREY: No, this is good stuff. Stefan here did an outstanding job of getting some estimates for the maneuverability and speed of flying saucers. They're all in here. We ran the numbers and actually came up with a proposed vehicle that's believable.

ROY: We made it unmanned. It might be described as a "super-drone."

JOHN: Could one actually be built? We all know there are a lot of other smart people who make rocket engines that will jump on this and tear it apart if it looks like Buck Rogers designed it.

STEFAN: Who is Buck Rogers?

Roy holds his palm up to Stefan.

ROY: Later.

JOHN: Based on your paper, if an announcement were to be made to the press – and I say, "if" – that America could have this "super-drone" in a back pocket to scare off the evil Martians, I wouldn't want any of our competitors like Space Engines, Advanced Thrusters, or Orbit Craft Industries shooting holes in it.

COREY: Could it be built? Sure! It wouldn't be easy, John, but it's doable. Although I wouldn't want the job.

JOHN (*looking down at the report, smiling*): I see you put it in a nice blue cover. Thanks, fellows. You've completed the mission. Consider this put to bed. You can forget about it and go back to whatever you were doing.

ROY: We're making a list of strategic materials we have to buy overseas or across our borders. I seriously suggest we start stocking up iridium.

JOHN: Iridium? Does Masterly know we might run short on that.

ROY: He will when he gets our survey.

JOHN: Flag that item for him. Now, if you gentlemen will leave me alone, I'm going to read what your concept paper says.

Corey, Roy, and Stefan leave the table and walk out of the room. John picks up the report, leans back in his chair, and begins turning pages.

INT. RTI. JOHN FULBRANE'S OFFICE. ADMIN AREA. DAY

Anita is pouring water from a paper cup into a small potted plant on her desk. She fluffs up the leaves and pushes the plant to the corner of her desk. John steps out of the doorway of his office to get the attention of Anita. She turns and looks up at him. John hands Anita the White Paper document.

> JOHN: Anita, find some kind of "Confidential" label and paste it on the cover. Then take it to the Mail Room. Give it to Stacey. She knows about it. She has a cover letter to enclose with it and a special envelope with an address I gave her. Remind her that it has to go overnight mail.

> ANITA: I didn't prepare any cover letter.

> JOHN: Don't worry, *I* did. It's hush-hush.

> ANITA: Outgoing data like this requires an approved Form twenty-three-A.

> JOHN: Oh, God, another form? I've got to have a talk with whoever is running Forms Control. Okay, fill out the form and I'll sign it.

Anita takes the document and watches John turn away to enter his office. She lifts the cover of the document and leafs through several of the pages. She raises her eyebrows and quickly closes the document. She pulls a sheet of white labels from a drawer, pastes one at the top of the cover and carefully prints the word CONFIDENTIAL. She holds the document up to study the placement of the label. She smiles.

INT. WHITE HOUSE. OVAL OFFICE. DAY

Thelma Grayfield sits at her desk staring intently at a single sheet of paper in front of her. Without looking away she reaches into a small apothecary jar of jelly bears on her desk and pulls out a blue one which she slides through her lips. She writes something on the border of the sheet of paper and places it in a tray at the corner of the desk.

A single KNOCK is heard. Thelma looks up to see Hazel Lazer enter the office swinging a large, thick, brown envelope.

> HAZEL: Another important piece of mail, Madam President.

> THELMA: Is this another one from the Ponca City Board of Commissioners? Give it to Lamar.

> HAZEL: No, it's from some company called "Repulsive Technology." There is a note on the front that says it is for your eyes only.

> THELMA (*holding out her hand to receive the envelope*): Oh, good. I guess Walter kept his promise.

Thelma picks up a pair of scissors and opens the envelope. The blue-covered document slides out. Thelma fingers through the first few pages.

> THELMA: This is great! Hazel, get Lamar in here.

As Hazel hurries from the room, Thelma keeps turning pages in the document. She reaches for another jelly bear. Lamar Ferret enters.

> LAMAR: If this is about your notes for the press conference in two days, I'll have them this afternoon.

> THELMA: No, but now that you mention the press conference, I have something that might be useful.

> LAMAR: What's that?

> THELMA (*waving the Repulsive Technology document*): This is what I told you I was after. I had my good friends in the aerospace business look into UFOs. They couldn't prove they don't exist, but they explained how you could build something to go after them – an interceptor. (*waving the document again*) It's all here.

Lamar drops his arms to his side and hangs his head in despair.

LAMAR: Thelma! In this coming press conference, you must say *nothing* about UFOs – *nothing*. There haven't been any reports of sightings or abductions *anywhere*. My news search company checked that out. In fact, the media has been unusually quiet on the subject.

THELMA: You realize, however, that smart aleck from Cover-Up, the tabloid, *will* ask about UFOs. I can just hear him: "Madam President, the senior groups of this country are concerned that you have issued no statement as to the steps your administration is taking to deal with this alien threat."

LAMAR: Your answer will be what I just said. *There are no reports*! There is insufficient information on which to take any action. That's a true statement.

THELMA: You're suggesting I make an outright denial?

LAMAR: Yes.

THELMA: I think you're right. But I predict my photo will appear on the cover of the next issue of Cover-Up. Some creature will be looking over my shoulder, grinning. In big, bold letters it will read: "Grayfield Denies Invasion from Other Worlds."

Thelma tosses the report into a tray marked FILE.

EXT. PONCA CITY TV STATION KPUT. ENTRANCE. DAY

The view is of two large, glass doors with the lettering KPUT TELEVISION. Orville Pressfit walks into the scene carrying a small cardboard carton. He pauses a moment to look at the lettering, peers inside, and grasps a large handle to pull one of the tall doors open. He enters and walks to the curved desk where a young woman RECEPTIONIST sits quietly.

Behind and above the receptionist on the wall is a TV monitor. It is tuned to the KPUT channel and is displaying a dog food commercial. The receptionist observes Orville and greets him.

>RECEPTIONIST: Welcome to KPUT television. What can I do for you?

>ORVILLE: Is Miss Flambeau here today? I would like to speak to her.

>RECEPTIONIST: Do you have an appointment?

>ORVILLE: No, but I have some important information for her. She knows me.

>RECEPTIONIST: What is your name?

>ORVILLE: Pressfit. That's my *last* name. She may not remember. Tell her Orville is here.

The receptionist picks up the handset of the phone beside her, punches in some numbers, and listens. She hears a voice.

>RECEPTIONIST: Leanne, a gentleman is here in the lobby who would like to speak to you. He is a mister Pressfit. He says you know him.

The receptionist nods as she listens. She looks up at Orville.

>RECEPTIONIST: Miss Flambeau asks if she could speak to you on the phone. (*she holds out the handset to Orville*)

>ORVILLE: Tell her what I have to say is very private, and I have something she should see.

>RECEPTIONIST (*into phone*): He says he wants to speak to you privately and show you something. (*she nods and looks at Orville*) She asks that you take a seat. It will take her a few minutes to finish a news report she is writing, but she will be out to talk with you.

On the TV screen an image of President Grayfield appears. There is a press conference taking place at the White House. The President stands in the Press Briefing Room in front of a lectern with ten microphones. Watching her is an agitated assemblage of seated and standing journalists.

The receptionist turns and peers over her shoulder at the TV monitor.

> RECEPTIONIST: Oh, look! It's the President. I didn't know there was a news conference scheduled for today. This must be something special.

CLOSE ON TV MONITOR

> THELMA (*pointing out toward the seated journalists*): I'll take the first question from Hank Keptiks of Cover-Up magazine.

HANK KEPTIKS, cover-up magazine staff writer, is one of the older newsmen, usually recognized by his tousled hair. He has given up learning anything new and he doubts half of what anyone reports to him. He is startled to hear his name and sits up abruptly in his chair.

> HANK: Madam President, the senior groups of this country are concerned that you have issued no statement as to the steps your administration is taking to deal with this alien threat. What action are you taking to protect our senior citizens?

> THELMA: Hank, I can see you're looking out for the best interests of the older people of our country, and I am as well. I have had my staff stay in constant touch with all of our security agencies for reports of extraterrestrial landings or atmospheric sightings and there are *no reports*! There is insufficient information on which to take *any* action.

> HANK: I would take that answer as a denial that there is a problem. Is that your position, Madam President?

THELMA: I am only denying requests – by any person or organization – that I assign any federal agency to investigate or pursue a menace that may not exist.

Hank looks down at a pad of paper in his lap and makes some hurried notes.

THELMA (*extending her hand toward the audience*): Let's hear the next question from Alice Allcaps of the Ponca Post. You've come a long way, Alice.

ALICE ALLCAPS, reporter for the Ponca Post, is twenty-five, has never attended a Presidential press conference before, and is nervous. She considers Journalism a sacred calling and is constantly thinking of ways to improve her abilities.

She adjusts her hair, clears her throat, and stands at her seat to respond.

ALICE: As you know, President Grayfield, the citizens of Ponca City – particularly the older generation – are overcome with fear in the belief that some foreign airborne gang could descend upon any of them at any time and carry them off. They feel helpless and are looking to you to assure them that you won't let that happen. Can I report back to my paper that you consider these abductions to be a recognized threat?

THELMA: Alice, I am aware of the reported incident in your area – a single occurrence – but you heard what I told Hank. If I had reason to believe there was a viable threat, I would have moved out on it long ago. I would like you to write a story for your paper assuring the people of Ponca City that there is nothing to be alarmed about.

Alice nods her understanding, and types some words on her lap-top computer.

BACK TO SCENE

Orville and the receptionist stare at the TV monitor, transfixed.

> ORVILLE: How can our President say that? Did you hear her? She said there is no threat.

> RECEPTIONIST: The people here in Ponca City will be glad to know that it's now official, especially the elderly. My mother is really afraid. She won't go to the supermarket.

From the back a door opens; Leanne Flambeau strides out briskly to Orville.

> LEANNE: Mister Pressfit, I'm glad to see you again. How are you? This is a very busy day for me. What did you have?

> ORVILLE: Can we sit in those chairs over there. I don't want to be overheard.

> LEANNE: All right, but we must make this quick.

Leanne and Orville move to an area next to a wall where two chairs and a small table are positioned. Orville places his carton on the table.

> ORVILLE (*breathing heavily*): They came again.

> LEANNE: *Who* came again?

> ORVILLE: The aliens came again in their ship last night, grabbed me, and took me for a ride.

> LEANNE: Last night? Where?

> ORVILLE: At the airfield where I work. The place you visited for your TV news story.

> LEANNE: Have you reported this to anyone?

> ORVILLE: No, I thought you might want an exclusive interview with me.

LEANNE (*sitting back, frowning*): You do realize, mister Pressfit, that the report of your first abduction was not widely believed. If we were to run a short announcement that you walked into our station claiming to have been carried off a second time – with no evidence or witnesses, – we would look foolish.

ORVILLE: I have some evidence; look at this.

He takes a leather pouch out of the cardboard carton and dumps the contents. A jumble of small parts rolls out and spreads across the table.

LEANNE: What is that?

ORVILLE: When they brought me into their craft, they showed me a pile of stuff like this in a cabinet. When they weren't looking, I jammed as much as I could in my pockets. These back up my story. These are spare parts from the alien spaceship.

Leanne picks up a small round black knurled object and examines it.

LEANNE: What is this? It looks like a knob from the stereo receiver I have at home.

ORVILLE: It *is* a knob. This one is a spare. They have them on the control panels for their ship. They didn't see me take it.

LEANNE (*shaking head in disbelief*): These could be things you bought at *any* hardware store. I don't think your evidence would convince any of our viewers.

ORVILLE: But what I'm telling you is the truth. Shouldn't you at least report that I made this claim?

LEANNE: Here's what I can do. I'll get a camera operator – maybe Woody – to shoot a brief interview. We might do it in the parking lot. I'll ask you on camera to repeat what you just said. I'll show it to our News Director. It's possible that even though it sounds crazy, he might like that angle. Wait here.

Leanne jumps up and heads toward the door she entered. She pauses and turns toward Orville.

> LEANNE: One more thing, mister Pressfit. Put that bag of stuff away. Don't mention it or show it during the interview.

Leanne leaves the lobby.

INT. SOONER STATE SENIOR CENTER. AFTERNOON

Octavia Genarian, Evita Añejo, Harold Versery, and Anna Versery are seated at a square collapsible card table in the Recreation Room playing rummy. Three other people are sitting, reading, in thickly upholstered chairs near the windows.

A television screen mounted on the wall is tuned to the KPUT Afternoon News, but no one is watching it. The male newscaster is describing a fire that has broken out in a welding shop in downtown Ponca City. The news camera shows black smoke billowing into the sky; fire trucks block the street; the owner of the shop is seen spraying the roof of the building with a garden hose, and the SIRENS of arriving POLICE CARS are heard.

> HAROLD: That TV is distracting. Shouldn't we turn it off, or at least turn off the sound?

> OCTAVIA (*reaching into a bowl of popcorn*): Sure, nothing is happening.

> EVITA (*rising from her chair*): I'll mute it. If anyone gets upset, blame me.

Evita walks to the small table under the TV set where the remote is lying and picks it up. She points the remote upward and clicks it. The TV goes silent. Suddenly Evita hears Anna Versery's SHRILL VOICE, and turns toward the table.

> ANNA (*excited*): Look! Look! It's Leanne.

The scene on the television has switched to the image of Leanne Flambeau seated at a desk in the studio, her lips move, but her words are unheard.

ANNA (*smiling*): I like Leanne; she's my favorite news reporter.

OCTAVIA: What is she saying? Evita, put the sound on.

Evita clicks the remote again. The voice of Leanne fills the room.

CLOSE ON TV SCREEN

LEANNE: As our viewers know, KPUT was the first to release the news three weeks ago that Orville Pressfit, an elderly aircraft mechanic, reported his abduction by aliens in a mysterious aircraft. In an exclusive interview with KPUT earlier today, mister Pressfit reported a second abduction. Here is the recording of that interview.

At the word "abduction", everyone in the room jumps up and rushes to stand in front of the TV. The view on the screen is the parking lot of TV station KPUT. Leanne stands facing Orville, holding her microphone. She speaks.

LEANNE: Mister Pressfit, you have reported to us for the second time within a short period that you have experienced an abduction by some form of extraterrestrial creatures, that you were again taken against your will into their spacecraft, subjected to a four-hour-long flight, and later released, apparently unharmed. Is that correct?

ORVILLE: Yeah. They looked like the same guys that came and got me the first time. As I explained before, you wouldn't call them creatures. And no, they didn't harm me. Their ship took off, flew around for a long time, and then landed. They opened a hatch, let me out, and then took off again.

LEANNE: Were there any witnesses to this event?

ORVILLE: No, everybody who works at the airstrip had gone home. It was late and very dark. Their ship doesn't make very much noise.

LEANNE: What did the aliens do to you during the flight?

As Orville begins to answer the question, a fire truck with its siren screaming roars by in the background, drowning his voice.

BACK TO SCENE

The seniors in front of the TV start waving their arms and shaking their heads in frustration.

EVITA: What did he say? What did they do to him?

HAROLD: I didn't' hear him. It's those damn fire trucks. Must have been that welding shop.

ANNA: That's not good. I want to know what they do to a person they've kidnapped.

CLOSE ON THE TV SCREEN

The street behind Leanne and Orville becomes empty and quiet. Leanne speaks.

LEANNE: Have you reported this second encounter to the authorities?

ORVILLE: Do you mean the police? I plan to go to the Police Department when we're done here. But they probably won't believe me again. When I told them about this the first time, I could see some of them laughing.

The recorded interview ends. The TV scene switches back to Leanne seated at a desk in the studio.

LEANNE: The authorities are now questioning mister Pressfit for additional details. When more information unfolds in this ongoing threat, KPUT will report it.

The image of Leanne goes dark and a COMMERCIAL for shampoo begins BLARING.

BACK TO SCENE

Evita picks up the remote again and turns off the TV.

> HAROLD: Well, it's happened again. I knew it would.

> ANNA: That mechanic didn't say very much.

> HAROLD: He probably wasn't allowed to. It's part of the hush-up by the government.

> OCTAVIA: They drugged him.

> EVITA: Who? The government?

> OCTAVIA: No, the aliens. Remember what he said the first time? They forced him to drink something once they got him in their spaceship.

> EVITA: He said they offered him a rum and cola. They didn't *force* him to drink it.

> OCTAVIA: That's what he *thinks* happened. I've read about what these aliens can do. They have advanced technology and can inject chemicals in you to erase your memory, chemicals that can't be detected in the bloodstream.

> HAROLD: Older people are being targeted by these visitors from space because we're helpless. The government is not doing anything. We've got to protest more vigorously.

> ANNA: We can march down on City Hall again.

> HAROLD: That's not enough. We've got to make our concerns known to the Federal Government. We've got to stage a protest in front of a Federal building.

> EVITA: Where are there any Federal offices around here?

HAROLD: Anna, hand me that phone book on the shelf.

Anna walks to the book shelf attached to the wall. She picks up the phone directory sitting on a stack of magazines, and hands it to Harold.

HAROLD: Let's see. There's the Bureau of Indian Affairs. I'm not sure they could do anything about this problem.

OCTAVIA: What about the Social Security office?

EVITA: The nearest one is in Stillwater; that's a forty-mile drive.

HAROLD: Let's just get together in front of the post office tomorrow. Do you all still have your signs?

Everybody in the room nods "yes."

HAROLD: Good. I'm going to stop by the newspaper office tomorrow morning and let them know we're staging a major protest. Maybe I can talk them into sending a reporter and photographer to cover it. By the way, I'll make some calls to the other senior clubs and retirement homes; we need a big turnout. We'll meet at the post office tomorrow after lunch – one-thirty, okay?

OCTAVIA: Could you move that to two-thirty?

HAROLD: Why?

OCTAVIA: Doctor Alvarez, the podiatrist, is coming to see me at one-thirty. You know him. He's the one that reminds me of Ricardo Montalban (*giggles*).

HAROLD: Do you have a metatarsal problem or something else? You seem to be walking normally.

OCTAVIA: No, it's my appointment for him to trim my toenails. Then he files them smooth and puts lotion on my feet (*giggles*).

> HAROLD: Okay. We meet at the post office at two-thirty.

The seniors that were reading nod in agreement and return to their chairs by the windows. Harold, Anna, Evita, and Octavia take their seats at the card table and resume their game.

INT. PONCA POST BUILDING. DAY

A YOUNG MAN stands behind a small wooden counter in the front entrance to the offices of the Ponca Post. He is about twenty. His neckwear is unevenly tied. He leans on his elbows on the counter, slowing turning the pages of the newspaper. He doesn't look up as Harold Versery enters and confronts him.

> HAROLD: Pardon me. May I speak to someone in the news room?

> YOUNG MAN (*startled, looking up*): I'm sorry. What did you say?

> HAROLD: I have a piece of important news. I'm here to see if the paper is interested.

> YOUNG MAN: Everyone's pretty busy right now. We're always working to deadlines, you know. What happened?

> HAROLD: It hasn't happened yet. A large group of citizens are planning to hold a protest today.

> YOUNG MAN: What are you protesting?

> HAROLD: Surely, you've read about it – you work on the paper. We're demanding that the Federal government – the President, in fact – do something to stop the abductions by space aliens.

> YOUNG MAN: I think you'll be wasting your time.

> HAROLD: What makes you think that?

YOUNG MAN: Haven't you heard?

HAROLD: Heard what?

YOUNG MAN: The President doesn't seem to believe there's a problem. Haven't you seen today's Post?

The young man picks up the paper from the counter and holds up the front page to show Harold the banner.

CLOSE ON FRONT PAGE

In very large, bold print are the words: GRAYFIELD DENIES ALIENS ARE HERE!

BACK TO SCENE

The young man runs his finger over an article at the bottom of the page.

YOUNG MAN: There's a great story here by Alice Allcaps, one of our people, explaining how the CIA and the FBI think this UFO stuff is all made up.

HAROLD (*taking hold of paper*): This can't be true. I'll have to show this to everybody at the Senior Center. May I have this copy?

YOUNG MAN: Sure. That'll be fifty cents.

Harold removes two quarters from a coin purse and gives them to the young man. He takes the folded newspaper and hurries to the exit.

INT. SOONER STATE SENIOR CENTER. DAY

Harold Versery stands in front of a cork bulletin board in the game room of the Senior Center. In his left hand, hanging to the floor, is the front page of The Ponca Post. With his right hand he takes two pushpins from the board. He lifts the newspaper up and pins each of the top corners to the board. The paper displays the headline Harold saw at the Ponca Post office: GRAYFIELD DENIES ALIENS ARE HERE!

Anna Versery steps up beside him, shaking her head as she looks at what he has posted.

> ANNA: I can't believe what I'm reading. Somebody's not telling President Grayfield what's going on. We've got to make a strong protest today.

> HAROLD: I've cancelled the protest at the post office and I've notified the other senior groups to stand down.

> ANNA: What! Why?

> HAROLD: I realize we've got to get the *President's* attention. You and I are going to take our protest directly to Washington – to the White House!

> ANNA: How can we do that?

> HAROLD: I talked with Lou, the treasurer of the Sunrise Seniors Club. Boy! Is he upset! We made calls to the rest of the Executive Board – Ned and Louise. I agreed to chip in half of our airfare – coach, of course. The board voted to pay the rest using the fund for the Christmas party. This is more important.

> ANNA: I'll start packing.

> HAROLD: Me too. Lou is going to send emails to other senior groups he knows of around the country that may be planning trips to DC this week. They just finished refurbishing the Washington Monument, you know. It's safe to go to the top again.

Harold presses in the pins holding the newspaper one more time, surveys his work, then walks quickly away with Anna.

EXT. WHITE HOUSE. NORTH LAWN. DAY

President Grayfield and Lamar Ferret are standing side by side under the north portico of the White House, looking out across the lawn toward Pennsylvania Avenue.

In the distance, behind the wrought iron fence, is a large crowd. Many in the crowd are holding large placards; those without placards are thrusting their arms up vigorously to attract attention.

> THELMA (*turning to Lamar*): What do you make of it?

> LAMAR *(holding binoculars up to his eyes)*: Let me see if I can read what's on some of those signs.

> THELMA: Last week we had those young college student protesters. I never did figure out what their complaint was. They put too many words on the cardboard they were holding up – and they print so small!

Lamar hands the binoculars to Thelma.

> LAMAR: It's what I thought. Take a look.

Thelma studies the crowd through the binoculars.

> THELMA: They look like they're all old people. Many are bent over. How did they ever make it here? I see three with walkers and two are in wheelchairs.

> LAMAR: Could you read any of the signs?

> THELMA: Yes, one says, "Where is Our Space Defense?" There's even a woman who's getting one of our Secret Service guys to help her lift up her sign. Her sign reads, "Old People Need Your Protection."

> LAMAR: The Secret Service is helping her? How do you know?

> THELMA: It's an overcast day, but he's wearing those expensive sunglasses*.

> LAMAR (*pointing*): There, that sign on the far right tells the story. Read it.

---

*Producer's note: Let's explore the opportunity for product placement here.

Thelma looks through the binoculars again.

> THELMA: I guess you mean the big one being held by the old couple. It says, "Remember the Alamo, Remember the Maine, Remember Ponca City."

> LAMAR: You see what this is, don't you? We shouldn't be surprised. Come inside; I want to show you some papers. It'll take me a minute to get them; I'll meet you in the Red Room.

INT. WHITE HOUSE. RED ROOM. DAY

Thelma hands the binoculars to Lamar. She turns and walks to the door. Lamar follows.

Thelma is sitting on a couch, tapping her finger on the arm in a manner of impatience. A door opens. Lamar enters carrying a stack of magazines. He places the stack on a table next to the couch. He pulls a chair up and sits down facing Thelma.

> LAMAR: Have you figured out yet who those people remonstrating* by the fence are?

> THELMA: I have a suspicion, but I can't believe it. You're going to tell me those old people are getting that worked up over an alleged abduction?

> LAMAR: It's gone beyond that. Look at this. It's a FAX Hazel received earlier today. It's a front-page article from the Ponca Post.

> THELMA: Read it to me.

> LAMAR: There's been a *second* abduction!

> THELMA: Where was it and who was carried off this time?

*Director's note: Isn't there a synonym for this word that more people will understand?

LAMAR: The same place – the Oklahoma airfield. And the same guy – the old mechanic.

THELMA: There you go! If it's the same senile, perhaps intoxicated, fellow claiming he was high-jacked under identical, questionable circumstances, isn't that even *more* reason to dismiss it as a hallucination?

LAMAR: Wait, there's more. Here's another FAX. It's a copy of a headline. The sender cut out the words and pasted them together on a piece of paper rather poorly, but it's legible.

Lamar holds it up to Thelma.

CLOSE ON FAX DOCUMENT

The FAX reads: GRAYFIELD DENIES ALIENS ARE HERE!

BACK TO SCENE

THELMA: I didn't actually say that.

LAMAR: But that's what they heard in Ponca City.

THELMA: You mean to say that this second, so-called abduction is being believed to a point where old people in Oklahoma – who should be in the park practicing tai chi – are boarding airplanes for DC to stand on the street and shout at me?

LAMAR: Yes, it's become a tempest in the state, and it's growing into a national uprising.

Lamar takes one of the publications from the top of the stack and holds it up.

LAMAR: Look at this one. (*reading title*) SENIOR ACTIVITIES. This magazine is published in Ponca City where this Orville what's-his-name is from. This issue ran a blistering article on the indifference of the local government to the safety of those over sixty-five.

THELMA: Are all of the people in the city that upset?

LAMAR: Let me repeat, Madam President, it's not just in *this* city. This panic, if I may call it that, has traveled throughout the state. During the last two days we've been receiving calls from the Oklahoma State Assembly and from the House of Representatives and the Senate in DC. And think about this: the two Senators and five of the six Representatives from Oklahoma are all from your party!

THELMA: Hmm.

LAMAR: Here's another one . . . SENIOR TRENDS . . . out of Portland, Oregon, with a two-page article suggesting aliens are introducing mind-altering drugs into the high blood pressure medication being administered at nursing homes.

Ferret hands another magazine to Thelma.

LAMAR: Look at the cover on this one. That's the GOLDEN YEARS REPORTER out of Tempe, Arizona. The REPORTER features a front-page story of an eighty-five-year old man who disappeared from his daughter's home and was found ten miles out in the desert standing next to a patch of mysteriously scorched earth. And there's more. Look! Here are more warnings of alien threats in these critical articles in SENIOR FUN, SENIOR TRAILS, and SENIOR AFFAIRS.

Ferret's enthusiasm and excitement builds as he comes across more articles in his stack.

LAMAR: This one's making the old-timers *really* upset. Check out this article in SENIOR HIJINKS, the one next to the report you see there on macular degeneration. It talks about alien implants.

THELMA: Where did you get all these?

LAMAR: People send them to me. Don't worry; they're free.

Thelma takes the copy of SENIOR HIJINKS from Lamar and reads the article.

LAMAR: They're all saying the same thing: The older generation – and that is a big voting bloc, Madam President – the older generation is asking the White House to treat these alien abduction reports seriously. You have to address these concerns, Thelma. This is the Silver Tsunami.

THELMA: Very well. I'll take care of it.

LAMAR: When?

THELMA: Soon. But I'm going to need some input from my Science Advisor, and I'll let her get things rolling. Call the Office of Science and Technology Policy. Have them notify Edith Wormbook, the Director, that I need to sit down with her tomorrow to discuss a critical issue. Don't mention the subject.

LAMAR: Shall I set up the meeting at her office in the Eisenhower Executive Office Building?

THELMA: No, have her come here. She's just down the street. The walk will do her good.

Lamar gathers up his stack of magazines and leaves the Red Room.

INT. WHITE HOUSE. OVAL OFFICE. DAY

Thelma sits in a couch, relaxing against the cushioned back, looking up across an oblong coffee table at EDITH WORMBOOK, Director of the Office of Science and Technology Policy, who has just arrived.

Edith, fifty-eight, has a hawk-like face. She is outfitted in an expensive blouse and charcoal slacks, and wears her hair pulled back in a bun. Edith has extensive training and experience in varied technical fields. She wishes she could be more of an influence on the government's scientific policies.

Edith has placed a dark brown vinyl case on the table, and is lowering herself carefully onto a similar couch opposite the President. On the table are two tumblers with White House emblems and a pitcher of iced tea.

THELMA: Edith, what do you think of the tan velour covering on these divans?

EDITH: I hope that question isn't the reason you have called me here.

THELMA: No, but I wanted your opinion.

EDITH: Did *you* pick out the color and fabric?

THELMA: They're not my choice; I inherited these pieces.

EDITH: In that case, have them re-covered; I'd suggest a floral pattern. (*sighs*) Can we get to why I'm here?

THELMA: First I have to ask another question: do you believe in flying saucers?

EDITH: On a personal level, no, but as Director of the OSTP I have to be open to evidence sent me, pro or con. I think I can guess where you're going with this.

THELMA: Then you've no doubt read the stories about the alien abduction in Oklahoma?

EDITH: A little. This excitement over extraterrestrial visits arises periodically. If you plot the frequency of reports over time, each surge is almost as periodic and predictable as the vernal equinox.

THELMA: The public firmly believes that we're being invaded from outer space. The attention these reports are getting has crowded out every other serious issue I'm trying to resolve in Congress. The pressure is on me to build and deploy some kind of vehicle that could chase after these UFOs – an interceptor. Is that possible?

EDITH: Well, no one has fully described these ships, let alone accurately gauge how fast they fly. That mechanic who supposedly was aboard one didn't know. Let's say their speed is slightly less than, oh, fifteen hundred miles per hour. You don't need any new spacecraft; you can use an F-twenty-two Raptor. It will catch up with a saucer easily. If the saucer tries to escape, the Raptor can follow it for eighteen hundred miles.

THELMA: I'm hearing that these craft must be incredibly fast if they're able to reach Earth from some planet we can't even see.

EDITH: In that case, you would need a rocket-powered vehicle. It must be ready to launch within less than a minute. It will probably have to use storable propellants. Radar spots the saucer, bang! Off it goes.

THELMA: That's what we need.

EDITH: The craft using the rocket propulsion wouldn't have the range of the Raptor, but you don't need it. The craft would be on the target in couple of minutes and able to take photos or shoot at it, whatever the plan is.

THELMA: Shoot at it? That's a little extreme; I was thinking more of threatening maneuvers. We don't know if they're hostile.

EDITH: Of course. Look, we're envisioning what would logically be an Air Force Space Command Contract. That department is in a better position to decide whether this ship should carry armament. Besides, the structure, weight limits, and avionics requirements could be written to allow emplacement later of whatever weapons might be needed in this application.

THELMA: Edith, you understand all these variables. I need you to carry this message to the Air Force. Tell them this is a specific request from the President of the United States. Get the Department of Homeland Security involved. I want the Air Force to publish a solicitation for an interceptor vehicle.

Edith pulls out a small planner from her case, hurriedly writes a note, then slams it shut.

THELMA: Which company do you think is best suited for a project of this type?

EDITH: Well, Repulsive Technology, Incorporated has an excellent track record. They've recently completed an anti-missile defense program, so they would have the time and the resources to take on a project of this kind.

THELMA: I agree. They prepared an excellent feasibility report for me describing a vehicle of the very type you suggested. Ask Hazel to give you my copy of the report before you leave. Show it to the Air Force. I'm sure Repulsive Technology is the company to contract with to build the vehicle we need.

EDITH: Very possibly, but if I know Walter Masterly, he would be reluctant to commit to an iffy, far-out task of catching flying saucers. I doubt that he would even bid on the job.

THELMA: I might be able to persuade him.

Hazel Lazer enters the office and pauses at the coffee table with hands folded at her waist looking first at Thelma, then at Edith.

HAZEL: Do you ladies need any more iced tea?

THELMA: You could pour some for us. When you get back to your desk, call the Office of Scheduling and Advance; tell them to arrange a trip to Repulsive Technology for me and Lamar.

Hazel fills each of the tumblers with tea and hands them to the ladies. Thelma raises her tumbler to Edith, toast-wise, in a gesture of dedication as Hazel turns and leaves.

EXT. MAJOR AIRPORT. DAY

An extremely large passenger plane is landing. As it touches down, the letters on the side become visible: AIR FORCE ONE. The plane comes to rest.

Portable air stairs are moved into position at the aircraft's forward cabin exit. The cabin door opens and six Secret Service agents in dark suits leap out. They pause a moment at the top of the stairs to scan the surroundings. Five of them trot quickly down the stairs and form a cordon around the base. One remains next to the open door.

There are only a few people in the vicinity – photographers, reporters, and men toting video cameras. A moment later a tall woman steps out, looks toward the terminal, shading her eyes with her left hand. It is Thelma Grayfield. She carefully steps down the stairs, waving to the nearly empty apron in front.

As she reaches the last step, the media people move in from the terminal until they are stopped by the open arms of the Secret Service agents.

> REPORTER: Madam President, what is the purpose of your visit today?
>
> THELMA: I have designated this week "A Decade of Progress in Space." I've dedicated my time during these seven days to traveling across America, presenting achievement awards to those great companies in the aerospace industry who have contributed so much to our progress in keeping America prominent in space.
>
> REPORTER: Whom are you visiting today?
>
> THELMA: Today I will be visiting Repulsive Technology, that great rocket engine developer, and then I will stop at Super

Structures, the company designing the space terminal on the moon.

Two black limousines roll up quietly to the crowd of news and television reporters. The drivers step out and open the rear doors of each. The rear doors are lettered in gold: ED'S RENT-A-LIMO.

>THELMA: I see my transportation is here. My schedule is very tight, people. I'm sorry. I wish I could answer more of your questions, but I must leave.

The Secret Service agents push the reporters aside, making an aisle for Thelma to reach the rear door of one of the limousines. She slides down into the seat, the door is closed, and the vehicle speeds off the landing area.

EXT. RTI. PARKING LOT. DAY

The President's limousine and the accompanying Secret Service limousine turn into a driveway of a large parking lot. In the background is a wide, two-story building. Except for a few windows on the ground floor, the building exterior has gray walls on all visible sides. Silver metal letters spelling out the company name jut out from the wall: REPULSIVE TECHNOLOGY, INC.

The limousines are stopped in their path by a strangely configured and motorized cart with a driver and TWO WORKMEN walking next to it. One of the workmen walks up to the driver's side of one of the limousines. The limo driver rolls down his window to speak to the workman.

>LIMO DRIVER: Where is visitor parking?

>WORKMAN: Right here, but you can't come any farther. We're re-striping the Reserved Parking area. You'll have to park in lot six.

>LIMO DRIVER: We have to park *here* and we have to park *now*!

>WORKMAN: I'm sorry, but we've got our orders. This job was supposed to be finished yesterday. We were told there are

some VIPs coming. Just park in lot six. We'll be finished in a couple of hours.

LIMO DRIVER: That's too far away. I have the *President* in this vehicle.

WORKMAN: Well, remind the President that he told my crew chief that he wants this lot finished *today*. And if he wants it finished, he'll have to park in lot six.

The re-striping machine driver guns the engine. The machine rolls forward, leaving a white strip as it moves.

LIMO DRIVER (*shouting*): This isn't the President of the company in this car! *This is the President of the United States!*

During the interchange of the limousine driver and the workman, the Secret Service agents have left their vehicle and are acting as a barrier to the other workmen and three RTI employees leaving for an early lunch. One of the AGENTS walks to the limo driver.

AGENT: Leave the car here, driver. (*looks to the rear seat*) Madam President, we recommend you get out of the car now and come with us inside.

The agent walks around the limo, opens the side door, and helps Thelma out. She stands up beside the car, pauses, and waves to the six people in the parking lot. Lamar steps out of the vehicle, straightens his jacket, and looks around.

In the distance, at the guard gate, a group of three men, graying executive types, and an attractive young woman wait. They are Walter Masterly, John Fulbrane, Angelique Del Mundo, and GREGORY KORJUL, Director of Government Relations.

Gregory is very old and actually past the normal retirement age. His suit is very business-like, but a little out of date. He wears a constant smile, and has developed an unctuous demeanor.

One of the Secret Service agents moves to join this group, talks with them briefly, and accompanies them across the parking lot to the limousine.

As the group approaches the vehicle, Walter walks faster to lead the pack. As he reaches the limo, he confronts the President.

> WALTER *(extending his hand)*:   Madam President, let me welcome you to Repulsive Technology, Incorporated. We're honored by your presence.

> THELMA: Please, just call me Thelma. It is I, Walter, who is honored to be here. As you know, I have a special presentation to make to your company.

> WALTER: Allow me to introduce your hosts for this visit. This gentleman to my left is Gregory Korjul, Director of Government Relations.

Gregory nods and smiles pleasantly.

> WALTER: This fine gentleman on my right is John Fulbrane, our Chief Engineer.

John nods and smiles grimly.

> WALTER: This very competent lady is my Administrative Assistant, Miss Angelique Del Mundo.

> ANGELIQUE *(bowing slightly)*:   *Senior* Administrative Assistant.
> WALTER: If you need any assistance during your visit, call upon Angelique. She is . . .

Walter's words are interrupted by a CHANT coming from off-screen. Everyone stops and turns to look to the sidewalk that borders the parking lot.

CUT TO: SIDEWALK

A group of three very elderly people are holding up a banner. The banner appears to be made from a white blanket, with large black sewn-on letters that read: STOP THE ALIENS.

BACK TO SCENE

>WALTER (*ignoring the protesters*): We're looking forward to your presentation. We have prepared a special area to accommodate the throngs of employees. Our entire workforce wants to hear what you have to say.

One of the Secret Service agents standing next to Walter quickly moves back to the gate to block fifteen employees who are leaving for lunch from straying near the limo.

>WALTER: We don't have far to go to the meeting area. Please come with us.

Thelma, Lamar, Walter, Gregory, John, Angelique, and the six Secret Service agents walk as a body to the gate.

INT. RTI. MANUFACTURING ASSEMBLY SHOP. DAY

A huge warehouse-sized room has been set up with hundreds of folding chairs. Most of the chairs are empty. Several dozen employees are scattered throughout the seating. In front of the sparse audience at one end of the room is a line of tables, set end to end. Seated at the tables in more folding chairs, facing the audience, are a dozen more people, some company executives, some city officials.
The space is a typical factory floor except that there are no machines. Overhead a bridge crane slowly moves away from the audience. The SCREECH of an occasional CHAIR movement and COUGH from the AUDIENCE echoes in the building.

One of the individuals at the table is the tired, aging DANIEL BRAZEWELL, Vice President of Manufacturing. Daniel recently passed sixty-three. He has dark, wavy hair and wears silver-rimmed eyeglasses. Daniel is not excited by his work at RTI. He is a thoughtful person, but treats most issues in a slow-going, matter-of-fact way

He has been sitting motionless, holding a cell phone. His boredom is obvious. The cell phone rings; he presses it to his ear. He rises and addresses the small crowd.

> DANIEL: I have received word that President Grayfield has arrived and is on her way now. (*pauses and frowns*) If you don't mind, I'd like the people toward the back to come up and sit in the front three rows. Would you do that? The press may be here to take some photos and we would like as many people in the picture as possible.

Daniel pauses in his remarks while the employees in the back, some muttering, stand up, push the chairs in front of them aside and make their way to the empty chairs near the head tables.

> DANIEL: When the President is introduced, please show your enthusiasm. Let's give her a really warm RTI welcome!

The resounding CLATTER of FOOTSTEPS on the cement floor of the area causes everyone to turn to look at the entrance at the rear. Two Secret Service agents enter, followed by President Grayfield, Walter Masterly, and the others in the party. The President and Walter make their way up the aisle between the chairs and take seats at the center table.

John and Angelique walk to the end table; they take empty chairs next to ALBERT GURITHUM, Director of Systems Analysis.

Albert is the only person at the table not wearing a suit; he prefers cardigans. He has a short, gray beard. He is often called upon to bring resolution to disagreements, sometimes bitter, among RTI management, using his skills as a mediator and pacifier.

Walter adjusts the chair for the President as she sits down. He remains standing next to her at a small lectern that rests on the table. The microphone at the lectern hangs off to the side like a tired serpent. Walter attempts several times, in vain, to get it to stay in a position near his chin, but it repeatedly falls back over the side. He holds it up while he is speaking.

> WALTER: Good afternoon to all you good people. Over the years at RTI we have had many important visitors, but none as important as the person who has chosen to honor us with her presence today. Fellow team members, it is with great pride I introduce the President of the United States, Thelma Grayfield!

Everyone in the three occupied rows of chairs in front of the tables applauds. One person in the second row waves a small stars and stripes.

Thelma Grayfield stands and moves sideways to the lectern at the center table. Walter gives her a warm handshake and seats himself beside her. She taps the microphone, notes the limp posture, and tilts it upward slightly.

> THELMA: Thank you, mister Masterly, mister Fulbrane, mister Korjul, RTI employees, and distinguished guests. My mission during this week has been to visit companies such as your's throughout America – companies that have not only made their mark in the aerospace world of the last century of the last millennium, but have already demonstrated that their ideas and skills have kept pace with the demands of the new technology required to build the more exotic missiles, spacecraft, and supporting equipment this millennium demands.

The approximately fifty employees present applaud. Someone in the audience takes a flash picture.

ANGLE ON END TABLE

> JOHN *(leaning over to Albert Gurithum and whispering)*: It was a bad idea to schedule this for the noontime lunch break. I think we could have had a better turnout during the work period.

ANGLE ON THELMA

> THELMA: Your company's successes in your development of the solar probe, the space taxi, the satellite search-and-rescue pod, and the low-earth orbit priority package delivery capsule prove your leadership in this field.

Thelma bends over and picks up the slim attaché case she has been carrying, places it on the table, and pulls out a plaque.

> THELMA: President Masterly, would you stand next to me, please?

CUT TO: THELMA AND WALTER

Walter stands and moves a little bit sidewise to join Thelma at the lectern.

> THELMA: President Masterly, representing the White House Committee on Industrial Excellence, it is with extreme pleasure that I present you and your fine company with this plaque of recognition.

Walter reaches to take it, but Thelma pulls it away.

> THELMA: Allow me to read to you the inscription. It says, "This award, given to Repulsive Technology, Incorporated by the President of the United States, symbolizes America's recognition of and appreciation for this company's achievements in rocket engine science."

Thelma smiles, turns the plaque toward the audience, moves it from side to side, and places her finger at the bottom of an etched plate.

> THELMA: Notice that it has your company logo, the Presidential seal, and my signature.

The audience applauds. She hands it to Walter.

> WALTER: Madam President, I gratefully accept this plaque on behalf of all of the great team members here at RTI. We will display this in a place of honor.

The audience applauds. Walter places the plaque gently on the table.

> WALTER: Madam President, at this time we have a short video presentation that tells the story of our company; can you stay long enough to watch.

> THELMA: How short?

> WALTER: About twelve minutes.

> THELMA: Fine. After that I have a brief announcement to make.

Thelma and Walter take their seats.

CUT TO: SIDE OF ASSEMBLY SHOP

LEONARD LENZ, a young man from the Media Services Department is sitting on the floor next to a cart supporting a large television monitor. He is inserting a DVD into the base of the monitor.

Leonard usually wears a tee shirt and jeans to work, but today he has on the dress shirt and bow tie he purchased for this event. Leonard is very creative in video productions for RTI, but he would rather be working in a motion picture studio. He looks up and realizes his manipulations are being carefully watched

> LEONARD: The equipment will be ready in a moment, folks.

BACK TO SCENE

Walter looks off to the side to check the progress with the television monitor. With a wave of his finger he beckons Leonard who jumps to his feet and rushes to Walter's side.

> WALTER (*speaking softly into Leonard's ear*): Take this plaque and find a place in Media Services to store it. (*holds out plaque; pauses*) No, better take it to the Graphics

Department and give it to Arthur Gumme. I think he has some display cases there or he can make one.

Leonard takes the plaque from Walter, and places it on the cart next to the television monitor. He pushes the cart up to the edge of the end table. He accidentally strikes the table, waking Albert Gurithum who has dozed off.

People seated at tables and in the audience turn their chairs slightly to view the monitor. Leonard walks back to the cart and presses the start button on the DVD player. Nothing happens. Albert turns in his chair and taps the cart to get the young man's attention.

    ALBERT: Check the power cord.

CUT TO: THELMA AND LAMAR

    THELMA *(whispering to Lamar)*: When is our appointment at
        Super Structures?

    LAMAR: Two hours from now. See if you can wrap this up.
        What's this announcement you're going to make?

    THELMA: I didn't have an opportunity to discuss it with you.
        Just go with me on this.

BACK TO SCENE

Leonard moves to the back of the cart and begins checking the cords.

    THELMA *(turning to Walter)*: How is it you have so much free
        space here on the factory floor?

    WALTER: This used to be the assembly area for the RT-thirty-
        three, the engine for the Anti-Anti-Missile. You cancelled
        the program last year, remember?

    THELMA: Oh, yes.

    LEONARD: Looks like I got it, folks.

CLOSE ON TV MONITOR

The screen glows and an image of the Milky Way forms. In the center three tiny letters appear that swell to fill the screen:

RTI

The letters fade and new words appear:

Our Heritage

The image changes to grainy black-and-white footage of three unidentified men in white lab frocks installing a narrow, four-foot long cylindrical propulsion system into a fragile looking launch cage. They speak to one another, but the film is silent. In the distance is a small, worn, concrete hut, the control center. The film is obviously very old, and the motions of the men are very jerky. The VOICE of a man, the NARRATOR, is heard off-screen. The voice is soft and the words are delivered in a measured tempo.

> NARRATOR: The year is nineteen thirty-one. The country is Germany. In an abandoned ammunitions storage facility in the city of Reinickendorf, a suburb of Berlin, starry-eyed young engineers and scientists have come together, tantalized by the dream of developing rocket propulsion. Their organization bears the name Verein für Raumshiffahrt, or VfR, which, in English, is Society for Space Travel. With meager resources this optimistic clan designed and built crude yet effective rockets, rockets that foretold the marvel of greater missiles and space vessels to come.

CUT TO: JOHN FULBRANE

John is leaning back in his chair with arms folded, looking at Albert.

> JOHN: I think this is the fourth time I've seen this video.

CLOSE ON TV MONITOR

The black-and-white film continues. The three men in white lab coats, using hand tools, make final adjustments on a rocket strapped to a launch fixture. They stop, examine their work, and walk quickly to the control hut.

The scene changes to the interior of the building. One of the men takes a position in front of a panel with dials and the faces of gauges. The second man stands before a small console with switches. The third man looks out of the window at the rocket launch stand. A caption appears at the bottom of the screen: "Die startvorbereitungen beginnen."

CUT TO: WALTER AND THELMA

> THELMA: What does that say?

> WALTER: That's German for "The launch preparations begin."

CLOSE ON TV MONITOR

The man at the window leans forward and waves his arm sharply. His lips make crisp, distinct movements as he speaks a one-word command. The caption reads FEUER! The video cuts to a close-up of a pair of hands on the small control console. A thumb pushes a toggle switch.

CUT TO: WALTER AND THELMA

> THELMA: Why is he talking about the Fuhrer?

> WALTER: He's not. He was giving the command to "Fire." That's the German word for "fire."

CLOSE ON TV MONITOR

As the camera cuts to the rocket, a white cloud gushes from the nozzle. The men, seeing this, crouch and back away out of the frame. The rocket rises slowly, explodes, and falls to the ground.

ANGLE ON ALBERT AND JOHN

> ALBERT: Their safety procedures give this business a bad name. You couldn't do that today.

> JOHN: Did that last launch you saw foretell of any tests we've got scheduled for next week?

CLOSE ON TV MONITOR

The camera pans over a large, mostly empty stretch of concrete dotted with a few tumbled-down buildings. Weeds are seen poking from cracks here and there. Four men stand outside the door of one of the shed-like structures holding unidentifiable parts. They smile at the camera.

> NARRATOR: This modest test site with its austere working quarters was named the Raketenflugplatz or rocket flying place. This cadre of young men who gave of their time to this exciting, but then-considered laughable pursuit, included those whose names would later stand out in this field: Willy Ley, Hermann Oberth, and the most famous of all, Wernher von Braun. Also, a member of this illustrious team was the youthful scientist who would later be transported to America with several hundred other German rocket designers at the end of World War II as part of Project Paperclip. He would start a company in America whose name would become synonymous with the conquest of space. That young man, a recent graduate of the University of Berlin, was Doctor Wilhelm von Streber.

The camera zooms in on one of the groups of four, Wilhelm Von Streber. All of the company executives applaud.

ANGLE ON THELMA AND LAMAR

> LAMAR *(whispering to Thelma)*: They're applauding a *video*. I've never seen that.

CLOSE ON TV MONITOR

The scene in the video switches to the interior of a crudely built and sparsely furnished wooden shack. Some of the men seen earlier, including von Streber and some new faces, possibly engineers or technicians, look first at a control console then out of a small window. The men talk to each other, but there is no sound of their voices, only some dubbed in classical MUSIC.

The scene changes momentarily to a distant view of a launch pad with a narrow silver tube held in place by four spider-like metal legs. Back inside the shack the men are seen making notes in journals they carry. One man slaps the back of the man at the console. He presses a large button.

The view changes again to the rocket sitting on the pad. An erratic flame issues from the bottom end. The rocket jumps from the pad, moves upward, then curves and disappears into a layer of haze.

Inside the shack von Streber begins cheering, jumping, and hugging the other men.

> NARRATOR: In May of nineteen thirty-one this brilliant team assembled a rocket employing liquid oxygen and gasoline as propellants. This rocket, christened Repulsor One, was launched successfully and reached an altitude of sixty-one meters. Later that summer, another version of the Repulsor design would reach a thousand meters. Doctor von Streber never forgot the thrill of those successes.

The scene is a small room with a tiny window. Shelves line the walls holding tools, paint cans, boxes, and bottles. Von Streber and an unidentified assistant are operating lathes. Small nozzles spin on the lathes. The men hold tools against the spinning metal as chips curl off and fall to the floor. Von Streber occasionally looks up, smiles, and returns his attention to the work on the lath.

> NARRATOR: In honor of the Repulsor engine, Doctor von Streber used the name when he started his rocket engine manufacturing shop in his garage in Huntsville, Alabama.

That tiny company moved to its present quarters, then grew and grew to become America's premier rocket developer: Repulsive Technology, Incorporated.

ANGLE ON THELMA AND WALTER

> THELMA *(leaning and whispering to Walter)*:   I always wondered how your company got its name.

> WALTER: It's part of our tradition. We have a lot of traditions here at RTI.

> THELMA: What is that ugly cut on Doctor von Streber's left cheek?

> WALTER: A dueling scar. He was lucky.

> THELMA: Lucky?

> WALTER: Yes, in Germany that scar was a badge of honor. He was able to arrange a duel with a fellow student at the University of Berlin. The trick was to get grazed enough to leave an impressive scar without being seriously injured. Von Streber wasn't all that good as a swordsman; he could have lost an ear. At least he didn't have to pay a surgeon to fake a scar. He *was* lucky.

> THELMA: When this video ends, I have a brief announcement. Would you introduce me again, please?

Walter looks her straight on and nods.

CLOSE ON TV MONITOR

The video changes to brilliant color and shows Repulsive Technology building, testing, delivering rocket engines.

The video ends with the RTI logo superimposed on an American flag rippling vigorously in a breeze.

ANGLE ON WALTER

Walter stands, slides to the lectern, and raises his arms.

> WALTER: You have been a wonderful audience; I know you are anxious to return to your work stations. President Grayfield has some final words for us before she runs off. Please take the microphone, Madam President.

ANGLE ON THELMA

Thelma pushes back her folding chair, places her attaché case on the table, straightens herself, steps sideways to the lectern, smiles graciously at Walter, and looks side to side into the faces of the employees.

She attempts to hold the limp microphone up.

> THELMA: Before I came here today, I thought I knew a lot about RTI. I listened to the information my staff supplied me on the company's accomplishments. This knowledge shaped the plaque I presented earlier. But now that I have talked with so many of your company's well-qualified executives, and now that I've met some of the people who work in the offices and at the drafting tables, my eyes have been opened to your skill and dedication.

ANGLE ON JOHN AND AL

> JOHN *(turning to Albert)*: Every designer in this company is on a computer terminal. Where did she see a drafting table?

BACK TO SCENE

> THELMA: And most important, now that I've seen this wonderful video of your company's past, present, and future, I know I've made the right choice for a special request I have for Repulsive Technology, Incorporated.

At these words, Albert Gurithum, who has dozed off again, opens his eyes in apparent shock, straightens in his chair, and turns briskly toward the President. Walter Masterly and Lamar Ferret look at each other and then turn their faces upward, poised for her next words.

> THELMA (*holding the microphone up*): It's not news when I mention that a recent incident involving the appearance of a UFO and an abduction in Oklahoma has generated serious concern across that state and, indeed, across America.

Thelma pauses, reaches down into her attaché, and pulls out a single page. She waves it at the audience.

> THELMA: I have here in my hand a resolution adopted by the Board of Commissioners of Ponca City, Oklahoma. This spells out pretty well the mood of the country. Our citizens, particularly our older citizens, who feel most at risk, are demanding to know what these UFOs are and who is piloting them. As your President, I, too, am equally concerned. I believe we must re-activate the investigations into these phenomena that we terminated in the past. I believe we must ask these questions again.

Lamar moves uncomfortably in his seat and takes a deep breath. He reaches for the paper with the resolution, but Thelma pulls it away.

> THELMA: To this end I have set some solutions in motion. I have passed my concerns on to my Chiefs of Staff and the Secretaries of the Air Force and of Defense, and I have their agreement. I also have agreement with the defense budgeting Committee in Congress to set aside sufficient funds for a contract to build a pursuit vehicle that will allow us to determine the nature of these UFOs and the possible threat they may pose. These vehicles will carry sufficient deterrent power to force these aliens to leave our airspace. A Request for Proposal will be forthcoming soon that defines the nature and scope of this effort.

Lamar places his forehead into the open palm of his left hand, his elbow resting on the table. A blank stare replaces the smile of a moment ago.

THELMA (*turning to look at Walter*): Walter, I want RTI to participate in the competition for this project. I want you to submit a bid. An Air Force Contracting Officer will be getting in touch with you shortly to assist your proposal team with any information on what we are looking for. This is your area of expertise, and I know you will come through for America.

Thelma steps back from the lectern and returns to her seat. Walter stands and replaces her at the microphone.

WALTER: President Grayfield, your words of recognition and praise of our work have humbled us and given us cause to do even better in the future. We will look forward to the issuance of the RFP of which you speak.

There is enthusiastic applause from the audience. Walter pulls back Thelma's chair as she stands. They begin walking to the exit. The Secret Service men converge on the pair and escort them out the large doors.

ANGLE ON JOHN AND ALBERT

ALBERT (*whispering to John*): Do we have anybody that knows anything about flying saucers?

John pats Albert's arm and nods reassuringly.

INT. RTI. SANDRA BINDING'S OFFICE. DAY

FLORENCE KAHDASILL, Deputy Director of Contract Administration, stands in an office doorway watching a woman stare intently at a computer monitor on her desk. Florence, who is very mature, is in good physical shape and would be at home on any golf course. She is great at conversation and is an inspiration to her coworkers.

She speaks only loud enough to be heard.

FLORENCE: Sandy, did you find the solicitation?

The woman at the computer looks up. It is SANDRA BINDING, Director of Contract Administration. Sandra is past middle age and looks it. She has a loose hair-do and a pinched face. Her eyeglasses hang on a silver chain from her neck. Sandra likes her job and is very good at it. She could not be lured away from RTI.

She shakes her head and raises her hands in frustration.

> SANDRA: No, I don't know how anyone could find *any* Request for Proposal on FedBizOpps.

> FLORENCE: Did you try FBODaily?

> SANDRA: Yes. (*glaring at computer screen*) I wish I could talk to the guy who designed this website. Walter asked me personally this morning to pull up this RFP and get it to the proposal team ASAP. I can't find it.

> FLORENCE: What did you put in as the keyword?

> SANDRA: That's the problem. I don't know how they've labeled this Interceptor thingy. I tried "UAV to pursue alien spacecraft," but that's too obvious. The Air Force has an obscure method of naming things.

> FLORENCE: Move over and let me at your computer. I think I can find the RFP. I've got the solicitation number.

> SANDRA: You do? Where did *you* get it?

> FLORENCE: The Air Force Contracting Officer emailed it to me.

> SANDRA: What! They've never done that before. (*pauses, reflects*) Somebody wants us to bid on this program – very badly. Flo, go ahead and try to find it yourself. I'm already logged in.

Sandra rises from her chair and gestures to Florence to sit down. Florence moves behind the desk, throws a small notebook on the table, falls back into the chair, and flips open the notebook.

FLORENCE: Here we go, A . . . F . . . (*punches in solicitation number on computer keyboard*) That should do it. Let's see what comes up.

SANDRA: If you're successful, print out the page.

FLORENCE: Bingo! Here's your RFP.

SANDRA: Surprise me. What will we be bidding on?

FLORENCE: The Air Force calls it the "Rocket-Propelled Response Vehicle for Unidentified Spacecraft."

Florence wiggles the computer mouse and clicks it. The PRINTER behind her on a small table begins HUMMING. A thin sheaf of pages slides out. Florence picks it up and hands it to Sandra.

SANDRA (*glances down at the sheets*): Great. I'm going to look this over, make a copy for myself, and rush a copy over to Al Gurithum who will be the proposal manager. He can do the follow-up on the RFP details.

FLORENCE: There's no need to hurry, Sandy.

SANDRA: Why's that?

FLORENCE (*speaking softly*): Don't repeat what I'm about to say or that I told you, but I have it from sources . . .

SANDRA (*interrupting*): Angelique told you. She blabs too much!

FLORENCE (*speaking just above a whisper*): That doesn't matter. The important fact is that Masterly doesn't *want* to win this contract. In fact, he doesn't even want to prepare a bid; he's only going through the motions because of the urging from the White House. I'm surprised he hasn't mentioned that to you.

SANDRA: Maybe he will. Usually he makes sure we're on the same page.

FLORENCE: *You* can understand the reason for secrecy. If that word got out, no one on the proposal team would seriously undertake the effort; they would settle for a crappy product, and God forbid, miss the deadline.

SANDRA: Very well. From this moment forward I will exhibit unrestrained enthusiasm in capturing the business for the "Rocket-Propelled Response Vehicle for Unidentified Spacecraft" and I will make sure everyone else on the team does also.

FLORENCE: That's the spirit!

Florence hugs Sandra.

INT. RTI. BLUE CAVERN ROOM. DAY

Ten tables have been arranged in the form of an oblong rectangle at one end of a huge meeting room known as the blue cavern. The room is on the first floor of the main building at the RTI complex.

The lighting is mostly indirect and very dramatic. The room has waist-high walnut paneling. Above the paneling, lining the four gray walls, are rectangles of blue velvet. The chairs are upholstered in a darker blue fabric. The colors were chosen by Walter Masterly. Thirty chairs are spaced around the rectangle.

Sitting alone at one of the tables is Albert Gurithum. He has called a meeting of the Interceptor proposal team. On the table next to him is a large stack of bound papers. Albert looks down at his wristwatch and then at the entrance doors. A man enters and strides toward the tables. It is Roy Cordu.

ROY: Hi, Al. When was the last time I worked on a proposal with you? Think this will be another big win for us? We need the work.

ALBERT: Big win? Not too sure, Roy. There are a lot of factors to consider in deciding how energetically we should go after a contract. That's what we'll be talking about today. Have a seat.

Six people appear at the doorway: BING CHANG, mechanical engineer; CHANDRA PATEL, purchasing agent; CELIA CAKPATI, financial analyst; KIMBERLY CHI, Manager of Materials Engineering; SUSAN SHI, systems engineering specialist; and STANLEY SNAPPI, ground support equipment designer. Stanley is carrying a large pink box.

Bing is one of the newer, younger engineers. He always wears a dress shirt and necktie to the office. Although he loves his job at RTI, he would rather be bicycle riding. He keeps excellent records.

Bing cocks his head and looks at Al.

> BING: Is this the proposal meeting?

> ALBERT: This is it. Come on in.

The six people file in and take seats around the table arrangement. Albert pushes the stack of documents to Roy who is sitting two chairs away.

> ALBERT: Roy, would you pass these around?

Roy lifts the heavy stack, walks along the tables, and drops a bound document on the table in front of each person.

> ALBERT: Instead of putting up some boring charts on a screen, I decided to put my thoughts down in hard copy. This way you can write sarcastic notes on each page.

Everyone begins leafing though the documents.

> ALBERT: For those who haven't run into me for a while, I'm Al Gurithum, Manager of Systems Analysis. I've been assigned as the proposal manager. You people have been selected as the proposal team. You represent the main disciplines that are involved.

Al points at Roy.

ALBERT: I'll try to stay deeply involved, but I may get called away. Roy, over there, will serve as the proposal team lead whenever I'm not around.

Chandra Patel leans forward, dips her finger toward each person at the table as she counts them, and looks over her shoulder at the doorway for any latecomers.

Chandra has worked at RTI all of her life. She is wearing her favorite sweater and the pearl necklace she received for thirty-five years of service. She often brings delicious home-cooked Indian dishes to the office parties. She is a careful listener, and people like to discuss their problems with her.

CHANDRA: Is this the whole of the team – eight people?

ALBERT: Yes, but each of you has the authority to call upon anyone, maybe even draft some subject matter experts for the team temporarily if you need input from them. (*looks over at Susan*) Sue, you will probably need some help in the system design area.

Susan nods at Albert's remark. She is sitting next to Chandra. Susan is middle-aged, has short curly blonde hair, and wears a fashionable watch. Susan always brings up the positive side of events at RTI that coworkers worry about.

SUSAN: Probably so, Al. You know, after we found out we were on the proposal team, Chandra, Kim, and I were chatting about the concept involved and our approach. The prospects are thrilling. We're only going on what info has been leaked, you understand; and we know you'll be giving us more details, Al, but we do have some terrific ideas for selling points.

BING: Yes, this is a fantastic opportunity for RTI. There never has been any program like this. The implementation of this program could result in verified alien contact. I was boning up on proposal strategy, Al. I have some suggestions of my own that I think will clinch the deal.

ALBERT: Hmm. (*smiles weakly*) Your enthusiasm is a plus, folks, but hold onto those ideas. The scope of the proposal and the aggressiveness that management has chosen to win this contract is covered in the handout in front of you. Let's go through it. Turn to the first inside page.

Everyone opens the handouts. Susan nudges Chandra.

ANGLE ON SUSAN AND CHANDRA

SUSAN: Did you notice that spiffy suit Stanley Snappi has been wearing all last week and this week? Usually he's so scruffy.

CHANDRA: There's a rumor going around that he's pretending it's his normal work outfit so he can sneak out for job interviews without calling attention to himself.

SUSAN: Leave RTI? He has told everybody he's a RepoTek guy for life.

CHANDRA: That was before this proposal came in. He was overheard saying that after he read the Statement of Work for this proposal, he doesn't think we have a snowball's chance in an autoclave to win. He says he wants to get a head start in the job search before the layoffs begin.

Susan nods knowingly.

CUT TO: WIDE VIEW OF BLUE CAVERN

Bing taps loudly on his handout.

BING: Roy, I have a question about the proposal title page.

ALBERT: Yes, Bing. What is it?

BING: The handout states the title of the proposal will be "Offer for Design, Development, and Delivery of IX Vehicles."

ALBERT: That is correct. What's your question?

BING: Why does it include the Roman numerals for nine? Are we proposing to deliver nine vehicles?

ALBERT: No, Bing. The IX is short for "Interceptor Experimental." Until the product goes into production and is assigned a name by the customer, it's customary to tack on the "X." Remember the MX missile? Everybody called it that for several years until President Reagan approved the name "Peacekeeper."

BING: Maybe we should put in a hyphen between the "I" and the "X."

ALBERT (*struggling not to frown*): We have some bigger problems. I suggest we leave the title as is. (*speaks slowly and distinctly*) This is a *very* important meeting, folks. Please pay close attention to what you're going to hear.

Celia Cakpati riffles the pages of the handout document in front of her. Celia was born in Nigeria, has the body of an active tennis player, but at the age of fifty-five, has not been on the courts for several months. She is meticulous, but patient, when she counsels employees who give her sloppy financial data.

Celia slides her chair back from the table, pushes herself to her feet, and walks to the thermostat on the wall. She studies it and looks over at Al.

CELIA (*smiling, shaking shoulders*): This room seems awfully cold, Al. Would you mind if I raise the thermostat a little?

ALBERT: Go ahead, Celia. (*turns to the group at the tables*) Is everyone on page two? You'll see the overall schedule there and the time allotted for each of your sections. Notice that we have ninety days to prepare and submit our proposal. Let that sink in, people. That is more than a desirable target; that is a *hard* date. Keep your eye . . .

Celia, back at her chair, has raised her hand. Albert's voice trails off as he looks up at Celia.

ALBERT: Yes, Celia.

CELIA: Al, I apologize, but I forgot to bring my sweater. Would it be okay if I raise the thermostat a teensy bit more?

ALBERT: Yes, Celia.

Albert falls silent. Celia gets up, trots over to the thermostat, peers at it, and makes an adjustment. Everyone turns to watch her.

ALBERT (*trying to recall the thread of his remarks*): As I was about to say, keep your eye on the schedule. If there is an indication that anyone may not meet the published inch-stones for their section, he or she will hear from me.

As Stanley Snappi observes Celia, his mouth tightens. Stanley is tall and lanky and is approaching thirty-six. He is wearing a dark double-breasted suit and a silvery silk necktie. He normally likes to talk a lot, is very friendly, and usually not argumentative.

He pats his forehead with his handkerchief, feigning discomfort from heat. He takes off his jacket and hangs it on the back of his chair.

Celia returns to her seat.

ALBERT (*showing the open handout*): The page budget for the proposal is in the back. As you will notice, there is not a lot of information in the handout as to what we will be actually proposing. The Air Force has been skimpy on their requirements. Frankly, they have no ideas about the necessary capabilities of a vehicle that has to catch a flying saucer. Officially they are asking us to help them derive those requirements for such a vehicle. Unofficially, they don't believe in flying saucers.

Albert notices Stanley has opened the box he brought and is holding it up.

ALBERT: What do you have there, Stan?

STANLEY: I wasn't sure how long your meeting would be, Al. I brought doughnuts for everybody.

ALBERT (*sighs*): Let's hold off on those until the meeting is over. (*taps on handout*) I know many questions will arise as we go along, but the rules and information set forth in the handout are a start and they *are* firm. (*looks over at Kimberly*) Kim, please read out loud the words on page seven that you see in bold type.

Kimberly flips the pages of the handout. She is a long-time, trusted member of the Materials Department. She is mature, has short black hair, and always displays a no-nonsense approach to the tasks at hand, but she does smile occasionally.

KIMBERLY: Sure. Let's see. "Above all, this proposal will be credible, responsive to the terms of the RFP, and internally consistent."

ALBERT: Those words express very succinctly what management wants delivered in this proposal. There are a few other important rules I have for you that aren't in the handouts. It is critical that you come away from this meeting with a strong understanding of what I am about to say; in fact, I suggest you write these words down in your copy.

Albert looks over at Celia who is waving at him again.

CELIA: Al, I don't think I pushed the little slider on the thermostat enough that last time. I'm still a little chilly.

Stanley jumps up, grabs his jacket from the back of his chair, and walks to Celia's chair. He offers her the jacket.

STANLEY: Celia, please wear this. Maybe you're coming down with something.

CELIA (*hesitating*): Well, okay. Thanks, Stanley.

Albert looks at his wristwatch while Celia dons the jacket.

> ALBERT: Yes, thank you, Stanley. By the way, you're in charge of the Risk Section.

Stanley throws up his arms in a display of joy.

> ALBERT: Here are some more "do"s and "don't"s to make note of. After submittal, we don't want to receive any ENs.

> BING: What are those, Al?

> ALBERT: Evaluation Notices. The customer sends them back during the review process. Masterly doesn't want the Air Force telling us about deficiencies.

> BING: What about a win theme? I don't see one mentioned in the handout.

> ALBERT: It wasn't forgotten, Bing. We didn't *plan* to invent one. The proposal has to stand on its own merits. If you'd like to suggest one, please do, but do it outside the meeting. Notice in the handout, you and Sue will be doing the Technical Definition Section. By the way, I'll write the Executive Summary and the Key Personnel section. (*looks at Celia*) Celia, are you comfortable now?

> CELIA: Yes, I'm going to get me a jacket like Stanley's.

> ALBERT: Celia, you and Chandra will be in charge of the Cost Section. Use the labor hours from the RTI one-thirty-five Engine Program and use the anticipated labor rates for the anticipated period of performance.

> CELIA: Okay, Al, but remember we received a load of complaints about the indirect charges on that program. Our overhead rates are killing us.

> ALBERT (*speaking with emphasis*): Keep this in mind as you get into the proposal process. We're *not* going to pretend we

have discovered more efficient ways to design, build, and test so we can underbid.

SUSAN (*waving her arm at Al*): We won the RTI one-thirty-five Engine program because we built a working prototype. It was rather crude because of the time limits, but it impressed the customer.

ALBERT: There is no time or company money for a prototype, Sue.

SUSAN: How about a mock-up?

ALBERT: No mock-up.

KIMBERLY: Our Materials Research sub-unit has come up with some great ideas for really strong, light-weight composites. They haven't been proven yet, but mentioning them as an alternative could show the customer we're keeping up.

ALBERT: Glad you brought that up, Kim. Pass this message to everyone working on the proposal. We're *not* going to advance the state of the art.

SUSAN: I have to say this, Al. After listening to all the things you rattled off that we are *not* going to do that might help win this contract, I find myself very de-motivated.

ALBERT: I understand your reaction, Susan. (*pauses, looks down*) Perhaps I should reaffirm our position. What I am about to state is not a secret, but it is not to be repeated outside of this room. (*pauses again, looks from side to side sternly*) Walter Masterly has carefully considered the risks and benefits to RTI that this program would represent and has judged it as having questionable value.

SUSAN: Then why are we going through all this effort?

ALBERT: Because the President of our company made a promise to the President of the United States.

Albert closes the pages of his handout, sits back in his chair, silent, and crosses his arms. The people at the table share questioning looks. Stanley offers the box of doughnuts to Chandra.

INT. RTI. PROPOSAL CENTER. DAY

The proposal center is a room in one of the smaller buildings on the RTI campus. It is windowless for security reasons. The room has nine hundred square feet of working space and is well-equipped.

A twenty-foot long conference table occupies the center; it is surrounded by many leather-upholstered, cushioned, mid-back, tiltable office chairs. There are computer terminals on the table, one in front of each chair.

Cork boards and white boards are spaced along the walls. Pinned on the cork boards are summaries of each of the sections of the Interceptor proposal in work and sketches of elements of the Interceptor vehicle.

A row of tall four-drawer file cabinets stands at one end of the room. They are secured with crashbars and heavy combination locks. A speakerphone sits on the center of the table. In one corner is a small table with a coffee maker, sugar, powdered creamer, cups, and stirrers.

At one end of the table are four people: Susan Shi, Bing Chang, Kimberly Chi, and Roy Cordu. They sit bent over the table as they pore through the pages of ring binders spread out in front of them. These binders have the completed sections of the proposal. Susan is studying a fold-out schedule chart.

> SUSAN: Wow! It's hard to believe that we've gone through *ten weeks* of our schedule. Let's see. Today is Friday. We have only two weeks left to wrap this package up. Do you think we'll make it, Roy?

> ROY: Sue, you don't want anyone to hear you even *ask* that question. What's worse, you're not paying attention to the completion date. Look again at that schedule.

Susan cranes her neck to find the event Roy is referring to.

> ROY: We don't have two weeks remaining; we have only twelve calendar days left to make the early submittal we're shooting for.

> BING: What's our job today?

> ROY: I want Sue to go over that layout of the proposed architecture of the vehicle – She helped create it. I want her to confirm that there are corresponding descriptions and rationale in the Technical Definition section that support our decision to include them.

Kimberly unfolds a large drawing and attaches it to a nearby corkboard with pushpins.

> SUSAN (*pointing to drawing*): There *could* be some holes.

> ROY: If there *are* any, you or Bing or Kim here will get on the squawk box there on the table with whoever is the responsible author and have whatever is missing completed pronto. If there is any hesitation on anyone's part, let Al Gurithum know. I have to report to him later this afternoon that we're on track. He was supposed to show up here today.

> KIMBERLY: I pinned the illustration of the system components up on the board, Roy. I checked off the one's we've already scrubbed.

> ROY (*looking at cork board*): Thanks, Kim. Okay, let's start with the overall vehicle shape.

> SUSAN: As you can see, we're proposing a vehicle that uses a lifting body concept with additional swept-back wings for added buoyancy. It is painted in dark earth tones so it won't be too visible to aliens looking down at it from above.

ROY (*squinting*): What is the significance of those rows of white, sharp streaks painted on the front?

SUSAN: Those are teeth.

ROY: Teeth?

SUSAN: Yes, that was Bing's contribution. Those are tiger teeth. He got the idea from the nose art on the P-forty aircraft flown by the Flying Tigers at the start of World War two. The purpose is to terrify the aliens.

ROY: The aliens may not have tigers wherever they come from. But let's move on.

BING: The vehicle will not be piloted; it is controlled entirely by either an on-board computer or by transfer to an uplink from a ground station. The Air Force requirements didn't include provisions for a pilot, and we're not proposing any.

SUSAN: You'll notice there are three thrusters. We determined that only two are needed for the scenario mission, but we added a third for some unanticipated maneuver and for engine-out capability.

KIMBERLY: The thrusters will be ablative; we'll be using the new phenolic resin my department has qualified. Embedded in the resin will be a new polymer fiber. The other bidders will have nothing comparable.

Roy leans back and raises his hands.

ROY: Hold on a minute. Remember, one of the ground rules is "nothing far out." How confident are you that this resin and fiber are compatible?

KIMBERLY: We've wrapped *many* combustion chambers with these two materials and test-fired them.

ROY: No delaminations after the cure?

KIMBERLY: Nope. And post-test we always found a uniform char everywhere – from the injector to the nozzle exit.

ROY: Bing, where do we stand on the propellant system?

BING: The propellants will be storables of course – hypergols.

ROY: Will the propellants be loaded at the launch site?

BING: No, there are no fill or drain valves – too much of a risk for leakage. The vehicles will be delivered with the propellants loaded. All the connections will be welded.

ROY: That makes sense, but how would the Air Force handle demilitarization?

BING: What is that?

ROY: The day will come, Bing, when the Air Force may take a vehicle out of service – you know, retire it – either because it's no longer needed or because it's unusable for some reason. For that operation they will have to deal with the challenge of unloading two tanks of toxic liquids that ignite on contact. They won't tolerate that.

BING: Oh, we anticipated that problem. Kim, pull out that artwork that shows the detanking operation.

Kimberly reaches over and picks up one of the binders, pinches a tab of a divider, and opens to a colorful drawing which she unfolds.

BING: You've got to see this, Roy. The manager of the Graphics Department, Arthur Gumme, personally created this drawing.

CLOSE ON DRAWING

A long stretch of paper with a drawing is seen. It has four panels. Bing's hand sweeps across the drawing. His finger points to the first panel which shows a man in a hazmat suit approaching the side of the Interceptor vehicle

A hatch on the side of the fuselage is open, revealing a red spherical fuel tank. The man is holding an appliance that resembles a large sawed-off shotgun connected to flexible tubing. He is pointing it at the tank.

> BING (*off-screen*): That's the insertion tool. It's pneumatically powered.

Bing moves his finger and touches the second panel that shows the man pressing the insertion tool against the side of the tank.

> BING (*off-screen*): When he pulls the trigger, the air pressure drives the drain fitting into the side of the tank. You know, like a nail gun.

ANGLE ON ROY AND BING

> ROY (*rubbing forehead*): That seems like an awfully aggressive design solution. Who came up with this?

> BING: Stanley Snappi.

> ROY (*rubbing forehead again*): Well, Stan's got the Risk Section. I wonder how he plans to sell this concept.

CLOSE ON DRAWING

Bing's hand points to the third panel. The man has backed away with the tool. A fitting is shown attached to the side of the tank.
> BING (*off-screen*): There. It's installed. The fitting is actually a valve.

The fourth panel shows the man connecting a hose to the fitting that leads to a large cylinder.

> BING (*off-screen*): Once the drain hose is attached the operator gives the fitting a half-turn with a wrench and presto, the propellant flows to the recovery tank. Of course, if there are any little spills, the operators have some neutralizing solutions handy for clean-up.

ANGLE ON ROY AND BING

> ROY (*speaking very slowly*): Remarkable! Who makes these fittings and the insertion tool?

> BING (*smiling*): Oh, neither of those items exists. We will have to design and build them.

> ROY (*looking closely at the drawing*): I'm going to have a talk with Stanley.

CUT TO: WIDE VIEW OF TABLE

Susan opens another binder and slides it in front of Roy.

> SUSAN: Here's our make-or-buy program. The big items to be farmed out are the tanks, the valves, and the guidance system.

Roy runs his finger down the list.

> ROY: Who will we be sub-contracting the valves to?

> SUSAN: The Hart Company.

> ROY: The name sounds familiar. Hmm. Hart Valves. Yes, however, the actual valve design will be done here at Repulsive Technology. Do they understand that?

> SUSAN: Yes.

> ROY: In fact, *I* will be creating the drawings.

Roy hears the CLICK of the LATCH on the proposal center door and looks up. The door opens, and Albert Gurithum enters.

> ALBERT: Hi, how's it going? Sorry I couldn't be here for the run-through. I just came from another meeting.

> ROY: There are a few things left to go over, but we're looking good.

ALBERT: That's great, because I have a task for you. I know it wasn't on the schedule, but I've called an early Red Team review of the Technical Definition for this afternoon.

ROY: That wasn't supposed to happen for another three days! We've got some open items. They'll be turning in a lot of deficiencies.

ALBERT: I know, I know. But I want to get this team familiar with the material. The team members were informed there will be gaps, and they will allow for those.

ROY: Can't you postpone the review for one more day?

ALBERT: (*shaking head*): I'm afraid not. Fulbrane himself suggested this special review. He's heard rumors that some features of the vehicle are being proposed that are beyond our core competencies. He wants to personally lead the team. In fact, he cancelled a trip to Washington for a NASA conference on safety so he could be here for the review.

ROY (*slapping hands on table*): Oh, boy. (*pauses*) What do you need?

ALBERT: Five copies of the stuff in those binders next to Sue. I need them in an hour.

ROY: Okay. (*starts stacking the binders and looks over at Bing*) Bing, take these to Repro. Tell them you want five copies – now!

Bing gathers up an armload of the binders and heads toward the door. Albert opens the door, and Bing disappears down the hall.

INT. RTI. REPRODUCTION DEPARTMENT. DAY

Bing stands at the counter of the Repro department. He steadies his stack of six thick white binders containing hard copies of the Technical Definition of the proposal. A thin equipment OPERATOR, the sole member of the department present, is tending a large, noisy copy machine that is spitting pages into a hopper. He is wearing jeans and a sport shirt with seagulls.

He is HUMMING some unrecognizable tune and swinging his head from side to side in time with the rhythm of the machine. Bing waves, but the operator's back is turned to him.

BING (*cupping his hand to his mouth*): Hello! Can you help me?

The operator turns to pick up a ream of blank copy paper and sees Bing over his shoulder. He puts down the paper and saunters over to the counter.

OPERATOR: Whatcha got?

BING (*tapping the stack of binders*): I need five bound copies of everything here. It's for a proposal in work. It's hot!

OPERATOR: *Everything* I get is hot. When do you *really* need it?

BING: I need them for a meeting that starts an hour from now.

OPERATOR: Can't do it.

BING: Why not? Just stop whatever you're running and start my job. I can get a priority.

OPERATOR: Can't do it. The job on the machine right now has a number one priority.

BING: What could that be?

The operator steps to another counter, picks up a piece of paper, and squints at it.

OPERATOR: Here's the repro work order. Let's see. It's for Mary Snackmeister. It's for some announcements and handouts for a big company party.

BING: A company *party*!

OPERATOR: It must be a big deal. It's counter-signed by the President of the company. Well, not actually the *President* – it's signed by Angelique Del Mundo, his admin. And you don't want to go up against *her*!

BING: What about that other copy machine over there?

OPERATOR: Oh, that one is turned off for maintenance. The laser printer guy will be here any minute now.

BING: Can't you just turn it on until he shows up?

OPERATOR: Ho, ho. Can't do that. See that calendar over there? Read what it says: "Machine twenty-one Maintenance." That's today. Wanna get me in trouble?

BING: The party job should be done in a few minutes.

OPERATOR: Yeah, but then I have to collate all those copies.

BING (*bows head in despair, looks up at operator*): Can I use your phone?

The operator gestures at the phone and walks back to the copy machine to load in more paper. Bing picks up the handset, shakes his head, and punches the keypad.

BING: Roy, is Al still there? (*listens*) What? He's going over the detanking procedure? He has questions? (*pauses*) That'll have to wait. I've got a little problem here at Repro. Tell Al he will have to re-schedule the Red Team review. I can't get the stuff copied. (*pauses*) Well, if he thinks he can pull some strings, he had better come here himself. I'll turn the job in.

Bing hangs up, reaches over to a stack of blank reproduction work orders, picks up a stubby pencil, and scribbles on the form. He slaps it on the stack of binders, waves to the operator, points to the work order, and walks slowly out the door.

INT. RTI. SANDRA BINDING'S OFFICE. DAY

Sandra is leaning over her desk, studying the cover of a thin booklet.

CLOSE ON BOOKLET

The cover of the booklet reads:

REPULSIVE TECHNOLOGY EMPLOYEE ACHIEVEMENT AWARDS

Below the cover title is a photograph of a bronze statuette: a Roman soldier, in uniform, holding a torch. Below the photograph is a description: Item Number 2785, Symbol of Dedication and Accomplishment, listed on page 3.

ANGLE ON SANDRA

Sandra lifts the cover, runs her finger down the next page, takes a pencil from a cup on her desk, and circles an image. She picks up the handset of her telephone, holds it to her left ear, and punches four numbers on the keypad.

> SANDRA: Angelique, this is Sandy – Sandy Binding. Is Walter there? Yes? Good. Can you put me through to him?

She continues to hold the handset close to her head, waiting for a response. She looks down again at the booklet. She circles another image on the page.

> SANDRA: Walter, good afternoon. Thanks for taking my call. I thought you would want to know that the Interceptor proposal was delivered.

She listens to Walter Masterly's response.

> SANDRA: Yes, it was submitted electronically, per Air Force instructions, using the DoD website. Yes, three days early! It cost us a little overtime, but we thought it would be worth it.

She frowns at what she hears.

SANDRA: Yes, I know the rule about overtime, but our IT people warned us that the DoD server might be tied up with some security operation. If that happens and the proposal doesn't go through, the Federal Acquisition Regulation states the Air Force won't make an exception. We'd be late and disqualified.

She listens more; a smile appears on her face.

SANDRA: You're welcome, Walter. I'll pass your words of gratitude on to all the members of the proposal team. In fact, the "great job" you mentioned is another reason for this call. While I have you on the phone, I want to run this idea by you.

The frown lines re-appear.

SANDRA: I *can* meet with you on this, but it's an easy question. Hear me out, if you will.

She pauses for Walter's reply.

SANDRA: Great! You may not have heard, Walter, but the proposal effort almost stalled out a couple of times. Yes, really. The Statement of Objectives in the RFP was vague. The Ponca City Resolution was no help at all. The guys and gals on the proposal team worked their tushes off to get it done on time and to make sure it was done right.

She nods as she hears Walter concur.

SANDRA: Here are my thoughts on that. I really think we should hand out some awards to these people. Don't you agree?

She smiles weakly, awaiting agreement.

SANDRA: Great! Right now, I'm looking at the RTI employee awards catalog. I know you probably haven't seen it lately, but you know what I'm talking about. That's the booklet we show to employees who have done something above and beyond. We let them choose a gift for themselves.

She pauses.

SANDRA: I believe that if the awards are to be meaningful, Walter, they have to go out in a timely manner. I thought about having a special design made, but that would take too long. These catalog awards are available now in our warehouse. I wanted your suggestion for an item to give to each person on the team.

She smiles broadly.

SANDRA: What do *I* suggest? Hmm. Let's see. I circled the digital desk clock.

She listens; her mouth begins to pinch.

SANDRA: Not too exciting, huh? How about the silver note keeper?

She presses the phone even harder against her ear.

SANDRA: Limited use? I guess you're right. Here's a portfolio; maybe the people would. . .

Her voice trails off as Walter breaks in.

SANDRA: You'd pass on that? The mini flashlight is popular. I have one.

Walter's reply is louder than expected. Sandra pulls the phone away from her head.

SANDRA: Not that? There's an umbrella. Rainy season is coming you know.

Pause

SANDRA: No? Okay, how about the lunch bag?

Pause

> SANDRA: Not good? Well, there are only a few items left that even *I* don't think would work out — like the barbeque apron. I tell you what, Walter, why don't we settle on some framed Achievement Certificates? They won't cost very much. The Graphics Department has a nice template and can run off the few dozen we need in an hour.

Sandra nods as she hears Walter's words.

> SANDRA: I'm glad we see eye-to-eye on this, mister President. We need to show our appreciation for the effort put forth by the team to produce the kind of proposal you could be proud of. I'll stay in touch.

Sandra carefully replaces the handset. She opens one of the drawers in her desk, throws the awards booklet in the back, and quietly closes the drawer.

INT. WHITE HOUSE. OVAL OFFICE. DAY

Lamar Ferret is sitting in a side chair next to the desk of President Grayfield. He has a grim look on his face; he holds a sheaf of papers in his lap.

Thelma Grayfield is holding her glass apothecary jar half full of jelly bears and is stirring the contents with her forefinger. The sunlight from the window behind her glints off the lid of the jar lying on the desk.

> THELMA (*looking down at the papers in Lamar's hands*): I take it those are the daily receipts of letters and emails with praise and complaints. Let me have the bad news first. Are there any letters from Ponca City demanding more action on curbing the space aliens?

> LAMAR: Of course, but the top letter is one from a seniors group there asking for assurance that the elevator in the Washington Monument has been serviced recently. They are planning another group tour. The last time they were in

DC, the elevator was out of order and they never got to the top of the monument.

THELMA: Most elevators have a small form on the wall with a date of the last inspection. Have someone go check that out and prepare a letter for my signature. Any new *alien* activity in Oklahoma?

LAMAR: No.

THELMA: What more do they want?

LAMAR: The senior citizens want to know the go-ahead date on the Interceptor Vehicle Program.

THELMA: As a matter of fact, I called the Assistant Secretary for Acquisition in the Department of the Air Force. He assured me that a Source Selection Decision Document would be ready for issue by tomorrow, noon. He promised to call me with that information.

LAMAR (*tapping stack of letters, looking up, deep in thought*): Hmm. We could capitalize on that announcement to boost your approval rating.

THELMA: How so?

LAMAR: Have you been invited to speak at any big gatherings in the next few days?

THELMA: Probably. There's always a waiting list. I'll have to ask Hazel who's currently clamoring for me. Why do you ask?

LAMAR: Envision this: *you*, the President of the United States, have made good on a pledge! On national television you will inform America that work will begin on a defense project unlike any attempted before – that our country will no longer sit and wait passively for intruders from another planet – or from who knows from where – to threaten our security.

THELMA: That does have a nice ring to it.

LAMAR: Remember Kennedy's "Moon Speech" at Rice University in sixty-two? Those words made people sit up and take notice. (*quoting*) "We choose to go to the moon, not because it's easy, but because it's hard." He said something close to that. Boy, I remember the hairs on the back of my neck gave a standing ovation.

THELMA: I was very young then. But I have seen that phrase quoted over and over.

LAMAR: Exactly! And when you make *your* announcement, *you* will be quoted, like JFK was – by all the major papers. I can hear it now: "We don't choose to seek out these invaders because it is easy; we seek them out because they don't believe we have the means to find them."

THELMA: Where do you propose the venue to be for this to happen?

LAMAR: Here's what I recommend. First, you must instruct the Secretary for Acquisition to notify you, *personally, and only you* of the selected Interceptor bidder and to withhold the release of the Decision Document for a few days.

THELMA: That's not their MO.

LAMAR: I know. Tell them you believe there's a clause in their procedures that *allows* that. I've read their Source Selection procedures. They're very wordy and complex. The current people in charge probably have never read all of them anyway. By the time they assign someone to go through the documents to find out whether that provision is actually there, you will have made the announcement.

THELMA: Then what?

LAMAR: Pick a club or group that's asking for you. *Any of them!* Have Hazel set it up. Have her tell the program chairperson flat out that your purpose in being there is to use that platform to announce the winner of the contract.

THELMA: All right, I'll prepare for that. How did you word that? "We are not hunting down these space terrorists because." How did that go?

LAMAR: I'll write it all down, Thelma. It will be the shortest speech you ever gave. Have Hazel begin setting up the meeting arrangements.

With two quick claps Lamar squares his stack of letters, rises from the chair, and leaves the office. Thelma presses a button on a unit on her desk and speaks.

THELMA: Hazel, bring me that list of organizations that have asked me to appear at one of their meetings. Highlight the ones that are serving dinner.

Thelma dips her fingers into the jelly bear jar. She looks up to see Hazel swing her office door wide and stride in. Hazel waves a sheet of paper at Thelma.

HAZEL: Here's a group that's meeting close by – Arlington. The meeting is in the evening two days from now. It's the American Society of Cosmetologists. They have no political agenda you would have to deal with. They also agreed you will be first to speak after dinner, and you can excuse yourself after that and leave early. Best of all they included their dinner menu. They're serving lobster.

THELMA: Sounds perfect. Call them with my acceptance. Make it clear that my reason for being there is to announce the winner of the Interceptor contract. Tell them to notify their members and the media well ahead of time. Oh yes, the television stations will want to show up.

HAZEL: Consider it done.

THELMA (*sitting back, sighing*): It will be a memorable evening.

Thelma pops a jelly bear into her mouth.

INT. HOTEL BANQUET ROOM. NIGHT

Our view scans the panorama of a large and magnificent banquet room in the Hyatt Regency Crystal City hotel in Arlington, Virginia. The dining tables are all filled, mostly with men. There is a range of dress from sports jackets to full tuxedos. Good-natured chatter, mixed with subdued laughter, fills the room. Waiters circulate among the tables with trays, placing glasses of wine before the guests and retrieving the empties.

At one side in the rear of the room television camera operators are setting up their equipment.

The head table, oblong and stretching about twenty-five feet, sits near one wall. On the wall, behind the table, hanging down from a massive bronze rod is a banner of burgundy satin. At the bottom is a gold fringe. In the center is an emblem, an oval with blue and gold shapes representing the oceans and continents of a flattened globe of Earth. In a semi-circle above the earth are the letters A S C.

Seated at the midpoint of the table in front of a bank of microphones is Dr. Clarence Peer. He looks anxiously from side to side. He taps his fork loudly on the side of his water goblet. The sounds of the diners' voices subside.

> CLARENCE: Good evening, ladies and gentlemen, members of the American Society of Cosmologists, and distinguished guests. My name is Clarence Peer – Doctor Peer. I am your host and master of ceremonies for our meeting tonight. (*continues looking from side to side*) We have many guests coming; one who has not yet arrived is very, very special. In fact, I have been pinching myself (*he pinches his arm to demonstrate*) to be sure I'm not dreaming.

INT. WALTER MASTERLY'S HOME. NIGHT

Walter Masterly and John Fulbrane are sitting comfortably in large, soft, leather-upholstered chairs in Walter's media room, looking up at an eighty-inch television screen set in a recess in the wall. The room and all of the furnishings are done in tones of brown. The room is paneled with matching paneled doors.

There is a bottle of whiskey and mixers on a small table in front of them. Each man is holding a tumbler half-full. On the screen is an image of the head table of a large dinner meeting.

> JOHN: Tell me again, Walter. Why are we watching this program?

> WALTER: Sandy Binding told me that she heard an announcement on the news this morning that the President was invited as a guest at a meeting of the ASC, that's the American Society of Cosmologists.

> JOHN: That's not news. Grayfield shows up at a lot of these functions. Last week she spoke at some veterans group.

> WALTER: I know, but on a hunch, Sandy called the ASC. One of our employees is a member, and Sandy told them we might send him and pay for his dinner. She used that as an excuse to pry into what was on the program. Whoever she talked to let it slip that Grayfield is going to announce the winner of the Interceptor contract.

> JOHN: Holy blue! Can she do that? It's my understanding that all awards have to be communicated by letter.

> WALTER: There are exceptions. She's the President and one of those exceptions. She's just making points with that herd of old geezers out there that have been hounding her to come up with something to scare off the space creatures.

Walter reaches over to the coffee table and pours a little whiskey into his tumbler.

INT. HOTEL BANQUET ROOM. NIGHT

Clarence Peer is standing at the head table in front of a cluster of microphones, each bearing the call letters of the radio and television stations covering this event. He is staring fixedly to his left. He smiles, his jaw drops, and he leans toward the microphones.

>   CLARENCE: Yes, our special guest has arrived! Let everybody stand and welcome the President of the United States!

The occupants of the room rise from their chairs. There is a loud MURMUR and enthusiastic APPLAUSE. From a door at the left of the dining room Thelma Grayfield strides in, accompanied by Lamar Ferret and three Secret Service men. Thelma and Lamar take seats at the head table. The Secret Service men move back to chairs at the side.

>   CLARENCE (*speaking into microphones*): I hope I'm not giving anything away by stating that our President will be making an announcement tonight of great importance – not only to our nation, but one that will add to our knowledge of the universe.

ANGLE ON THELMA AND LAMAR

>   THELMA (*whispering to Lamar*): That's putting it awfully strong, don't you think?

ANGLE ON CLARENCE

>   CLARENCE: I'm sure there is agreement when I say that the knowledge sought daily by the members of our group is that which informs us of the origin, evolution, structure, dynamics, and fate of our universe. Perhaps to a lesser extent, many members also believe that the observation of humanity elsewhere in the cosmos is part of our charge. That is why I am excited about the prospects of what Thelma Grayfield will announce this evening.

ANGLE ON THELMA AND LAMAR

>   THELMA (*whispering to Lamar*): What's he talking about? What has the Interceptor contract to do with cosmetology?

>   LAMAR (*startled*): Cosmetology?

BACK TO SCENE

Clarence notices the furtive conversation of Thelma and Lamar with a puzzled expression. He stops speaking. There is an awkward silence throughout the room as everyone focuses on the interchange between the President and her Chief of Staff.

ANGLE ON THELMA AND LAMAR

>   THELMA (*whispering*): Something's fishy here. Why are there so few women at this table? Don't they hold important roles in the American Society of Cosmetologists?

>   LAMAR: (*exasperated, but struggling to speak softly*): Thelma, we are at a meeting of the American Society of *Cosmologists.*

>   THELMA (*whispering*): Hazel told me it was *Cosmetologists!*

>   LAMAR: She got it wrong.

Thelma shows Lamar some small cards she has been gripping.

>   THELMA (*whispering*): What do I say? These are my notes. All of my remarks are directed at hair dressers.

>   LAMAR: Everyone's waiting to hear from you. Just stick with the words I wrote for you.

CUT TO: WIDE VIEW OF HEAD TABLE

Lamar puts on a fake smile and waves to Clarence. Clarence nods, taking the wave as a signal to proceed.

>   CLARENCE: At this time, Ladies and Gentlemen, the dinner will be served. During the dinner you will be entertained with talks by some of our more prominent members. One presentation that is especially thought-provoking will reveal data recently acquired that links micro-particle disks to planetary formation. At the conclusion of the speaking program we will hear from our President.

Clarence sits down; the waiters move in and begin setting plates of food along the table.

INT. WALTER MASTERLY'S HOME. NIGHT

Walter has muted the television. The speakers at the ASC meeting, taking their turns, can be seen gesturing and mouthing words, but their voices cannot the heard. Walter has placed his drink on the table; he is lying back in the chair, eyes closed. John is watching the silent movements of the speakers and the reactions of the audience on the screen.

JOHN: Walt, there's still time before our President makes the big announcement about who has been awarded the contract for the Interceptor. Would you care to make a small bet as to who that will be? Who *is* bidding, by the way?

WALTER (*stirs from his rest, looks over at John*): All the biggies are in: Space Engines, Advanced Thrusters, and Orbit Craft Industries. But I won't take that bet; that would be unfair. Sandy also passed along to me a little G-two on the front-runners she snagged from her contacts.

JOHN: You mean she actually told you who's going to get the contract and you're holding back on me?

WALTER: No such luck. But she *did* find out that the source selection board was highly impressed by the low maintenance costs submitted by Space Engines. They may have low-balled that figure, but I doubt it.

JOHN: I would have bet on Advanced Thrusters. They've got a good handle on forming the kind of ablative nozzles the Interceptor would use.

WALTER: I think everyone in this business is high-tech enough. The selection is going to hinge on ways to save money. The Air Force has been stung on out-of-sight maintainability on

a few programs. Low life-cycle costs are what will sell this
program.

JOHN: How do you think *we* will do?

WALTER: The numbers we proposed were on the high side, but
realistic. I really think Space Engines is a shoo-in.

JOHN (*looking up at TV*): Hey, the other speakers are finished.
That Peer guy is about to call on Grayfield.

WALTER: All I can say is God help the company that wins this
bid and has to deliver a vehicle to chase down UFOs that
we're not sure even *exist*! That CEO has my deepest
sympathy.

*Walter picks up the TV remote from the table, points it at the screen,
and presses a button. There is a burst of SOUND; the reverberation of
the standing OVATION of the meeting attendees surrounds Walter and
John.*

They lean forward, watching, struck by the enthusiasm on the diners.

*The television image zooms in on the figure of Thelma Grayfield
standing at the microphones, waving, waiting for the applause to die
down. At a moment of complete stillness, she smiles and begins to
speak.*

THELMA: Thank you, Doctor Peer. And more thanks must go to
the ASC for allowing me to appear before such a
distinguished assemblage this evening. (*pauses, looks down
at the stack of cards in her hands*) I'm not qualified to bear
witness to the great work your organization has done, but I
must say I was greatly impressed by all the fine speeches I
heard. As a result, I will be looking forward to all future
advances in Cosmetol . . ., excuse me, *Cosmology*.

There is scattered APPLAUSE, then silence.

THELMA: Now let me turn to the reason I am here this evening. Doctor Peer alluded to the word that is out there, word that you may have heard, that the Air Force is in the process of acquiring a vehicle to engage and study unidentified extraterrestrial spacecraft that have been reported and are believed to have abducted one of our citizens. What you have heard is true.

Some MUTTERING disturbs the silence.

THELMA: We don't choose to seek out these invaders because it is easy; we seek them out because they don't believe we have the means to find them.

Every person in the room rises and applauds. The OVATION is continuous. Thelma nods and smiles to acknowledge this show of approval. She waves to them. The applause tapers off. The guests return to their chairs.

THELMA: The vehicle to be designed, built, and deployed has been termed the Interceptor X. I must say, there has been fierce competition to capture that prize task by all of the companies prominent in aerospace. The winner of that competition has been chosen. That decision has not been easy. Tonight, I am pleased to announce that the company which our nation will look to for the realization of this bold countermeasure is Repulsive Technology, Incorporated.

Walter stiffens, drops the hand holding his drink to his knee, almost spilling it. He lowers his head, touches his fingers to his brow. John sees his distress and places his hand on Walter's shoulder. Again, the renewed APPLAUSE from the television saturates the room.

INT. RTI. EXECUTIVE DINING ROOM. DAY

The executive dining room at RTI is a cozy enclosure located adjacent to the large employee cafeteria space. There are double doors leading to the kitchen and double doors leading out to the courtyard. There are nine circular tables, dressed with blue tablecloths, each with seating for seven. Twelve restless people occupy three of the tables.

They are here for a meeting. Some are chatting quietly. Some are fiddling with notepads, anxious for the meeting to start.

Seated at one table is MICHAEL HEADKNUCKLE, Manager of the Performance Analysis Unit. He has called the meeting.

Michael has plump, somewhat ruddy features and short, graying hair with a bald spot on top; he is wearing suspenders. He usually carries a tired, grumpy look and laughs only when he hears someone has goofed up. Most of the time he can be very caustic.

Behind him is an easel with two-foot by three-foot flip charts. The first chart has very large, hand-written letters that read: INTERCEPTOR PROGRAM CHARTER AND ASSIGNMENTS.

Another person steps in furtively and pulls out a chair. It is Stefan Espacamore. Michael glares at him.

> MICHAEL: Espacamore, you're *late!* What's more, your presence puts thirteen bodies in this room (*shakes head*) As if this program didn't have enough ill omens already visible.

Stefan looks from side to side sheepishly and shrugs. He rises and pretends to leave.

> MICHAEL: Sit down. You can stay. In fact, none of you will be allowed to jump ship. If we go down, we're all going down together.

Stefan quickly sits.

> MICHAEL: As you have undoubtedly heard, I've been saddled with the job of Chief Program Engineer for this wild-eyed project (*points over his shoulder to his charts*). I called this meeting to let you know who the players are and to give you an idea of where we're headed.

A woman at the table, MARY SNACKMEISTER, materials engineer, picks up her cup and waves it at Michael. Mary is forty-two, has short dark hair, and is a tad bit overweight. She is a gadabout, enjoys food, and believes frequent office parties are critical to worker morale.

> MARY: I thought the email announcing this meeting mentioned coffee and doughnuts. Where are they?

Michael looks around.

> MICHAEL (*pointing to the side*): They were supposed to be on that table over there. (*waves at Stanley Snappi*) Stan, go into the kitchen and get the cafeteria manager out here.

Stanley pulls himself up from his chair and saunters through the double doors into the food preparation area.

Michael pushes his chair back, stands up, and flips over the first page of his charts. The page underneath reads: STATEMENT OF TASK: DESIGN, BUILD, TEST, DELIVER, AND SUPPORT AN UNMANNED ROCKET PROPELLED VEHICLE CAPABLE OF INTERCEPTING AND ENGAGING SPACECRAFT OF UNKNOWN ORIGIN.

> MICHAEL: In my opinion this is an over-simplified description of the job ahead, but this is what the Air Force thinks it wants.

Michael flips over the second page of his charts. The next page has a crudely drawn organization chart done with a red felt-tip pen.

> MICHAEL: Here's the Engineering org. This setup goes into effect tomorrow.

Michael leans a little and places his hand on the shoulder of Steven Acheever sitting next to him.

> MICHAEL: By the way, Steve Acheever is the Program Manager. Do you have anything you want to say, Steve?

STEVEN ACHEEVER, Manager of Advanced Concepts, looks a bit younger than fifty-three; his hair is combed straight back; his brow is a tiny bit furrowed and his eyes seem to question people's remarks. He always wears a solid color sport shirt, open at the throat. He is very likeable and carries out his job responsibilities with intensity.

Steven looks up at the ceiling and pauses a moment before he answers.

STEVEN: I'm not as pessimistic about the success of this program as I feel you are, Mike. We've proven over and over again that we have the know-how to build propulsion systems that work every time.

MICHAEL: Yeah, but there was never any waffling about the mission of any of our earlier products. Here's the Air Force Statement of Work. (*picks up a thin booklet from table and angrily waves it*) You've read it! We don't got no hard numbers for how fast and maneuverable this bird is supposed to be.

STEVEN: True, true. But on the other hand, our vehicle may *never* be put to a severe test. *Is there* an alien craft out there to be intercepted? There have been sightings by only *one man!* And those occurrences are questionable. The Interceptor could sit on the launch pad forever.

The doors from the kitchen swing open wide; Stanley returns with TIMOTHY FERNWAY, cafeteria manager.

Timothy has a very light frame, a narrow face with almost invisible eyelashes and eyebrows, and very light hair combed straight back. He is most at ease with repetitious schedules and avoids innovation.

TIMOTHY: I'm Tim, the manager. I was told someone has a question. Was it about the menu for lunch today?

MICHAEL (*sharply*): No! We ordered coffee and doughnuts to be here at nine. Where are they?

Tim reaches into a pocket inside his jacket and retrieves a slip of paper. He stares at it for a moment.

TIMOTHY: Here's a note that was handed me this morning. The cook that took the call didn't put your name or number on it. The note says "one dozen doughnuts and an urn of coffee to the EDR." I assumed that meant Engineering Design Records, the loft with all of the file cabinets.

MICHAEL (*controlling obvious irritation*): EDR? I never used those words. I clearly said *Executive Dining Room*. Why would we hold a meeting in that cramped file space up in the Engineering Building mezzanine?

TIMOTHY (*shrugging*): I don't know. No one ever holds meetings here in the dining room either. You people are mostly engineers; it made sense to me to send the food over there. (*pauses, smiles*) Well, I *do* know the coffee and doughnuts *were* delivered. Do you want to move your meeting over there?

MICHAEL (*breathing heavily*): We will proceed at this location, thank you. Please have the doughnuts and coffee re-delivered.

TIMOTHY (*smiling*): We're really occupied with the lunch preparations, but I'll try to break someone loose and have your food brought over.

Timothy turns and walks through the doors to the kitchen. Michael waits for the doors to fully close.

MICHAEL: That guy has got to be replaced. Who do I talk to?

MARY: I think you have to call Plant Services.

STEFAN: That's right. By the way, they changed the name of that department to Facility Maintenance.

MARY: Why do they have to keep changing the names of departments?

Michael looks up at his chart.

MICHAEL: Getting back to the Engineering Organization: let's see. Mary will be responsible for materials, Corey will take care of Electro-Mechanical, Valve Design will be directed by

Roy, and Al will be doing Systems Analysis. I won't go through the rest. I believe all of your names are up there.

STEVEN: You've got a really capable group there, Mike.

MICHAEL: Without a doubt, Steve. I just wish I didn't have that uneasy premonition that this is doomed project. Looking at that chart is like looking at the passenger list of the Titanic.

STEVEN (*trying to be positive*): That's understandable in the beginning of a new program, Mike, when we're still uncertain about the size of our obstacles. But I'm sure that when we get rolling, we'll be up to whatever challenge arises.

MICHAEL: Yeah, when things get tough, we can always do what General Patton ordered: "Circle the tanks."

STEVEN: I don't think Patton said that. The phrase is "Circle the wagons."

MICHAEL: Okay. (*attempting a smile*) Whatever happens, I'm confident everyone here has the skill to ensure success in the end. But I should add, don't put in a request for transfer out of the program. It will be rejected.

COREY: Can you give us a hard copy of that chart, Mike?

There is a BANG as the DOORS to the cafeteria swing inward. One cafeteria worker rushes in with a pink carton. A second worker follows carrying two white plastic pitchers. They place their load on a small table at the side. One of the workers waves to get Michael's attention.

CAFETERIA WORKER (*stammering*): The doughnuts, uh, and, ah, the coffee.

MICHAEL: Great! The food arrives after the meeting is over.

Mary and Stefan rise and start to walk to the table with the doughnuts. Several people head for the door.

MICHAEL: Stick around, folks. I have one more chart.

Mary and Stefan sneak back to their chairs. The few at the exit turn and look at Michael.

Michael flips another page of his charts. The heading reads SECURITY. He slaps the chart.

MICHAEL: Oh yeah. (*shakes his head in dismay*) This program is subject to *all* sorts of classifications. That's going to add to the fun. I won't try to go into the details. Rudy Vault is going to hold a special meeting on the rules. Here's the date, the place, and the time. (*slapping chart again*) Write them down.

Everyone takes out a pad and jots down the words and numbers from the chart. Michael folds back the pages of the large pad, takes the pad off the easel, and collapses the easel.

Many in the group are helping themselves to the doughnuts and coffee. Steven joins Michael as the group leaves the dining room. Steven makes a remark that is not heard. Michael shrugs.

INT. RTI. PROPOSAL CENTER. DAY

RUDY VAULT, Manager of The Data Classification Group within Plant Security, looks up at the wall clock in the proposal center from his chair at the long conference table. He buttons his jacket and adjusts the badge attached to his left breast pocket.

Rudy is thin, has a very mature, square face, a high forehead and light brown hair. He likes to wear a charcoal gray pinstripe suit. He prides himself for being methodical. He realizes employees are irritated by his security restrictions, but tries to overcome any resentment by being exceptionally helpful.

Seated next to Rudy is LEO MEERTZ, Deputy Manager of Data Classification within Plant Security. Leo looks to be sixty-six, is clean-shaven, and has a narrow face; his gray hair is combed straight back.

He is somber and frequently scowls. Leo keeps to himself most of the time. He usually talks in questions.

A loud CLICK is heard as the LOCK on the door disengages indicating someone has waved a badge over the lock sensor. Rudy turns his eyes to the door as Steven Acheever walks in.

>STEVEN: Hey, good afternoon, Rudy. You should get a good turnout for this meeting. All of the key program people will be here. Mike Headknuckle made sure of that.

Steven pulls out a chair at the conference table and collapses into it. Another CLICK is heard. The door swings wide and a crowd pours in – the same group from Michael Headknuckle's earlier meeting. As they enter, Leo checks their names off from a list on the table.

After everyone is seated Rudy begins to speak solemnly.

>RUDY: It should come as no surprise to anyone here that the Interceptor Program launched this week is classified. Those of you who have never worked on a secure program have some hard lessons to learn; those with previous exposure on this kind of program know the drill, but there will be a few new twists in how we will operate. I'm sure you all want to do whatever is necessary to guard the information that will be generated.

Everyone in the room nods in agreement.

>RUDY: I chose to hold this meeting here in the proposal center for that very reason. This room is sealed off from any surveillance. I want you to know that the Air Force has assigned higher levels of classification on the elements of this program than I have seen in a long time.

HAP CAWSHUN, one of the group at the table, frowns slightly. He is the lead test engineer for the program. He is wearing a knitted company shirt with the RTI logo. He is forty-two, has short curly black hair and a youthful face. He is imaginative and an avid motion picture devotee.

HAP: Why do you suppose that is, Rudy?

Rudy doesn't respond immediately. He looks down, taps his finger on the table, then looks back at Hap. There is an uncomfortable period of silence.

RUDY: Hap, your question touches on one of the most sensitive areas of this program. I'll come back to that. First, let's talk about how data will be handled.

Leo hands Rudy a thick booklet with a faded green cover. Rudy holds it at his chest.

CLOSE ON BOOKLET

The cover of the booklet reads: AIR FORCE CLASSIFICATION GUIDE FOR INTERCEPTOR X PROGRAM.
BACK TO SCENE

RUDY: This will be our Bible. This book defines how we must treat information and activities associated with the program. Some pieces of data will be Unclassified; some will be only Confidential; some will be Secret.

Rudy flips through the book.

RUDY: Here are some examples. Let's see. The engine cut-off impulse has an "R" after it; that means it's "Restricted" information. (*flips page*) The fuselage material has a "C." Any document mentioning the fuselage material would have to be stamped and treated as "Confidential." (*flips page*) Here we go. "Electronic Counter-Measures." That has an "S" after it, so that information is "Secret." Pretty straight-forward, right?

Steven Acheever holds out his hand, indicating his desire to look at the booklet.

STEVEN: Can we get some copies for the different groups here today?

RUDY: Unfortunately, the Air Force sent me a single copy and I am prohibited from making any more copies. They apparently want to control the distribution.

HAP GROANS, puts his head in his hands, and rests his arms on the table.

RUDY: That won't be a problem. I'm going to hold a separate meeting in which I'll go over all the categories for labeling data and designs. (*smiling*) And if you ever have a question, I'm just a phone call away. I'll keep this guide handy.

Rudy pauses and looks down at a list of topics scribbled on a pad on the table.

RUDY: Oh, by the way, everybody in this room will require Secret clearance. (*pauses to watch reactions*) My associate, Leo Meertz, will submit the applications for you. Some will require Top Secret.

He holds up stack of forms.

RUDY: Here, Corey, pass these around. Find the form with your name on it and take it.

He hands the stack of forms to Corey Layt who is sitting to his right. Corey flips through the pile, takes one, and passes the stack to Daniel Brazewell who passes it to Albert Gurithum. The stack is moved around the table. Everybody takes one.

RUDY: These are the security questionnaires. You can fill out these hard copies and return them to me or do it electronically on-line.

Stanley Snappi shakes his form at Rudy.

STANLEY: Speaking purely hypothetically, Rudy, would getting traffic tickets compromise a person's ability to get a clearance?

RUDY: Stan, we're concerned about your loyalty, not your driving record.

STANLEY (*smiling*): Oh, of course.

RUDY: I have assigned two document custodians for the program: Roy Cordu and Stefan Espacamore.

Two soft GROANS are heard.

RUDY: The document custodians will ensure that all classified material is placed in an approved security container at the end of each work day.

Rudy points to the file cabinets with padlocked crashbars at the back of the room.

RUDY: Like one of those. (*pauses*) And I might add that sticking a classified document in your desk drawer while you go on a coffee break is considered a violation!

Rudy looks directly at Roy and Stefan.

RUDY: There will be periodic audits by members of my department, such as Leo here, to verify that all classified material is either in a file or that there is a signature of the person who has checked out the material on a log in the file. You have to use Form thirty-four B.

Rudy waves a sample form.

STANLEY: I never saw that one before. Can't we just use a piece of paper?

RUDY: No, the log *has* to be on Form thirty-four B. You can get a stack from Forms Control.

Stanley SIGHS and makes a note.

RUDY: The document custodians will be present during the audit. Remember, gentlemen, unauthorized disclosure of classified material is punishable under Federal Criminal Statutes.

More GROANS are heard.

STANLEY: What do I do with a secret document that I want to get rid of?

RUDY: There are special rules for the destruction of classified documents explained in the Classification Guide. I'm glad you asked that question.

STANLEY: I'm sorry I asked that question. What *are* the rules?

RUDY: Fortunately, you have a number of choices for the method of destroying paperwork. You can use burning, cross-cut shredding, wet-pulping, melting, mutilation, chemical decomposition, or pulverizing.

STANLEY: *Fortunately*? Do we have the equipment to do *any* of those? Other than shredding, I'm not familiar with those other methods.

RUDY: The equipment has been ordered. You all will be invited to demonstrations and you will become proficient in the processes.

A WHIMPER is heard.

RUDY: But to make it easy, Leo has volunteered to perform the destruction for anyone who doesn't have the time or the skill. Just give your obsolete documents to Leo.

A chorus of YES, YES is heard. Leo breaks out into a smile.

STANLEY: Let's see if I understand this. When I'm working at my desk, and I finish using or preparing some classified paperwork, I have to get up, find a document custodian, and get him to unlock a file for me.

RUDY: That won't happen, Stan. Special rooms have been designated as the work spaces for design activity, document preparation, and any technical discussions pertaining to this program. They will be labeled and kept locked at all times.

Rudy holds up a small sign that reads INTERCEPTOR ONLY.

Stefan waves his badge at Rudy.

STEFAN: Will we access the rooms using our radio-frequency identification badges like we do for this room?

RUDY: Good question. The answer is "No." The Security Committee studied that aspect. There is a concern that those badges could be hacked. For the Interceptor rooms we're going to install retinal scanner locks. Very expensive ones, I might add.

Rudy takes a company badge out of his pocket and holds it up.

RUDY: You will be issued new badges that are color-coded for your classification.

STANLEY: Can I have a new picture taken? Mine is terrible! I think it's the same one they took when I hired in fifteen years ago. I look like a teen-ager!

STEFAN: I hear they can make badges using the Dorian Gray effect.

STANLEY: What's that?

STEFAN: The photo on your badge grows old; you stay young forever.

EVERYBODY in the room LAUGHS except Stanley, Rudy, and Leo.

RUDY: While we're on that topic, be aware that every person on this program shall remove the badge when he or she steps off the company premises. I personally do not want to see any of you on the street with your badge showing, and if I even *hear* that any were seen, that person and I will have a little talk.

Daniel Brazewell waves his hand.

DANIEL: This is not meant to be a smart-aleck question, Rudy, but can I show my badge to my wife?

There is some muffled LAUGHTER.

RUDY (*smiling*): Of course! She knows you work at RTI. (*his smile fades and his face becomes stern*) I say this to all of you. Other than allowing your badge to lie exposed on your dresser at home, you will *not* tell your spouse that you are assigned to the Interceptor Program or *what* you are doing!

There are muffled MURMURS. Albert Gurithum raises his hand.

ALBERT: Rudy, I plan to be extra careful in what I say about our progress, but aren't these measures being defeated? Did you see that article in yesterday's paper by that aerospace writer, Frank Remarques? He reported that the Air Force is procuring a "flying saucer chaser" and spelled out the *range and speed from the proposal*!

RUDY: I saw it. Remarques must have a pipeline to somebody in the Air Force who is allowed to leak stuff like that.

ALBERT: What do I say to people who come up to me and ask if that's all true?

RUDY: That *will* happen. And when it does, you will neither *confirm* nor *deny*.

Hap Cawshun pushes himself back from the table, crosses his arms, and angrily shakes his head.

HAP: Rudy, can you get back to that question I asked earlier? When are you going to let us in on why this program is so super hush-hush?

RUDY: Hap, we're up against a dilemma.

Rudy tightens his jaw and looks around. His lips move slightly, but no sounds come out, as though he were searching for words.

RUDY: Do any of you remember reading the details obtained from that guy, Orville Pressfit, the aircraft mechanic that claims he was taken aboard the spaceship?

STEVEN: Yeah, a little.

RUDY: He was asked over and over by the Air Force Investigation Team to describe the aliens.

STANLEY: You mean, like, "were they four feet tall, green, with three fingers?"

RUDY: Exactly, he *didn't* describe them that way. And that's the crux of our dilemma.

STEVEN: Why do we care what they look like?

RUDY: Think about it, Steve. Pressfit's description indicated that there was *nothing* distinctive about the appearance of the aliens. (*waves his arm across the group*) One could be sitting in this room and you wouldn't notice.

The attendees exhibit shock. Many eyes widen and many mouths drop. They turn and look at one another.

HAP: Are you suggesting that there could be an alien operative among us? Not likely. Everybody here knows everybody else on the program.

RUDY: Yes, but RTI has been hiring new people every day for less *visible* jobs. For example, we haven't been running extensive background checks on replacements for the maintenance crew or the cafeteria or for the warehouse.

> HAP: I see what you're saying. We could tighten up our screening procedure, but it may be too late already. There *could be* some of them among us.

The attendees move nervously in their chairs; they began looking around.

> RUDY: Here's the question that our Security Committee wrestled with: do we spread the word throughout the company that we may have been infiltrated? We would then initiate full-time surveillance by *every* employee to detect possible sabotage or espionage. But if we do, any mole that's working here now would be put on guard and may not show his hand. (*chuckles*) Pressfit *did* say they have hands.

Hap nods to signify his understanding.

> RUDY: Or do we play it dumb, conduct business as usual, pretend it's not a problem, and hide any outward signs that we are watching for an alien spy? This might embolden them to attempt some data theft.

> STANLEY: Wow! That's a tough choice. Don't keep us in suspense, Rudy. What did the Security Committee say we should do?

> RUDY: We decided on the first course of action. We are planning an all-out campaign to warn our people of the potential danger of an alien sleeper. We will enlist every man and woman at RTI as an extension of Plant Security.

Everyone at the table nods in agreement. Rudy picks up his material and walks to the door. He stops, turns, and speaks.

> RUDY: I'll say this one more time: Everything that takes place in the Interceptor Program must stay within this group. From this day forward, we must ensure that what we do and say is kept from prying eyes and ears.

Everyone nods again; Rudy and Leo stride out the door.

INT. RTI. ALBERT GURITHUM'S OFFICE. DAY

The office of Albert Gurithum, Manager of the Systems Analysis Group, is unfortunately one of those rooms at RTI without windows. Albert has compensated for that by decorating his walls with nature calendars and framed photographs of colorful scenes of forests and distant mountain ranges. Albert is seated at a small table in the office.

Seated around the table next to Albert are Mary Snackmeister, Corey Layt, Roy Cordu, and BERNARD BLASTOF, Senior Technical Fellow in Advanced Propulsion. Bernard is medium height, sixty-one, and wears only dark sports shirts. He is a former Marine which may explain why he is gruff.

Mary unwraps a granola bar. She notices she is being watched.

> MARY: Anyone here want a honey date oat bar? I also have a chocolate peanut.

The men at the table shake their heads or wave away the offer.

> ALBERT (*looking around*): Welcome, everyone, to the Interceptor Requirements Derivation Team. I don't have to tell you we've got a long, hard road ahead of us.

> COREY: Where do we start, Al?

> ALBERT: Well, our contract makes it very clear that we have to follow a disciplined systems engineering approach. For those of you that haven't been exposed to that, we have a company procedure.

> BERNARD: Yes, I'm well aware of the process, Al, but I personally think we'll end up generating more paperwork than we need.

> ALBERT: Your comment on paperwork, Bernie, reminds me of an announcement I'm supposed to make. The company is

discontinuing the TFP, the Target Focus Plan for goal-keeping.

Mary begins CLAPPING.

MARY: Hooray! I always felt it was wasteful to have to spend an hour at the end of the day to write down all of the tasks I had completed. I'm glad that's over.

ALBERT: Not quite. The TFP has been replaced with the Navigator Action Process, the "NAP."

MARY (*grimly*): What's that?

ALBERT: For each program, the major goals are laid out as ports-of-call on a chart. The Project Manager, the "Captain," navigates the "ship" to each port. When the goal is completed, the Captain "drops anchor."

MARY: Who thought that up?

ALBERT: That new guy in Business Development, Lou Cannon.

BERNARD: Does that affect the work we're doing? I mean this requirements derivation step.

ALBERT: Yes, we have designated sets of requirements to finalize by certain dates. The approval of each set is a "port."

COREY: Is "finalize" really a word, Al? What's wrong with "complete"?

BERNARD: "Finalize" was invented sometime in the sixties. It was generally accepted around ninety-seven.

COREY: If Mary didn't hear about "NAP," she probably hasn't heard about "NIP" yet.

MARY: No, I haven't. What's "NIP"?

COREY: Another handiwork of Business Development.

MARY: What does it do? What is it for?

BERNARD: Well, Repulsive Technology wanted to incorporate the kaizen principle of continuous improvement into the quality portfolio, but as always, our innovative thinkers in BusDev couldn't bring themselves to adopt the system as currently practiced; they *had* to modify it and give it a new name. Our version will be known as the "Never-Ending Improvement Program" or "NIP."

MARY: Maybe it will be a good thing.

Roy moves restlessly in his chair. He reaches over and touches the sleeve of Bernard's shirt.

ROY: Sorry to interrupt, Bernie. Look, Al, I want to start designing some valves for this system. When do I get *my* requirements?

ALBERT: Not for a while, Roy. First, we have to do a complete mission analysis for the Interceptor. We'll need some functional flow block diagrams.

MARY: I've heard of those. What does one look like?

Albert points to a box in the corner of the office.

ALBERT: Those are records from the Anti-Anti-Missile Program. I pulled them from storage. The systems engineering documents that were generated are there. You can use them as an example of the format.

Corey twists uncomfortably in his chair.

COREY: When you say "mission analysis," Al, you're asking us to put down on paper *all* of the events that occur when a UFO of some unknown shape comes out of the blue in some unpredictable flight pattern, (*waves arms in frustration*) and when our ship takes off after it.

ROY: Nothing like that has ever happened. We have no examples to draw upon. We'll have to *invent* that scenario. I don't feel comfortable doing that!

MARY: Can't we get that stuff out of the proposal?

ALBERT: Out of the proposal? (*pauses, looks her in the eye questioningly*) That's right, Mary, you didn't work on the proposal. But that's okay; I made copies of the Technical Definition section for everyone.

Albert taps a stack of documents on his bookcase.

ALBERT: They're here. Take a copy when you leave. Read it carefully; there's not much there to go on. (*gestures for attention*) Oh, by the way, I've included the Ponca City Board of Commissioners Resolution.

MARY: What's that?

ROY: Ponca City is near the airfield in Oklahoma where the flying saucer supposedly landed. The Board of Commissioners in the city drew up the Resolution to get the Federal Government to take action. It was part of the Statement of Work in the RFP. The proposal *had* to say we *would* respond to the Resolution.

ALBERT: Yeah, the Resolution really says nothing, but somehow we've got to work it into the description of what we're doing.

BERNARD: What about the Air Force requirements?

ALBERT: I've said this before, Bernie: the Air Force *doesn't know* what it takes for a spacecraft to tail and observe a flying saucer. They want *us* to tell *them*.

COREY: Oh, boy! All it takes is one off-the-cuff, irrelevant function laid on the system to trigger a dozen goofball requirements that will ripple through the stack of specifications we will have to design and build to.

ALBERT: I think we have enough smart people in this room to come up with some valid requirements. Some of you *surely* have seen photographs of alleged overflights by saucers, or videos of UFOs.

MARY: I remember seeing the movie, *The War of The Worlds,* *b*ut that was a long time ago.

BERNARD (*frowning intensely*): We shouldn't be guessing about the configuration or the maneuverability of whatever the heck this "alien machine" is supposed to be. (*pleading*) Al, we need some direct answers from the guy who started this whole thing.

MARY: Who's that?

Bernard pounds the table.

BERNARD: That airplane mechanic!

ALBERT: You mean Orville Pressfit?

Bernard pounds the table again, more vigorously.

BERNARD: Yeah, him! Get him in here for an interview!

ALBERT: I think you're right, Bernie. Masterly has an in with the White House. I'll tell him our team *has* to hear a full account from Pressfit before we can intelligently assess the threat of the alien vehicle.

Bernard stands and slaps the table again.

BERNARD: Let's get to it!

ALBERT: Hold on, everybody. Before you go, I have one last assignment.

ROY: What's that?

ALBERT: Our little group here has been appointed as the nominating committee for the Engineer of The Year Award for next year. We've got to come up with a name.

COREY: I forgot. Who *is* Engineer of The Year this time around?

ALBERT: Roy, here.

COREY: Oops. Sorry about that, Roy.

Mary displays a confident smile.

MARY: How about Murray Jaysize, the designer?

ROY: He got that award two years ago.

COREY (*looking down in thought*): Okay. I nominate Stanley Snappi, the Ground Support Equipment guy.

BERNARD: Stan was selected three years ago.

COREY: This is tough!

There is silence as everyone ponders.

COREY: We have to nominate *someone*!

MARY: I know. I nominate Corey.

ROY: Someone on this committee? That wouldn't look too cool, Mary.

COREY: Thanks, Mary. How about Bing Chang? He has been doing some very good work. He likes to get involved in everything.

BERNARD: I don't think so. He's a recent hire and hasn't been around long enough. I suggest Susan Shi. She's one of your people, Al.

ALBERT: I thought about her. Wouldn't that smack of favoritism?

Bernard sits erect in his chair and looks soberly at Albert.

BERNARD: Let the record show that it was *my* suggestion, Al, not *yours*. Everybody who agrees that Susan Shi should be nominated for Engineer of the Year raise your hand.

All of the hands go up.

ROY: If that's it, I want to get back to my valve design.

ALBERT: Yeah, let's all get back to work.

Mary, Corey, Roy, and Bernard jump from their chairs, grab a copy of the documents from the box in the corner, and shuffle out the door of the office. Albert returns to his desk, looks down at a schedule chart, picks up a pen, and marks a big "X" over one of the "bubbles."

INT. RTI. TAPESTRY ROOM. DAY

Five people sit at one end of a long, wide conference table in the Tapestry Room, one of the larger and more elegant conference rooms at RTI. In one corner, on the wall, hangs a five-foot high, three-foot wide tapestry. Woven into the fabric is a crude depiction of the RTRE-1, the first rocket engine developed by RTI.

Next to the tapestry is an oil painting of the founder of the company, Wilhelm von Streber, standing next to the Repulsor rocket. Around the room, spaced along the walls, are framed photographs of rocket engines emitting bright plumes of flame and smoke, and missiles emerging from silos.

The five people present are Orville Pressfit, Albert Gurithum, Corey Layt, Angelique Del Mundo, and Bernard Blastof.

Orville's hands cover a soiled leather drawstring pouch that lies in front of him on the table.

Miss Del Mundo has a voice recorder and a bottle of water. Each of the engineers has a pad of paper and pencil. A tray sits in the center of the group with a dish of doughnuts, a pot of coffee, canisters labeled powdered milk and sugar, a box with plastic stirrers, and a stack of white foam cups.

Albert clasps his hands and leans forward at the table toward Orville.

> ALBERT: Mister Pressfit, I'm Albert Gurithum, Manager of the Systems Analysis Group here at Repulsive Technology. We really appreciate your taking time off to accept our invitation to come to RTI and tell us about your experiences in connection with the alien visitors that seem to be focusing on you.

> ORVILLE: Well, I wasn't that busy. As long as your company is willing to pay for my airfare and motel room, I'll talk as long as you like. By the way, you can call me Orville.

> ALBERT: Great! Everybody knows me as Al. I'll let the people here introduce themselves. Care for a cup of coffee?

> ORVILLE: Sure. I always accept free coffee.

> COREY: Orville, I'm Corey Layt. (*shakes hands with Orville*) Call me Corey. I'm an Engineering Specialist with the Electro-Mechanical Devices Unit; I'll pour you that coffee. Cream and sugar?

> ORVILLE: Just cream.

While Layt is pouring coffee into one of the cups, Bernard reaches out his hand to Orville.

> BERNARD: Orville, I'm a Senior Technical Fellow in Advanced Propulsion. My name is Bernard; call me Bernie. This nice lady next to me is Miss Del Mundo. She's the Administrative Assistant to Walter Masterly, our President.

> ANGELIQUE: *Senior* Administrative Assistant.

BERNARD: Yes, Miss Del Mundo knows everything about everything. If you want to get anything done, you see her.

ORVILLE: It's a pleasure to meet you, Miss Del Mundo.

ANGELIQUE: I understand you're from Oklahoma. I've never been there, but I flew over it once.

Orville looks over at Corey as he stirs in some white powder into a cup of coffee.

ORVILLE: Oh, mister Layt, I didn't want powdered milk in my coffee, I take cream.

COREY: We don't actually have cream; that's just an expression.

Orville accepts the cup from Corey, looks down at it for a moment, then sips it.

ORVILLE: You wouldn't have any Irish coffee, would you? (*laughs*) I really enjoy Irish coffee!

Corey looks at Orville, questioningly, then at Bernard. Corey knits his brow, then makes a note on his paper pad.

ALBERT: Orville, we're going to ask some questions, and cover some ground today that may not have come up in previous interviews you've had. As a matter of fact, we'd like to know if you've talked to very many people since your, uh, abductions.

ORVILLE: There were the police officers on the two nights when I got carried off, there was the TV lady, and three Air Force guys questioned me. But all *they* wanted to know about was what the aliens looked like. Nobody has ever asked me about how their ship was built or how it was operated.

BERNARD: And that's all?

ORVILLE: Yup.

ALBERT: Well, we want to get into some technical details today, Orville. I'm going to ask that you don't repeat what we have discussed when you leave here. Is that acceptable?

ORVILLE: Yup.

ALBERT (*looking at the others*): In fact, this meeting is classed as Confidential. Is there anybody here who isn't cleared for Confidential?

They all shake their heads side to side, indicating "no", except Angelique who nods.

ALBERT: Angel, is that a yes or no?

ANGELIQUE: Well, the way you worded the question, I'm not sure.

Angelique looks down at her badge.

ANGELIQUE: I have the little red stripe on my badge. Does that mean I can handle Confidential or Secret? Did you say this meeting is Secret or Confidential?

COREY: She has a point, Al. Should this meeting be Secret?

BERNARD: Want me to check with Plant Security?

ALBERT: Bernie, please close the doors and then call Security.

Bernard gets out of his chair, walks to each of the two entrances to the conference room, and closes the double doors. He walks to the rear of the conference room to a small table with a telephone. He picks up the handset and punches the keypad.

INT. RTI. SECURITY OFFICE. DAY

The Manager of the Data Classification group in Plant Security, Rudy Vault, is standing in front of a file in his office. The top drawer is open. He is going through the folders one by one. The TELEPHONE RINGS. He picks it up.

RUDY: Vault here. (*pauses*) Oh, hi, Bernie.

The scene now alternates between Rudy Vault's office and the Tapestry Room.

INTERCUT RUDY/BERNARD

BERNARD: I'm in a meeting, and I need some help on classification levels. Have you got the Vehicle IX Classification guide handy?

RUDY: I should have it right here in my file.

He opens a top drawer in an adjacent file cabinet and pulls out a one-inch thick booklet with a pale green cover.

RUDY: Hold on a minute. Yeah, here it is. What do you want to know?

BERNARD: We're interviewing that Pressfit guy . . . the one you signed the pass for . . . we have to know whether this meeting is Confidential or Secret.

RUDY: What are you talking about?

BERNARD: We're having a meeting with Pressfit. We're questioning him.

Rudy shakes his head in frustration

RUDY: I *know* you're talking about the meeting. I need to know the subjects of your questions.

BERNARD: Well, one of the questions is going to be about size – the size of the alien spacecraft. Another question we have is about the materials of construction, and another question is about his estimate of the speed of the craft.

Rudy cradles the phone between his head and shoulder as he flips pages in the classification guide.

RUDY: Let's see. The guide has a big "C" next to "Size." That means that data on spacecraft size is Confidential. And "Materials" are "C," also Confidential. But "Speed," unfortunately, has an "S" so it's Secret. Sorry, Bernie, but your whole meeting is Secret. Are the doors closed, and have you posted monitors? (*pauses*) Good!

The view returns to the Tapestry Room. Orville, Albert, Corey, and Angelique watch Bernard as he slowly lowers the telephone handset. Bernard looks directly at Albert.

BERNARD: Al, this meeting has to be Secret.

ANGELIQUE: Does that mean I have to leave?

COREY: You're okay, Angel. The red stripe on your badge means you're cleared for Secret.

ALBERT (*almost whispering*): Angel, would you take some shorthand notes on Orville's responses.

ANGELIQUE: I don't take shorthand, Al.

ALBERT: Right. Then turn on the recorder for this. (*turning to Orville*) Orville, what questions did the police ask you and what answers did you give them?

One of the entrance doors is pushed open suddenly and forcefully. A short, somewhat STOCKY MAN wearing a white apron and white paper garrison cap walks into the room with a piece of paper in his outstretched hand. He is from the cafeteria.

CAFETERIA MAN: Who signs this?

ALBERT (*visibly annoyed at the intrusion*): Signs what? This meeting is Secret!

CAFETERIA MAN: Somebody has to sign for the coffee and doughnuts.

ORVILLE: They didn't ask me any questions other than . . .

Albert holds up his palm in Orville's face.

> ALBERT: Don't say anymore, Orville. Would somebody take care of this gentleman from the cafeteria?

> COREY: I'll sign for the food.

Corey takes the paper from the cafeteria man and scribbles his name across the bottom. The man turns and leaves room.

> ALBERT: Okay. What were you saying, Orville?

> ORVILLE: The first time I called the police department the officers that drove up didn't ask me anything other than my name and where I lived.

> ALBERT: What happened the second time?

> ORVILLE: The second time I called them they drove up, recognized me, wrote something down, gave me the Breathalyzer test, and drove away.

> ALBERT: The *Breathalyzer* test?

> ORVILLE: Yeah. I guess I passed it.

Corey makes another note on his pad. Bernard notices Corey's pad.

> BERNARD: Corey, when we get to the question on spacecraft speed, the data is Secret. You'll have to put the word "SECRET" on the top and bottom of your page. And you'll have to lock up your notes in the special file.

> COREY: I'll put the Confidential and Unclassified answers on separate sheets. Remember the guide says you must not over-classify.

> BERNARD: Good idea!

Corey rips two more sheets off his pad and labels them CONFIDENTIAL and UNCLASSIFIED.

ALBERT: Orville, how long would you estimate you were aboard the alien spacecraft?

ORVILLE: The first time or the second time?

ALBERT: Both times.

ORVILLE: Well, it seemed like two hours the first time and about four hours the second time.

ALBERT: Ah-huh. How much of the inside did you get to see?

ORVILLE: The ship had only two rooms – compartments, I guess you'd call them.

ALBERT: What was in these compartments?

ORVILLE: The one in the front was the cockpit, or whatever they called it. The pilot and co-pilot sat there and steered the thing. The one in back was part workshop and part living quarters.

BERNARD: How much time did you spend on the ground and how much time were you aloft?

ORVILLE: Well, the first time, they took off quickly. They seemed nervous parked there on the runway with the overhead hangar lights on. They landed right away in an area with lots of trees. We sat there for a long time. Then they took me back to the airfield.

BERNARD: Where were you while they were flying and after they landed?

ORVILLE: They rigged up a little seat for me on a cushion and strapped me in for the flight. They unstrapped me when we landed, offered me a rum and cola, and showed me around their ship.

COREY: What kind of sounds did they make?

ORVILLE: They didn't make any *sounds*. They talked with me.

ALBERT: *They talked to you?*

ORVILLE: Yeah. It was broken English, but they said a few words I understood. Most of the time they just pointed at things.

ALBERT: What did they point at?

ORVILLE: Well, on the second flight, they wanted me to look at a rod sticking out of the floor. It looked like a gear shift to me, but I know spaceships don't use gears. It had broken loose. They showed me some spare parts, but they weren't serviceable. So, when we landed back at the air strip, I scrounged up a nut, washer, and bolt from my tool box and re-connected the rod for them.

COREY: Did you talk to them about anything else?

ORVILLE: Yeah. I asked, "Where ya from?"

COREY: Did they show you any kind of star chart or celestial map?

ORVILLE: No, the pilot said to me, "We are from planet Peoria."

ALBERT: You mean he made a sound something like "Pura" or "Pora"?

ORVILLE: No, he clearly said "Peoria."

Corey hastily writes on his pad. He looks up at Angelique.

COREY: Angel, are you getting all this?

ANGELIQUE: My recorder has been on all of the time.

BERNARD: Orville, what else can you tell us about the layout of the control room of the ship?

ORVILLE: Well, it needed a lot of work.

BERNARD: Work?

ORVILLE: A lot of things were coming apart. Some panels on what I'd call their dashboard were loose. The pilot's seat was rocking. I'd describe the area as being held together with baling wire.

BERNARD: I was looking for more specific information on the ship's control system.

ORVILLE: I don't know if this will help you, but on the second flight I got some parts from their ship.

ALBERT: Parts?

ORVILLE: Yeah. I keep some spare nuts and bolts in this here leather pouch you see. I brought it into the ship to fix their gear shift. When they weren't looking, I gathered up a bunch of *their* spare parts and snuck away with them.

Orville releases the drawstring on the pouch and pours the hardware on the table. Corey, Albert, and Bernard quickly lean forward to study the pieces that fall out. There are some knobs, nuts, bolts, connectors, switches, and pieces of linkage.

ALBERT: Orville, we would like to study those parts. If we give you a signed, detailed receipt for what you have there, would you let us keep them for a couple of weeks?

ORVILLE: Sure. You can mail 'em back to me.

ALBERT: Angel, when the meeting's over, draw up a list of these items mister Pressfit brought. I'll sign it. Make two copies.

Corey lifts the coffee pot and offers it to Orville.

COREY: Orville, can I warm up your coffee?

ORVILLE: Sure.

BERNARD: Orville, I'd like to go back to the beginning of your access to the alien spaceship. Think carefully. What do you remember about the size of the ship, both inside and out? What kind of sounds and motion did you feel when it lifted off? Do you remember what displays were being used by the pilot or co-pilot?

Bernard and the others sit back, remaining silent. Orville sips his coffee, puts the cup down, and begins making wide swooping gestures with his arms. Dramatic orchestral MUSIC begins that rises in volume. The scene fades.

INT. RTI. GRAPHICS DEPARTMENT. DAY

Stefan Espacamore stands in the doorway of a large room at RTI. Overhead a sign reads GRAPHICS. Within, several men and women are seated at computers manipulating images. They lean forward, scrutinizing the layouts on the monitors. As they finger a keyboard or slide a computer mouse, lines and blotches of color move around the monitors.

Off to one side ARTHUR GUMME, graphic designer, leans over a table. He is studying several large pieces of artwork done on paper.

He is middle-aged. He is wearing a short-sleeved sports shirt decorated with huge palm trees and clouds. The thick blonde hair on his heavy arms matches the short tufts on his head. Arthur is a chronic improver and likes to keep busy.

Stefan notices Arthur and walks into the room to the table. Arthur looks up at him.

CUT TO: STEFAN AND ARTHUR

> STEFAN: You're mister Gumme, right? Roy Cordu assigned me to work with you on some posters.

> ARTHUR: That's me, but you can call me Art. That's what I do. (*laughs*) I understand you're in the valve design group with Roy.

> STEFAN: That's right. He was supposed to be mentoring me on a valve project this afternoon, but he told me that the company's concerns for ensuring data integrity and preventing intrusion by outsiders take priority. So here I am.

ARTHUR: Yeah. Rudy Vault is on a mission to recruit every wage-earner in this company for his security network. He has a fixation on the idea that we could be infiltrated by beings from another planet.

STEFAN: I guess that's a possibility, Art. What do you need me for?

ARTHUR: I've been directed to prepare a set of posters to alert everyone that there *could* be strangers among us gathering information about the projects we're working on – the Interceptor Program in particular. The posters will be hung throughout the buildings. Here's some that need your input.

Stefan looks down at the stack of drawings on the table that Arthur is pointing at.

STEFAN: I've had no art training. I don't know how I can help you.

ARTHUR: Roy said you might give me some ideas on how to depict aliens from outer space. He said you had studied them a lot.

STEFAN: Well, I studied what *literature* is available on them. I wrote an essay on extraterrestrials that won an award.

ARTHUR: Ever meet one?

STEFAN: Of course not. That's the problem. The reports by people who claim they actually encountered a space alien are not really credible.

ARTHUR: What about that Orville what's-his-name who was here to be interviewed? Do you think he was telling the truth? He claims he spent several hours with the aliens. He said they were human in every respect and they came from some planet named *Peoria*! Can you believe that?

STEFAN: I wasn't in the meeting when he was questioned. I wish I had been. I could have asked him whether the beings he saw did things or had characteristics similar to what other people have related – people who claim to have been abducted. I doubt that Peoria bunk. There are no planets in our solar system that would be habitable for humans.

ARTHUR: Stefan, take a look at these.

Arthur pulls out two more sheets of drawings from under a brown paper cover.

ARTHUR: I made these sketches using drawings of aliens I found on the internet.

CLOSE ON DRAWINGS

One drawing shows two men peering into a window; in the other drawing they are listening at a door. They have normal human frames, but their heads are large at the top, their chins are very narrow, their eyes are abnormally large and dark, and their skin is olive.

CUT TO: STEFAN AND ARTHUR

STEFAN: They're certainly striking!

ARTHUR: These images have to do more than create an emotion; they have to carry a message.

STEFAN: What kind of a message?

ARTHUR: As I said, Rudy Vault is taking a *personal* interest in how these pictures turn out; he gave me a long lecture on how he wants the employees to be *constantly* reminded by these posters that there *could* be alien agents planted here in the company. They could be listening and watching everything we do on the Interceptor Program.

STEFAN: If you want some recognizable and menacing creatures like Martians, you could just copy some old movie posters.

ARTHUR: That occurred to me and that would be easy. But that's why I had Roy put me in touch with you. How does the anatomy and features I used to portray these creatures match with what *you* have read abut them?

Arthur gestures toward his drawings on the table. Stefan bends over the table and cocks his head to get a second look.

STEFAN: I don't mean to be critical, Art. You're good at what you do. But these space creatures you sketched have the usual egg-shaped head, slanted eyes, and green skin you see in cartoons. They're scary, but they don't look anything like *people*.

ARTHUR: I can draw people all day long, but they're not going to get any attention. Rudy Vault wants to scare the pants off everyone.

STEFAN: I wasn't invited to Vault's meeting, but I heard that he *emphasized* that the spies, if you want to call them that, look like run-of-the-mill employees. If they were weird creatures, like you show here, they would be easy to spot.

Arthur pulls out another drawing and holds it up to Stefan.

ARTHUR: How about these? Here is a face you might see on the street, but I gave it a threatening expression.

CLOSE ON DRAWING

The drawing depicts a man with a camera photographing an open notebook. The pages of the notebook have mathematical equations. He has an evil, glaring countenance.
CUT TO: STEFAN AND ARTHUR

STEFAN: That's better. I think that's what Vault had in mind. However, the alien reminds me of his right-hand man, Leo Meertz. I don't think you want to imply that.

ARTHUR: Oops! I see what you mean. I'll fix that.

Arthur scribbles a note on the face in the drawing.

> ARTHUR: Here's one that's almost finished. I used the "alien" features on this one also, but I'll change those faces to look more human. Notice the alien is listening in on a conversation between two engineers on a coffee break.

> STEFAN: That's good. And it's true. Engineers like to discuss their design problems even when they're relaxing. They might accidentally reveal some sensitive information. You should put that poster in the break rooms.

> ARTHUR: Here's another one.

Arthur pulls out another drawing and holds it up to Stefan.

CLOSE ON DRAWING

The shadowy figure of a man is standing in front of an open file drawer in a darkened room. One hand holds a flashlight; the other holds a folder. The tab on the folder reads CONTROL SYSTEM – SECRET. The light reflected from the folder illuminates the man's features. There is a villainous grin on his face.

> ARTHUR: It's not finished. It needs a footer. I'm looking for a catchy phrase.

> STEFAN: A catchy phrase?

> ARTHUR: You know, like the kind they used for security posters during World War II – "Loose lips sink ships." Ever hear that one?

> STEFAN: No, but it could be revised a little. Try this, "An unlocked file makes a Peorian smile."

> ARTHUR: That's good!

Arthur writes it on the bottom of the drawing and sets it aside. He pulls out another poster.

ARTHUR: Here's one. Notice the two engineers are walking away from a large whiteboard that shows a system schematic they finished drawing. They forgot to erase it. The alien is off to the side making notes.

STEFAN: Will *any* of the aliens in these posters be female?

ARTHUR: I was hoping *you* would tell *me* about that.

STEFAN: I'll have to give that some thought. When will these posters be finished?

ARTHUR: I told Vault that I would have them drawn, printed, framed, and mounted around the plant by the end of next week.

STEFAN: If that's it, I'll tell Roy I gave you everything you needed.

ARTHUR: Yeah. Tell him we reached an agreement on how these are going to look; I'm in good shape.

The two men shake hands. As Stefan walks away, he notices a plaque leaning against a stack of books on top of a file cabinet. He pauses to study it.

STEFAN: Art, isn't this the award plaque President Grayfield gave to Masterly?

ARTHUR: Oh, yeah. I was going to put it in the display case in the lobby, but there isn't enough room there. I've got to find a place for it.

Stefan continues out the door. Arthur signals to one of the women working a computer. She joins him at the table. He waves his hand over the drawings and points out details.

INT. MARY SNACKMEISTER'S CUBICLE. DAY

Mary is seated at her work station, checking the email on her computer monitor. She taps the delete button several times. She hears a noise, turns, and sees Kimberly Chi in the aisle. Kimberly is holding a small stack of documents.

> MARY: Kim, c'mon in. Have a seat.

> KIMBERLY: I brought the specs.

Mary pulls a chair out from a small table in the cubicle. She takes the documents from Kimberly and sets them on the table. Kimberly sits down.

> MARY: Sue and Bing should be here in a minute. Thanks for stopping by Repro.

Mary riffles through the pages of one of the documents Kimberly delivered.

Susan Shi and Bing Chang walk up to the entrance of the cubicle.

> SUSAN: We're here, Mary.

> MARY: Let's see. We will need two more chairs. Grab them from those empty cubicles down the aisle. The facilities guys just finished furnishing them for the two new people we hired for our group. But they won't start until next week.

Susan and Bing drag chairs into Mary's cubicle. Mary notices how new they are and puts her hand on one.

> MARY: Hmm. These look better than mine. Maybe I'll switch.

> BING: What are we doing today?
> MARY: Al Gurithum told me that Steve Acheever wants to get closure on the System Specification for the Interceptor. We have to scrub it for terminology. Al says there are too many acronyms.

Mary points to the documents on the table.

> MARY: And, oh, yeah, Steve was looking over the functional analysis and thinks there are some gaps.

Mary reaches down next to her bookcase and grabs a large, rolled document. She spreads it out for the group to inspect.

CLOSE ON PAPER

The paper has a long flow chart that consists of a string of large boxes with wording inside, connected by arrows.

BACK TO SCENE

> MARY: This is the Functional Flow Block Diagram for the level six flow, the one Steve is unhappy with. Let's see, the title is "Vehicle Reaches Intercept Distance."

> SUSAN: Looks good to me.

> MARY: Steve says there's a function missing right here after block six point eight, the one that reads "Arresting Vehicle Characterizes Target." He says something has to occur before the final function, the six point nine block that reads "Alien Vehicle Surrenders."

Mary puts her finger on the diagram.

> KIMBERLY: That makes sense.

> SUSAN: How about adding a function "Arresting Vehicle Fires Warning Laser Beam Across the Bow of Target"?

> KIMBERLY: That seems overly confrontational. We don't know if the aliens are belligerent or not.

> BING: Before our vehicle fires it could first issue an order to the target vehicle to land.

> SUSAN: How would it do that?

> BING: Our vehicle could display a big, flashing red arrow that points down.

Bing makes a gesture downward with his index finger.

> MARY: Would aliens know what a flashing red arrow means?

> KIMBERLY: I would think that's a universal sign.

> SUSAN: Well, they *are* flying over *our* territory and *should realize* they are not welcome. Besides the Air Force *suggested* we provide for weapons. If we stick that function in here, it will drive out that requirement.

> KIMBERLY: Where did the Air Force specify anything about weapons?

> SUSAN: The Statement of Work in our contract invokes the Ponca City Resolution.

> KIMBERLY: The what?

Susan opens a case she is carrying and pulls out a two-page document.

> SUSAN: Let me read it to you. "Therefore, be it resolved that the Ponca City Board of Commissioners demand that our nation's President initiate a program to pursue, identify, and combat any spacecraft and their operators that threaten our population."

Kimberly, Bing, and Mary lean forward, straining to see what Susan is quoting.

> SUSAN: The functional analysis already includes provisions for "pursuit" and "identification." "Combat" is the operative word here.

> KIMBERLY: Yes, but that doesn't mean the Interceptor has to *shoot* at them. That word could have other meanings, like "exercise helps combat stress." There's no report of their ship shooting at us.

BING: True, but I think we have to assume that they are up to no good. Why else would they kidnap someone? Why haven't they landed somewhere and sent out a party with the message, "We come in peace"?

MARY: Even if they would, that's just a ploy. Did you see the movie, *Mars Attacks*? The show of friendship by the Martians was just a pretense. I do believe aliens would take over Earth at the first opportunity. You can't trust them.

SUSAN: Bing is right. The interceptor has to have the capability for deadly force. First a warning shot, then "bang," we blow them out of the sky.

MARY: I agree. Sue, take a red pencil and add that block in the functional flow diagram. Give it that title you suggested: "Fires Warning Laser Beam, etcetera."

Mary hands out copies of the documents Kimberly brought.

MARY: This is a draft of the IX System Specification. Take a copy with you after we're done. Look through it carefully for the usual goofs. Make sure all the "shall"s, "should"s, and "will"s are properly used. But while we're all here let's find those acronyms Al was talking about and spell them out.

BING: Here's one that pops up immediately and seems to be used everywhere. Section One, Scope refers to the Interceptor as a "UAV." I'm not quite sure what that stands for.

MARY: I think it means "Unarmed Attack Vehicle."

BING: That wouldn't make sense. If it's unarmed, how would it be able to attack? Besides, the Interceptor *will* be armed.

MARY: There will be no pilot in the Interceptor. Change it to "Uninhabited Armed Vehicle."

SUSAN: Well, *that is* what it is, but I don't think those words are exactly correct either.

KIMBERLY: Someone told me it stands for "Unusual Air Vessel."

MARY: I can see we're not making any progress on that one. I'll contact the Procedures Group. I think they'll know what the heck it means. Let's move on.

SUSAN: Here's another one. The three point nine requirement says "The AGCS shall withstand the ground handling vibration environment."

MARY: That's an easy one. Those letters stand for the "Aircraft Guidance and Control Set." Corey Layt explained it to me. That's the box with the expensive Inertial doo-hickey in it.

BING: Hold on a minute; the three point seventeen requirement says "The AGCS shall be capable of thirty minutes of continuous operation." That stands for the "Axial Gimbal Coolant System"; I know, because I'll be designing it!

KIMBERLY: So, spell it out!

BING: Sure, except that "AGCS" appears twenty times. Which is which?

MARY: I see we have a problem. Let's throw that one back at Al. Anybody found another acronym?

SUSAN: Here's a double one. Requirement three point thirty-two says "The EEC shall be capable of removal with standard hand tools during the A&CO operations." Anybody know what those mean?

Bing leans back and taps his finger on the table. Susan looks at Kimberly and shrugs. Mary turns the pages of her copy to the requirement Bing mentioned; she holds it up to read it and frowns.

MARY: Some of these are going to take a little thought. Let's just red-line those entries that need review.

Bing, Susan, Kimberly, and Mary open the documents and begin circling words.

INT. RTI. BUILDING 102. HALLWAY. DAY

Corey Layt, Roy Cordu, and Bernard Blastof are standing at a closed door looking up at a sign that reads IX HIGH SECURITY DESIGN SUITE No. 3.

> COREY: This must be the place.

> ROY: They sure made it easy for spies to find it.

> BERNARD: We've never had a security system as tight as this before. I wonder if Rudy knows something he isn't telling us.

The three men look down and study a small box with a dull silver finish installed at shoulder height. The box has a dark, circular opening in the center. Corey points to the box.

> COREY: And there's one of those new retinal scanner locks.

> ROY: Yeah, Rudy Vault's contribution to program security. I suppose Rudy told you what he told me when he captured our retina images in the security office. He said he would insert the recognition data into all the boxes around the facility. Let's hope he did. Go ahead, look into the lens and push the button.

> COREY: Here goes.

Corey puts his face to the box and peers in at the lens. He presses a small black button; there is a HUM from the BOX, a CLUNKING SOUND from the DOOR, and a piece of paper spits out from the underside of the box. Corey pinches the paper and pulls it away.

> ROY: What does it say?

> COREY (*reading*): It has my name, badge number, the date and time of day. It also says we're supposed to do this one

person at a time. I'll go in, close the door, and you can follow.

Corey pushes the door open and enters. He lets it close. There is a loud SNAP.

Roy looks into the lens, presses the button. The door unlocks, and another slip of paper protrudes from the bottom of the scanner. Roy takes the paper and pushes the door open.

After Roy has entered, and the door has closed, Bernard holds his eye to the box and activates the scanner. There is a HUM, a CLUNK, and a paper slides into his hand. He enters the room.

INT. RTI. IX HIGH SECURITY DESIGN SUITE 3. DAY

Corey notices that Bernard is staring intently at the slip of paper printed by the retinal scanner.

> COREY: Is the information correct, Bernie?

> BERNARD: Well my name, ID number, and the date are okay, but there's a note at the bottom that says, "You have traces of incipient cataract."

> ROY: Better look into that.

> BERNARD: Why have you boys invited me to this get-together?

Corey holds up a thick notebook.

> COREY: We want your input on the system architecture. Based on the functions we've assigned to the Interceptor and the requirements in the System Specification, we had the design group prepare these representations of the components that satisfy those functions and requirements.

> ROY: We want you to go over them.

> BERNARD: Do you have something that shows me how they come together? I'd like to see that first.

Corey opens the notebook to the first page and holds it out for Bernard to see.

> COREY: Yeah. Right here in front is an exploded view of the aircraft.

> BERNARD (*visibly disturbed*): I guess you weren't in that meeting with Masterly. He handed down the rule that we are *never, never* to use the phrase "exploded view" of anything we design or build. It has a bad connotation.

Roy and Bernard look at the page Corey has offered.

> ROY: Notice the vehicle has easily removable panels for access to the radar equipment, the guidance system, the pressurant and propellant tanks, and the engine.

> BERNARD: Show me the pressurant tank.

Corey flips some pages.

> COREY: Here it is. It will carry about four thousand psi of helium. It is designed to leak before burst.

> BERNARD: It looks familiar. Wasn't this tank used for the RT-twenty-eight vehicle?

> COREY: Yes, it was.

> BERNARD: Why are we resurrecting that design?

> COREY: Out illustrious Chief Program Engineer, Mike Headknuckle, has flowed down the directive that we are *not* to reinvent the wheel. He didn't say this, but I think he believes this program will be cancelled, and doesn't want to invest too much effort.

> BERNARD: Hmmm. Show me the propellant tanks.

Corey flips more pages.

COREY: This is the tank. The same configuration is used for the inhibited red fuming nitric acid and the unsymmetrical dimethylhydrazine. It's a bladder tank for positive displacement.

BERNARD: Looks good. (*pauses*) Wait a minute; wasn't that tank used in the RT thirty-four vehicle.

COREY: Actually, yes.

Corey flips more pages.

COREY: This is the engine. It is a zero field-maintenance design.
He points to a feature in the drawing.

COREY: These connections on the side provide the fuel injection pulse thrust vector control.

Bernard nods in approval.

COREY: It will have a cast aluminum injector and a forged steel thrust chamber body with an ablative liner.

BERNARD (*wearing puzzled expression*): Wait a minute. Will this be a new design?

COREY: Yes, why do you ask?

BERNARD: We've already designed an engine like that.

COREY: Which one was that?

BERNARD: The number escapes me, but I'm sure it was one we delivered ten years ago. Roy, you should remember. Wasn't it the RT seventeen?

ROY: Possibly. But that program was cancelled, and we destroyed all the drawings.

BERNARD: Are you sure? That would be tragic.

ROY: The Print Crib said they were running out of space.

BERNARD: There must be some drawings around. Check with Murray Jaysize, the designer. He's a packrat. I think he has a secret stash of drawings. What's next?

Corey turns a page in the notebook.

COREY: Here's the list of flight instrumentation and the locations of the transducers.

BERNARD: That needs a close look. Usually you guys have too little or too much.

Corey lays the notebook on the table. Bernard bends over the notebook and begins making notes on a pad. Corey and Roy look at each other and raise their eyebrows.

INT. BARBER SHOP. DAY

The view is of the brightly lit interior of a small, single-chair neighborhood barber shop near the RTI facility. The BARBER is sitting in the barber chair, leafing through a magazine. He is wearing a light brown, zippered, barber jacket. He has bushy hair and a heavy moustache.

Roy Cordu opens the glass door and pauses in the doorway to look in. The barber jumps from the chair and tosses the magazine on a small table next to several customer chairs. He waves Roy in and points toward the barber chair.

BARBER: Come in. Have a seat. I can take care of you right now.

Roy walks to the barber chair, raises himself into it, and leans back.

ROY: I took some personal time off from the office. I thought I might squeeze in a hair cut.

BARBER: For sure. I'll have you out of here in twenty minutes.

The barber picks up a blue-striped cape, shakes it out, and prepares to toss it over his customer, but stops when he sees Roy quickly reach up and unclip his RTI badge from his pocket protector and jam it into a pocket. The barber takes notice, finishes casting the cape like a net over Roy's chest, and quickly fastens it around his neck.

> BARBER: I see you work for that high-tech company down the street.

> ROY: Uh-huh. I'd appreciate it if we would talk about some other topic – especially if another customer comes in. Company Security frowns on employees wearing badges off the property.

> BARBER: That secret, huh? Don't worry. Tuesday afternoons are very slow for some reason. Nobody is going to walk through that door.

The barber ties a neck strip on Roy.

> BARBER: How do you want your hair?

> ROY: Trim a little around the ears, cut a little off the top, and leave it long in back.

The barber picks up his electric CLIPPERS and flicks the switch. There is a loud BUZZ. He begins by touching the clippers to Roy's temple.

> BARBER: I guess you can't talk much about what you do.

> ROY (*changing the subject*): If Tuesdays are always slow, maybe there's some way you can drum up a little business.

> BARBER: Like what?
> ROY: Well, you know. Offer a Tuesday special. Charge a few bucks less on a haircut.

The barber stops, grimaces, and shakes his head.

> BARBER: Can't do that!

> ROY: Why not?

BARBER: I'm a professional. I have to charge professional rates for my services.

ROY: I see.

BARBER: I can understand all the secrecy in your work. But I would bet that if the public found out about some of the things going on at your company – what's it called, RepoTek – somebody might get really upset.

ROY: The company name is Repulsive Technology. What'd you hear?

BARBER: Maybe it's just a funny coincidence, but just before you came in, I was reading an article in Cover-Up magazine over there on the table. It was written by that guy, Hank Keptiks. He's good. He seems to know what's going on. He must have talked to someone at RepoTek.

ROY: What'd you read?

BARBER: His article states that your company has parts from the alien ship that landed in Oklahoma. That mechanic, Footpress, gave them to you. The article says you're using them to build a similar ship.

ROY: *Pressfit.*

BARBER: What?

ROY: Pressfit is the last name of the mechanic, and he didn't give us enough parts to build a spaceship.

The barber picks up a pair of shears and begins combing and clipping the top of Roy's head.

BARBER: I also read about the anti-gravity smoke-screen.

ROY: What smoke-screen?

BARBER: Keptiks also confirmed that your company acquired the method for anti-gravity from the aliens, but you're suppressing it. I heard that even *before* I read the article. *Everybody* knows that. My other customers tell me that too. It's been going around.

ROY: That's not true. Besides, if we had a device to create anti-gravity, why would we keep a lid on it?

BARBER: Cuz no one would need a rocket engine to get into space anymore. You wouldn't be able to sell any. You'd go out of business.

ROY: That's just a dumb rumor, but I don't think I can convince you.

BARBER: That's okay. I understand; you have to keep the doors open and meet the payroll. I'm a businessman too.

The barber brushes Roy's face and holds up a mirror.

ROY: That'll do.

The barber removes the cape. Roy steps out of the chair, pulls a twenty-dollar bill from his wallet, and hands it to the barber. The barber opens the cash drawer on the counter and pulls out some small bills that he hands to Roy.

BARBER: I may not be an injuneer, (*chuckles*) but I have what I think are some good ideas you guys could use in your rockets.

ROY: Such as?

BARBER: I was reading about how you have to build those big, heavy, expensive stands to test the rockets because of the high thrust they put out.

ROY: True.

BARBER: Well, if you stuck the top of the rocket engine into the ground and fired it pointing downward, it couldn't go anywhere. You wouldn't need a big test stand.

ROY: That would create design problems. Besides, space vehicles and missiles don't fly in that direction. We test the engine in the attitude in which it will be used.

BARBER: Who can I call at the company to give them these ideas?

ROY: Call the Public Relations office; ask for Joyce Plaisant.

The barber scribbles on a pad on his counter.

BARBER: Thanks.

Roy walks to the door of the shop. He pauses and turns.

ROY: And give some thought to Tuesday specials.

INT. WALTER MASTERLY'S OFFICE. DAY

Angelique leans into the doorway of Walter's office. She taps on the door frame. Walter looks up.

ANGELIQUE: Stefan Espacamore from Valve Design wishes to speak to you.

Walter nods approvingly.

WALTER: Send him in.

Stefan enters and stands next to Walter's desk.

STEFAN: I work with Roy Cordu. He's out getting a haircut. He called me and asked me to drop by. He told me you have some paperwork to give him.

WALTER: Well, I wanted to speak with him personally, but you can pass along what I have to say.

Walter opens a drawer in his desk and pulls out a large piece of paper with a sketch on it. He lays it on his desk and waves Stefan over.

> WALTER: Take a look at this.

Stefan studies the sketch.

> WALTER: Since you work with Roy, Stefan, you must be aware that the bi-propellant valve for the axial engine did not pass the preliminary functional testing. The report said the valve did not move linearly and was not closing fully.

> STEFAN: Yes, Roy explained that. In fact, when he gets back, he plans to initiate the necessary changes to the valve to cure those problems. He said he wants to issue a Design Change Request before he leaves work this afternoon.

> WALTER: That's admirable. But I want to offer a little help. (*smiles*) Most of the RTI people think of me only as the President, a desk jockey. They forget that many years ago I started as a designer. I still consider myself pretty good at that job.

Feigning a show of interest, Stefan picks up the sketch and looks closely at it.

> STEFAN: I'm just learning, but it seems to be an excellent design, mister Masterly.

Walter leans back, smiling. He is evidently pleased by Stefan's comment.

> WALTER: It's a balanced-force pintle valve. Give it to Roy. He'll recognize the features I've added.

Stefan slides the paper into a large envelope he is carrying under his arm.

> STEFAN: I'll get it to Roy immediately, mister Masterly.

Stefan hurries out of the office door.

INT. RTI. IX HIGH SECURITY DESIGN SUITE 3. DAY

A man is sitting at a small, square table looking at a computer terminal. It is MURRAY JAYSIZE, lead designer.

Murray is forty-eight with a head of hair that needs combing. The sleeves of his white shirt are rolled up. Murray is exceptionally careful in his work, but is sometimes a plodder.

Over his shoulder we see the door of the room swing open. Stefan walks in.

> STEFAN: Murray, have you started yet?

Murray looks up.

> MURRAY: I'm booting up the software now.

> STEFAN: Roy told me the design change on the propellant valve *has* to be completed by today.

> MURRAY: Where *is* Roy?

> STEFAN: He'll be here any minute. He went to get a haircut.

> MURRAY: Oh, great! He couldn't pick a better time! (*frowns*) And on top of it this terminal is *really slow*.

ANGLE ON MONITOR

The screen is a deep blue, with large yellow letters that read:

PROPULCAD
Computer Aided Design for All Propulsion Products

CUT TO: STEFAN AND MURRAY

> STEFAN: Did you finish those changes Roy requested?

> MURRAY (*growling*): Did I? I was here until nine last night!

Stefan points to monitor excitedly.

STEFAN: There it is!

CLOSE ON MONITOR

A many-colored three-dimensional image of a somewhat cylindrical valve body is rotating slowly on the screen.

CUT TO: STEFAN AND MURRAY

MURRAY: I'll go to a cutaway so you can see the changes to the interior. The differences between the old and new valve are mainly in the clearances and the seal type.

CLOSE ON MONITOR

The image has changed. The valve is shown cut in half like a melon. The moving parts of the valve are displayed. Then the image becomes a black and white two-dimensional engineering drawing of the surfaces seen a moment ago.

BACK TO SCENE

STEFAN (*pointing to image*): Can you give me a print of that? I'll need it to attach to the DCR, you know, the Design Change Request. In fact, I'll need before and after drawings.

Murray taps a few keys. The PRINTER next to him HUMS and a paper slides out. He grabs it and also grabs another paper lying next to the printer.

MURRAY: Here you are. One of each.

As Stefan compares the two drawings handed to him by Murray, the door to the room opens and Roy walks in.

ROY: Sorry I'm late. How's it going?

MURRAY: I'm done. I just gave Stefan the drawings for the DCR.

ROY: Great. Let me fire up this computer over here to open the draft of the DCR I started. I also want to see if I have any emails.

Roy walks to the computer, bends over, and presses the power-on button. A TELEPHONE on Murray's table RINGS. Murray picks it up.

MURRAY: Hello, Jaysize here. (*pauses*) Oh, Hi, Joyce.

Murray listens for a while, nodding. He offers the phone to Roy.

MURRAY: It's Joyce Plaisant in Public Relations. She's asking for you. She's got some guy on the line that says he has a great product idea for our company that could make us a lot of money.

Roy grabs the phone from Murray.

ROY (*under his breath*): I have a terrible feeling. (*speaking into the handset*) This is Roy, Joyce. Who called you?

INT. RTI. PUBLIC RELATIONS OFFICE. DAY

Joyce Plaisant is standing next to a wall of her cubicle, holding the handset of her phone to her ear. She turns her head side to side despairingly.

JOYCE: Hi, Roy. I'm *really* sorry about bothering you at this time, but I've got another one of those callers that has a suggestion. I have him on the other line. He gave me your name. He says he knows you. He says he cut your hair. Can you take the call?

The scene now alternates between Joyce's cubicle and the Design Suite.

INTERCUT JOYCE/ROY

Roy listens for a moment, places his palm over the mouthpiece of the handset, and whispers to Murray.

ROY: It's the *barber*! He must have remembered my name from my badge.

He painfully holds the phone to his mouth.

ROY: I'm working against a deadline for a critical design change, Joyce. I don't have time to talk to this fellow. Does he have a question or what?

JOYCE: He's suggesting that RTI make something he called a "devil nozzle" to put on the ends of tail pipes on cars to give them extra speed.

ROY: Look. Tell him this, if you can remember it. What he's talking about is a "de Laval" nozzle. That's what we use on our rocket engines to expand the combustion gases. Tell him that any added speed from the thrust of that small nozzle would be immeasurable. What's worse: tell him the nozzle throat would increase the back pressure to the car's engine. I'm not an automotive engineer, but I believe that could have undesirable effects. Tell him to call up an automobile manufacturer and offer them the idea.

JOYCE: Thank you so much, Roy. I've made some notes here. I'll try to tell him all that.

Joyce punches the keypad of the phone cradle. She begins reading from a scrap of paper.

The view returns to the design suite. Roy replaces the handset on his phone. He notices Stefan is looking at a computer monitor in an agitated state.

STEFAN: Oh – oh! Roy, take a gander at this! I put "Interceptor" into the search engine. This is what came up.

Roy steps behind Stefan and looks over his shoulder at the monitor.

ROY: Holy cow! Murray, stop a moment and come over here.

> MURRAY: Wait, I'm making sure I save this file. This better be important.

Murray presses a key at the CAD terminal with determination. He watches the screen fade, and slides back his chair. He steps over to Roy and squints at the image on the monitor in front of Stefan.

CLOSE ON THE COMPUTER MONITOR

The screen has an image of a diminutive version of the Interceptor vehicle.

BACK TO SCENE

> ROY: Can you believe it? The Plastiknack Company has come out with a kit to build an Inceptor model.

> MURRAY: They did a good job.

> ROY: Yeah, they even have the attitude control thrusters in the new location near the nose.

> STEFAN: Where are they getting this information?

> ROY: Somebody in the Air Force must be leaking the details.

> MURRAY: That's nothing. Take a look at this month's issue of Aerospace Progress.

Murray reaches into a pile of magazines next to the coffee maker and pulls one out.

> MURRAY: Read the article on page twelve. It's a report on the background of the Interceptor Program and the design and testing progress. It's all there.

Roy takes the magazine from Murray and flips the pages.
> ROY: Oh, no! It even mentions our propellants – inhibited red fuming nitric acid and unsymmetrical dimethylhydrazine – and they're *secret*!

MURRAY: It gets even worse. The next paragraph says that getting the IRFNA in the concentration and quantities we need may be difficult.

Roy circles the text in the magazine and hands it to Stefan.

STEFAN: Maybe some branches of the Air Force use a different classification guide than the one Rudy Vault showed us.

ROY: I'll speak to Rudy about that later. In the meantime, we've *got* to get the DCR for the valve mods completed *today*.

Roy sits down at the computer. With a few taps on the keyboard, a blank form appears on the monitor.

ROY: Murray, what's the valve drawing number that's being revised.

MURRAY: EX-VC- twelve-thirty-one-A. You'll be creating the "B" change.

Roy inserts numbers onto the form on his screen.

ROY: Murray, I'm trying to describe the old and new configurations. Do I use "from" and "to" or "was" and "is"?

MURRAY: Aren't those terms on the form?

ROY: No.

MURRAY: Maybe you should check with Forms Control. They're very strict.

ROY: Stefan, would you give a call to Forms Control and ask them what I need to use to complete this Design Change Request. I've got to finish this *today*!

STEFAN: Hold on. I just received a priority email. You guys should check *your* inboxes. It says the attachment *must* be read *now* and you *must* acknowledge *now* that you read and understand it.

MURRAY: What's the attachment say?

STEFAN: The email is from Rudy Vault. It says the attachment has a set of instructions for reporting any suspicious persons or activity of extraterrestrial origin. It includes tips for recognizing an alien.

Stefan opens the email attachment. The three men study the wordy document on the screen.

MURRAY: I assume Vault composed all this. How the heck does he know what an alien looks like?

STEFAN: Look. There at the bottom. There's a charge number for reporting alien activity – and another charge number for evacuation of the building in case of an alien attack.

A piece of paper emerges from the printer. Roy takes it and hands it to Stefan.

ROY: Forget that. Here's the completed DCR. Make about a dozen copies. I had Kimberly Chi call a special meeting of the Engineering Change Board first thing tomorrow morning. She chairs it. I've got to have them approve this change.

STEFAN: I'll take it down the hall. There's a copy room there.

ROY: I don't want anyone to see you carrying it. It's stamped CONFIDENTIAL. Here, put it in that large envelope you're holding.

Stefan opens the flap on the envelope to slip in the paper Roy gave him. As he peers inside, he notices another paper.

STEFAN: Oh, my God!

ROY: What is it?

STEFAN: I was supposed to give you this. Walter Masterly asked me to deliver it. I forgot.

ROY: Let's see it.

Stefan tips the envelope to let the paper with the sketch slide out. Roy catches it and looks down at it.

STEFAN: Masterly said it was his solution to the valve problem. It's a re-design he came up with.

Roy drops his hand with the sketch to his side. He takes a deep breath and stands motionless, looking at the wall.

ROY: Murray, we have a problem.

Murray looks up from the computer monitor and walks over to Roy. Roy holds up the sketch.

ROY: What do you think of this alternate valve design?

Murray snaps it from Roy's fingers and rotates it slightly as he studies it.

MURRAY: We tried that. It won't work. Where did you get this?

ROY: It's Walter Masterly's brainchild.

MURRAY: Great. He wants to get back into designing things. I'd toss it in the wastebasket. Do you want to break the news to him?

ROY: Before I do that, is there any little feature of what he's suggesting here that you could incorporate into the design we just finished? You know, so I could throw him a bone.

MURRAY: Possibly. But it would be a kluge. I'll need some time to do some calculations and re-do the model. What do *you* want to do?

Roy lets go with another long sigh. He stands thinking for a long time. Murray runs his hand through his hair nervously, waiting for an answer.

ROY: See what you can do, Murray. I'm going to call Kimberly Chi and cancel tomorrow's Engineering Change Board. Stefan, hold off on those copies.

Roy collapses into a chair. Murray begins to punch keys at the CAD terminal. Stefan returns to the computer and looks with fascination at the website with the Interceptor model kit.

INT. RTI. BREAK ROOM. DAY

The Building 102 break room, the largest in RTI, bustles with employees carrying in trays of snacks, bottles of beverages, paper plates, napkins, and plastic cutlery. The break room is completely outfitted for preparing and serving food. A large white refrigerator stands against the wall. There is a large, double, stainless steel sink.

On a long counter is a toaster oven, a microwave oven, a large chrome coffee urn, and other appliances. The large table in the center of the room is overflowing with pizzas, vegetable crudités, dips, meat appetizers, salads, cakes, and other pastries.

The NOISE LEVEL erupts as employees on their lunch period wander in and begin talking to each other.

Across the top of the wide entrance door to the room a banner has been stretched. The banner reads THE INTERCEPTOR TEAM — CHAMPIONS ALL.

Mary Snackmeister and CONSTANCE HARMONY, Manager of Training, are directing the activities. They are standing off to the side, watching.

Constance is forty-one. Her dark garnet hair circles her face. She has high cheekbones and a small mouth that is usually pulled into a smile. Constance has developed many strong relationships at RTI over the years. She is very adaptable.

CONSTANCE: Everything seems to be in place and everyone seems to be here, Mary. Why don't you use this opportunity to make your announcement?

Mary walks to the center of the room and cups her hands over her mouth.

> MARY (*loudly*): Attention, everyone!

Some of the employees waiting in the food line turn toward Mary to listen. Most of those scooping food onto their paper plates pay little attention.

> MARY: I hope everyone is in a celebratory mood today. Repulsive Technology is doing great. The Interceptor Program is on schedule, meeting all objectives, and getting ready for a big program review with the customer.

Mary pauses to applaud. Many of the employees put down their paper plates to applaud along with Mary.

> MARY (*excitedly*): We have *many* reasons to be happy and positive today. Let's use this opportunity to share our good feelings with each other.

There are several shouts of YEAH! The employees begin mingling and scarfing food between their greetings to one another. All of the departments are represented: Engineering, Quality, Purchasing, Finance, Health & Safety, Plant Security, Human Resources, Customer and Public Relations, Media Services, Business Operations, Manufacturing, Warehousing, and Facility Maintenance.

CUT TO: JOYCE AND EDWARD

Joyce Plaisant and Edward Confirme are leaning on the counter next to the coffee urn, poking at small piles of salad on their plates.

> JOYCE: Well, Ed, do you feel especially joyous today?

> EDWARD: No, do you?

> JOYCE: Not really. It seems as though the tone of this organization is changing. I feel many of the people here are getting uncomfortable, if not outright frightened, by the

prospect that other-worldly creatures are working here among us. Do you think that's possible?

EDWARD: Rudy Vault seems to think it's possible.

JOYCE: These creatures are supposed to be here from the planet Peoria.

EDWARD: I don't believe there is any such planet.

JOYCE: Have you seen all those alien posters he had made? They've got me going to bed at night thinking about those eyes, those vile expressions!

EDWARD: Yes, Art Gumme outdid himself promoting the fear that Rudy wanted to get across.

JOYCE: Rudy even had some of those posters hung in the ladies room.

EDWARD: Everywhere I go in the plant I run across people conversing about possible aliens in the plant.

JOYCE: Yes, and I'm starting to get strange phone calls. People want to know what we're *doing* about the aliens. How is word about that getting out to the public?

EDWARD: Apparently Rudy wants everything kept secret except the possible alien threat.

JOYCE: I'm probably over-sensitive to the subject of aliens. My mother told me that when I was very little, I was always imagining that there was a troll under my bed. I guess I never outgrew that fixation. Let's just hope that most of our Repulsive Technology employees are mature enough to keep these rumors about ET visits in perspective.

Edward nods and Joyce stirs the salad on her plate nervously.

CUT TO: HAP AND LEONARD

Hap Cawshun is pouring ginger ale into two tall plastic cups; one is for himself and one is for Leonard Lenz. Leonard picks up his cup and raises it in a salute to Hap

>LEONARD: Cheers.

Hap picks up his cup and looks at Leonard glumly.

>HAP: I suppose I *should* be cheerful, but I've been having some uneasy feelings about what's been happening here.

>LEONARD: What's bothering you?

>HAP: It's kind of difficult to explain.

>LEONARD: That's okay. I'm listening.

>HAP: Maybe this will make sense: you work in our video department. Are you a big movie fan?

>LEONARD: I've seen a few. Why?

>HAP: Do you remember any of the body snatcher films?

>LEONARD: The subject sounds familiar, but they were made before my time. What do they have to do with your uneasy feelings?

>HAP: Well, the premise of these movies is that aliens come to Earth in the form of long plant-like pods. The pods bloom and create a human-looking shape that takes over people that are sleeping.

>LEONARD: Well, that *is* a frightening prospect. But then all of these stories about being invaded by life-forms from other planets are really far out. After all, it's just a movie. Those things don't really happen.

HAP: I'm not so sure about that. When I pulled into the parking lot this morning, I saw a truck backed up to the street entrance to the cafeteria kitchen. A man was opening the rear swing doors. He was acting suspiciously. He reached in and brought out what looked like a large green pod. He carried it into the cafeteria. He came out several times and carried in three more. On each trip he kept looking around to see if he was being watched.

LEONARD: Now you've got me worried. Mary Snackmeister has been in and out of the cafeteria all morning organizing this party. Maybe she has seen something. Let's ask her.

HAP: Okay, but let's be careful of what we say. I don't want to start a panic.

Leonard waves at Mary to come over. She steps away from Constance and joins the two men.

HAP: We just wanted to congratulate you, Mary, on the wide variety of foods you ordered for the party. The fruits and pastry look delicious and healthy. We want to try *everything*. Someone said they saw some big green vegetables being delivered this morning. Were they for our party?

MARY: You mean the watermelons? Yeah, I thought four would be enough. They're cut up and in the bowls over there on the dessert table. Have some.

Hap and Leonard look to the table where Mary is pointing. They turn to look at each other and laugh boisterously. Then the smiles fade from their faces, and they stare again at the table for a long time.

CUT TO: STANLEY AND ANITA

Stanley Snappi and Anita Guardley bump into each other as they both reach for cupcakes from a large, round, aluminum platter. Anita backs away quickly.

ANITA: Oh, excuse me, Stan. I didn't mean to be greedy.

STANLEY: No, you go first.

Anita smiles and picks up a thickly frosted cupcake. She cradles it in a napkin in her hand. Stanley picks up a cupcake, eyes it for a moment, then takes a bite.

ANITA: As Mary said, Stan. We should *all* be happy today. Do you have any reason *not* to be happy? You're a key player in the Interceptor Program. I overheard John telling someone on the phone today that he was very satisfied with the progress we're making.

STANLEY: It's not all that simple. I do believe we have done a darn good job so far with the design, production, and testing of the Ground Support Equipment – the GSE, but I somehow keep feeling that there's something holding us back.

ANITA: Holding us back? What does *that* mean?

STANLEY: I haven't mentioned this to anyone, Anita, because I can't prove it, but I *do* believe that there are alien beings right here – among us.

ANITA (*gasping*): My God, have you seen some?

STANLEY: No, but I've felt them.

ANITA (*growing more emotional*): What did you feel?

STANLEY: I do believe that they are exerting a narcotic influence over everyone connected with the Interceptor Program. I'm seeing that influence at work here every day!

Anita's mouth drops open; her eyes widen; she sets the uneaten cupcake on the table.

STANLEY: I was reading reports of alien control tricks in Cover-Up magazine. First, they take over your mind. It happens slowly so it won't be too obvious to the person or to coworkers.

Anita moves her head side to side slowly in disbelief.

STANLEY: The employee becomes sluggish, dull-witted, indifferent to responsibility, and resistant to company procedures.

ANITA: Now that you mention it, I can think of times I *have* encountered that behavior in some of the people here. The things I ask for are never being done correctly. The other day I ordered some two-inch ring binders and they delivered one-inch. The maintenance guy isn't emptying the wastebasket in Fulbrane's office anymore. Do you think *you* have been affected?

STANLEY: Normally I wouldn't repeat something like this. (*hesitates*) Yesterday I was reviewing a drawing of an engine dolly. I was checking tolerances. I felt very sleepy and leaned back and closed my eyes. Wouldn't you know, your boss, Fulbrane, came by and caught me doping off. He was probably ticked off, but he didn't show it. He only said, "Keep at it, Stan." I *knew* it was the alien narcotic influence, Anita.

ANITA: That's frightening. Maybe you should report your condition to John.

STANLEY: Let's keep this between you and me until I collect more evidence.

Anita nods in agreement as she picks up her cupcake and nibbles it slowly.

CUT TO: SANDRA AND FLORENCE

Sandra Binding and Florence Kahdasill walk under the banner into the break room. Sandra looks around slowly. Her face reflects a sense of disappointment.

SANDRA: I expected Walter to be here. I thought I had better make an appearance. Besides, this could be an opportunity to get his interpretation of some of those Interceptor contract clauses.

FLORENCE: This is a *big* turn-out. Apparently, a lot of employees felt the same as you about being seen by Walter.

SANDRA: Yes, but who *are* all these people? I don't recognize half of them!

FLORENCE: There were a lot of new hires for the Interceptor Program.

Sandra swings her head from side to side, surveying the room. She zeroes in on a lone MAN. He looks to be about fifty. The hair on his head is disheveled; he is wearing silvery-gray coveralls with a vortex-like emblem on the shoulder.

SANDRA: Look at that fellow over there. I've never seen *him* before. He's dressed strangely. I wonder what he does.

FLORENCE: The purpose of these get-togethers is to know each other better. Let's introduce ourselves and ask him, Sandy.

Sandra and Florence move through the clumps of people juggling paper plates and plastic tumblers to confront the man they have spied. He is standing off by himself. He is looking down at the food on his plate as if puzzled. Sandra attempts a smile.

SANDRA: Good afternoon. I see you're enjoying some of Mary Snackmeister's delicacies. It may not be the most healthful food, but it *is* tempting. I haven't seen you at any meetings. Are you one of our newer employees?

MAN: Yes, yes, I am.

SANDRA: I'm Sandra Binding, Director of Contract Administration. This lady next to me is Florence Kahdasill, my deputy. What's *your* name?

MAN: Oh, I'm John Smith.

FLORENCE: How do you like working at Repulsive Technology, John?

JOHN: It's a wonderful company, and I really enjoy my job. I'm in Facility Maintenance and I work outside a lot. The weather in this part of the country is much milder than where I came from.

SANDRA: Where is that, John?

JOHN: Peoria.

Sandra and Florence are stunned by the word. They take a step back and look at each other. Their faces are paralyzed by shock.

SANDRA: Excuse us for a moment, John. I think I see someone I have to speak to. (*lying*) Look, Florence, isn't that Walter Masterly over there?

Sandra and Florence quickly turn away. Sandra pulls Florence by the arm to a corner of the break room.

SANDRA (*breathing heavily*): Did you hear that? *Peoria*!

FLORENCE: He's one of *them*! Isn't that some kind of space suit he is wearing? Imagine — taking the name *John Smith*. I knew that was phony when he said it.

SANDRA: Yes. (*in a low voice in Florence's ear*) Do you remember what Rudy Vault said in one of his security briefings? The company has *not* been doing extensive background checks on people being hired for *maintenance* jobs! And I think I detected some kind of accent when he spoke. Let's ask him a few more questions. I have a way to trick him.

The two women merge back into the crowd of merrymakers and sidle up to John.

SANDRA: Well, John. I'm happy to know you prefer our weather here. How does it compare with the weather in Illinois? You know, where you came from.

JOHN: I've never been in Illinois. I like it here because there's always a cool breeze. I work in the sun a lot. The place I came from is too hot and arid.

Sandra's neck stiffens. Her face contorts. She tightly grips Florence's arm. Florence winces in pain.

SANDRA (*in a wavering voice*):   We have to go.
Sandra pushes her way through the thickening crowds, dragging Florence along. They pass under the banner into the adjoining office area where they halt abruptly. They take deep breaths.

SANDRA: You heard him, Flo. *He took the bait*! These aliens must think we're stupid. He says he's from Peoria, but he isn't smart enough to make up a story about Illinois. Hot and arid, huh. The planet Peoria must be like *Mars*!

FLORENCE: We've got to notify Security!

SANDRA: There are three Security guys in the break room. See if you can get the attention of one of them.

Florence steps inside the entrance to the break room. She sees the uniformed SECURITY GUARDS holding pastries and coffee. They are engaged in lively conversation.

Florence waves frantically. One of the guards notices her gestures, nods, and walks to the entrance where she is standing. She backs into the office area where Sandra is waiting. The guard follows.

SECURITY GUARD: You need me?

SANDRA (*panting*):   There is a suspicious person here at the company party. See, that fellow over there – in the silvery suit.

Sandra's hand shakes visibly as she points at the man.

SECURITY GUARD: Yeah, you mean John?

SANDRA (*hyperventilating*): You *know* him?

SECURITY GUARD: He's new here – John Smith. I ran into him the other day when he changed some of the fluorescent tubes in our office. He's from Peoria, Arizona. What's suspicious about him?

Sandra places her hand in the wall to steady herself.

SANDRA: I'm a little confused. Flo, let's go sit down somewhere.

Sandra and Florence walk away. The security guard returns to the party.

CUT TO: STEFAN AND KIMBERLY

Kimberly Chi is standing at the large food table, sorting through the tray of meat appetizers. Stefan Espacamore slides over next to her and reaches into the tray for a small sausage with a toothpick in it. Kimberly notices him.

KIMBERLY: Good afternoon, Stefan.

STEFAN: Oh, hi, Kim. As you can see, I'm in the partying mood.

Stefan swings around to face Kimberly. He spreads his arms and displays his torso. He is wearing a deep blue T-shirt. In the center of the shirt in large, white, block letters is the company logo: RTI. On the breast pocket is a small image of the Interceptor vehicle. It is angled upward. A flame spills out the tail. Below are the words, INTECEPTOR GO!

STEFAN: What do you think?

KIMBERLY: Is that new? Where did you get that?

STEFAN: I put it on for the party.

KIMBERLY: Is that a sample?

STEFAN: No, our full order came in yesterday. This is the design our committee agreed on. We knew Masterly would go for the blue color. Everyone on the program gets one. They'll be distributed later this afternoon.

KIMBERLY: Doesn't that sort of tell the world we're working on an interceptor vehicle?

STEFAN: That's right! We thought it would bolster employee spirit. You know, motivate everyone.

KIMBERLY: I thought the idea was to keep the program secret.

STEFAN: We'll be launching an IX soon. It won't be any secret.

KIMBERLY: Mmm.

Stefan and Kimberly look down again at the tiny sausages speared with the toothpicks.

CUT TO: CHANDRA AND SUSAN

Chandra Patel and Susan Shi are standing close to the counter. Chandra is pouring root beer from a plastic bottle into two paper cups on the counter surface. Susan holds them to steady them. Chandra finishes pouring and sets the bottle down. They pick up the cups and sip.

SUSAN: Thanks, Chandra. Should we drink a toast to our successes in the Interceptor Program? You must be very busy in Purchasing.

CHANDRA (*with a sour expression*): I could be busier, but they've just issued a new bunch of procedures for our department. They don't make sense. The Procedures group claims these rule changes implement new government procurement regulations. They're too restrictive. I can't get a purchase order out the door.

SUSAN: You don't look too happy. Don't let Mary Snackmeister see you.

CHANDRA: And we can't use our existing PO forms! Forms Control said the new procedures require additional authorization signatures.

SUSAN: I guess you *aren't* happy.

CHANDRA: I wish I *were* President of this company. I'd sure straighten things out.

SUSAN (*looking around*): Don't let Masterly hear you.

CHANDRA: I'll bet even *he* doesn't know what's going on. (*getting angrier*). Look at that banner over the door. What does it say? The Interceptor *Team*! There's no teamwork here! Look at the words on this cup.

Chandra holds her paper cup to Susan's eyes.

CLOSE ON CUP

There is a phrase in red letters on the side of the cup: DRINK TO THE ONGOING SUCCESS OF THE RTI TEAM.

CUT TO: CHANDRA AND SUSAN

CHANDRA: In all of the company meetings and in the company brochures and newsletters we're always addressed as "the team members." So why do the company procedures only refer to us as "employees"?

SUSAN: Yes, it is contradictory – and kind of sad. But smile; I think I see Mary coming this way.

Susan raises her cup of root beer as a salute.

CUT TO: ALBERT AND BERNARD

Albert Gurithum and Bernard Blastof walk side by side, at a leisurely pace, to the entrance to the break room. Bernard stops and looks up at the banner. Albert surveys the crowds of people at the food table.

ALBERT: Well, Bernie, it looks like a lot of enthusiasm is being generated here today.

BERNARD (*with sarcasm*): Sure. As though this spread will resolve all of the problems in the Interceptor project. Maybe, if everyone here gets back to work at one o'clock. Who's paying for this shindig?

ALBERT: The Business Development Group. They have a discretionary budget for customer social events that also let's them sponsor office parties.

BERNARD: I thought so. And I know *who* in that group is behind this – their idea-guy, Louis Cannon.

ALBERT: What makes you think so?

BERNARD: I was sitting at a table next to him in the cafeteria while he was lecturing the Director of Personnel. He was going off on one of his usual sermons about increasing productivity.

ALBERT: What did he say?

BERNARD: He was relating an article in a science journal. Some guy named Pfluggleman ran experiments in which he fed rats different kinds of foods to see which type motivated them the most.

ALBERT: I would think anything you offer a rat would motivate it.

BERNARD: Apparently some foods are better than others. Pfluggleman put the rats in pens with a supply of twigs, paper, plant materials, and other debris. The rats would use the trash to build nests, but they would do that slowly and would frequently stop and lay down. When he fed them certain foods, they began actively working without interruptions.

ALBERT: What did he feed them?

BERNARD: That was one of the discoveries of the research. It apparently depends on the DNA of the rat. Some rats were motivated by glazed doughnuts, some by cheese dip, and some by pigs-in-a-blanket.

ALBERT: Why do you bring that up?

BERNARD: Don't you see the connection? Cannon views these "banquets" for the RTI workforce as an extension of that experiment.

ALBERT: Maybe that was just a coincidence.

BERNARD: Maybe, but look carefully at what all those people are devouring. I'd be willing to bet that when Cannon gave Mary Snackmeister the money for the food, he also gave her a *menu*.

Bernard raises his arm and sweeps it across the break room. He nods and smiles knowingly at Albert.

BERNARD: The experiment is working, Al.

ALBERT: That could be, Bernie. Give everybody a little sugar, a little protein, and they turn to. That carrot cake does look savory, but I've got to get back to my office. Let's go.

The two men walk leisurely away.

CUT TO: BING AND COREY

Bing Chang and Corey Layt are standing at the coffee urn. Corey has his RTI mug under the spout and his thumb on the valve handle. Coffee is flowing slowly into the mug.

COREY: I think there's enough here for both of us, Bing. May I pour you a cup?

BING: Sure.

Corey takes Bing's mug from his hand, slides it under the spout, and begins filling.

COREY: Well, *you* have reason to celebrate; you've been in the Interceptor Program for a year. You've probably got a good handle on your job by now.

BING: I'd like to think so, but I'm not in a good frame of mind. I have a performance review tomorrow.

COREY: You should do okay.

BING: I've never gone through a performance review. Some of the older guys told me what the boss will ask me and what to say.

COREY: Such as?

BING: Well, my boss, Warren Neadle, is going to ask me what my goals are for the coming year.

COREY: That should be easy. You look at your job description and pick out some of your task areas. Think up an accomplishment in each.

BING: That's the problem. I don't have a job description.

COREY: After a year?

BING: Yeah, Neadle says he's hesitant to put one in writing as it would be too restrictive and would limit the assignments he might have to give me as new problems come up.

COREY: Why not write your own using the jobs you've been doing?

BING: I'm not that brave. Got any other ideas?

COREY: What you could *also* do, Bing, is look at your department org chart. See who your lead person is and tell Neadle you plan to work toward advancement to the next level. Managers like to hear that. They're supposed to groom people to take *their* job so *they* can be promoted.

BING: That's *another* problem. When I first hired in, Neadle handed out a rough organization chart, but he pulled it back. He told us he's working on a new one. He says it's difficult because he wants it to be flexible and responsive to the company vision. So, we don't *have* an organization chart.

COREY: I see the spot you're in. Bing. Well, maybe there's something else we can celebrate.

Corey and Bing look at each other glumly.

CUT TO: ARTHUR AND ANGELIQUE

Arthur Gumme, graphic artist, is bending over the large round tray of chopped vegetables. He is picking up some celery sticks and placing them on his paper plate. In the distance seen sweeping into the break room is Angelique Del Mundo. She threads her way between the milling employees to stand next to Arthur.

ANGELIQUE: Anything left?

ARTHUR: Oh, sure, lots. Have some these veggies with the ranch dip.

ANGELIQUE: Walter's phone wouldn't stop ringing. Normally people know better than to call him at lunch. Finally, he showed up and ordered me to take a break. He said he would man the phone.

ARTHUR: Isn't he coming to the party?

ANGELIQUE: He said he wanted to make an appearance, but he's expecting a call from Washington, from the Air Force Interceptor Project Office. He wants their concurrence on the date for the upcoming program review.

Angelique piles some thin stalks of carrots and tiny sprouts of broccoli in a paper boat. She takes the ladle sitting in the dip and pours some over the vegetables. She picks up a carrot stick to sample it. As she raises her head and holds the morsel to her mouth, she pauses and looks at the side of the room, aghast. She punches Arthur on his shoulder. He turns, startled.

ANGELIQUE: My God! Do I see what I *think* I see?

ARTHUR: What?

She points to a plaque mounted on the wall above the refrigerator.

CLOSE ON PLAQUE

The plaque has a highly polished brass plate at the top of a dark walnut base. Engraved on the brass plate is the RTI logo and the words: "THIS AWARD, GIVEN TO REPULSIVE TECHNOLOGY, INCORPORATED BY THE PRESIDENT OF THE UNITED STATES, SYMBOLIZES AMERICA'S RECOGNITION OF AND APPRECIATION FOR THIS COMPANY'S ACHIEVEMENTS IN ROCKET ENGINE SCIENCE." Below that is the United States Presidential Seal and at the bottom is an engraved signature: THELMA GRAYFIELD, PRESIDENT.

ANGELIQUE: What's that plaque doing *here*?

ARTHUR: I thought it would be appropriate for everyone at the party to see it and admire it.

ANGELIQUE: Look, it's getting dusty. If Walter shows up and sees it here, he will be *very* upset. Why isn't it in the display case in the lobby?

ARTHUR: There's no room there.

ANGELIQUE: Well, *make* room!

ARTHUR: There *would* be room if I could transfer that stupid plaque from the Chamber of Commerce. All it says is "To Repulsive Technology, a good member of our community."

They gave it to us because Masterly sponsored their chili cook-off with a five-hundred-dollar donation.

ANGELIQUE: For heaven's sake, don't touch *that* plaque. Walter's brother-in-law is a member of the Chamber Executive Board.

ARTHUR: I'll see what I can do. Some party this turned out to be.

Arthur walks to the refrigerator, reaches up to the plaque and removes it, making unintelligible GRUMBLING noises.
CUT TO: MURRAY AND DANIEL

Murray Jaysize strolls into the break room, pauses, and gazes at the commotion at the food table. He sees Daniel Brazewell shaking a toaster on the counter and twisting the knobs. He saunters toward Daniel.

MURRAY: Hey, Dan. What are you doing there? Fixing the toaster?

Daniel hears his name and turns to face Murray.

DANIEL: I can't seem to get it to work. I'm trying to toast this crumpet.

MURRAY: What's that? I've heard the name, but I've never eaten one.

Daniel takes the crumpet out of the toaster and shows it to Murray. It is a flat, spongy square.

DANIEL: These are from New Zealand; I wonder where Mary got them. I was trying to make this one nice and crisp before I put the butter and jelly on, but I can't get it crisp enough.

Murray takes the toaster from Daniel and peers inside.

MURRAY: And the toaster won't do that?

Daniel inserts the pale, cream-colored crumpet into one of the top slots and depresses a lever, lowering the crumpet into the toaster. The elements turn red. After a minute the toaster CLICKS and the tray rises. The crumpet is still pale.

> DANIEL: See, the toaster turns on, all right, but doesn't stay on long enough. These crumpets take forever to brown.

Daniel depresses the lever again. The crumpet descends.

> MURRAY (laughing): They must have some heat resistant ingredients.

> DANIEL: As a matter of fact, you just reminded me of a suggestion I had.

> MURRAY: For what?

> DANIEL: I was going to turn in a suggestion that these crumpets be used as heat-resistant tiles for the skin of the Interceptor. You know, to withstand the extreme re-entry temperatures.

> MURRAY: Did you get that idea from one of those crazy guys that call Joyce Plaisant with their design schemes?

> DANIEL: No, this occurred to me when I was toasting a crumpet this morning. I have the same problem at home.

> MURRAY: Dan, I have to tell you this. The Interceptor doesn't fly high enough to experience any re-entry conditions.

> DANIEL: Oh. (*shrugging*) It's just as well. That circumvents a problem I might have.

> MURRAY: Which one is that?

> DANIEL: I was wondering how the boys in the shop would glue them on.

The toaster emits a CLICK and the crumpet pops up. It is still cream-colored.

Daniel picks up the crumpet, breathes a SIGH of despair, and tosses it into the wastebasket. Murray looks at the wastebasket and shakes his head.

CUT TO: MICHAEL AND CLARA

Michael Headknuckle is staring at a framed poster on the wall of the break room. Near him, CLARA CLOSCHEK, of the Travel Audit Department, is reaching into a bag of potato chips, popping a few into her mouth.

Clara is a mousy woman. She wears trifocals and tends to move her head up and down a lot depending on what she is looking at. She is a cat lover and likes to volunteer for charitable activities.

She notices Michael's intense concentration on the poster and steps over next to him.

> CLARA: What are you thinking?

> MICHAEL: Look at that! I don't know which label it deserves
> the most – stupid or offensive.

He throws his arm toward the poster.

CLOSE ON POSTER

The poster is a large drawing of two men in space suits seated at what appears to be a monitoring center. They have elongated faces; their mouths are turned up slightly at the edges in a grim smile. They are wearing headphones and making notes in a journal. Above the men are the words:

> *THE ALIENS ARE LISTENING*
> *They want to know what <u>you</u> know'*
> *KEEP IT TO YOURSELF*

CUT TO: MICHAEL AND CLARA

> MICHAEL: It's not even original! Those words are left over from World War II.

> CLARA: These posters have been hung *everywhere*.

> MICHAEL: These are the product of Rudy Vault's neurotic preoccupation with spying. Vault is a reversed check valve in the pressurizing line of life.

> CLARA: And that Deputy of his, Leo Meertz, is just as bad. He came by our area yesterday and wanted to know if we were storing our data properly. I told him we don't *keep* any classified data.

> MICHAEL: What did he say?

> CLARA: He ignored me. Then he asked me to show him where we file the figures for maintenance costs on the Interceptor. I told him there hasn't been any *maintenance* because we haven't finishing *building* the darn thing!

> MICHAEL (*frowning*): I wonder why he would ask to see that information.

> CLARA: Meertz is a rounding error in the financial ledger of life.
Michael looks up again at the poster and slowly shakes his head.

INT. RTI. TAPESTRY ROOM. DAY

The room has been darkened. At the end of a long conference table at the front of the room is the silhouette of a lone man facing a large projection screen. The screen is brilliantly illuminated with a chart that has at the top the RTI logo in electric blue. Below are the words: INTERCEPTOR X PROGRAM REVIEW – COMPLETION PHASE. The faint notes of a DRAMATIC ORCHESTRAL SCORE are heard. The view zooms in on the man and the screen. The music grows in intensity.

The man turns. The scattered rays from the overhead projector light up his face. It is Steven Acheever, the Program Manager.

As Steven watches, more silhouettes glide into the scene, taking seats at the conference tables. After a period of time the tables are filled.

Steven looks along the tables at the meeting attendees. Holding his gaze steady, he raises his right arm and points over his shoulder at the chart. The dramatic music fades. He smiles and speaks.

> STEVEN: This is it, folks. Next week we have a major program review with the customer. Today we will go over the charts I've asked you to prepare. I want these charts to be complete and truthful, but I want us to look good.

Steven turns his head from side to side as he checks his audience. His smile turns to a frown.

> STEVEN: We're missing a couple of managers and a director. Does anybody know where Ed Confirme is? I want to make sure that any sensitive customer relations issues that come up are handled properly.

> VOICE FROM THE REAR OF THE ROOM: He had to attend the Participative Leadership Training session.

Steven shakes his head; makes a note on a pad.

> STEVEN: Al Gurithum will be giving the rundown on the Integrated Master Plan and Integrated Master Schedule. That's important. (*looking around*) Where *is* Al?

Susan Shi waves her hand

> SUSAN: He's in the Participative Leadership Training session. I'm covering for him.

> STEVEN: Sandy Binding is supposed to show up to fill us in on the contract phase compliance. I heard that some status reporting was questioned. I don't see her.

Florence Kahdasill, at the back of the room, looks up.

FLORENCE: Sandy is taking the Participative Leadership Training, Steve. She directed me to assure you she will be prepared for the actual review. I'm ready to present her charts today.

Steven makes another note on a pad.

STEVEN: I want this review to be very professional. Don't be too casual. All of you know *I'm* easy and will overlook flubs. But the Air Force delegates won't be that forgiving. I expect each of you to use this planning meeting to practice the actual approach and the words you will use in the formal review. Okay?

Several OKAYs are heard in reply.

STEVEN: There obviously will be some wording changes necessary. We don't have the luxury of taking these charts back to our offices and thinking about them. Any corrections or additions will be made here in real time. Bing back there will do that.

Steven waves a finger toward the rear of the room.

STEVEN: Are you set to go, Bing?

Bing Chang, seated in the distance, tilts the screen on his laptop.

BING: I'm ready.

STEVEN: Good. Bring up the agenda.

Bing's hands fly over the keyboard of his laptop. A chart appears with the words REVIEW TOPICS.

STEVEN: For the purpose of this review I don't have to follow the exact order of the subjects. Roy Cordu has asked if he can go first with his presentation on the main propellant valve. He has to leave to prepare for the critical design review of that part. So, go ahead, Roy.

Roy joins Steven near the screen.

> ROY: Thanks, Steve. This part was added at the last minute. We want to assure the customer that the valve will be fully functional. Some Air Force rep at the preliminary design review had heartburn over possible excessive combustion loads on the pintle. I've made several design changes since then. We want to explain how the problem was addressed.

Roy looks at a note card in his hand.

> ROY: From the beginning we chose to go, basically, with a pintle valve for the main engines. A pintle valve, rather than a poppet valve, basically, permits variable control. The use of a poppet valve would, basically, require precision timing of the open and close movements.

> STEVEN: Sorry to interrupt, Roy, but I notice that the words you are using to explain are not on the chart. All you have is a sketch.

> ROY: I thought it would be easier for everyone to understand if I explain it in simple language as I go, rather than hit them with a chart full of technical jargon.

> STEVEN: I see. Well, try to keep it short and simple.

> ROY: Basically, I started with a conventional pintle design. But that had drawbacks. For example, the face of the valve is, basically, subjected to high loads imparted by combustion products passing over the pintle valve and through the nozzle throat.

Roy points to a tiny area on the chart. The attendees lean forward to view the area indicated.

> ROY: To overcome those loads, the actuation mechanism would, basically, have to be large and heavy. As you might expect, the extra size and weight would, basically, degrade the performance and maneuverability of the engine.

STEVEN: Was that the drawback that the Air Force guy was concerned about at the preliminary design review?

ROY: Basically. But I fixed that. Bring up the next chart, Bing.

A sketch, similar to the first, one is shown. It is bigger and more detailed.

ROY: Notice the changes to the design. I've basically added some bleed passageways that admit gases to the opposite side of the pintle head portion that will, basically, counterbalance the loads on the face.

STEVEN: That's it?

ROY: That's it.

Roy returns to his chair at one of the tables. Steven stands up and looks at a pad in his hand.

STEVEN: Ah, yes. I have a chart I *must* show you. It's not part of the presentation, but it's relevant. You've seen this message before but it needs to be repeated. Bing, show us number thirty-six.

A very plain chart appears with this sentence: "Title 18 United States Code Section 201(c) makes it a crime to offer or give a gratuity to a public official for or because of any official act performed or to be performed by such public official."

STEVEN: I know you want our Air Force visitors to feel welcome and enjoy themselves, but no one is allowed to invite them to dinner at the end of the day or suggest entertainment. In fact, do not even offer to buy them lunch. They will be treated to a meal in the cafeteria.

Michael Headknuckle slams the conference table.

MICHAEL: If there is anything that results in the Air Force contingent leaving this review next week with negative feelings, lunch in the cafeteria will do it.

Steven ignores Michael's remark.

> STEVEN: We decided to include some charts detailing the results of the combined pressurant, propellant, and main engine hot-fire tests. Hap Cawshun will present those. Come on up, Hap and show us what you have.

Hap Cawshun hands a CD to Bing and walks to the front. Bing slides the CD into the drive at the side of his laptop.

> HAP: I don't have a lot to report. I prepared only one chart. Can you find it on the CD, Bing?

A chart is projected that reads: "Five thirty-second duration firings of the complete system were conducted. In four tests all subsystems performed perfectly. In the fifth test, the main engine pintle valve operation experienced a failure. The valve did not close fully at cutoff."

> STEVEN: I guess that says it all, Hap, but we have to make a couple word changes.

> HAP: Which words?

> STEVEN: This is in line with our new company policy on terminology. We don't say the subsystems performed "perfectly." We say, "They performed as expected."

> HAP: Oh, sure. Bing, can you fix that?

Bing taps the keyboard. The words on the projected chart are replaced.

> STEVEN: And we don't say, "The pintle valve operation experienced a failure." We say, "The pintle valve operation exhibited a *departure*." You know, it departed from normal operation.

> HAP: Makes sense. No failures. Bing, can you fix that?

Bing taps the keyboard a second time. The words on the projected chart are revised.

STEVEN: One more thing, Hap. Dig up some photographs of the hardware being tested. Major Ogeny, who will be one of the people at the review representing the Air Force, likes lots of pictures.

HAP: I have some pinned on my cubicle wall. I can use those.

STEVEN: The charts will be perfect, Hap. Use them for the review next week.

Hap smiles, nods, and walks back to Bing to pick up his CD.

STEVEN: I'd like Chandra to come up next and give us her summary of supplier performance. I understand you have a single chart.

Chandra slides her chair back slightly, lifts up slowly, and joins Steven at the front.

CHANDRA (*speaking loudly to Bing*): My chart is twenty-one.

On the screen a large horizontal bar graph is seen. At the left of each bar is the name of a supplier. Next to that is the name of the component purchased from the supplier. To the right of each component name is a long bar in color. Chandra has a laser pointer in her hand. She moves the red dot around the screen.

CHANDRA: I've color-coded each bar to indicate how the vendor is doing on delivery percentages. Notice that the Miller Company, to date, is on schedule. So, I made that bar green.

The red laser dot is moved to a bar labeled SHORT AND SWEET.

CHANDRA: The Short and Sweet Company indicated they may encounter delays in production, so their bar is yellow.

The red laser dot is moved to a bar labeled ABLE CABLE.

CHANDRA: The Able Cable Company is behind with only eighty-seven percent of their order on schedule, I made their bar red.

Sandra Binding raises her arm.

SANDRA: I think the red you chose for Able Cable brings too much attention to a problem area. It really strikes the eye. The Miller bar is the one we want to brag about. I suggest you change that bar to red to flag it. I'd give the Able Cable bar some less distinctive hue, like, say, purple.

CHANDRA: Bing. Did you hear that? Try those color changes.

Bing's hands fly over his keyboard. The bars are highlighted on the image. The colors change. Kimberly Chi waves her arm excitedly.

KIMBERLY: Sandy, I have to disagree. The color red communicates trouble. I think the Miller bar should be orange. It's bright and cheerful.

CHANDRA: Orange on the Miller bar, Bing.

Bing highlights the Miller bar on the screen. It changes to a vibrant orange. Michael Headknuckle brings his palm down LOUDLY on the conference table.

MICHAEL: Why do we need any *special* colors? The percent completions are easily read on the graph. Make them all blue; Masterly would like that color.

STEVEN: In the interest of time, I suggest we accept the chart as originally submitted by Chandra. She has your comments. She has a week to take your ideas under consideration.

Chandra smiles and returns to her chair at the table.

STEVEN: Bing. Punch up chart sixteen. Dan, this is your area.
The next chart reads INTERCEPTOR BUILD STATUS.

Daniel Brazewell, waiting to the side, moves over to the center of the screen. The blinding light makes him aware he is blocking everyone's view of the chart. He puts his arm in front of his eyes and steps aside.

> DANIEL: Before I get into the details, let me summarize by saying that the machining of parts, and the assembly of the first unit of the Interceptor are going very well. We've had a few problems, and I will cover those. I want to complement Chandra Patel in Purchasing. She has done a remarkable job of keeping the suppliers on track and has not let us down on the delivery of the long-lead items.

He pinches the remote. The chart changes. The next chart reads: INJECTOR PROPELLANT CHANNEL MILLING: TWO DINGS and TRANSDUCER HEAT SHIELD MOUNTING: THREE SQUAWKS.

> DANIEL: As stated, during the milling operation on the propellant channels on the backside of the injector, we suffered two dings. The defects were referred to the Material Review Board and were found acceptable.

Michael Headknuckle waves, but Daniel keeps talking.

> DANIEL: The installation of the heat shield for the pressure transducers was a bit of a problem, but those squawks were worked off.

Michael holds up a piece of paper on which he has written in large letters: QUESTION!!!

> MIKE: Dan. For the last many months now I've been looking at charts out of your department that talk about "dings." We need better definition. What were *these* dings?

> DANIEL: I'm not sure. They could have been scuff marks, or maybe scratches during the milling. Or maybe a dent.

> MIKE: Then let's say that in the chart.

DANIEL (*making note on pad*): Okay, we'll make that change. I'll send someone over to the shop to get better handle on those dings.

MIKE: Fine. Now can you explain what generated the squawks?

DANIEL: I don't know. That's the term they always use in the manufacturing record. (*looks at man at the back of the meeting room*). Nick, do you know what these squawks were about?

Nick shrugs.

DANIEL: I'll have someone find the inspector who wrote these up. I'll get back to you this afternoon, Steve. (*smiles as he makes a note on his pad*) They could be something minor – like surface preparation for painting.

MIKE: Or they could be something serious like weld porosity!

Daniel frowns then looks at Steven questioningly. Steven nods and returns to the front of the room.

STEVEN: I'll take over.

Daniel departs the room.

STEVEN: If you all don't mind, I'm going to use this opportunity to squeeze in a short presentation on a program planning methodology that the Business Development Group wants us to consider for use on the Interceptor effort. It wasn't originally included in the program review agenda, but if you think it has value, we will introduce the topic to the customer at the review. Any objections?

Steven waits for a reaction from the group. Everyone is leaning back in boredom or resting, head down, on the table in detached silence. Steven notices that Michael Headknuckle is tilted to the side in his chair with his eyes closed.

> STEVEN: I take that as a positive response. Lou Cannon will explain. You're up, Lou.

A young man strides confidently to the front. It is LOUIS CANNON, a junior analyst in Business Development.

He is twenty-eight and slim. His dark hair is matted, but he otherwise looks very businesslike. He is jacketless; a pinstripe vest covers an expensive dress shirt with silver cuff links. He is very self-motivated, and tries hard to be a walking advertisement for RTI.

He is carrying a three-foot piece of wooden dowel.

> LOUIS (*talking toward Bing*): Fire up my charts. When you hear me slap the screen – like this – go to the next chart.

He strikes the screen with the dowel. The sharp RAP stirs everyone at the tables.

The first chart is the title page. It reads: KARATE MANAGEMENT – SPARE BUT DURABLE TOOLS.

Michael Headknuckle sits up, stares at the chart, and shakes his head in disapproval.

> LOUIS: The Interceptor Program has been very successful to date and more success is ahead. But we, in Business Development, believe in the principle that you have to run twice as fast if you don't want to stay in one place.

The people at the tables begin to look at one another. Their lips start moving, but the words spoken are too soft to be heard.

He strikes the screen again. POW! Many of the people at the tables flinch. He takes long steps in front of the new chart, touching the words on the screen with his stick as he goes.

> LOUIS: As it says on the chart, "This forward-looking set of proposed operational directives ensures that company talent and energy will be channeled into optimal tasks. These directives will be known as Plan Top-Notch. The

Interceptor Program will serve as the pathfinder for this strategy for the whole of RTI."

CUT TO: BENARD AND GREGORY

Bernard Blastof nudges Gregory Korjul who is sitting next to him. Bernard points to the screen.

>   BERNARD: Did you hear that? *The whole of RTI*? That's pretty ambitious.

>   GREGORY: That's very frightening.

BACK TO SCENE

Louis raises the dowel to slap the screen. Bing observes Louis's arm movement and keys in the next chart in mid-swing. Louis looks startled.

>   LOUIS: The first idea is this: "The mission statement for RTI will be fine-tuned to reflect empowerment of our stakeholders and enhanced accommodation of the customer base. Drawing upon that optimized goal, the mission statement for each sub-organization within RTI will be re-visited for correlative alignment with the parent statement."

CUT TO: BERNARD AND GREGORY

>   BERNARD (*with frustration*): He's just reading the charts! He's not explaining anything. Why doesn't he just clam up? Didn't anyone ever tell him that his delivery is lousy? I'm able to read the charts perfectly well.

>   GREGORY: I don't understand what he's recommending.

BACK TO SCENE

Louis holds his stick still, stands poised. He taps the screen lightly and looks at Bing. The earlier chart accidentally appears. An OOPS is heard from Bing. The correct chart is projected.

LOUIS (*reading*): "Once Plan Top-Notch is activated, an exposition will be disseminated that delineates the final state of performance integration in which RTI will operate. This position paper will explain how the high realization paradigm interacts with the cutting-edge success factors. To bring this final state into fruition, transformation of all individual company sub-units to the paradigm-cognizant mode must be initiated and that transformation must be verified. On a periodic basis, that is, monthly, each group will submit up-flow reports citing their achievement and compliance scores."

Several OH, NOs are heard.

Louis begins to raise his stick; instead he waves it at Bing. Bing responds. The image is changed.

LOUIS (*reading chart*): This is a key step: "RTI must be staffed and organized to react to exigencies that arise in the marketplace and in the supply pipeline. Our responsive posture must possess capabilities that go beyond the concept of agile. There must be a fluidity of skills throughout the departmental network. To accomplish this, there will be rotating assignments across functions."

CUT TO: CHANDRA AND CELIA

Chandra Patel and Celia Cakpati, seated side by side, are paying rapt attention. Celia turns to Chandra with a look of confusion.

CELIA: What did he say?

CHANDRA: I think he's saying that you might have to give up your job and intern in my department. I might end up interning in *your* department.

CELIA: This guy is *dangerous*.

BACK TO SCENE

Louis raps his dowel on the screen twice. Bing looks up, confused, then changes the chart.

> LOUIS: As this chart states: "One element of this proposition will be the scrutinizing of staffing levels to eliminate redundant or sub-standard effort. Many functions will be combined allowing a reduction in force. This is essential because overcoming the competition in the aerospace arena requires that the enterprise be trimmed down to fighting weight."

CUT TO: CHANDRA AND CELIA

> CELIA: Did he really say what I think I heard?

> CHANDRA: He's saying that when the new plan forces you to start work at another job and you don't do well at that, you will be surplussed.

> CELIA: Surplussed?

> CHANDRA: You will be riffed.

> CELIA: Riffed?

> CHANDRA: You will be shown the door.

BACK TO SCENE

Louis is standing erect next to the screen, leaning on the dowel. He is smiling at the attendees. Some soft GRUNTS in the back are heard.

> LOUIS: That is the plan we propose. If you give me the go-ahead, I will make this presentation at the Program Review.

Michael Headknuckle pushes his chair back and lifts himself to a slightly bent posture.

> MICHAEL (*looking at Steven*): Mister Program Manager, that was, indeed, an impressive portrayal of heads-up

management by mister Cannon. However, we must consider that Repulsive Technology has also done an admirable job to date in developing a state-of-the-art vehicle that many observers predicted would not be feasible and, I might add, we did it by using our traditional management practices. I suggest we continue as we have. I remember General Jimmy Doolittle's advice: "Don't change flight formation mid-route to the target."

STEVEN: I don't think those were General Doolittle's words, Mike, but I respect the significance and the applicability.

Steven turns to Louis who has stopped smiling.

STEVEN: Lou, we really appreciate all the work you and your department have done to formulate this exciting new business plan. But until we've all had time to assess it, I don't want to reveal it to the Air Force.

Louis nods, thinks a moment as if to speak, then turns without a word. He walks to the doorway, waving his dowel weakly.

INT. WHITE HOUSE. OVAL OFFICE. DAY

Edith Wormbook is seated in one of the couches in front of the President's desk. She is fingering one of the cushions.

Hazel Lazer enters the office and steps quickly to Edith.

HAZEL: The President will be here shortly. Would you like some tea?

EDITH: No, thank you, Hazel. I have some paperwork to go over while I'm waiting.

Edith flips open a planner she is holding and runs down the page with her finger. The office door swings open, and President Grayfield appears. Edith closes the planner and looks up.

Thelma takes a seat in the opposite couch.

EDITH: I see you took my advice and had these couches re-covered in a floral pattern.

THELMA (*winking*): Fortunately, I was able to do it within my Repair and Restoration budget. (*looking serious*) Edith, I really appreciate your breaking loose from whatever you were doing to meet with me today.

EDITH: I was told you wanted to talk about the Interceptor Program.

THELMA: Yes, what's your assessment of the progress so far at Repulsive Technology?

EDITH: I'm not following the program that closely. The reports sent me indicate they are on schedule, within budget, and meeting all technical objectives.

THELMA: I'm sure they have, but that doesn't address my concern.

EDITH: What *does* concern you?

THELMA: From the very beginning, Walter Masterly, the company President, told me that he can only guarantee that the vehicle he delivers will meet the mission requirements. What troubles him is that there may be contingencies that were not planned for. He said there is very, very little known about the "threat"; the alien ship may have unexpected capabilities that the Interceptor may not be prepared to deal with.

EDITH: Thelma, you know my feelings in this matter. I've always believed from the start that this project was unnecessary. In all of the months since this program was funded there have been no new sightings of this "threat." I'm sure that Repulsive Technology will deliver a well-designed, workable product for the money. We just won't need it.

THELMA: Nevertheless, here's why I asked you over. The reports I get from the Air Force Project Office tell me what you just said: "on schedule, on budget, blah, blah." Walter Masterly notified me that they are having a key program review next week. The Air Force will be there, but I want *you* to attend as *my* representative – ask questions, listen closely. Then I want you to get back to me with your honest opinion as to whether you think the Interceptor in work will do the job.

EDITH (*forming a pained expression*): My schedule for next week is full. Can't you have them push the review date forward a week or so?

THELMA (*nodding*): I anticipated there might be a conflict with your timetable, so I asked Walter that. He says he can't move the date.

EDITH: Why?

THELMA: It's a port-of-call in their NAP

EDITH: What in the world is *that*?

THELMA: Walter explained they have a Navigator Action Process method of scheduling. Once a date is picked, it's sacrosanct.

EDITH: The dates I work to are pretty firm too, Thelma. There must be *some* arrangement that will work. Maybe I'll call Masterly myself.

THELMA: Good! See what you can do.

Edith picks up her planner, pats Thelma on the arm reassuringly, and storms out of the office.

INT. RTI. LOBBY. DAY

The SECURITY GUARD is seated behind an expansive lobby reception desk. Behind him on the wall are the huge letters: RTI. He sees the figures of two men appear at the glass door entrance. He rises quickly to greet them.

The two men are dressed in the uniforms of Air Force officers. One is CAPTAIN BARRY HAGGARD, Interceptor Project Officer. Barry is forty; has close-cropped brown hair and wears small, rimless glasses. He is nervous, fussy about details, and needs constant reassurance.

The second is MAJOR PHILLIP OGENY, Barry Haggard's Commanding Officer and a representative of The Air Force Space Command. Phillip is sixty-five. He has a prominent chin, a small gray moustache, and two patches of matching hair on each side of an otherwise bald head. Phillip is self-assured, somewhat pompous, stand-offish, and removed from details.

They move to the desk and lay their briefcases on the counter.

> PHILLIP: We're here for a program review. Do you have badges for us?

> SECURITY GUARD: I'm sure I do; may I see your identification please?

Phillip and Barry reach into their pockets, bring out wallets, and flip them open for the guard. The guard gives each wallet a quick look and a nod. He reaches into a drawer beneath the desk and pulls out two plastic badge holders with clips which he hands to each of the officers. He then immediately picks up the phone, punches a few keys, and begins talking.

Phillip and Barry fumble a little attempting to fasten the badges to their uniforms. They attach them slightly sideways on the collars of their jackets.

> SECURITY GUARD: I've called for your escort.

Phillip and Barry turn and study the furnishings of the lobby. They notice a large, ceiling-high, enclosed display case and walk to it. Within the case are small models of engines built by RTI over the years. There are some trophies and plaques.

The two men hold their faces close to the glass to read the inscriptions. Phillip moves sideways to look closer at one of the plaques.

> PHILLIP: Barry, come over here for a second. See if you can read what's on this award.

Phillip points to a large group of plaques. Barry crouches to get a better look.

> BARRY: It says "To Repulsive Technology, a good member of our community." It's from the Chamber of Commerce.

> PHILLIP: No, not that one – the one that's hidden behind it. The one that fell down and is lying on its side.

> BARRY (*moving head side to side*): Let's see, I think it says, "This award, given to Repulsive Technology, Incorporated, something, something," then "America's recognition, something, something," then "rocket engine science." That's all I can make out.

> PHILLIP: Look further down. Isn't that the signature of Thelma Grayfield?

> BARRY: It is! It's a Presidential Award Plaque and they put it where you can't see it!

> PHILLIP: That is *not* good. Is anyone from the White House coming to the meeting today? God help Masterly if Grayfield hears about *this*.

> BARRY: Yes, there *will* be some one here. The President sent a note over to the Project Office that Edith Wormbook will be here to represent her.

PHILLIP: Maybe we can tip off Masterly to straighten up that mess before she sees it.

A door to the lobby opens. Bing Chang strides in. He sees the two officers and walks up to them, smiling.

BING: Good morning. I was told you gentlemen are from the Air Force Project Office. I'm Bing Chang. If you'll follow me, I'll take you to the meeting room.

Bing holds open the door to the hallway. Barry and Phillip exit the lobby with Bing.

The three walk the length of the hallway, Bing leading. They reach a large meeting room doorway. Bing stops, faces them, and raises his arm to direct them into the room. They nod and enter.

INT. BLUE CAVERN ROOM. DAY

Steven Acheever, the Interceptor Program Manager, is sitting on the edge of a conference table at the front of the blue cavern meeting room in which the lights have been dimmed. He is looking down and speaking to Walter Masterly seated at the same table facing the blank projection screen on the wall. Steven hears the footsteps at the doorway, looks up, and sees the two officers. He jumps to his feet and walks to meet the visitors. Walter rises from his chair and joins Steven. The men shake hands. Steven points to chairs at the front table.

STEVEN: Captain Haggard and Major Ogeny, it's good that you could come. We have two seats reserved for you here.

Steven pulls out two chairs. The officers sit down.

Bing takes a seat off to the side to operate a laptop computer. He begins typing; an image appears on the screen. At the top is the RTI logo. The chart reads: INTERCEPTOR X PROGRAM REVIEW — COMPLETION PHASE.

John Fulbrane and Michael Headknuckle enter the room; John walks to the front and takes a chair next to Major Ogeny. The two men begin a conversation.

A few casual remarks are heard as a large group quietly enters the room: Daniel Brazewell, Albert Gurithum, Chandra Patel, Celia Cakpati, Hap Cawshun, Harry Handover, and Leo Meertz.

Steven checks off the attendees on a sheet he has been holding. He looks over at Hap.

> STEVEN: Hap, you're nearest the door. Would you please close it? (*pauses*) This is an important review, and we have a lot of material to cover. So, let's settle in and get started.

> WALTER (*looking around*): Is everyone here, Steven?

> STEVEN: Not quite, Walter. Stanley Snappi is late. And our most important guest has yet to arrive.

> WALTER: Who's that?

> STEVEN: Edith Wormbook, Director of the Office of Science and Technology Policy. President Grayfield has asked her to attend.

> WALTER: This meeting *has* to start. When will she arrive?

> STEVEN: We had to make special arrangements. She has unalterable engagements later today in Washington, so she can't be here in person, but she will be in virtual attendance.

> WALTER: What does *that* mean?

> STEVEN: We have obtained some very sophisticated electronic conferencing equipment. At this moment the Director is sitting in a chair in her office in DC watching our charts on a monitor. She is being picked up on video; a hologram of her will be projected into that chair over there.

Steven points to a special large chair at the rear and at the side of the first table in a space that has been cleared.

STEVEN: Let me get her on the phone.

Steven reaches to the center of the table. He pulls the speakerphone over and hits a button. There is a dial tone. He keys in a number. There is a RING and a VOICE.

FEMALE VOICE (*on phone*): Director Wormbook's office.

STEVEN: This is Steve Acheever calling from Repulsive Technology. Please notify Director Wormbrook we are ready to start transmitting. Also, please have her turn on *her* speakerphone.

There is a minute of silence.

DIFFERENT FEMALE VOICE (*on phone*): Good afternoon, Steve. This is Edith Wormbook. Can you hear me?

STEVEN: Everyone present can hear you, Director. Is the video equipment at your end in operation?

EDITH (*on phone*): You can call me Edith, Steve. Yes, the men are working the equipment.

Suddenly a luminous figure of a woman is seen sitting in the chair that Steven pointed to. The image solidifies and appears more realistic, although somewhat transparent. There are gasps from the meeting attendees. The image flickers and disappears for a moment. The image returns.

EDITH (*on phone*): The technicians in my office tell me I should be visible in your meeting, Steve.

STEVEN: Yes, you are, Edith. There was a glitch just then, but you're back with us. Please ask your operators to double-check their connections. We'll do the same here.

At the side of the cavern, the men in charge of the hologram projection equipment run their hands along the power cables and tighten the fittings.

The door to the meeting room swings wide and Stanley Snappi sweeps in. He bumps into the men at the controls of the image projector. The hologram of Edith fades.

Stanley is busy apologizing to the technicians. He isn't aware of what is taking place in the meeting. He swings his head back and forth looking for a vacant chair in the darkened room. He notices one off to the side in a shadowy area. He stumbles over and falls into it.

> STANLEY: Sorry I'm late, everybody.

The three-dimensional image of Edith reappears in the chair, the chair Stanley has chosen. The projection light blinds Stanley; he raises his forearm over his eyes. There are loud GASPS from the ATTENDEES.

> STEVEN (*shouting*): Stanley, Stanley! Get up. You're sitting in Director Wormbook's lap!
>
> EDITH (*on phone*): I heard my name. Was there a question? There seems to be a lot of noise at your end.

Stanley jumps from the chair, turns to view the image of Edith, and backs away in shock.

> STANLEY: I apologize, ma'm.

Steven waves him toward another chair.

> STEVEN (*talking at speakerphone*): We were having some technical difficulties, Edith, but everything is under control.
>
> EDITH (*on phone*): As you know, Steve, I have been asked by our President to sit in on your program review to assess the viability of this venture. I've never attended one of these reviews before. I'm concerned about your ability to meet your schedule and to hold costs down.

STEVEN (*talking at speakerphone*):   Those topics will be covered, Edith.

He looks out at the people seated at the table and begins pointing to each.

STEVEN (*looking down at an agenda sheet*): Al Gurithum will go over the Integrated Master Plan and Integrated Master Schedule. Let's see. Chandra Patel will cover supply chain management and tell us how we're doing on supplier qualification. Celia Cakpati will present the section on budgets.

EDITH (*on phone*): I forgot to ask if you will discuss how the vehicle assembly is progressing, and, oh, yes, how is the testing going?

STEVEN: We have a very capable person who will describe the assembly and other manufacturing tasks. That will be Dan Brazewell. Our testing program is in the good hands of Hap Cawshun. He will describe that as well as fill us in on the details of the upcoming Interceptor launch plans.

EDITH (*on phone*): Yes, I'm particularly interested in the results of the first launch. Please proceed with the review.

Phillip leans closer to John Fulbrane and begins speaking energetically. His words are not heard. John nods in understanding. John waves at Steven, and says something to him. Steven steps aside, and John stands at his chair to face the group.

JOHN: Major Ogeny has made a request of me just now to hold off on the planned program review for a few minutes to allow him to give a short, but very special presentation. He assures me that what he has to report will add emphasis and context to the serious work underway here. I agreed to that, so I'll turn control of the meeting over to him.

Phillip reaches into his case and pulls out a small object.

PHILLIP: I have the presentation on this flash drive.

Phillip leaves his seat and hands the drive to Bing. Bing slides it in the side of the laptop and looks at the screen.

A chart comes up with SECRET in large black letters at the top and bottom. In the center is the title: INTERCEPTOR RURAL BASING MODE AND ANTI-DETECTION STRATEGY.

Phillip walks from Bing to the edge of the screen and points at the chart.

PHILLIP: What I'm going to show you now is a system that has been proposed for spotting the vehicle in key locations around the country. It has been carefully thought out; I'm confident the Air Force will go forward with this plan.

He looks over at Bing and nods. Bing depresses a key on the laptop and a second chart comes up. It is a photograph of a dilapidated barn. The roof of the barn is a dirty gray color; the sides are a very weathered brick red; the wood is heavily cracked and splintered.

A puzzled expression appears on many of the meeting attendees, but no one speaks.

PHILLIP: Yes, what you're looking at *is a barn*. Clever, wouldn't you say? The plan is to house – and I might add hide – the Interceptors in these deceptive shelters.

John Fulbrane raises his hand.

JOHN: Major, do you believe we have to *hide* the Interceptor?

PHILLIP: Definitely. Once the aliens are alerted to the fact that the Interceptor is operational – and we believe they *will* find out, they may have means to detect and disable the Interceptor on the ground. In fact, the second part of this briefing addresses that.

The image of Edith stirs restlessly. She raises her hand. Her voice emits shrilly from the speakerphone on the table.

EDITH (*on phone*): Major, Major. Do you really think you can find enough abandoned barns to accommodate the fleet?

PHILLIP (*speaking loudly*): Director Wormbook, to answer your concern: these will not be *existing* barns; these will be *new* barns.

JOHN: I take it the Interceptor will remain in the barn at all times.

PHILLIP: Yes. When an approaching UFO is detected, the vehicle will launch *from* the barn.

JOHN: If your picture is representative, the doors of the barn aren't wide enough for the Interceptor to go in or come out.

PHILLIP: The doors you see are just for appearance, John. Adequate clearance has been designed in. Next chart, please.

Bing taps his laptop. A new image of the barn appears. This one is a drawing also. The front of the barn is wide open. The full width of the Interceptor, poised inside, is visible at the opening.

PHILLIP: This is an artist's rendition showing the "shelter," as I'll call it, after being activated. Activation occurs when the radar unit inside picks up an incoming alien ship. The doors you saw are fake and do not open. Actually, the complete front moves back inside on rails like a roll-up garage door. Then the Interceptor launches from within.

Steven Acheever raises his hand.

STEVEN: Barns are always seen in farming areas. Wouldn't it be a giveaway if you place one within a residential community?

PHILLIP: I'm sure we can find enough open areas. In fact, we already have a choice of locations near Ponca City where all the sightings have occurred.

Leo Meertz rises from his chair to get Phillip's attention.

LEO: Major Ogeny, could you send me a list of where these chosen locations will be?

PHILLIP: That's very sensitive information. Why would you need to know?

CUT TO: DANIEL AND ALBERT

Albert turns to Daniel with a strained look.

ALBERT: Why is Meertz asking that question? He's Data Classification. I'm beginning to wonder about him.

DANIEL: He has a reputation for being nosy.

CUT TO: LEO

LEO: If a vehicle needs servicing, our Field Support group will need to know where to send a technician.

BACK TO SCENE

PHILLIP: If that contingency should arise, I assure you that mister Handover will be supplied with the location.

Michael Headknuckle taps his finger noisily on the table.

MICHAEL: You said these "shelters" would be *new*. The barn in the picture looks about a hundred years old. A new barn will stand out like a three-legged chicken.

PHILLIP: We anticipated that. The specifications for the fabrication of these units will state that the outside finish shall be fully oxidized and demonstrate surface weakness typical of extreme age and exposure of wood to sun and rain.

CUT TO: DANIEL AND ALBERT

Daniel leans his head close to Albert.

> DANIEL: Where do you suppose they came up with the idea for *barns*, Al?

> ALBERT: Well, they've been using *silos* for years. Maybe somebody figured the aliens would start looking there first. Besides, the Interceptor wouldn't fit in a silo.

> DANIEL: I wouldn't want the contract to build *those* huts. Did you hear what Ogeny said? The outside has to exhibit *full oxidization and surface weakness*. How would you know if a barn would pass a delivery quality check? I can just hear the inspector: "You can't ship. This wall isn't *defective* enough."

BACK TO SCENE

> PHILLIP: As effective as these imitation barns will be in fooling any alien ships that are scouting for our launch sites, the Air Force has gone a step further. Many of these barns will only contain a decoy Interceptor. These will draw the alien ships away from the real Interceptors.

Hap Cawshun, who hasn't been paying much attention, is suddenly brought to life by Phillip's words.

> HAP: What would lure an alien ship to a decoy that you can't see from the air?

> PHILLIP (*smiling broadly*): I'm *glad* you asked that question, mister Cawshun. That allows me to move into the second part of my briefing on the anti-detection measures. Next chart, please.

On the screen an organization chart springs up. The box at the top contains the words PROJECT INTERCEPTOR SAFEGUARD. There is a hierarchy of five boxes below. One box contains the words ENCLOSURE

ACQUISITION. One box contains the words DECOY DEVELOPMENT. The other three boxes are empty.

> PHILLIP: Within the Space Command we have formed a very special group dedicated to ensuring the security of the Interceptor. This is a very "black" project and not even known about by most of the Command.

> HAP (*pointing*): The chart isn't complete; is the organization still being set up?

> PHILLIP: No, those boxes were intentionally left blank. Those are some very, very secret activities within this project. I'm not even allowed to reveal their titles.

> EDITH (*on phone*): Major Ogeny, I need a little more information to complete my report to the President.

> PHILLIP: Of course, Director Wormbook. As you might expect, the staff of the Enclosure Acquisition sub-unit will develop the requirements for the "barns" and will arrange for their procurement. That part is somewhat straight forward. Implementation of the Decoy Development effort, however, requires a *lot* more analysis. I'll show you our approach. Next chart, please.

The projected chart shows the same ancient barn seen on the first chart. Hovering over the barn is a typical UFO symbol, a silver, round, domed craft. Emanating from the UFO, heading to the barn, are curved lines signifying some kind of rays.

> PHILLIP: We are working with the premise that the aliens have enough advanced technology to be able to electronically interrogate the contents of the shelter during a flyover.

> HAP: Why not just line the shelter with some barrier material that shields the Interceptor from examination?

> PHILLIP: The Enclosure Acquisition team may very well have considered that feature. But that's all I'm permitted to say

about *that*. The solution we are seeking is to create a decoy that is *irresistible* to the aliens – a decoy that displays more Interceptor characteristics than the Interceptor *itself*! Next chart, please.

Bing has been sitting back with his eyes closed. He hears the word "chart." He quickly hits on the laptop keyboard; a new image comes up.

The new chart has the same huge SECRET title at the top and bottom. The content is a list of nine words:

DENSITY	*TEMPERATURE*	*REFLECTIVITY*
VOLUME	*EMISSIVITY*	*ODOR*
MASS	*COLOR*	*RADIOACTIVITY*

PHILLIP (*tapping chart with hand*): The Decoy Development honchos will characterize each of these properties for the Interceptor. These tell-tale traits will then be incorporated in the decoy in spades. To the aliens the decoy will stick out like a neon sign.

CUT TO: DANIEL AND ALBERT

Albert leans his head close to Daniel.

ALBERT: I don't understand why *that* chart is labeled "secret." That same list of physical properties was in my high school physics book.

DANIEL: Maybe Ogeny left some properties off that we're not supposed to know about, for the same reason some of the boxes on the org chart were not labeled.

ALBERT: You may be right. I'm going to ask about that.

CUT TO: VIEW OF MEETING ROOM

Albert stands to gain the attention of Phillip.

ALBERT: Major Ogeny, I have a comment and a question. The physical properties you've listed that the decoy will exhibit seem very basic and are common knowledge, but the chart is *"secret."* My question is: have you considered that the aliens might have psychic powers?

Albert takes his seat. A hush falls over the room. Phillip leans forward, speaks quietly, with a focused look at Albert.

PHILLIP: All of the properties being considered, mister Gurithum, are *not* yet on that list. As to your question about our intelligence on the psychic talents of aliens, (*pauses in thought*) there are some things we don't talk about.

Excited MURMURING is heard.

ALBERT: I understand.

PHILLIP: That concludes my presentation.

Phillip returns to his chair. The screen goes dark. Bing slides along the chairs and hands the flashdrive to Phillip.

Steven takes the floor.

STEVEN: Major, we thank you for a very informative account of other important work taking place behind the scenes that adds emphasis to what we're doing here at Repulsive Technology.

Steven looks at his watch.

STEVEN: Let's take a ten-minute break, and when you return, we'll begin the Program Review.

There is a rush by the attendees to the door.

INT. RTI. IX HIGH SECURITY DESIGN SUITE 3. DAY

The room has been darkened. NORMAN NEVERCUTT, test engineer, is sitting at a table, and is working a laptop computer. A duplicate of the image on his monitor is being flashed by the overhead projector onto a wall screen.

Norman is thirty-eight. His hair falls over his forehead. He has a small moustache. He wears dark-rimmed spectacles. Norman is a very cautious person who strictly follows procedures.
Sitting across the table from Norman is Hap Cawshun, Lead Test Engineer. Hap is watching Norman's creation of a chart on the screen.

The image is a page of small boxes in which Norman is inserting numbers and words.

> HAP: I'd like to get the Interceptor test plan wrapped up in the next day or two. What am I seeing here?

> NORMAN: This is the test matrix. The first column has the requirement number from section three of the System Specification. The second column is a statement of the requirement, and the third column has the section four Quality Assurance Provisions describing how that requirement is verified. These are the tests that will be performed on the components, the subsystems, and on the complete vehicle.

> HAP (*looking uncomfortable*): You're using a spreadsheet. Why aren't you using that expensive new software we bought for requirements traceability? You know, ComplyTool. I use a spreadsheet only when I have to do number-crunching.

> NORMAN: I was having trouble learning how to enter stuff in that program. Besides, the spreadsheet has all the little boxes ready to go.

> HAP: Yeah, but now somebody else has to insert all that material into ComplyTool in order for it to generate the Verification Plan.

NORMAN: Susan Shi is working that software. Maybe she can copy and paste.

HAP: Get with her on that.

Hap points to an entry on the chart on the screen.

HAP: How do I read that valve cleanliness requirement – the three-point-twenty-five you've got up there?

NORMAN: Oh, yeah. Valve Cleanliness. You mean the line that says that for particles over twenty-five microns in size only thirty shall be allowed per square foot of flow surface.

HAP: I understand that one. Read the next one.

NORMAN: That one says that for particles less than twenty-five microns in size, sixty shall be allowed per square foot of flow surface.

HAP: I understand that also. But what if a cleanliness check turns up particles of *exactly* twenty-five microns?

NORMAN: That's a good question. (*pauses to think*) On the other hand, Hap, what's the chance of ever having that many particles of exactly twenty-five microns? Besides, the valves in this engine don't have anywhere near a square foot of flow surface.

HAP (*frowning*): I can see you're not a valve man. You better run that wording by Roy Cordu, he *knows* about valves.

NORMAN: Check.

HAP: Frankly, Norm, I'm more concerned about the tests on the complete vehicle. Can you bring up the pages of your matrix where you spell those out?

NORMAN: Sure.

Norman taps the keyboard of his lap-top. The image on the screen changes. The wording in the cells of the spreadsheet is much longer.

> HAP: Hmm. Those are all good, but those are verification tests, you know, such as the time from Launch Start to lift-off, and the flight duration. Where do you have the validation tests?

> NORMAN: Like what?

> HAP: For example, where is the flight test that demonstrates that the vehicle can actually maneuver and stay in range of an unidentified craft that's being evasive?

Norman begins punching keys frantically.

> NORMAN: I was just about to add that test statement to this group somewhere.

> HAP: That's my point. It shouldn't *be* there. I want you to insert a separate Validation test category at the end of section four.

> NORMAN: What's the difference between Verification and Validation?

> HAP: The Validation shows the Interceptor satisfies the customer's mission. It has a different meaning.

> NORMAN: Not so fast. Stand by.

Norman does some more frantic typing on the lap-top keyboard. The screen image changes from the matrix to a website with page of words.

> NORMAN: This is my on-line thesaurus, Hap. See, Verify and Validate are synonyms!

Hap looks up at the screen, then looks down at the table solemnly and clasps his hands.

> HAP (*quietly, to himself*): I need an aerospace dictionary.

NORMAN: What did you say?

HAP: Never mind. I'll handle that little specification detail myself. Just make sure you state there *will* be flight demonstrations.

Norman begins typing again.

NORMAN: Where will these flights take place?

HAP: White Sands Missile Range.

NORMAN: Has it been set up? Do we have approval to do that? Can I actually say that in the specification?

HAP: Sure, why not? Masterly made the arrangements personally. I think he got a little support from President Grayfield, but he has been in direct contact with the Test Center Commander at the Range. There's one little caveat though.

NORMAN: What's that?

HAP: There are protected wild bighorn sheep in the San Andres Mountains near the Missile Range. We have to do an environmental impact study to show that a failure in an Interceptor flight will not result in any harm to the sheep.

NORMAN: I know there are *oryx* in the area. What about them?

HAP: That's not a problem; there are too many of them, anyway.

NORMAN (*thinking out loud*): You mean someone is worried that an Interceptor could fall out of the sky and hit a sheep? You know, Hap, I have a terrible feeling this contract is going to be cancelled.

Hap says nothing in reply. He watches the screen as Norman fills in the cells of the spreadsheet.

HAP: I have another question. Were you planning to print out that matrix?

NORMAN: Yeah, for my records. Why do you ask?

HAP: Because you will have created a new form. You can't do that unless you go through Forms Control and have them issue you a number.

Norman stops typing, turns slowly, and stares at Hap in silence.

INT. RTI. MANUFACTURING ASSEMBLY SHOP. DAY

Corey Layt, Roy Cordu, and Murray Jaysize are standing at the open doorway to the RTI assembly shop. The morning light is streaming in. They each hold a cup of coffee and are looking outside from right to left.

MURRAY: Where's our man?

COREY: I was told he would be here at nine, sharp. He's probably signing in at the lobby. I told our receptionist to send him over here.

ROY: What's his name? What's his company?

COREY: I don't know the answer to either of those questions. Our Director of Quality made the pick.

ROY: I've never been through a First Article Inspection, Murray. How do you think we'll do?

MURRAY: I'm sure we'll pass with flying colors. I've participated in the Preliminary Design Reviews, the Critical Design Reviews, the Qualification Reviews, and the Production Readiness Reviews. I think we've covered every base.

ROY: I hope you're right. Now and then I hear rumors about program cancellation.

MURRAY: That's negative thinking. I don't want to hear *anything* about that!

The soft click of shoes on the pavement is heard.

MURRAY: Here comes somebody.

A small, thin MAN carrying a heavy catalog case appears at the corner of the building and walks briskly to the entrance. He has a high forehead with light-brown hair. He is wearing a tweed jacket and a bright red tie. There is a look of intense concentration on his face that identifies him as a man on a mission.

He stops in front of the RTI men, sets down his case, and offers his business card.

MAN: Good morning, gentlemen. My name is Arnold Trouver. I represent Lotaqual Consultants. I'm here to conduct a third party first article inspection.

COREY: We're really happy to see you, mister Trouver. May we call you Arnie?

ARNOLD: No, my name is Arnold.

COREY (*flustered*): Oh, of course. Well, my name is Corey Layt. This fellow is Roy Cordu, and this is Murray Jaysize. We're engineers assigned to assist you and provide you with whatever information you need for your inspection of our product.

ARNOLD: Yes, I *will* need quite a bit of information.

ROY: I'm not familiar with Lotaqual Consultants. I don't believe we have ever used your company before.

ARNOLD: No, you haven't, but these first article inspections are what we do and we're quite proficient. Where is the item we will be working with this morning?

COREY: It's over in the next bay. Follow me.

The four men leave the doorway, walk down an aisle between several large pieces of machining EQUIPMENT HUMMING loudly, and enter a spacious unlit area.

COREY: This is it. Let me turn on some lights.

Corey leans over to a wall and flips a large switch. A dozen floodlights come to life in the ceiling far above the men. Revealed in the glare is a large form, shrouded by several pale blue cloth blankets.
Cory and Roy grab edges of the blankets and pull them to the floor. The shape of the Interceptor vehicle is revealed.

ARNOLD: This vehicle is certainly larger than I imagined. This inspection will take quite a few hours.

Arnold reaches down into his case and pulls out a stack of forms.

ARNOLD: This is the Form AS nine-one-zero-two A that I will be using. Where do you have the records I will need?

MURRAY: All of the build books and drawings are there on the table.

ARNOLD: I hope they are sufficient. I find many contractors underestimate the importance of good record-keeping. You understand that this item is not deliverable until this inspection is complete and fully documented in accordance with the AS nine-one-zero-two A standard. Have you gentlemen been involved in these inspections before?

ROY: I have, but that was years and years ago. Corey here hasn't, and I don't think Murray has either.

Murray shakes his head to indicate "no."

MURRAY: Management thought the exposure would be good training for us.

ARNOLD: I hope that you and your management realize that the purpose of this inspection is to provide objective evidence that all engineering design and specification requirements are properly understood, accounted for, verified, and documented.

COREY (*trying to sound positive*): We're here to make that happen.

Roy picks up a pad of paper from the table.

ROY: If you need any information that isn't in the manufacturing records, I will make a note here and we will get it for you.

ARNOLD: Very good; let's get started.

Arnold holds a clipboard with a form close to his face, studies it for a moment, and looks at Corey.

ARNOLD: Here's the first block on the form. I can get that datum out of your build records over there, but if you can tell me, it will save time. What is the part number?

MURRAY: You mean the drawing number?

ARNOLD: That comes later; I want the *part number.*

MURRAY: I don't think you'll find that in the manufacturing sheets. I guess the part number would be "RTI one-thirty-six," wouldn't you say, Roy? Our last program was the RTI one-thirty-five. The numbers go consecutively, don't they?

ROY: I think so, but I'm not positive. I've always wondered about that.

Murray looks at Arnold; reaches over and taps on his clipboard.

MURRAY: Put down "RTI one-thirty-six."

Arnold sighs, shakes his head, and enters a number on the form.

ARNOLD: Perhaps I had better get the rest of the information directly from the Manufacturing Inspection Records.

Arnold walks to the table, opens the top book, and begins copying the information there. The three men watch nervously. Arnold then walks to the vehicle and places his hand on a small protuberance on the nose of the structure.

ARNOLD: There is an antenna under this radome, correct?

MURRAY: Yep, that's part of the fire-control radar.

ARNOLD: The antenna is a purchased part, correct?

MURRAY: Yep.

Arnold holds up the open Manufacturing Inspection Record book page for Murray.

ARNOLD: I need the supplier code; it's not in the book.

COREY: Write that down, Roy. We'll get it for you, Arnold.

Arnold begins flipping pages faster and writing at a furious pace.

ARNOLD: Oh, oh.

COREY: Is there a problem, Arnold?

Arnold taps on the side of the vehicle.

ARNOLD: There's an aluminum frame behind this hatch panel, correct?

MURRAY: Yes, in fact that's one of my designs.

ARNOLD: Who supplied the aluminum?

MURRAY: Let's see. I think it was Choice Alloys.

ARNOLD: "Think" isn't good enough.

MURRAY: Write that question down, Roy.

ARNOLD: Next question. What mine did the aluminum come from?

COREY: What mine? Arnold, I admit I haven't participated in a First Article Inspection, but I don't think that's one of the questions.

ARNOLD: Gentlemen, I've been performing these inspections for years. Trust me; I know what information is required. If you expect to deliver this vehicle to the Air Force any time soon, you had better treat these questions seriously.

Roy writes on his pad.

ROY: I've made a note of your question, Arnold.

ARNOLD: I see the brackets supporting the propellant tanks are welded to the outer structure.

MURRAY: Yes, a solid mount.

ARNOLD: When was your welder last certified?

Roy makes another entry on his pad.

ROY: I'm sure we can find that date, Arnold.

ARNOLD: I notice on these records that there is drill press operator with the same first letters in his name as the welder, Frank McCoy, who initialed the build sheet when he was done.

COREY: Yes, that's Fred Moran. He's been with RTI for fifteen years.

ARNOLD: Is Fred Moran certified to weld?

COREY: He couldn't weld two pins together, but he can make that drill press stand up and salute.

ARNOLD: We have to be *sure* who did the weld. Get me a sample of Frank McCoy's handwriting.

COREY: Arnold, are you *sure* that information is *really* called for in the AS nine-one-zero-two standard?

Arnold drops his clipboard to his side in a gesture of despair, and stares at Corey, Roy, and Murray.

> ARNOLD: Gentlemen, I sense there is lack of diligence in retaining traceability in your records on this project, and I also sense there is a disregard by management for that lack.

> COREY: Arnold, the information you are seeking may *not* be in those books on the table, but I am *confident* that RTI has it stored *somewhere*, and we *can* find it.

Arnold ignores Corey's pleas and begins keying in numbers on his cell phone.

> ARNOLD: Please excuse me for a minute while I call my hotel. Based on this small sample of problems I'm encountering with record referral I see I will have to extend my stay here for several more days or even longer.

> ROY: Arnold, speaking for myself, and for Corey and Murray here, and for the company, for that matter, we will do *whatever* is necessary to achieve a timely completion of this inspection. Our personal reputations and that of the company rest on delivery of this bird to the Air Force on the promised date.

Arnold looks at his clipboard and shakes his head.

> ARNOLD: In fact, there is a possibility that this vehicle may never leave this floor.

Corey, Roy, and Murray look grimly at each other in silence. Roy makes a note on his pad.

> COREY: Roy, I'm going to have to make a call to our Director of Quality.

Corey picks up a telephone handset on one of the workbenches near the vehicle, punches in four numbers, and stares into the distance.

Murray taps Roy's shoulder

> MURRAY: Maybe you should tell me a little of what you heard about the program cancellation.

Roy gives Murray a concerned look, but says nothing.

EXT. WHITE SANDS MISSILE RANGE. DAY

It is a slightly breezy, but gorgeous morning in the Tularosa Basin of south-central New Mexico. The location is the White Sands Missile Range. We see a panorama of mountains and desert as the view moves from West to North, then to the snow-like dunes of gypsum in the East.

The scene zooms in to a somewhat remote area of the range. As the image enlarges, a crew of men wearing hard hats of various colors becomes distinguishable. There is an atmosphere of excitement as they move aggressively among small buildings, metal structures, large propellant and pressurant tanks, and trailers spaced across a wide flat area of desert. This is Launch Complex 17 Able. Vibrant, stirring BANJO MUSIC* begins softly, and then grows.

Several hundred feet to the west is a small viewing area, empty except for some men unloading a truck. At the center of the Launch Complex is a large concrete pad the size and shape of a baseball diamond. Located at intervals around the edge of the pad are light standards and water nozzles. In the center of the concrete pad a spacecraft sits, poised for launch. It looks like a giant gray moth at rest. It is the Interceptor, the IX

Two men stand next to the craft, talking. One is Steven Acheever, the Program Manager; the other is Hap Cawshun, Lead Test Engineer.

> STEVEN: Where do we stand in the preparation ladder, Hap?

---

*Director's Note: Make sure the tune is "Fireball Mail."

HAP: The last time I checked with the Control Center they were half-way through the calibration checks on the instrumentation. (*looking at clipboard in hand*) That should take about another half hour, then we'll load the flight program into the onboard controller. After that we go into a fifteen-minute countdown.

STEVEN: I can't emphasize how important this launch is. If you see or hear of anything that is the least bit out of the ordinary, let me know – immediately. And there's one more thing – we haven't talked about it yet.

HAP: What's that?

STEVEN: I wasn't allowed to say anything about this until it was cleared with Security, but all personnel involved with this launch are being monitored for the presence of possible intruders planning espionage or sabotage.

HAP: What kind of intruders?

STEVEN (*quietly and solemnly*): Aliens.

HAP: You mean, like, from across the border?

STEVEN: No, from another planet.

Hap lowers his clipboard to his side, pauses, and stares Steven in the eyes.

HAP: What do they look like?

STEVEN: Nothing special. One could look like you . . . or me!

HAP: No one told me. What precautions are we taking?

STEVEN: Every precaution. Rudy Vault, our Manager of Data Classification at the plant, is here today, and will have extra security personnel stationed among the people out there in the viewing stands and around the facility. Most of the security guys are out-sourced so you won't recognize them.

HAP: Well, I'm personally familiar with all of the test personnel assigned to this operation. I would know if there's any strangers present – unless . . .

STEVEN: Unless what?

HAP: Do you remember the movie, *The Thing,* with Kurt Russell?

Steven looks down in thought.

STEVEN: A little. It's been quite a few years.

HAP: Maybe this will ring a bell: an alien spacecraft is discovered by some research guys working in a remote Antarctic base. Some alien creature that you never see is present. The creature starts taking over the bodies of the base personnel. (*nudges Steven*) Members of the team never know if the guy working next to them is a friend or the *Thing*!

STEVEN: I don't think that's our problem, but it's something you might plan for. Look, I've got to get over to the Control Center to use the phone.

HAP: I'm going to rent a copy of that movie and show it at our staff meeting tomorrow.

STEVEN: I wouldn't do that. If you've got an alien working here, it'll put him on notice. Didn't they figure out who was taken over by the Thing by doing some kind of a blood test on each person?

HAP: That's right. We could take a blood sample from everyone. We don't have the equipment, but we could bring in the Red Cross.

STEVEN: That's right. You could tie it in with the blood drive.

Steven walks toward a car parked at the corner of the launch pad.

STEVEN: I've got to get back to the Control Center.

Hap stands alone, looking out into the distance.

HAP (*soliloquy*): Why are aliens always hostile to Earth people?

CUT TO: OBSERVATION AREA

John Fulbrane and Walter Masterly watch as workmen complete the assembly of a large portable grandstand. Across the backs of their coveralls are the words ED'S RENT-A-BLEACHER.

JOHN: Apparently the Missile Range is expanding its facilities. It seems foolish to increase the seating capacity out here, considering the limited number of visitors we'll have for this test launch.

WALTER: When you see Rudy Vault, *a*sk him if those workmen have been cleared to be in this area.

A late model gray sedan pulls up and parks next to the newly erected grandstand. On each of the front doors in large letters are the words AIR FORCE. Below them in smaller letters are the words HOW'S MY DRIVING? CALL 1-800-CAR POOL.

The driver, in the uniform of an Air Force Officer, steps out. It is Captain Barry Haggard.

Another officer, also in uniform, slides out from the passenger side. It is Major Phillip Ogeny.

Barry and Phillip walk over to John and Walter. Barry gestures toward Phillip.

BARRY: I believe you've already met my boss, Major Ogeny, at the last program review meeting.

The men nod and shake hands with the Major.

BARRY: How is the launch prep going?

JOHN: Steve Acheever is with the Test Engineer now at the pad. I expect a call any minute now.

John picks up a binder of papers lying on the grandstand seat.

JOHN: In the meantime, Captain, let me show you the flight paths for the Interceptor and the drone it will be tracking.

John walks off with Barry, flipping the pages of a report.

PHILLIP (*talking privately to Walter*): You *do* understand the importance of this launch?

WALTER: My aerodynamicists tell me the data we hope to get on control surface efficiency and drag will really anchor their flight model.

PHILLIP: I don't mean that. I'm talking about the *politics* of this program, Walter. Failure to launch today could critically affect future funding of the program. *Critically!*

WALTER: I understand. I will pass that along to my people.

PHILLIP: I realize there are risks and uncertainties you have to deal with when you press the Ignition Start button, but when I report to Congress next week, I want to be able to say I saw that bird *airborne!* Do I make myself clear?

John and Barry return.

JOHN (*addressing Phillip*): Major, would you like to see the test plan I showed the Captain?

PHILLIP: By all means. I hope there are lots of pictures.

John begins turning the pages of the test plan for Phillip. Phillip becomes focused. Barry uses this opportunity to take Walter by the arm and pull him aside.

BARRY: I need to speak to you privately, Walter. *You* understand the importance of this launch?

WALTER: The Major was explaining that to me.

BARRY: Good. Then you know it's a *political* thing. Walter, those committees in Congress that hold the purse strings don't know or don't care about the value and technical significance of what we're accomplishing here. They're only thinking about the money tied to this project. They can't deal with news reports about failures, and angry emails from taxpayers. They're only interested in positive results.

WALTER: Understood, but even a launch that doesn't quite make it teaches us things we need to know.

BARRY: I understand that; it's the nature of engineers to learn from their mistakes, but politicians don't think in those terms. If the Interceptor launch were to be delayed today for, say, a hairline crack in a panel, it would be simply mentioned over morning coffee at Space Command Headquarters. But if the Interceptor were to catch fire or land out in the gypsum, there would be Congressional hearings and investigations. And I would be called to those hearings!

WALTER: Right. You want to see a successful flight. But every developmental flight has some measure of risk.

BARRY: I think you read me on this. As we move toward the countdown today, stay in touch with what's going on. Listen to Acheever. He seems to know his stuff. If he or *anyone* feels there is the smallest potential glitch, *don't launch*!

WALTER: Run that by me again.

BARRY: I know you'd like to see the Interceptor lift off as much as I would. But there are people in Congress that would use the excuse of a flight failure to move the money for this program to their priorities. (*whispering*) What I'm suggesting is – and this is not an official Project Office directive – don't take any unnecessary risks. If there's *any* chance this launch won't complete the mission, – the intercept – *scrub it*!

WALTER: Have you discussed this with the Major?

BARRY: No, my contacts in Congress asked me to limit this concern to specific individuals and events; otherwise the word will get out to the media and be interpreted as Air Force policy.

WALTER: I'll talk to Acheever.

Their conversation is interrupted by the arrival of a black van with an antenna on the roof and large bright letters on the side: KPOW – CHANNEL 3 – LAS CRUCES. The doors swing open on each side. A man and a woman step out. The woman is Leanne Flambeau. Instead of her usual dressy outfits she is wearing a wide-brimmed straw hat, a long-sleeve western shirt, jeans, and boots. She walks over to Walter. The man follows. Walter, Barry, John, and Phillip converge on them.

LEANNE: Good morning, gentlemen. I'm Leanne Flambeau *(turns and points to the van)* with that television station. *(taps her partner on the shoulder)* This is my camera operator, Burt.

BURTON COYEL, KPOW news cameraman, is steadying his camera on his shoulder with both hands. He is wearing a brown safari jacket and shorts. Burton's long, graying hair is loosely combed. His mouth is turned down slightly at the edges, a solemn look. Burton has adopted a pessimistic outlook toward most ventures in life.

He lets go of his camera with his left hand to offer a quick salute to Walter, Barry, and Phillip.

Leanne walks up to Walter.

LEANNE: You could be mister Masterly since you're not in uniform.

WALTER: Yes, I'm Masterly. How did you get through the gate? This is a classified project.

LEANNE: I've got papers.

She pulls out a letter from a small case she is carrying and hands it to Walter. He takes it, flips it open, and scans it quickly. Phillip leans toward Walter to look at the paper he is holding.

PHILLIP: Let me see that.

He grabs the letter from Walter and reads it.

PHILLIP: This is an authorization from the Space and Missile Systems Center. It gives her and her associate, Burt, clearance. I don't recognize the name of the officer that signed it.

WALTER: What are you here to do?

LEANNE: I'm supposed to cover the launch of some kind of spacecraft. When does it go off?

Walter turns to Phillip and pulls him aside. He turns his back on Leanne.

WALTER (*in soft tones*): What do you think, Major?

PHILLIP (*in a husky whisper*): This is not good. If I thought I could raise someone at Peterson Air Force Base, I would get that authorization retracted. Let's see if I can reason with her.

Phillip walks over to Leanne.

PHILLIP: Allow me to introduce myself, young lady, I am Major Ogeny. What is about to happen here today is part of a very secret Air Force Program. If you were to televise these testing activities or videotape them for later viewing, the security of our nation could be compromised. Can't I appeal to you as an American citizen? You are a citizen?

LEANNE (*with indignation*): Of course!

PHILLIP: Then I think that you, as a loyal citizen should . . ."

Phillip's lecture is interrupted by the distant ROAR of automotive ENGINES coming from the direction of the facility entrance. Phillip, Walter, John, Leanne, and Burton turn and look down the access road.

CUT TO: LAUNCH SITE ACCESS ROAD

Four large buses speed along the road and stop at the gate to the area. The driver of the first bus reaches out his window and hands a piece of paper to a security guard. The guard looks at it briefly and waves him through. Each of the buses, in turn, pulls up to the gate and stops before continuing on.

CUT TO: OBSERVATION AREA

The caravan of four buses moves along the road to the Observation Area. They park next to the grandstand. Phillip, Walter, John, Leanne, and Burton watch, somewhat bewildered, as the throngs of men, women, and children step down from the bus door.

> JOHN: I see some of the visitors have arrived. There seems to be quite a lot. More than should be here.

> PHILLIP: My daughter, Lisa, and my grandchild, Robyn, should be on one of those buses.

> JOHN: Your daughter? Is she on the program?

> PHILLIP: No, they're in New Mexico on vacation. They've never seen a launch. I made special arrangements for her and Robyn, but I don't know who those other people are.

Leanne overhears the conversation between John and Phillip. She strides over to Phillip and looks up at him sternly.

> LEANNE: Major Ogeny, if this event is so secret, why are those other people allowed to be here?

> PHILLIP: Our security team will be checking on the credentials of all visitors.

JOHN: Your team may accept her letter, Major. I think you should take the initiative and direct miss Flambeau to pack up and leave.

Leanne bristles at John's remark.

LEANNE: You saw my papers, Major. I have been directed to cover this event by my employer and I have the authority. I intend to ask my camera operator to start shooting. When is the launch scheduled to go off?

PHILLIP: I'm not required to reveal that, Miss Flambeau. It may not occur for a long time. Perhaps you should change your plans and leave. Or, you could shoot a package showing the visitors you see.

Leanne turns to Burton. They walk back to their vehicle. Burton sets his camera down in the interior of the van.

LEANNE: This is turning out to be another one of those fruitless assignments.

Leanne and Burton lean against the van. Burton lights up a cigarette.

LEANNE: Did I tell you I got a call from KPUT in Ponca City? They want me back.

BURTON: You told me that gig was a dead end and not suitable for your career path.

LEANNE: I thought so at the time, but they made me an attractive offer.

They continue leaning on the van and watching the buses disembark the visitors.

CUT TO: DOOR OF THE SECOND BUS

The bus door opens. A MAN wearing a burgundy blazer and tan trousers steps out and onto the dusty ground followed by a long stream of people, mostly elderly men and women. Some youthful parents with children emerge. They are chattering, pointing.

ANGLE ON MAN IN BLAZER

We see a colorful badge pinned to the man's left breast pocket that reads LAS CRUCES FUN TOURS. He raises his arm and directs the throng to the grandstands.

CUT TO: GRAND STANDS

The crowd surges to the stands and begins climbing the rows of seating, filling up the structure.

CUT TO: WALTER AND BARRY

> WALTER (*pointing away*): Excuse me, Barry. I've got to make a phone call.

Walter walks a few yards to a tall, weathered pole. Attached to the pole is an equally worn and weathered box with a telephone handset inside. Walter picks it up and punches some of the buttons.

> WALTER: Control Center? Is Steve Acheever there? Good. Put him on. (*pauses*). Steve? Can you leave and meet me here at the Observation Area? I've got some issues here we have to discuss.

CUT TO: JOHN AND PHILLIP

John stands close to Phillip with his hands raised shoulder-level, palms down. He swings one beneath the other, simulating an aircraft maneuver.

> JOHN: Phil, as I was explaining to you earlier, the plan for this intercept is to have the IX craft approach and close on the target drone from its underside. Our craft will take photographs and video recordings. In actual encounters this maneuver will be valuable in getting details of the alien propulsion method. However, if the IX doesn't remained engaged sufficiently long. . .

John is interrupted by a MAN in a red and white clown outfit.

CLOWN: Is this the place where the Interceptor party is being held?

JOHN: May I ask who you are, and your business?

CLOWN: I'm Clipper, the Clown. I was hired to appear here as part of some kind of launch celebration.

JOHN: Have you checked in with mister Vault?

CLOWN: Who's he?

PHILLIP (*inserting himself*): I think I know about this, John. My daughter told me they had some other activities planned today to keep the children occupied. You know how restless kids can get if the countdown becomes protracted.

JOHN: I suggest you join those people on the stands over there.

Clipper runs to the stands, waving excitedly at the crowd.

CUT TO: WALTER

Walter Masterly stands at the edge of a paved road that leads to the launch pad where the IX vehicle sits. In the distance an automobile speeds toward him. It pulls off onto the shoulder and stops. Steven Acheever steps out from the driver's seat. He is still wearing a hard hat, and takes it off as he reaches Walter.

WALTER: How are the preparations going?

STEVEN: They're having the usual problems. Nothing I'd call critical. They're changing out a thruster compartment thermocouple.

WALTER: I've just had some discussions with our Air Force friends. They'll probably ask you the question I just did. Be careful what you tell them. Tell them the truth, but be careful how you say it.

STEVEN: How so?

WALTER: The Major wants me to believe that we *must* launch under *any* circumstances. The Captain, however, states that the word out is that we must *not* have any glitches in the launch. He's telling me that if any system is less than perfect, cancel!

STEVEN: Well, that will be a first. I've never been involved in a development program test launch where I felt comfortable about everything. Have you?

Steven looks toward the viewing stands and is struck by the crowds.

STEVEN: Who are all those people? This is a classified operation!

WALTER: That's what I'm trying to find out. I haven't caught up with Rudy Vault to ask him who invited this group.

STEVEN: Let's have a seat in the stands. The control center won't have an update for about fifteen minutes.

Walter and Steven walk to the viewing stands, look for an empty spot, and sit down. Immediately a man wearing a bright yellow jacket covered with embroidered emblems confronts them, pushing a carton containing more of the same emblems under their noses.

VENDOR: Interceptor patches, gentlemen. It's your one and only chance to have a piece of history.

Acheever picks one of the patches out of the carton.

STEVEN: Look at this Walter. This one has got the Interceptor in detail. My God, I can even make out the special antenna for the back-up control link!

WALTER (*holding patch out to vendor*): Where did you get these?

VENDOR: We make 'em at El Paso Stitchery. Neat, huh?

WALTER (*turning to Steven*): Does Vault know about this?

The vendor moves on, calling to the rows of visitors.

VENDOR: Interceptor patches! Get chur authentic Interceptor patches here!

A series of rings are heard coming from the beat-up telephone on the post near the stand where Steven and Walter sit. Steven stands up; looks down at Walter.

STEVEN: That's probably Cawshun calling. I didn't expect to hear from him this soon. It must be another problem.

Steven walks to the old post, picks up the phone, and speaks.

STEVEN: Observation Area. Acheever here. (*pauses*) Is this you, Hap? What's going on?

INT. WSMR. CONTROL CENTER. DAY

Hap Cawshun stands next to a large panel with flashing lights, TV monitors, gauges, and switches. He is pressing a telephone handset to his ear.

Next to him is a short, stocky man in coveralls holding a flashlight and a clipboard. He is about fifty-eight, has a square face, blond hair, and bushy eyebrows. He is RALPH RIGID, Air Force inspector. The man has a calm, but serious expression that arises from frequently having to convince engineers that they have a problem.

HAP: Steve, we have a situation that's going to hold us up. I don't have the resources to deal with it. There's an open squawk we just picked up on the vehicle. I'll let you speak to the inspector.

Hap offers the telephone to Ralph.

HAP: Ralph, I've got Steve Acheever here on the line. He's the Program Manager. Explain what you're concerned about.

Ralph takes the handset and speaks very firmly.

> RALPH: Mister Acheever, I'm Ralph Rigid, Air Force Quality. I've had to red-tag your bird.

Ralph presses the handset to his ear to hear Steven's response. He raises his clipboard and studies a form on the top of a stack.

> RALPH (*speaking into phone*): You're asking me what that means? It means you can't conduct this test until you clear this discrepancy. (*pauses*) Yes, that's what I said, you can't launch. (*studying the form intently*) I'll have Hap, here, get one of his technicians to run the discrepancy record over to you. You can read it for yourself.

The scene now alternates between the observation area and control center, showing close-ups of each man gripping the phone tightly, shouting into the mouthpiece.

INTERCUT RALPH/STEVEN

> STEVEN: I do appreciate your sending the written description and I will read it, but until then, could you summarize for me what the problem is?

> RALPH: The main thrusters are not grounded to the vehicle. MIL-STD twenty-eight twenty-five requires a grounding strap from the engine to the fuselage.

> STEVEN: Fuselage?

Steven pauses, drops the handset to his side, looks down, and again raises the handset to his ear.

> STEVEN: Ralph, why do you think that requirement applies to our vehicle?

> RALPH: From my years of experience, mister Acheever. Every plane in the Air Force inventory has that requirement.

> STEVEN: I'm sure that's true, but the IX is not like every plane the Air Force owns.

> RALPH: That may be true also, but you'll have to show me some evidence that you aren't subject to that requirement. Then I'll pull the red tag.

> STEVEN: Ralph, would you tell Hap I request that he personally deliver your discrepancy record to me.

> RALPH (*handing the form to Cawshun*): Here. Mister Acheever wants you to deliver this to him.   ·

The view returns to the Control Center. Hap grabs the form and starts to walk out of the door. He stops, turns to Norman Nevercutt, Test Engineer, standing at a control console and taps him on the shoulder. Norman, somewhat scowling because he has been interrupted, looks over at Steven.

> STEVEN: Norm, I'm leaving for the observation area for a few minutes. Announce we're in a hold. You had better tell them it will be at least an hour.

CUT TO: OBSERVATION AREA

There is a great activity at the observation area. Some people have left the stands and are standing in groups talking, laughing, eating, and drinking. Most of the children are running up and down the stand seating. Vendors are walking along the front of the stands selling hot dogs, popcorn, cans of soft drinks, small inflated replicas of the Interceptor, and balloons imprinted with the words FIRST INTERCEPTOR LAUNCH.

Clipper the Clown is attempting a head-stand for a group of very young girls.

A loud SCRATCHING sound emanates from the LOUDSPEAKER perched at the top of the pole with the telephone. A man's voice is heard.

LOUDSPEAKER: Your attention please. Because of technical difficulties, there will be a hold in the countdown of approximately one hour.

CROWD OF VISITORS (*in unison*): Aww!

CUT TO: OBSERVATION AREA CALL PHONE

A vehicle pulls up near the pole where Steven is standing. Hap Cawshun jumps out, clutching a piece of paper.

HAP: Steve, here's the squawk.

Steven grabs the paper; reads it quickly.

STEVEN: I've got to call Blastof.

He pulls a cell phone out of his pocket and begins punching in numbers. He raises the phone to his ear.

INT. RTI. BERNARD BLASTOF'S OFFICE. DAY

Bernard is sitting at his desk sorting through a pile of images of high-frequency recordings of rocket engine combustion chamber pressure waves. The PHONE RINGS.

BERNARD: Repulsive Technology, Blastof speaking.

The scene now alternates between the White Sands observation area and Bernard's office.

INTERCUT STEVEN/BERNARD

STEVEN: Bernie. This is Steve. I'm at the launch site. We're in the middle of the countdown. We've got a problem. Have one of the teams go into the requirements database and see if we have any specification invoked on the system that requires a grounding strap from the main thrusters to the vehicle frame.

BERNARD: We don't have any military or DoD specifications in this contract! Remember? That's called Acquisition Reform.

STEVEN: We do have one, Bernie. It was snuck into the statement of work during the last phase of contract negotiations because the contracting officer had a sentimental thing about it. Remember? It's that old, old manual issued by the Air Force Systems Command – AFSCM ten-forty-nine. I think the title is "Quality Assurance Elements of Procured Flight Articles."

BERNARD (t*hinking*): You're right. But that one has only ten pages, and the content is all motherhood. There's nothing in it about electrical grounding.

STEVEN: I know that. But find a copy. Look at Section 2, under Compliance Documents. There are other sub-tiered specs listed. Dig those out and see if any talk about grounding. The inspector here claims the requirement is called out in MIL-STANDARD twenty-eight twenty-five.

BERNARD: Okay. When do you want this done?

STEVEN: Now!

BERNARD: Now?

STEVEN: You heard me. There's a lot at stake here.

BERNARD: Aren't you going to scrub the launch for today?

STEVEN: Not if I don't have to. The Air Force is breathing down our necks. Make a list of those sub-tiered specifications. Assign each one to a different engineer and have them read them carefully. Be sure they look for any other sub-tiered specs. Call me back with status as you go.

BERNARD: Okay. I'll call you back in an hour on your cell phone.

Bernard hangs up the phone and makes an entry in his daily planner. He picks up the phone again, enters the number for Angelique Del Mundo.

BERNARD: Hello, Angelique? This is Bernie. Our admin has taken the day off. Would you set up a meeting for me? Track down Corey Layt, Al Gurithum, and Mary Snackmeister. Tell them to get to my office immediately!

Bernard hangs up the phone again, closes his eyes, and places his hand on his forehead.

INT. RTI. BERNARD BLASTOF'S OFFICE. DAY

Three people are sitting in upholstered office chairs facing the desk of Bernard Blastof who is not present: Corey Layt, Roy Cordu, and Mary Snackmeister.

Corey is sipping coffee from a cup with a picture of Repulsor I on the side. Roy is making notes in his daily planner.

Mary is eating a cookie she retrieved from a red tote bag next to her chair.

MARY: Do either of you have any knowledge of what this meeting is all about?

COREY: It's probably about the launch. (*looking at wristwatch*) It should have gone off by now. If so, Bernie has received word from Acheever or Fulbrane. Let's hope it's positive.

ROY: I predict Bernie is going to announce the flight was a success, but there was a departure – the main oxidizer valve didn't close completely.

Bernard Blastof strides into the office carrying a stack of documents, walks around his desk to his chair, falls into it, and throws the pile on the desktop.

BERNARD: People, we have a priority assignment. I have to ask you all to stop whatever you're doing and turn to on this.

MARY: I was planning a pizza outing to celebrate the launch. You told me *that* was a priority.

BERNARD: Unless we resolve this problem, there isn't going to be a launch.

ROY: Bernie, are you're telling us they've scrubbed the launch?

BERNARD: Not yet, but they've called a Hold.

ROY: What is it, weather? Avionics?

BERNARD: Worse. They have some kind of specification non-compliance and they expect *us* to get them out of it.

COREY: I'm not good at trouble-shooting a bungle that occurred hundreds of miles from here. What's the problem?

BERNARD: We have to go through all the specs on this program. I want to know if MIL-STD twenty-eight twenty-five is invoked anywhere in this contract!

COREY: I don't think that's likely. I believe we have only one specification called out in Exhibit A of the contract. If I recall, it's AFSCM ten-forty-nine.

BERNARD: That's correct. That's what Acheever told me. So, I went to the spec crib and was able to get a copy. I made three more copies; one for each of you.

Corey *holds up his copy of the standard and reads the title.*

COREY: "Quality Assurance Elements of Procured Flight Articles"

MARY: Where does the problem come in?

BERNARD: I'm coming to that. Turn to page six in your copy. That will be section two.

Bernard pauses while the others flip through the handouts.

BERNARD: What do you see?

MARY: I see three other specifications listed.

BERNARD: Exactly, and what does the sentence read that's just above those three?

ROY (*reading out loud*): "The following documents of the exact issue shown form a part of this standard to the extent specified herein."

BERNARD: Exactly. Those words mean that the three sub-tiered specifications are also invoked. Get the picture? We have more standards than AFSCM ten-forty-nine to deal with on this program, if you want to get technical.

Mary holds up the page of specification for Bernard to see.

MARY: Sure, but, look, none of them is MIL-STD twenty-eight twenty-five.

BERNARD: Exactly. Now let me answer Mary's question about the problem. The title of Military Standard twenty-eight twenty-five is "Grounding, comma, Air Vehicle, comma, General Specification For." The Air Force inspector at Launch Complex seventeen Able at White Sands . . . the guy who has red-tagged the Interceptor test vehicle . . . claims that the requirements of that standard apply to *our* vehicle. He says the standard requires that there be a grounding strap from each main thruster to the vehicle frame.

COREY: Each thruster *is* grounded to the frame. It's bolted metal-to-metal.

ROY: In fact, Bernie, we have a requirement in the vehicle-to-thruster interface control drawing that the bonding resistance at that connection be less than two and a half milliohms at initial installation. Actually, it's a dead short.

BERNARD: I know that. But we're dealing with the facts of life in the aerospace world. We have a problem here that has to be resolved. Unfortunately, because you three are on the

Launch Support Team, you're the stuckees. Now here's what I need you to do.

Mary reaches into her tote bag and pulls out a candy bar she slowly unwraps.

BERNARD: Corey, take the first spec listed. Get a copy, either on-line from that service we subscribe to, or from the spec crib, if they have any left. Roy, you find a copy of the second spec. Mary, you take the third spec. See if any of those three reference MIL-STD twenty-eight twenty-five. Let's meet here in my office in fifteen minutes.

Roy makes a note in his daily planner. Bernard watches with interest.

BERNARD: Roy, do you always make entries for fifteen-minute assignments?

ROY: I want to ensure I get everything right. Besides, this note will be a record for my NAP progress report.

Corey, Roy, and Mary hurriedly leave Bernard's office.

INT. RTI. BLASTOF'S OFFICE. ONE HOUR LATER

Corey, Roy, and Mary have returned to Bernard's office. The three stand around the desk facing Bernard.

BERNARD: Where were you all? I expected you back forty-five minutes ago!

MARY: We have *problems*!

ROY: You had better place a call to White Sands, to Acheever.

COREY: This search you've got us on is going to take a couple of hours, Bernie.

BERNARD: I didn't say it would be easy. What have you got so far?

COREY: I found the military standard you asked me to look up. It invokes four other standards. I was able to dig up those four. One of those four invokes three more, the second calls out three more, the third calls out six more, and the last one invokes two more. That makes fourteen more documents I had to pull. Based on a quick look at them I would say there are twenty more called out I have to dig up.

BERNARD: I assume from your remarks none of them is MIL-STD twenty-eight twenty-five.

COREY: Unfortunately, no. But it could be lurking in any one of those twenty sub-tiered documents.

BERNARD: Mary, how many have you been through?

MARY: About fifteen. And those reference about thirty more!

BERNARD: How many more specs did you find, Roy?

ROY (*eyeing a stack under his arm*): Let's see, I'd say only six . . . but they invoke twenty-two more. God knows how far this chain of specs stretches. This could go on for days.

Bernard looks at his watch.

BERNARD: It's eleven a.m. in White Sands. I'll tell them we need more time, a lot more time. (*looks at Corey, Roy, and Mary*) But don't stop working. Keep pulling those specs.

ROY: Bernie, what if we find that MIL-STD twenty-eight twenty-five *is* called out somewhere?

BERNARD: You're asking if I have a plan B?

ROY: I know it doesn't make any engineering sense, but what if . . . *what if* . . . there really *is* a requirement for a grounding strap?

Bernard looks silently at Roy, then picks up his phone, punches in five numbers. There is a pause. He speaks.

>   BERNARD: Is this Murray Jaysize? Good. Murray, this is Bernie Blastof, with Advanced Propulsion. I've just now assigned you to the Interceptor Launch Support Team. That's right, just now. Stop whatever you're doing. I need a design for a piece of hardware.

INT. RTI. IX HIGH SECURITY DESIGN SUITE 3. DAY

Murray is sitting at a computer terminal, holding the handset of his telephone with his left hand. He is chewing on a piece of candy nervously.

On the screen before him is a three-dimensional silver image of an S-shaped duct. He stares at the screen, tapping the keyboard with his right hand, rotating the image while responding to Bernard's words.

The scene now alternates between the Design Suite and Bernard's office.

>   MURRAY: Whaddya need?

INTERCUT BERNARD/MURRAY

>   BERNARD: Murray, you worked on the drawing of the interface of the Interceptor main thrusters to the vehicle attach frame, right?

>   MURRAY: I would say I've worked on almost everything, Bernie.

>   BERNARD: Well, since you know the configuration, Murray, this should be easy. I need a grounding strap to go from each thruster to the frame.

>   MURRAY: That doesn't make sense.

>   BERNARD: I know. How long will it take you to work up a drawing?

MURRAY: This is your lucky day. There's a strap in the Standard Parts Manual that will probably work. Better yet, you can buy one today just down the street.

BERNARD: I'll send someone there to get one, but we'll still need paperwork to put one on the system. I'll get the parts but you have to add them to the engine-to-vehicle interface drawing. I'll get the manager of Configuration Management to approve it as an Out-Of-Board Mandatory Change and release it.

Bernard turns to Corey.

BERNARD: Corey, make out a Form fifty-six D Petty Cash Voucher for about fifty bucks. Go to Ed's Electric World on Contingency Avenue and buy three eighteen-inch braided grounding straps – the kind with a bolt hole in the flange at each end. Show them to Murray Jaysize, then take them to Shipping and get them wrapped. Send the package by overnight delivery to Acheever.

COREY: Forms Control revised Form fifty-six D this morning and they're still in Repro.

BERNARD (*reaching in pocket for wallet*): Here are three twenties. I'll get reimbursed later.

Corey lays down his armload of specifications and standards, takes the bills from Murray, and heads out the door. Bernard picks up the telephone again and vigorously punches the keypad.

BERNARD: Steve, it's me, Bernie, again. It's come down to this. Proving that MIL-STD twenty-eight twenty-five is *not* called out is going to be an unwieldy if not impossible task. It could be days before we really convince ourselves the requirement is not buried somewhere, and even then, the amount of documentation I'd have to prepare to prove it to the Air Force could take weeks. There's no other option for now, Steve. Cancel the launch.

Bernard stops talking to hear Steven's response.

> BERNARD: I *know* you have to launch *sometime*. I've put in motion a plan to get you the required grounding strap. (*pauses*) I'll have it shipped by the end of the day.

Bernard hangs up and collapses in his chair.

11.4 INT. WSMR. CONTROL CENTER. LATE AFTERNOON

Steven replaces the handset of the telephone on the base. He turns to Norman Nevercutt.

> STEVEN: Norm, secure everything. We're going to have to cancel the launch. Make the announcement.

Norman takes off his headset, places it on the control console, and picks up the microphone, looks at it, and shakes his head.

EXT. WSMR. OBSERVATION AREA. LATE AFTERNOON

Only a few people remain seated in the makeshift viewing stands. Most are wandering in the open space nearby. Some people are picking up small pebbles and examining them, some are photographing each other or the mountain ranges. The children are running back and forth, laughing and screaming. Some of the people have returned to the buses and are napping in the seats.

> LOUDSPEAKER: Your attention please. Because of technical difficulties the launch has been cancelled. Be careful as you exit the area, and be sure to gather up your personal possessions.

> CROWD OF VISITORS (*in unison*): Aww!

The men from Ed's Rent-A-Bleacher quickly jump from their truck and begin disassembling the stands.

Leanne and Burton are sitting on a blanket next to the van, leaning back with their eyes closed. They hear the announcement and look around.

LEANNE: It's all over, Burt. Let's go home.

Leanne struggles to her feet and gets in the cab of the van. Burton folds up the blanket and throws in inside next to his camera. He walks around and slides into the driver's side. The van moves slowly at first and then speeds off to the gate.

EXT. WSMR. INTERCEPTOR LAUNCH PAD. NIGHT

It is the evening of the following day. The banks of lights surrounding the launch pad at Launch Complex 17 Able have been turned on. We look down on a flurry of activity that surrounds the Interceptor vehicle, glistening under the strong illumination. Helmeted technicians are seen opening panels on the craft and making adjustments.

Men in Air Force uniforms encircle the launch pad, some taking notes, some bending to inspect the undercarriage of the vehicle. The view turns slowly to the Observation Area in the distance, lit by a small lamp on the pole; it is totally empty. The view turns back to the launch pad and zooms in on two figures standing at the rear of the vehicle, next to the rocket nozzles that provide the propulsion. It is Steven Acheever and Hap Cawshun.

> STEVEN: Well, mister Cawshun, we have been granted another day of work and a second chance to try out this baby. Have you encountered any delays so far?

> HAP: None. The grounding straps arrived and were installed late this afternoon. We tracked down Ralph, the Inspector, and he has withdrawn the discrepancy report. We were able to use the extra time to install some additional flight instrumentation. We're good to go. Actually, we could launch right now.

> STEVEN: Let's go to the Control Center and do just that.

> HAP: Let me tell the leadman here to clear the area.

Hap strides over to a man wearing a headset. He says a few words and gestures toward the Control Center. The man nods and turns to the technicians standing idle at the edge of the pad and shouts a few words. The men pick up their gear and begin boarding vans in a small parking area. Steven and Hap jump into a nearby compact car and drive away.

INT. WSMR. CONTROL CENTER. NIGHT

About a dozen men and women – engineers and technicians – have entered the Control Center and have taken seats at two sets of long tables. Each station has a monitor displaying a parameter that characterizes the state of the components and subsystems on the Interceptor: pressures, temperatures, voltages, events. Some stations have control panels with switches. Each person dons a headset with a mouthpiece. Some are flipping pages in a notebook; some are making adjustments to the image on their monitor.

In the back of the room Steven Acheever, Barry Haggard, Walter Masterly, and Phillip Ogeny have taken seats next to each other.

Stanley Snappi, who has been drafted to assist in the launch operation, is being prepped by Norman Nevercutt.

Hap Cawshun stands in the center of the room. He holds a microphone in one hand and a clipboard in the other.

> HAP (*on PA system*): Listen up, everyone! We have been directed to proceed with the test launch of the Interceptor X.

Scattered CHEERS are heard.

> HAP (*on PA system*): This is the scenario of the exercise: the Interceptor will launch and engage a drone that will be flown in from a remote location on the Missile Range. The drone will simulate the approach of an alien vehicle. The azimuth, altitude, and time of arrival of the drone will be selected by an Air Force Observation Team at the drone's launch site and will be kept secret from us.

Two technicians are standing at the power distribution panel.

TECHNICIAN #1: It's really dark outside. How are we supposed to see it?

HAP: No problem. The air search radar outside feeding the control center scopes and the radar system in the Interceptor are linked. Stanley Snappi will be monitoring the scope. He has a lot of shipboard experience in distinguishing valid contacts from clutter.

Hap points to a Plan Position Indicator display console at the front of the room where Stanley Snappi sits twiddling the knobs and wiping the face of the display.

HAP: Whichever radar detects the approach of the target first will transmit the coordinates to the other. However, the Launch Control Officer – that's Norman Nevercutt, over there by the terminal – will determine if and when the Interceptor is to be launched to pursue the target.

More CHEERS are heard as Norman shakes his fist in the air.

ANGLE ON SECTION OF CONTROL PANEL

TECHNICIAN #1: I wish this test was being conducted during the day. We won't see any of the action.

TECHNICIAN #2: This could be a long night.

ANGLE ON WALTER, PHILLIP, STEVEN, AND BARRY

BARRY: Walter, I want your honest opinion. How comfortable do you feel about the launch tonight? Is there any condition that might compromise the flight performance? Should we have done more subsystem tests?

WALTER: I feel very confident. All of the systems have been through Qualification.

PHILLIP (*looking at his watch*): I hope they don't wait too long to deploy the drone. I'm sure this is going to be a memorable display of the value of this project that we've been waiting for.

Phillip leans over, touches Walter's shoulder, and speaks close to his ear.

PHILLIP (*almost whispering*): Keep in mind what I told you yesterday about the impact of this launch. A successful flight will not only be a political boost for President Grayfield, another feather in the cap of RTI, but (*hesitates*) – perhaps I should have been more open – this flight could mean a promotion for me.

WALTER: Really?

PHILLIP: "Lieutenant Colonel Ogeny", how does that sound?

CUT TO: WIDE VIEW OF CONTROL CENTER

There is a loud THUMPING noise on the PA SYSTEM as Hap taps the microphone he is holding.

HAP: Attention again, everyone. I will go through the pre-launch checkout ladder. Be sure your headsets are on and working. When all checks are complete, I will notify the AF team that they can release the drone at any time.

Hap works his way down his checklist on the clipboard, talking by headset to the engineer in charge of each subsystem, marking off their assurance that their system is "go." Phillip leans out from his chair and crooks his first finger to get Steven's attention.

ANGLE ON WALTER, PHILLIP, STEVEN, AND BARRY

PHILLIP: Steve, when the Interceptor reaches and locks on to the drone, will it fire at it and disable it?

STEVEN (*controlling a smile*): That could be expensive. We've told the Air Force we won't do that. The Interceptor does have the necessary weapons, the high-energy laser beams – you authorized them. But in this simulation the

Interceptor will only illuminate the target with the low-power beams. Sensors on the drone will confirm a "kill."

Phillip sits back in his chair, nodding and smiling.

CUT TO: WIDE VIEW OF CONTROL CENTER

HAP: (*on PA system*): All pre-launch checks are complete. The Observation Team has been notified. From this point on we just have to sit and wait until they decide how and when to send the drone our way.

ANGLE ON SECTION OF CONTROL PANEL

TECHNICIAN #2 (*leaning toward Technician #1*): This could be a long night.

CUT TO: WIDE VIEW OF CONTROL CENTER

The engineers at the tables begin leaning back in their chairs, looking at the clock on the wall, and nervously shaking their coffee cups.

HAP (*on PA system*): I know this is tedium, but stay focused, everyone.

ANGLE ON BARRY AND WALTER

Barry looks around nervously. He puts his hand on Walter's shoulder and points toward the long row of engineers slumping, watching the flickering changes on their monitors.

BARRY: Walter, I know Hap has gone through the pre-launch sequence, but as we sit here, will the launch team continue to monitor things?

WALTER: If anything falls out of bed, somebody will let Hap know.

BARRY: What about *after* Ignition Start?

WALTER: There's about five seconds of hold-down. We still have time to hit a cut button if anything looks questionable.

BARRY: Does everybody have one?

WALTER (*pointing at the tables*): No, only the guys watching the critical parameters. For example, see that technician in front of us? Notice, he's holding a small case with a little red plunger at the end of a long cord.

BARRY: Yeah. What's *that* cut button for?

WALTER: He's watching the boat-tail temperature. If it gets too high at ignition start, he will abort the launch. It could mean a fire in the engine compartment.

BARRY: Shouldn't there be more? As I mentioned yesterday, if there's anything the *least abnormal*, the test should be terminated. I'd feel better if you could pass that along to your people. You've heard the saying: "He, who cuts and walks away, gets to test another day."

WALTER: Barry, I assure you. From what we learned in our subsystem tests we have a very good handle on the potential problem areas.

ANGLE ON PHILLIP and WALTER

Major Ogeny is listening to voice mail messages on his cell phone. He overhears a few words of Walter's remarks to Barry and drops his phone into a jacket pocket. He leans over to Walter.

PHILLIP: What were you saying about "cut buttons"?

WALTER: I was explaining that those cords you see with the little red knobs at the end are cut buttons. The engineers can press them to shut down the engine and secure the vehicle if any measurement or event is outside the nominal limits.

PHILLIP: Why are there so many?

WALTER: Well, there are actually very few compared to, say, the number we would hook up to any of the pump-fed propulsion systems we've developed. This engine is pressure-fed; it's simpler.

PHILLIP: I know that seems reasonable to you, Walter, but there *could* be some nervous Nellies out there on the floor who wouldn't think twice before pressing that red button.

WALTER: As a matter of fact, Phil, none of the cut options in place here were ever exercised during development. It's just a matter of adding extra safety to protect the hardware.

PHILLIP (*shaking his fist*): As I have stressed again and again, yesterday and today, many elements depend on a successful launch tonight: funding, national security, reputations. I would like you to get the word out to your people, Walter, that termination of this test would be acceptable only if there is a clearly recognized and severe condition.

WALTER: I'm sure that Steve and his crew have that understanding.

PHILLIP: Let me put it even *more* strongly, Walter. Failure to launch tonight could be fatal. We're talking *program termination*!

CUT TO: WIDE VIEW OF CONTROL CENTER

The room is silent. Everyone's eyes are on Stanley Snappi who is hovering over the PPI display.

STANLEY: C'mon, drone. Show yourself!

The minutes drag on. Many heads begin nodding. Steven Acheever paces slowly back and forth. The display on the large digital wall clock flashes tirelessly.

Stanley Snappi, who has been sitting, eyes half closed, head resting on one arm, suddenly lunges over the radar screen.

STANLEY (*jumping up, knocking over his chair*): *Target! Target!*

HAP (*presses headset close to ear*): Where?

STANLEY: Ten miles away, due east, moving directly toward us at about five thousand feet – and it's closing fast.

HAP: Does the Interceptor have the same fix?

STANLEY: Yes.

HAP (*looks quickly around the room*): Prepare to launch Interceptor!

There is intense activity and SCRAPING of CHAIRS as the engineers and technicians position themselves at their stations.

ANGLE ON NORMAN NEVERCUTT

Norman sits hunched over his place at a table, staring intently at the screen on the Launch Control Terminal. Hap races to his side.

HAP (*loudly*): Do it!

Norman punches the LAUNCH key on the pad in front of him.

CLOSE ON MONITOR

A small rectangular image appears on the center of the monitor with the message: "Do you really want to start an interplanetary war? ☐ Yes ☐ No"

CUT TO: NORMAN AND HAP

NORMAN (*looks up at Hap, points to the message on the monitor*): What's this?

HAP: That's just an Air Force precaution. Ignore it. Click on "Yes."

Norman pushes his finger on a key with great emphasis. The occupants of the Control Center look up at the televised image of the

Interceptor on the wall-mounted television monitor, bracing themselves for the expected ear-crushing ROAR and the brilliant orange plume of flame from the nozzle. The craft sits quietly on the pad. Nothing happens.

> HAP (*looking to the left and right*): Did anyone chop it?

CUT TO: WIDE VIEW OF CONTROL CENTER

There is a chorus of NO and NOT ME; many of the engineers shake their heads and wave their arms to communicate their puzzlement. Walter Masterly, Steven Acheever, Captain Haggard, and Major Ogeny leap from their chairs and stride quickly to join Hap at the Launch Control Terminal.

CUT TO: LAUNCH CONTROL CONSOLE AREA

> NORMAN (*pointing frantically at the monitor*): There it is. We got a launch command chain interrupt.

Norman's fingers fly over the keypad, entering a query.

> NORMAN (*pointing at the monitor, speaking loudly*): Read it for yourself. The helium manifold pressure switch didn't pick up!

ANGLE ON PHILLIP AND STEVEN

> PHILLIP: What does that mean?

> STEVEN: There is a pressure switch downstream of the pressurant tank valve. When the tank valve opens, the pressure switch closes to indicate that pressure is available for the propellant tanks.

BACK TO SCENE

Stanley's voice is heard in the background.

> STANLEY'S VOICE: The target is eight miles away.

> WALTER: Steve, what failed?

STEVEN: The pressure switch. The flight instrumentation readout tells me both propellant tanks are pressurized. We could still launch.

WALTER: Can you override the pressure switch?

STANLEY'S VOICE: The target is six miles away.

Steven types frantically on a keyboard next to the Launch Control Terminal

STEVEN: I'm trying to re-program the launch command chain.

STANLEY'S VOICE: The target is three miles away.

Steven leans back abruptly and throws his hands up in frustration.

STEVEN: It won't work. The control of the Interceptor at this point has been handed over to the on-board computer. We didn't anticipate this.

STANLEY'S VOICE: The target is one mile away.

HAP: How could this have been allowed to happen? We have a pressure switch failure and a software failure.

WALTER (*with resignation*): A *dual malfunction*!

STANLEY'S VOICE: The target is overhead and seems to be hovering there.

BARRY: That's impossible. The drone the Air Force is sending can't hover. Somebody has to go outside and see what the radar is picking up.

HAP: Stanley, you know what might give a false return. Go outside and see what's there. Maybe it's a buzzard

Stanley throws his headset on the floor and dashes out the door.

EXT. WSMR. INTERCEPTOR LAUNCH PAD. NIGHT

Stanley is seen running from the main entrance of the Control Center. The outside area is extremely dark. His face is illuminated by the light from the Control Center windows. He looks up and freezes. His face reveals his state of shock.

There is a large, saucer-shaped vehicle above him, lit by panels around the rim. The VEHICLE emits a loud HUM as it lowers itself to the ground. A hatch on the side opens; two men in dark suits climb out through the hatch and begin pointing at Stanley and the door to the Control Center.

Stanley turns and runs back into the Control Center; once inside he slams the door and sets the lock.

INT. WSMR. CONTROL CENTER. NIGHT

Stanley staggers in and collapses on a chair next to Walter, Steven, Hap, Barry, and Phillip.

> HAP: What did you see?
>
> STANLEY: It's a ship.
>
> HAP: The drone?
>
> STANLEY: No, an alien spaceship. It's the saucer everyone is talking about. It landed!
>
> STEVEN: Walter, what do you want to do?
>
> WALTER: We must take a look to know what we're dealing with.
>
> STANLEY: Don't go outside. There are aliens out there!
>
> PHILLIP: I think we should stay locked inside and call for reinforcements.
>
> WALTER: How many aliens did you see?

There is a heavy POUNDING on the main entrance DOOR. Some of the WOMEN start SCREAMING.

> HAP: They may have ways of breaking in we don't know about.
>
> PHILLIP: We don't have any weapons to defend ourselves.
>
> STANLEY: Isn't there a company procedure that covers a situation like this?
>
> WALTER: There are twenty of us here. We might have a better chance if we open the doors, make a run for it, and scatter. They can't catch us all.
>
> STEVEN (*over PA system*): Here's what we're going to do, people. We're going to surprise whoever is out there. I'll stand by the main door, and open it quickly. Stanley, you and Hap run out first to draw their attention. The rest of us will have to run out as fast as we can. Each person must take a different direction. Those who make it should rendezvous at the Observation Area.

Steven steps quickly to the main entrance and places one hand on the door handle and the other on the lock knob.

> STEVEN (*shouting*): Now!

In one brisk movement, Steven swings the door open wide. Stanley and Hap surge out into the night.

EXT. WSMR. INTERCEPTOR LAUNCH PAD. NIGHT

As Stanley and Hap pound the earth in long, fast strides, they see ahead the figures of the two aliens standing motionless by their ship. White beams stream in the dusty air from their hands to the soil in front of them. Stanley and Hap come to an abrupt stop and stare.

> STANLEY: Oh, my God. They've got lightsabers!
>
> HAP: You've been seeing too many Star Wars movies. Those are flashlights.

Behind Hap and Stanley, the engineers and technicians flee the Control Center with their hands over their heads. They see the light beams the two aliens are pointing their way and they stop moving. Some fall to their knees.

SCATTERED CRIES: We surrender! We surrender!

The aliens walk slowly to Stanley and Hap. One of the aliens raises a face shield on his helmet. He reaches into a breast pocket of his spacesuit and pulls out a piece of paper that he unfolds. He shines his flashlight on it and reads it carefully. He speaks to Stanley.

FIRST ALIEN: Take me to your leader.

STANLEY: You speak our language?

FIRST ALIEN: A little. Where is your leader?

STANLEY: You mean our President?

FIRST ALIEN (*pauses, thinks for a while*): Yes.

STANLEY: Let's see, it's close to eleven p.m. here in New Mexico. So, it's nearly one a.m. in Washington, DC – about sixteen hundred miles away – where our President, Thelma Grayfield is probably asleep.

FIRST ALIEN: No, take me to the President of your company.

HAP: Why do you need to see *our* President?

The second alien has joined the first alien. He has removed his helmet. He speaks to Hap:

SECOND ALIEN: We want to meet him. We come in peace.

HAP: Stanley, go find Walter and tell him what's happening here.

Stanley turns and hurries back to the group standing outside the Control Center. He sees Walter at one side talking with Phillip. He works his way through the milling Control Center crowd and confronts Walter.

> STANLEY: For some reason, Walter, the aliens want to talk to you.

Phillip grabs Walter by the shoulder and pulls him away from Stanley to get his attention.

> PHILLIP (*breathing heavily*): Walter, I'm going to use this opportunity to make a dash for it. My car is around back. I'm going for help. The situation is hopeless. Salvage what you can, but this incursion by the aliens is too much. The Interceptor is finished!

Phillip steps sideways until he reaches the edge of the building, then breaks into a run, disappearing into the darkness. A minute later an automobile ENGINE is heard TURNING OVER, then there is a ROAR. The tail lights of the Air Force car are seen bouncing along the access road toward the exit. Walter watches the car for a few minutes, then trudges with Stanley toward Hap and the aliens.

> WALTER (*staring intently at the second alien*): What is it you want from me?

> SECOND ALIEN (*reading from small piece of paper*): My Flight Commander wants to meet with you.

> WALTER (*pointing at first alien*): I will do that. Is that him?

> SECOND ALIEN: He is not with us. He would like to meet with you in a few days at another place.

> WALTER: Very well, where do I have to go?

> SECOND ALIEN: He will come to you. What is your address?

> WALTER: What?

> SECOND ALIEN: What is your home address?

WALTER: I don't believe this.

Walter reaches into his pocket, pulls out his wallet, opens it and displays it to the alien

WALTER: My address is on my driver's license.

SECOND ALIEN: Would you hold my light for me? (*hands flashlight to Walter, strains to look at wallet; laboriously copies address from driver's license*) Thank you.

The two aliens lower their face shields, turn, and walk back to the spaceship. They climb through the hatch, and close it behind them. The HUMMING resumes, the vehicle rises slowly, and then speeds away into the dark sky, disappearing among the blanket of stars. The Control Center personnel watch in silence.

INT. RTI. MARY SNACKMEISTER'S CUBICLE. DAY

Mary is in her office chair, leaning slightly forward, staring numbly at a stack of folded cardboard cartons next to the cubicle wall. She has a blank look and sits motionless. Her computer has been turned off. Next to another wall is a tall stack of papers and documents that has spilled over. She picks up a notebook, glances at it indifferently, and throws it down. Soft, sad VIOLIN MUSIC is heard.

Susan Shi swings into the entrance to the cubicle and peeks at Mary.

SUSAN: Hey there, Snacky. Do you have a minute to help a fellow employee?

MARY (*bitterly*): You mean a *former* fellow employee?

SUSAN: Cheer up. Nobody said you've been fired.

MARY (*shaking head despondently*): I can't believe the Interceptor Program has been cancelled. There were always rumors, sure, but everything was going so *well*.

SUSAN: Yes, all of the hardware was qualified, and we were delivering everything on time.

MARY: I was sure that NIP and NAP would get us through successfully.

SUSAN: Something else will come along.

MARY: Not likely. You saw the graph Masterly presented in the last general meeting. The projected business line was *flat*. He admitted there are *no new projects* on the horizon. The Interceptor was the only account I was charging to!

Mary picks up a piece of paper next to her printer and waves it at Susan.

MARY: Did you see this latest email on the layoffs?

SUSAN: No, I haven't read any emails for the last two hours. I've been updating my résumé. What does it say?

MARY: Let me read the first part to you. "We are sorry to inform you that RTI will be reducing staff during the next month because of cancellation of the Interceptor contract. Affected employees will receive notification with their paychecks. Laid-off employees will receive one month's severance pay."

SUSAN: That's sad. Has your boss, Kim, given you any indication of who will be let go in your department?

MARY: She avoids me. What about *your* manager, Al Gurithum? Has he said anything in meetings about how bad the layoff will be?

SUSAN: Al said that none of the managers, like him, can offer any assurance to the people on their staff because they're uncertain about their *own* survival.

MARY: What was that help you said you needed?

SUSAN: I've been trying to pack up my Interceptor documents for storage as we've been directed. I can't figure out how to fold the cartons together. I've never seen this kind before. Where did *they* come from?

MARY: Repulsive Technology contracted with a new company – Hilltop Record Repository. They delivered them early this morning. Maybe the two of us we can figure out how to assemble one.

Mary holds up one of the flattened cartons, and shows it to Susan. Susan reads off the red lettering printed on the underside of the lid.

SUSAN: It says here, "Fold flaps A inward. Pull flaps B down. Lift up flaps C." I tried that and it doesn't work.

MARY: I did too. I even asked Diane Cratewright to come over to my cubicle to explain how these are supposed to come together. I thought *she* would know. She gave up and left. And she's the *packaging engineer*!

Susan takes the carton from Mary and begins unfolding and folding the sides and ends.

SUSAN: Maybe the instructions were written out of order. Let's try pulling the B flaps down first.

Susan struggles with the carton, swinging it side to side. She knocks over Mary's wastebasket. Mary grabs one end of the box to steady it and reaches inside.

MARY: Well, the B flaps are down, but the C flaps won't move.

Susan lets one end of the carton fall to the floor. She leans against the cubicle wall, exhausted.

SUSAN: This is not working. I need some boxes. I have all of my systems engineering documents to store.

MARY (*pointing*): That pile you see over there are Interceptor material specifications and the results of vendor sample tests; they're all waiting to be packed.

SUSAN: What'll we do?

MARY: I've already called Security. I told them I have this giant stack of paperwork sitting out here, exposed. They connected me with Leo Meertz. He said he would send someone over to pack the records and haul them away. No one's shown up yet.

SUSAN: Good. I'll have them do mine too. Did you fill out the complete itemized list of documents on Form sixty-seven E? And don't forget to specify the correct retention period. The contract requires only five years, but the company lawyers said we should make it ten.

MARY: I didn't have time. I just wrote "specifications." I doubt anyone will ever retrieve those from dead storage.

SUSAN (*looking worried*): I'm not expecting to be fired, mind you, but are there any plans to assist those who are?

MARY: Yeah. That's covered in the second part of the email. Let me read it to you. "Following the notifications, a meeting for affected employees will be held in the Tapestry room. We will discuss severance benefits, health insurance, retirement plan distributions, unemployment benefits, counseling, and re-training opportunities. We urge all interested to attend. The date and time will be announced."

Two men in dark coveralls arrive at the cubicle. One sees the stack of cartons and begins separating them. The other looks first at Susan, then at Mary.

MAN: Are you Mary? We're here for the records.

Mary points to the sloppy pile of reports and specifications.

MARY: There they are. Susan, here, has some for you to pack also. She's four cubicles down the aisle.

The men quickly assemble the cartons. They dump the records into the cartons carelessly, close the tops, and stack them on dollies. They leave and disappear down the aisle.

> MARY: That's strange. Those guys didn't have "HILLTOP" on the back of their coveralls like the guys who delivered the cartons this morning. I'm wondering if Meertz is using the right company to store that data.

> SUSAN: Let's hope so. I wouldn't want my stuff to get into the wrong hands. By the way, did the email say anything about being hired back in if things turn around?

Mary picks up the copy of the email again.

> MARY: I'll read you the last paragraph. "We truly appreciate your years of service at RTI. Unfortunately, this layoff was unavoidable. We wish you success in your future endeavors."

> SUSAN: That's not too encouraging, Mary. (*sighs*) Well, now that the records are taken care of, let's finish polishing our résumés.

Susan walks out of the cubicle. Mary reaches over and presses the power button on her computer. She stares into the distance.

EXT. WALTER MASTERLY'S HOME. ESTABLISHING. DAY

The home is a wide, two-story mansion, mostly gray in color with blue columns supporting the roof of the portico at the entrance. The building is surrounded by wide stretches of well-kept lawn.

In the center of the circular driveway in front are a flower bed and a fountain. Parked in the driveway is Masterly's royal blue Ferrari.

INT. WALTER MASTERLY'S HOME. DAY

Walter Masterly stands at the window of his study, looking out across the front of his property, a grassy meadow-like expanse bordered by a wide bank of trees, A road leads from his front door out into the forest that surrounds his estate.

Walter looks down momentarily at his wristwatch then back at the road. Over his shoulder in the distance can be seen a small black object that grows larger. It is an approaching scooter-like vehicle with the dark outline of a man on board.

The scooter is without wheels and floats about a foot above the ground. It moves rapidly to the front of the house, stops, and settles to the driveway.

The driver dismounts: a man in a dark gray jumpsuit with silver stars on the collar, and a matching cap with silver stars on the visor. He rests the vehicle against a planter, steps away, and walks to the front door.

The RING of the DOORBELL is heard. Walter turns and leaves the study.

CUT TO: INTERIOR FRONT DOOR

Walter opens the door. The stranger stands silent and motionless as Walter surveys him. The hair peeking from beneath the visitor's cap is silvery white; he has a large, lined face, prominent cheeks, upturned eyebrows, and a broad smile. He radiates a temperament that is good-natured, curious, and adventuresome.

Walter speaks.

> WALTER: Do I have the pleasure of meeting the Flight Commander of the Peorian Squadron?

The man smiles broadly and nods in agreement. Walter holds up a large piece of paper.

> WALTER: This was shoved under my door during the night. It has a message introducing you, and it states you would be visiting me today – alone, as I see you are.

Hearing no comment from the visitor, Walter pauses.

WALTER: Perhaps I should have asked first, but I assume you speak *some* English.

MAN: Yes, I do. My full name is Sigmondis Dredcoast, but you can call me Sig.

WALTER: Pardon me if I seemed startled, Sig, but you bear an amazing resemblance to a famous actor, Ernest Borgnine*.

SIGMONDIS: I consider that a compliment; I hope I meet your expectations.

WALTER: Please come in, Sig. We can talk in my study.

The two men walk from the doorway into the house; Sigmondis follows Walter across the entry way through another door into the study. Walter points to a chair.

WALTER: Have a seat. May I offer you a cup of coffee?

SIGMONDIS: I will pass on the coffee; I am still getting adjusted to Earth beverages.

WALTER: Where is your ship? Did anyone see you coming?

SIGMONDIS: During the night we landed our ship in a clearing in the trees down the road. We apparently did not attract attention, so we stayed there.

WALTER: You speak English well; you must have spent a lot of time studying us.

SIGMONDIS: Yes, but we found English to be a difficult language with many conflicting rules. Our language, Peorese, has similar problems.

*Writer's note: This saves having to add a lot of character description.

Sigmondis reaches into a briefcase at his side and brings out a copy of an English dictionary.

SIGMONDIS (*quickly flipping pages in the dictionary*): As an example, our crew had a major discussion as to why "caught" and "draught" are pronounced so differently when they are spelled so alike.

WALTER: Your message said you wanted to arrange a business deal. Before we can get to that, I think we need to find out more about each other.

SIGMONDIS: I know enough about your country, your company, and you. I'm sure, though, you have to satisfy yourself as to who you will be dealing with.

WALTER: For starters, where are you from?

SIGMONDIS: We are from the planet Peoria. We share this solar system.

WALTER: I am not an astronomer, but I know of no other habitable planets in our solar system. Where is it located, what orbit?

SIGMONDIS: We are in the same orbit as Earth, but on the opposite side of the Sun. You would never see our planet.

WALTER: Hmm. Many people have hypothesized there could be a planet there, but that's only possible in science-fiction literature.

SIGMONDIS: How so?

WALTER: Well, the astronomy experts claim that the presence of another planet, say of comparable size to Earth, would be revealed by its gravitational effect on other planetary movements – and on our space probes.

SIGMONDIS (*shrugging*): What can I say? Check your data.

WALTER: I need to know more about this business deal. Why did you pick *my* company?

SIGMONDIS: You were selected by your government to build a ship that could match the maneuverability of my ships. I was impressed by your accomplishments.

WALTER: We never got the opportunity to prove our propulsion system could perform the mission. The Interceptor Program was cancelled by the Air Force yesterday morning. The failed launch and the presence of your crewmen were the fatal blows.

SIGMONDIS: Yes, I know. It was reported in today's Wall Street Journal. I assumed you would be receptive to new business.

WALTER: What do you need my company for?

Sigmondis reaches down again into his briefcase and brings out a copy of Aerospace Progress magazine and opens to a folded page.

SIGMONDIS: There is an article here that states your company, Repulsive Technology, has an outstanding quality program. It states that all of your components exhibit extremely high Mean Time Between Failure. There is an advertisement for Repulsive Technology on the next page that says the same thing.

WALTER: Well, we bought a full-page ad so the editor ran a nice write-up, but it is true. We place a big emphasis on quality. We have an operation we call NIP, Never-Ending Improvement Program. When a recurring lapse in quality is reported, we NIP it. Did you want us to teach your people our methods?

Sigmondis reaches again into his briefcase and withdraws a thick sheaf of papers that he hands to Walter.

SIGMONDIS: More than that. I want, or should I say my *planet* wants, to enter into a contract with you. (*he points to papers that Walter holds*) You have it in your hands. Our fleet of ships is sorely in need of restoration. The contract has *four* major provisions: *First*, your company, Repulsive Technology, would provide the tools and components for repairs of our vessels. *Second*, your company would provide service manuals so that we could perform these repairs ourselves. *Third*, your company would re-design and replace those components and systems in our ships that exhibit high failure rates.

Sigmondis pauses as if to get a reaction from Walter.

WALTER: That's *three*.

SIGMONDIS: The last and perhaps most important clause, if you will, states that some of our people will be hired to work on this project alongside your people. We need to learn the techniques you use.

WALTER: That could be arranged.

SIGMONDIS: Well then, what remains to be done before the contract can be signed?

WALTER: I have to know the scope of the work. I have to have a detailed Statement of Work.

SIGMONDIS: That's attached to the contract. The details are all there: the quantities, the degree of completion. I leave the cost and schedule estimates to you. I trust you.

WALTER: I realize you are not that familiar with aerospace contracting procedures, but it would be unfair to you and unfair to me to have too many loose ends. For example, since we would be preparing service manuals, as you mentioned, the contract should have a CDRL.

Sigmondis leans back, puzzled.

SIGMONDIS: Why would I want a sea drill?

WALTER: That isn't what I meant. The word "CDRL" is an acronym. It stands for "Contract Data Requirements List."

SIGMONDIS: Can you formulate one and put it in for me. I trust you.

WALTER: Sure, but then the contract will need some DIDs.

SIGMONDIS: Some deeds? There is no property involved.

WALTER: No, a DID means "Data Item Description." The DID would describe what goes into the service manual and how it would be formatted.

SIGMONDIS: I'm sure the manuals will be fine if they look like your other manuals.

WALTER: I'll get with my people tomorrow. I'll need input from Manufacturing, Engineering, and Field Support groups.

SIGMONDIS: One critical item is missing from the contract.

WALTER: What's that?

SIGMONDIS: The method of payment.

WALTER: I was coming to that. Do you suppose we could conjure up some kind of trade agreement? Is there anything you make on Peoria we might need, something we could buy in exchange?

Sigmondis shrugs.

WALTER: That could be a problem. I'll bring it up in my meeting tomorrow. How can I get back in touch with you when I have the complete plan laid out and costed? This will take about a week.

SIGMONDIS: I was able to acquire one of your cell phones. Call me. Here is the number (*hands slip of paper to Walter*).

Sigmondis rises from his chair and offers his hand to Walter. Silently, the men shake hands in agreement. They walk from the study, out the front door, to the driveway. Sigmondis moves on toward his vehicle, pauses, turns, and waves.

INT. RTI. WALTER MASTERLY'S OFFICE. MORNING

The brilliant morning sun cascades through a large picture window and across a circular conference table next to the desk where Walter bends, gathering a stack of papers. Walter moves to the window and closes the louvers to remove the glare.

Seated around the table are POLLY PROPALEAN, Director of Processes and Materials, Daniel Brazewell, John Fulbrane, HARRY HANDOVER, Director of Field Support, and Sandra Binding. In front of each person is a blue coffee cup with the letters RTI in gold. Walter picks up a carafe from under the brewer.

> WALTER: Would anyone like their coffee warmed up? Angelique made a fresh pot.

Walter waves the carafe at Harry.

Harry has worked at RTI almost as long as John. He has strong features and rippled brown hair. His shirt is custom tailored. He sometimes appears lost in thought, but his staff knows he takes note of everything going on.

> HARRY: I take it this meeting is going to be very short.

> WALTER: Why do you say that, Harry?

> HARRY: It has been rumored that you use the technique of serving large quantities of liquids to your meeting attendees to hasten their need to use the restroom rather than prolong the meeting with long-winded opinions.

> WALTER: I can't believe my generosity has provoked that speculation. I'm always interested in what *anyone* has to say – as long as it's to the point.

SANDRA: On the subject of rumors, it was whispered to me that this get-together was discuss some new business we are about to capture.

WALTER: That's right on, Sandra. It's no secret that I've had a conversation with the leader of the aliens – a conversation that could turn out to be lucrative for us. I must say, they already have been responsible for a good bit of work being thrown our way.

DANIEL: Yeah, but the Interceptor Program is history – cancelled. We have an insufficient backlog of contracts. Unless we can latch on to something to fill in, I have to start preparing a layoff list.

Walter picks up the papers from his desk and distributes them around the table.

WALTER: This may do it for you, Dan. The Peorians want to enter into an agreement with us for an upgrade to their ships, for refurbishment of some subsystems, and for some maintenance procedures. This is their version of the contract; I made copies for everybody.

Each of the people in the meeting begins reading, turning pages.

WALTER: Some of the words and the phrasing may seem strange. They're still learning the language. Sandra, you can have your people clean it up. And you'll notice that a lot of exhibits you're used to are missing. Add whatever we need; just make up what you think is reasonable.

JOHN: Unbelievable! (*reading from contract*) It says here they're going to deliver every one of their ships to us for inspection. They're actually going to let us *look* at them?

WALTER: I'll bet that's tempting to you.

HARRY: What do you want us to do with all this stuff?

WALTER: Dredcoast, the Flight Commander, did a pretty good job of quantifying and itemizing the amount of hardware we will be either fixing or replacing, and he seems pretty savvy as to the amount of servicing that is needed. I want you people to get together and come up with a timeline and some cost figures for the work in each of your areas. Sandra will coordinate that team and collate your input. I'd like it back in a week.

DANIEL: I don't mean to be funny, Walter, but do you want the cost in Peorian dollars? If so, what is the exchange rate?

WALTER (*heaves a long sigh*): I was coming to that. Dan has touched upon the one fly in the ointment here. I haven't figured out how they are going to pay us.

Walter's remark gets Polly's attention. Polly is comely, middle-aged, but looks younger, perhaps due to her eternally happy expression. She wears a conservative business suit and a small choker. She has short, curled, dishwater blond hair and uses very little makeup. She is known for her excellent memory and strong influence on Walter.

POLLY: Walter, an idea just germinated in my brain. But I have to ask this first: did you read the report my group issued on the materials analysis of the parts and fittings turned over to us by Orville Pressfit – you know, the stuff he lifted from the spaceships while he was abducted?

WALTER: It was a little dry, but I read it. It said you found all of the parts incorporated the wrong choice of metals.

Polly nods in agreement, waves at Walter, rises from her chair, and steps from the table to a corner of the office.

POLLY: Walter, may I have a few words with you privately?

Walter walks to Polly and stands facing her with his arms crossed; a questioning look alters the lines on his face. Polly beckons him closer with her forefinger. Walter bends his head. Polly speaks softly into his ear for several minutes. Walter nods. He returns to the table.

JOHN: Well, what was that all about?

WALTER: Polly gave me a crazy idea. But if I tell you now, they'll lock up all of us.

DANIEL: When do you want this contract all done up and ready to sign?

WALTER: In a week. And to answer your question, Dan, for now, price everything in dollars.

DANIEL: I don't think a week is enough. We will have to think about contingencies.

WALTER: Don't worry. Sandra is good at putting in some clauses that will allow us to renegotiate if the going gets tough. Dan, you've got a week.

Polly, Daniel, John, Harry, and Sandra pick up their copies of the contract and leave the room, shaking their heads, MURMURING.

EXT. WALTER MASTERLY'S HOME. NEARBY WOODS. DAWN

A dazzling blue pickup truck drives slowly down an unpaved road *through a stand of trees. The early morning sunlight streaking in from just above the* horizon casts long shadows of the trees across the road.

A clearing appears in the distance where a silvery gray dome sits. It is the alien spaceship that had landed a few days before at the Interceptor launch site at the White Sands Missile Range. A subdued but OMINOUS THEME begins playing in the background*.

The truck rolls near the spaceship and parks. The door of the cab opens, and Walter Masterly climbs down. He is wearing jeans, a plaid shirt, and a blue cap with the letters RTI in gold. He reaches back into the cab and withdraws a large, thick, brown paper envelope. He looks down at the face of the envelope.

*Producer's Note: Let's not use any more banjo music. For this scene get a real orchestra.

CLOSE ON ENVELOPE

A large label on the envelope reads REVISED CONTRACT – PEORIAN VEHICLE UPGRADES AND MAINTENANCE AGREEMENT.

BACK TO SCENE

Walter walks to the spaceship, stumbling slightly on the uneven ground. The ominous MUSIC grows louder. He pauses, peering back and forth across the exterior of the hull. There is no sign of life.

Suddenly many small lenses set in a ring that encircles the hull of the craft begin pulsing with light, slowly, on and off. The ominous MUSIC grows even louder. The pulsing of the lights accelerates. An antenna-like rod appears on the dome and extends skyward. The CRAFT begins to vibrate and generates a HUM.

Walter backs away, startled. He crouches and moves toward the hull with short, slow steps. He reaches up and knocks on what appears to be a small hatch. The hatch lid flips up, and a sleepy face of an alien crewman appears. The crewman squints at Walter.

> WALTER (*holding up the envelope*):   Give this to Sig. He's expecting it.

The face moves back into the darkness of the interior, and a hand reaches out and grabs the envelope. The hatch closes. The ring of lights goes dark. The antenna retracts. The vibration and the hum stop. The ominous music subsides.

Walter walks slowly back to the pickup truck, climbs up into the cab, and closes the door. The truck pulls away, turns around, and heads back up the road.

EXT. WALTER MASTERLY'S HOME. PATIO. DAY

Walter Masterly and Sigmondis Dredcoast are leaning back in padded patio chairs next to a large, glass-topped table. On the table is a coffee pot, a small pitcher of cream, two blue coffee mugs with the letters

RTI in gold, and the large, brown envelope Walter had delivered to the spacecraft earlier that day.

Set against one of the patio columns is the scooter used by Sigmondis. The men are looking out at the back of Walter's estate. The view is a vast area of deep green turf, surrounded by lush conifers in the distance.

Walter stands, picks up the coffee pot, and begins to pour the dark beverage into the mug in front of Sigmondis.

> WALTER: I know you're still getting used to Earth coffee, Sig, but you've got to try this. It's Jamaican blue mountain – fifty dollars a pound.

> SIGMONDIS (*picks up mug and sips*): Yes, this *is* good. Walter, your home is in a beautiful location. The arrangement and the vegetation remind me of my own home on Peoria. I am eager to return.

> WALTER: You should be able to – at any time now. You have the contract you wanted – right there.

Walter points at the brown envelope.

> WALTER: At Repulsive Technology Incorporated we're primed and ready to move out once we get the go-ahead. As the result of this additional work, we'll need a few more heads. As you requested, Sig, we can place at least fifteen of your people in positions in Manufacturing, Quality, Design, Materials, Systems, and Software to work your project.

> SIGMONDIS: Didn't any of your people object to our having access to some of your proprietary technology?

> WALTER (*smiling*): No, there were no objections. It *is* a real concern though. We're *always* on guard for industrial espionage by our competitors down the street, but we aren't challenged by any agency in a similar endeavor on a remote planet like Peoria.

SIGMONDIS: Good. We want to feel welcome.

Hearing the words of Sigmondis, Walter abruptly leans back in his chair. He places his hand to his chin and rubs it, exhibiting unease. He stays silent for a long time, obviously composing some thoughts.

WALTER: What you said brings up a point, Sig. I want you and me — *and* our planets — to have a cordial and open relationship in this venture. But there *was* an issue, and I'll bring it up now so that it can be discussed and put behind us.

SIGMONDIS: Of course, Walter. What is it?

WALTER: In spite of the absence of any overt evidence, my security specialist, Rudy Vault, insisted that there was a Peorian spy within our company. I ask you now, Sig. Was that true?

SIGMONDIS: Yes, Walter, there was. But his assignment was not to inflict any damage. He was placed there to gather information on your quality control methods so we could improve our products. He was able to secure a large quantity of records. He is gone now.

WALTER: Who was it, Sig?

SIGMONDIS: His real name on Peoria is Leogeok Immertzif. You knew him as Leo Meertz.

Walter takes a deep breath.

WALTER (*in a husky whisper*): Leo Meertz. (*pauses, shakes his head*) Our Deputy Manager of Data Classification. A most trusted employee.

SIGMONDIS: Yes.

WALTER: I have to think how I can break this news to Rudy Vault.

Walter rubs his chin again, slowly, as if in great pain.

> SIGMONDIS: As you said, Walter. That is history. There is nothing now to stand in the way of our agreement.

> WALTER (*raising his hand for emphasis*): There *was* one other potential problem: Federal export control over hardware and services. We're subject to International Traffic in Arms Regulations, or ITAR – those apply to defense articles – and subject to Export Administration Regulations, or EAR, for commercial stuff. So, I sat down for an hour with the company Counsel and we agreed, based on the wording, that the regulations apply to foreign nations, not other planets.

> SIGMONDIS: I see you feel very strongly and positive about this business arrangement.

> WALTER: We made sure we accounted for everything you asked for. (*makes sweeping gesture*) Plus, we expanded on a few provisions to cover some marginal condition in your equipment that you may have overlooked. And, most important, Sig, I signed the contract.

Sigmondis picks up the envelope, removes the contract, and leafs through it.

> SIGMONDIS: That's the first thing I noticed when I read it this morning. The statement of work is very thorough and straightforward. You are a man of great integrity.

> WALTER: Integrity. That's the key word in this whole deal, Sig. I will see to it that we keep our part of the bargain; I know you will too. Now, all you have to do is sign as well.

> SIGMONDIS: I came prepared to do that. But, as you surely know, the financial details had to be glossed over in *my* original draft. I didn't know how to begin; I thought *you* might work out some arrangement for payment. (*holds up a page of contract*) I did see that you specified elsewhere

that there would be progress payments, which is good, but otherwise the page labeled "CONSIDERATION" is left blank. (*pauses, looks down at page in his hand*) Wait, I see there is a note at the bottom that says, "Insert Barter Terms." What does that mean, Walter?

WALTER: I was coming to that.

He picks up the coffee pot and fills Sigmondis's mug.

WALTER: Here, have some more blue mountain.

SIGMONDIS: It is rather good. Perhaps you could spare some of whatever it is you use to brew it; I'd like to my crew try it. Didn't I read that coffee makes you more alert? My men have been sitting out in the woods for several days now, confined to the ship, with very little to do. They're getting languid.

WALTER: So I noticed. Yes, it might perk your men up a little; I'll package up some beans for you to take when you leave. But let me switch gears here and talk about a business arrangement by which we both will benefit measurably.

SIGMONDIS: As we say on Peoria, "Unfold your road map and show me your route."

WALTER: We noticed on most of your spaceship parts that came into our possession that many of the materials you use, particularly the alloys, were – let me say it politely – substandard.

SIGMONDIS: You mean they lacked strength?

WALTER: Yes. (*pauses*) Are you familiar with what we call the Periodic Table?

SIGMONDIS: Yes, that's a pictorial presentation of the elements on your planet. I've seen it and studied it. You've grouped your elements on the basis of their atomic numbers, electron configurations, and recurring chemical properties. We have a similar chart, but we may not have every element you show, although we predicted their existence. Also, we've grouped them slightly differently.

WALTER: Are you familiar with the element with the atomic number twenty-six?

SIGMONDIS: That's the one you call "Iron," but it's labeled "Fe" on the table. Why is that?

WALTER: It's from the Latin "Ferrum." Do you use it much on Peoria?

SIGMONDIS: It's a wonderful metal and has wonderful properties, but iron deposits are very rare on Peoria. Actually, we refer to it as one of our "precious metals." It's mostly reserved for women's fine jewelry.

WALTER: You're saying it's only affordable by the very rich and only used for special applications?

Sigmondis takes off his cap and shows the peak to Walter.

SIGMONDIS: Here's a good example. Take a look at those stars. Most of our lower rank uniforms have buttons and bars made out of what you call "brass." But when you get promoted to Fleet Commander, like me, you get to trade them in for these.

He waves the stars close to Walter's face

SIGMONDIS: Those are iron, Walter — *one-hundred per cent pure*! In your language I guess they'd be called "sterling iron."

WALTER: I see you've put a nice polish on them, but don't they get rusty?

SIGMONDIS: Chemically pure iron doesn't rust.

WALTER: Yeah, you're right. I see why you treasure it. From what you're telling me, Sig, you seem ready to go to any lengths to find and acquire a source of that metal.

SIGMONDIS: Definitely, yes. We'd like to develop alloys with this element for our ships, but there just isn't enough to go around.

Sigmondis taps the stars on his cap lovingly.

WALTER: We're a little more fortunate in having a better supply of iron here on Earth. Why do you suppose it's so rare on Peoria?

SIGMONDIS: I wondered about that. I'm not very learned about the origin of the solar system, but I'm told that Peoria was created at about the same time as Earth, from the accumulation of material left over from the creation of the Sun. Apparently Earth ended up with more iron than we did.

WALTER: Well, what *are* your most common elements?

SIGMONDIS: That question is easy. Getting back to your periodic table, are you familiar with element number seventy-nine, the one labeled "Au." We have a tremendous amount of that one.

WALTER: That stands for Aurum, the Latin word for Gold. We noticed it was used for quite a number of parts on your craft. You say you have a lot of it?

SIGMONDIS: Oh, yes. It is very easy to locate and to mine. There are large deposits all over the planet, usually close to the surface. The few alloys we are able to prepare from gold are extremely corrosion resistant, but unfortunately too soft.

WALTER: I would imagine your bolt threads often fail.

SIGMONDIS: Yes.

WALTER: I have a proposal for you that should easily take care of the funding problem with our contract. It was suggested by Polly Propalean, my Director of Materials and Processes.

SIGMONDIS: If I agree, will you have to take back the contract and revise it? Are we looking at another few days?

WALTER: No, I have the amendment right here – all printed out and ready to go. If you are in accord with it, I can simply add it to replace the blank CONSIDERATION page.

Walter reaches into a thin black leather case resting against a planter on the patio and retrieves a single piece of paper. He displays the paper to Sigmondis.

WALTER: I'll let you read this, but let me summarize what's here. This will be the barter arrangement that you noted. There will be two exchanges going on. First, we will remove all gold fittings, struts, fasteners, beams – anything subject to stress, and maybe paneling too – and replace them with an appropriate iron alloy. Those are generally referred to as some kind of "steel." There will be no charge for the labor or materials. You get the new part; we get the gold.

SIGMONDIS: We'll have quite a few ships for you to refurbish.

WALTER: Here's the second deal: This will cover the other contract costs including documentation, quality control, testing, logistic supply chains, and, of course, all the "ilities."

SIGMONDIS: "Ilities"?

WALTER: You know, Reliability, Vulnerability, Affordability, Availability, Maintainability, and so on. Those processes review the overall suitability of the design. You wouldn't want to accept a product that was less than optimal, would you?

SIGMONDIS: Of course not. So, what is the second deal?

WALTER: Each of your ships sent from Peoria to RTI for refurbishment will carry a cargo of gold. For ease of handling the gold should be cast in twenty-seven-pound bars. We will replace your gold with our iron, which your ship will take back to Peoria in trade. You can specify whether you want your metal in tubes, rounds, sheets, or bars. But we will swap you iron for gold, pound for pound.

SIGMONDIS: You're willing to do that?

WALTER (*displaying the page again to Sigmondis*): It's all here in black and white.

SIGMONDIS: Unbelievable! (*looks down in deep thought and back again at Walter*) Pound for pound you say?

WALTER: That is the agreement. By the way, how big is your supply of iridium?

SIGMONDIS: Which element is that?

WALTER: The Atomic Number is seventy-seven; it's located between osmium and platinum.

SIGMONDIS (*thinks for a moment*): Oh, yes, we have very large reserves of iridium as well.

WALTER: Hmm, interesting. I'll get back to you on that.

SIGMONDIS (*pounds the table top joyously*): Our fleet will be *restored*! We will have new sources of materials. What an achievement for me! I can't wait to get back to the Metal Resources Council with this news. They will be overjoyed. I will probably be awarded the Space Fleet's Medal of Honor. Where do I sign?

Walter places the single sheet with the amendment on the table in front of Sigmondis, takes a fountain pen from the plastic pocket protector in the breast pocket of his shirt, and lays it on the sheet.

CLOSE ON PEN

The name on the pen is a very expensive brand*.

BACK TO SCENE

Sigmondis picks up the pen and begins writing.

> SIGMONDIS: I am truly proud to be part of this project and to add my signature to this milestone in Peorian history.

He holds up the paper to examine the pen strokes.

> SIGMONDIS: Very readable! I should explain that I received an award in penmanship when I was very young. I have always tried to retain in my writing the elements that I was taught – you know: spacing, slant, alignment.

Sigmondis shakes head and frowns.

> SIGMONDIS: Recently some idiots on Peoria have actually suggested that cursive writing be dropped from the curriculum of the elementary schools.

Walter takes the paper from Sigmondis and slides it into the envelope with the other pages of the contract.

> WALTER: I'll inform everyone at the plant that your ships will be arriving and work is to start immediately. We have an organization plan that goes into effect the moment I give the word. If you have any drawings of your craft that you keep aboard, we could surely use them.

Walter escorts Sigmondis to the front door. Sigmondis turns to Walter and shakes his hand.

Sigmondis walks to the scooter, replaces the cap on his head with a helmet, mounts the machine, and floats off toward the trees.

---

*Producer's Note: This looks like another excellent opportunity for a product placement.

INT. RTI. AUDITORIUM. MORNING

At one end of von Streber Hall, an auditorium at the center of the main RTI building, a projection screen is being lowered down the wall at the rear of a stage.

At the front of the stage, off to the side, sitting in a folding chair is TERENCE TALLTREE, Director of Financial Services. Having a stature of six feet six inches he is often kidded about his name. He very handsome and never lacks a haircut. He is well-educated, sometimes aloof, and procedure-oriented.

Employees are filing into the room, chatting, taking seats. When most of the seats are filled, Terence picks up a cordless microphone from a small table next to his chair, stands, and walks to the front of the screen.

> TERENCE (*loudly, over speaker system*): Good morning, everyone. (*waits for chatter to stop*) This is the first of a series of meetings we're holding today to tell everyone about new business. I'm only going to take about thirty minutes. To avoid crowding I've spaced four meetings throughout the day. This meeting is for team members with last names beginning A through F. If you know of anyone in that group who isn't here, remind them to come to one of the later meetings.

CUT TO: VIEW OF AUDIENCE

Most of the auditorium is occupied. Three more employees enter holding coffee cups; they slide carefully along the rows, stepping over feet, inching toward empty seats. Heads are turning side-to-side in the search for familiar faces.

ANGLE ON FRONT ROW

Mary Snackmeister is seated next to Stefan Espacamore. She turns to him.

MARY: I'm not supposed to be at *this* meeting, but I'm taking time off this afternoon. I see you heard the announcement.

STEFAN: I almost didn't come. At first, I thought I heard the announcement over the PA system say that people with names K through S were supposed to show up. The words were a bit muffled. Those speakers need to be replaced.

MARY: Apparently a lot of other people heard the same message. (*pointing*) There's Stanley Snappi.

CUT TO: VIEW OF STAGE

Terence waves to the side of the auditorium where Leonard Lenz from the Media Department is seated at a small table punching the keyboard of a lap-top computer.

TERENCE (*into microphone*): Len, you can fire up the projector now – and go to the first chart.

An image fills the screen behind Terence. A long string of digits runs across the white background.

TERENCE: This is the charge number for this meeting, folks.
There is a RUSTLE of PAPERS and MUMBLING in the AUDIENCE as people open notebooks or take out small pads to jot down the number.

ANGLE ON FRONT ROW

STEFAN: Gee, you need a charge number for everything you do around here. I guess if you have the right charge number, you can do *anything*.

MARY: Didn't somebody already say that? "Give me a charge number and I shall move the world."

STEFAN: That was Archimedes. He said "Give me a fulcrum."

CUT TO: VIEW OF STAGE

> TERENCE: I'm sure the word has gotten around that we are in possession of a new contract – a contract with the planet Peoria. I'm here today to give you the details.

Several of the people in the audience immediately raise their arms.

> TERENCE: Please hold your questions until later. The presentation will probably cover the information you want. Len, the next chart, please.

A chart appears on the screen with an artist's rendition of the Solar System. Ten spheres are shown circling the Sun; an arrowhead labeled EARTH points to one in a third orbit from the Sun. A second arrowhead with the word PEORIA indicates a planet positioned in the same orbit on the opposite side of the Sun.

Terence takes out a laser pointer and directs the red beam at the chart.

> TERENCE: This is our Solar System; these are the planets. Here *we* are (*places red dot on Earth*) and *here* is Peoria. (the *red dot is moved to the other planet in the orbit*) This is the location of the aliens, excuse me, the people, we will be doing business with.

A man in the audience waves his arm frantically. It is Roy Cordu.

> TERENCE: I see you have a comment that can't wait, Roy. What is it?

> ROY: You're showing Pluto on the chart. Pluto is no longer considered a *real* planet.

> TERENCE: You have a point there. Len, did you get that? Moving on. As a result of this new venture, there will be some organizational changes. Obviously, a Program Office will be established to direct all activities. The Program has

been named "Peorian Equipment Provisioning" or "PEP." We expect members of the program to be "peppy."

He smiles broadly and chuckles. The audience remains silent and solemn-faced. Mary Snackmeister fans her hand at Terence.

> TERENCE (*exhibiting a tired frown*): I'll take your question, Mary.

> MARY: Will any of us be expected to make trips to the customer's site?

> TERENCE: At this time the program schedule only shows customer meetings at *this* facility, but as the work progresses, I suppose issues could develop that warrant off-site conferences; (*frowning*) we would have to give that some thought.

A woman in the audience raises both arms. It is Clara Closchek.

> TERENCE (*pointing at woman*): Folks, I want to introduce Clara Closchek who was recently brought into Travel Audit, one of my departments. What is your question, Clara?

> CLARA: If trips to Peoria, which Mary asked about, *are* a possibility, Terry, would our current company procedure, RTOP seven point nine, "Reimbursement for Transportation, Food, Lodging, and Incidental Expenses," still apply?

> TERENCE (*hesitating*): I'll raise that question at the next meeting with our CFO. By the way, Travel Audit will now be known as Transit Expenditure Review.

> CLARA (*softly and sadly*): Oh, dear. Another name-change. I'll have to revise all the forms.

More raised hands appear throughout the audience.

> TERENCE: Believe me, I do want to answer all those questions that may be troubling you, but I must get through my agenda. Put up the next chart, Len.

An organization chart is thrown up on the screen. Shown is a hierarchy of little boxes with names and titles. Some boxes lack names.

> TERENCE: This is the latest company organization chart. I've added the structure that reflects this new endeavor. As you can see, not all of the slots have been filled. The PEP Program Manager will be Harry Handover, who has been Director of Field Support and does a wonderful job. We believe this program has a major element of customer integration and logistics in it; Harry has the experience for that assignment. (*looking back and forth across chart*) Let's see – the Chief Program Engineer will be Steve Acheever, who has moved over from the Interceptor Program which, as you know, has been cancelled.

There is scattered APPLAUSE.

> TERENCE: I hope that applause was for Steve and not the fact that the Interceptor work has ended. That contract termination could have been a knockout punch to our policy for keeping everyone here occupied. If it weren't for the innovative and aggressive steps by our President, Walter Masterly, to bring in this new program, we would have had to start down-sizing. In fact, I expected a dozen questions this morning about possible cut-backs. I haven't heard *any*.

A man raises his hand. It is Murray Jaysize

> TERENCE: Was that *your* question, Murray? I don't think you have to worry about being laid off.

> MURRAY: No, I wanted to hear about the safe.

> TERENCE: The safe?

> MURRAY: Yes, the safe that's being built under the warehouse.

> TERENCE: I wouldn't call it a safe. It's a secure storage room.

MURRAY: I was asked to assist Facilities Engineering in preparing some drawings. I noticed that the design for this "storage room" meets the Underwriters Laboratories Class Three Standard. The door has twenty-two one-and-a-half-inch locking bolts. It sure looks like a safe to me.

TERENCE: President Masterly is taking steps to ensure that we have a cushion in our supply of rare earth minerals that are critical to our operations, rare minerals that we will be laying in. The world demand is increasing and our overseas sources are in doubt.

Terence takes on a stern expression. He waits for a nod of agreement from Murray.

TERENCE: The Facilities Engineering people are just making extra sure that their design for the storage area is unbreachable. There are clever people out there, Murray. If they are desperate enough to steal manhole covers for the metal, they will work even harder to get their hands on our precious minerals.

Murray waves his hand again.

MURRAY: There's been some talk about our proposing on a combination space truck and excavation module to mine asteroids. Wouldn't this interplanetary alliance be a great opportunity for us to exploit mineral recovery from Peoria?

TERENCE: I'm sure President Masterly has considered that and is exploring every avenue.

MURRAY: Considering the thickness of the door shown on the drawings for that basement space, you'd think they were going to store gold there!

TERENCE: Let's move on.

Terence points to the organization chart on the screen.

TERENCE: You probably noticed we have a couple of organization name changes.

GROANS from the AUDIENCE are heard.

TERENCE: The Procedures Group will now be known as Enterprise Documentation.

MURMURS circulate in the AUDIENCE.

TERENCE (*turning to audience*): I should mention that as part of the contract agreements some of the Peorians will be working right here at RTI in program functions.

Louder MURMURS emanate from the AUDIENCE.

TERENCE: Fortunately, all of the Peorians with whom you will be working speak English fluently. However, as back-up, some of our paperwork that involves critical rules and processes will include a Peorian translation.

Loud GROANS are heard from the AUDIENCE. A man raises his hand. It is Stefan Espacamore.

TERENCE: Oh, there's Stefan Espacamore. What is your question?

ANGLE ON STEFAN

STEFAN: Your mention of the incorporation of Peorian language addenda raises this thought: Will the drawings and specifications for the PEP Program be in Standard or Metric units? In fact, do we even know if the Peorians have their own measurement system? If we use theirs or go Metric, we will have to depart from our Parts Standardization Policy.

An ominous UMMM rises from the AUDIENCE.

ANGLE ON TERENCE

> TERENCE: Well, being a Finance person, I can't pass judgment on *that* question. I'll leave *that* one to Harry Handover and Steve Acheever.

Terence again looks up at the organization chart.

> TERENCE: Oh yes, another department name change. Human Resources will henceforth be known as Employee Processing.

CUT TO: AUDIENCE

A woman raises her hand. It is Angelique Del Mundo. Terence recognizes her.

> TERENCE: Yes, Angelique. Did you want to add something about the name changes?

ANGLE ON ANGELIQUE

> ANGELIQUE: Yes, why was that department name changed? Was it because our work force will *now* include hirelings who *aren't* human? I haven't seen any of the Peorians yet, so I don't know what to expect, but based on the posters that were hanging around here until last week and the warnings on the company intranet, those people don't look too amiable.

ANGLE ON TERENCE

> TERENCE: Those posters and the intranet images were, unfortunately, based on a misperception. Our President, Walter Masterly, who has seen the Peorians personally, and conferred with their local leader, assures me that they are friendly, cooperative, and trained to do the jobs they will be assigned.

ANGLE ON ANGELIQUE

>ANGELIQUE: Maybe so, but I and many other employees here this morning, will feel very uncomfortable in their presence.

ANGLE ON TERENCE

>TERENCE: Thank you, Angelique. That brings me to another announcement. We *will* have Peorians, these people from a faraway world, among us. We want them to feel welcome and comfortable here. We considered resuming our Diversity Meetings. Mary Snackmeister is working with Constance Harmony, our Manager of Training, to set those up.

Terence holds his hand out to the audience

>TERENCE: I call upon Mary to tell us how that effort is going.

Mary Snackmeister stands at her seat, turns, and faces the audience.

>MARY: Well, Terry, Constance interviewed most of the new hires and discovered there isn't enough diversity to discuss. (*shrugs*) In spite of what you may have read or heard, they're not any different from the people here.

The people in the audience begin looking at one another.

>MARY: Instead of Diversity Training, Constance and I are planning a Peoria Welcome party. Everyone is invited. The company is footing the bill.

CHEERS and APPLAUSE are heard from the AUDIENCE.

CUT TO: VIEW OF AUDITORIUM

Terence looks down at a man sitting in the front row of seats; he waves him up to the stage. He is MELVIN WHOLEHAM, Cafeteria Manager. He is forty years old, five foot ten in height, and weighs about two-hundred-twenty-five pounds. He has curly reddish hair and rosy cheeks. His necktie has images of carrots, beans, corn, and potatoes. He is quick to give praise to staff members, and is always thinking of ways to delight cafeteria diners.

> TERENCE: As you may know, National Edibles, the company that provides our cafeteria service, has appointed a new manager. I invited him to speak today. He has some exciting things to tell us about changes to the operation of the cafeteria. Please welcome Melvin Wholeham.

Melvin is smiling broadly as he hurries up the steps to the stage. Terence hands him the mike and returns to his folding chair.

There is scattered APPLAUSE from the BACK of the auditorium.

> MELVIN: I want to tell you how honored I am to have been appointed to serve as your cafeteria manager. I know Repulsive Technology sets high standards for its products and it will be my job to be sure the food available in your cafeteria meets those same standards.

He pauses, waits for applause, and continues smiling. The audience is silent.

> MELVIN: Many employees choose to bring bag lunches and many of you *do* eat breakfast or lunch every day in the cafeteria. I recognize some faces. Will those who prefer to use the cafeteria please raise their hand?

About half of the people in the audience raise their hands.

> MELVIN: Great! As Terry said, I'm here today to tell you about some innovations I'm incorporating to make your dining experience more adventuresome.

Melvin looks down at a list written on a card in his hand.

> MELVIN: First, we have received feedback that employees are getting tired of the same old chicken noodle, clam chowder, and Italian wedding soups, so we will be offering a new selection, including (*his voice becomes spirited*) *cream of asparagus* and *carrot bisque*!

The audience remains quiet; Terence applauds briefly. Melvin smiles and nods at Terence.

> MELVIN: Second, I fortunately have a reliable source of monkfish. And I've got a great bunch of ways to prepare it. (*pauses, bends down to peer at the front row*). The monkfish, you must have heard, is known as "the poor man's abalone." (*laughs vigorously*)

Members of the audience turn and look at each other questioningly.

> MELVIN: Third, we've added a touch of upscale elegance you won't find in other company cafeterias. All of the salad forks will *be chilled*!

A man in the audience begins to raise his hand, but pulls it back sharply.

> MELVIN: Fourth and most important: I and my crews in the kitchen and on the serving line felt the cafeteria should have a name. So we "cooked up" a contest. (*laughs vigorously at his choice of words*) That's right, we "cooked up" the idea of a contest to choose a name. Every employee will be allowed to submit one name. The winner will receive a voucher for a full week of lunches. There will be entry forms at the cafeteria entrance tomorrow. See you then; *Bon Appetit*!

Melvin waves and offers the microphone to Terence. Terence jumps from the folding chair and takes the microphone. Melvin walks off the stage.

> TERENCE: Next chart, Len.

A chart appears filled with dense text and numbers.

> TERENCE: Here are some new rules that I thought I should include. The first one is about the use of coffee warmers at your desks. And, oh, yeah, our Information Technology Department has upgraded the website for submitting your

timecard. It takes a little learning, but they tell me you'll love it once you get the hang of it.

Everyone in the audience begins to stir, uncomfortably. Many are pointing at the chart. An angry HUM begins to swell. The scene fades.

EXT. RTI. COURTYARD. AFTERNOON

The large courtyard within the building complex of the Repulsive Technology, Incorporated campus is filled with colorful blue canvas pavilions and RTI employees.

Three workmen are adjusting the legs of one of the large aluminum frames that support the canvas covers. The backs of the coveralls have the words: ED'S RENT-A-TENT.

Some of the employees are setting up tables under the covers. Others are bringing out trays of food and large plastic bottles of carbonated beverages from the cafeteria.

Mary Snackmeister and Constance Harmony stand side by side surveying the preparation of the tables. Mary turns her head toward one the tables that is bare except for a stack of foam cups. Mary grabs Constance's arm.

> MARY: Have they brought out the coffee urns yet?

> CONSTANCE: They're coming. I have to ask. Why are we serving coffee on a sweltering day like this?

> MARY: Well, *I* won't be drinking any, but I was told that the Peorians specifically asked for it. And it *has* to be blue mountain.

CUT TO: COURTYARD ENTRANCE

A small platform, draped with red, white, and blue bunting, has been set up near the entrance to the courtyard. A set of unpainted, crude wooden steps has been placed next to it. A microphone stand and a folding chair have been placed on the platform. At its base on each side is a large, black speaker box.

Next to the platform Leonard Lenz bends over a metal cart on which rests a CD player he is adjusting. He inserts the leads running from the two speakers into the unit. After surveying the wire connections, he nods in approval, and presses a button on the CD player.

From the speakers comes the BLARE of the United States Marine BAND playing the marching piece, UNDER THE DOUBLE EAGLE*.

The crowds of employees are startled; they turn to stare at the stage as if something were about to happen. The rhythm of the music takes over. Everyone starts swinging heads and waving arms in time with the beat of the melody.

*Director's note: Can we make this the Roy Clark guitar version?
Stanley Snappi, who has been eating a doughnut under one of the tents, walks over to Leonard.

ANGLE ON PLATFORM AREA

> STANLEY: Len, I know the music is stirring, but isn't it a little loud?

> LEONARD: Think so? I'll drop the volume a little.

Stanley walks over to Mary Snackmeister who is placing stacks of white foam cups next to bottles of orange soda. She looks up at him and smiles.

> MARY: Oh, Hi, Stanley. Isn't this an exciting day?

> STANLEY: I'm not so sure. I only came for the food and to get a good look at these Peorians. I've met two of them already in the desert in New Mexico. I'm not convinced yet they can be trusted to work here.

> MARY: I don't think you have anything to worry about. One of them will be speaking this afternoon. (*looks at Stanley's shirt*) Oh, I see you are wearing the special pin the company issued to celebrate the new program.

STANLEY: Yeah, someone dropped one off at my desk this morning. Couldn't they afford something better? If this program is going to be as profitable as Terry Talltree predicted it will be, they could have spent a little more money on the pins. This looks chintzy.

MARY: I thought it was nicely designed. It shows the two planets, Earth and Peoria, circling the Sun – they did a nice enamel job. Look at the big letters at the top: P E P.

STANLEY: But look at it closely, Mary, it's made out of *cheap metal*. And it's not even plated! I couldn't believe my suspicions, so I showed it to my buddy in the Materials Lab. He had already tested the metal on *his* pin. He confirmed what I guessed. It's plain *iron!* Why couldn't they have made it out of gold?

MARY: Joyce Plaisant in Communications ordered them. She told me Walter Masterly designed the pin himself. Joyce wondered about the material, and she told Masterly the pin company thought she was nuts, but Masterly was *very* specific about using iron. Here she comes now.

Joyce Plaisant walks through the entrance and stops next to Leonard Lenz. She touches his shoulder, speaks to him, and points to the CD player. Leonard nods and turns off the music. Leonard helps her up the wooden stairs to the platform. Joyce pushes the switch on the microphone and taps it. Hearing a THUMP, she begins speaking.

JOYCE: Welcome, Repulsive Technology team members. On this day we kick off the Peorian Equipment Provisioning Program. I can't remember ever feeling as keyed up and optimistic about the future as I have at this moment. Our President, Walter Masterly, will be here shortly to share his vision with you. Oh, here he is now. Please come up, Walter.

Walter Masterly navigates his way through the crowd of employees at the entrance to the platform. He moves up the wooden stairway sprightly and grasps the microphone stand. Joyce lowers herself into the folding chair.

> WALTER: This is truly a good afternoon that I wish you, my fellow RTI colleagues. I will make this short; I know you want to use your lunch break to avail yourselves of the great drinks and snacks that I see waiting for you under the tents.

Walter points at the tables of food. The CROWD CHEERS.

> WALTER: We are on the verge of a unique and solid program. The contract is firm; the funding is in place. We know what our customer wants, and our customer knows he will get what he is paying for. And you people out there will make that happen. The good visitors from Peoria that have been selected to participate in this fantastic program will be able to watch miracles take place, miracles that we do regularly. (*taps the pin on his lapel*) I hope everyone received this special program pin. Wear it every day with pride.

Walter waves to the employees, turns, and steps down from the platform. EVERYONE APPLAUDS vigorously. Joyce takes up a position at the microphone again.

> JOYCE: As you know, we will have many skilled technicians, designers, and engineers from the planet Peoria working side-by-side with us on the PEP Program. You probably want to know how they feel about their new duties and new surroundings. Here this afternoon to tell us about their reactions is one of the men who will be working in valve design.

Joyce looks down at a young man standing off to the side, and she gestures at him to come forward. He is DOX ALTURI, a Peorian. His features are youthful; his frame slender. The Earth-style clothes he chose for his employment are not well coordinated. He entertains many doubts about his ability to fit in and carry out his assignments, but he is careful not to reveal them.

He moves quickly up the steps, and joins Joyce at the microphone. He is holding a foam coffee cup and a scrap of paper.

> JOYCE: I'm pleased to present Dox Alturi. Everybody is waiting to hear from you, Dox, please tell us what is going through your mind on the brink of this new adventure for you and for Repulsive Technology.

Dox takes a sip from his cup and looks down at the piece of paper he has been clutching.

> DOX: Good afternoon, RTI team members. Basically, I am honored to have been chosen to represent my fellow Peorians here at this great company on this day, and allowed to express our gratitude and positive feelings about this program and our future here. (*raises the coffee cup in a salute*) I do believe, basically, this is the greatest aerospace company in America!

The EMPLOYEES flocking in front of the platform CHEER and APPLAUD.

> DOX: Every person I have met has made me feel welcome, which is good, because, basically, we *are* strangers to this planet.

Someone in the crowd raises a crude banner that reads WE'RE ALL FRIENDS.

> DOX: Basically, I plan to work diligently at my assignment, to follow your procedures, to study your methods, and to learn your secrets of success (*laughs*).

The crowd is quiet. Some WHISPERED comments are heard.
ANGLE ON STANLEY AND MARY

> STANLEY: What does he mean by "learn your secrets"? I'm worried. These guys are up to no good.

> MARY: Shhh!

CUT TO: VIEW OF PLATFORM AND CROWD

> DOX (*sips from the cup*): I want to say thanks to the many people here who, over the last few days, have helped me adjust. Basically, I can't remember their names or point them out right now. As the saying goes on Peoria, "All Earthlings look alike." (*laughs*)

The people in front of the platform remain silent.

> DOX (*pointing out at his audience*): I do want to thank Roy Cordu over there who has improved my English. He basically spent many hours with me, teaching me the right words and the right pronunciation.

Off in the crowd Roy raises his arm.

> DOX (*pointing at Mary Snackmeister*): I must give my thanks also to Mary Snackmeister who has opened my eyes. Basically, she has made me aware of the many things I can do and the many places I should visit in this great country while I am here.

Mary waves at Dox.

> DOX (*looking down at the paper in his hand*): Mary has also shared her vast knowledge of food with me. Basically, after hearing her descriptions, I can't wait to try her recommended list of authentic American dishes – (*looks again at paper*) hot dogs, sushi, pizza, tacos, and chop suey.

Several PEOPLE in the crowd eating pizza slices wave them in the air and CHEER.

> DOX: Most important of all, I am thrilled to receive this pin.

He pauses and touches pin attached to the lapel of his jacket.

> DOX: It has been basically designed to memorialize our alliance and our program. It is unbelievably beautiful and expensive. Basically, I can't wait to show this pin to my friends and

family on my next trip home to Peoria. Usually you have to work for at least thirty-five years at the companies on Peoria to receive a pin of this quality. I got mine my first day at work. (*laughs*)

Dox stops speaking and turns to Joyce with a questioning look. Joyce smiles and, with a wave of her hand, signals for him to leave the platform. She replaces him at the microphone. Dox runs down the steps and heads toward the coffee urn to refill his cup.

> JOYCE: Thank you, Dox. That was inspirational. You truly set the tone for our festivities this afternoon. Have fun, everyone.

Constance Harmony holds a note up for Joyce to read. Joyce bends over and squints at the piece of paper. She grabs the paper and waves it.

> JOYCE: This is a note from Melvin Wholeham, the Manager of our cafeteria; he reports that his team of judges has selected a winner of the cafeteria naming contest. The winner is Chandra Patel.

There is scattered applause, a few CHEERS, and an enthusiastic YELL, "Yaaah, Chandra!"

> JOYCE: The cafeteria will now be called "The Chilled Fork." And, oh, yes. Please throw your empty plates and cups in the trash containers.

Leonard presses the button on the CD player. The martial NOTES of Under the Double Eagle fill the air again. The RTI employees wave their arms and step in unison. The view pulls back to encompass the entire complex; the happy crowd shrinks and disappears in the distance.

INT. PONCA CITY. SOONER STATE SENIOR CENTER. DAY

Octavia Genarian, Evita Añejo, and Anna Versery are leaning back in a plump, well-worn couch, staring at the television mounted on the wall. Harold Versery sits beside them in an equally well-padded, high-

backed chair; his eyes are closed, his head is resting on the wing of the chair.

The television set is tuned to ANNN, the All Nation News Network. The view moves toward the TV until it fills the screen. The face of Leanne Flambeau appears. She is wearing a white hard-hat, and standing in front of the Interceptor vehicle. She gestures toward the vehicle with her microphone and speaks.

> LEANNE: Oklahoma and the nation no longer need fear the intrusion of visitors from other worlds. The vehicle you see behind me, the Interceptor – sometimes known as "the Moth" – has proven itself to be the shield that will protect us from aliens and forever prevent a recurrence of the abductions that terrorized the citizens of Ponca City. Although it does look like a moth, we can think of it as our guardian angel, thanks to the know-how of the American Aerospace industry.

ANGLE ON THE COUCH

> ANNA (*leaping forward, pointing at the TV*): It's Leanne! There she is. (*waves the remote at the TV, clicks frantically, and raises the volume*)

> EVITA: What's she doing on the ANNN channel?

> ANNA: Didn't you read about her in the paper—in the entertainment section? She got promoted. She's in the big time now.

ANGLE ON HAROLD IN THE CHAIR

> HAROLD (*waking, looking around*): Can't you ladies watch without having the TV blaring?

ANGLE ON THE COUCH

> OCTAVIA (*ignoring Harold*): She's right. Now that we have that Interceptor thing, there have been no more kidnappings of

old people. The aliens know we can blast them out of the sky, so they've gone back to where they came from. I feel a lot safer now.

EVITA: I've been sleeping better at night.

ANNA: Blast them out of the sky? I thought I read in the papers that they captured one of our Interceptors when we tried to launch it.

OCTAVIA: They *thought* they captured one, but when they examined *our* ship, they realized how technologically advanced it was over theirs. The aliens didn't know what to do. I read that their leader met with the President of the RTI Company and surrendered.

ANGLE ON HAROLD IN THE CHAIR

HAROLD (*waving at his wife*): Could you turn the sound down just a *little*, please?

ANGLE ON COUCH

OCTAVIA: Might as well turn it off. What's-her-name is gone. They're showing that insurance commercial.

EVITA (*quietly*): No! No! Pretend we're still watching. If we turn it off, somebody will put on the noisy sports channel.

ANNA: There's nobody else here now.

OCTAVIA (*whispering*): Only that new guy, the one over there.

She jabs her finger toward her left.

CUT TO: WINDOW CHAIR

A gray-haired man is seated in the overstuffed chair by the window. He seems preoccupied with some activity outside the building.

EVITA (*leaning over to Octavia to speak directly in her ear*): You mean the strange one. I've never seen him in a crafts class.

He never watches TV or wants to play cards. He started coming here two weeks ago, but he doesn't socialize at all.

ANNA: I don't remember ever seeing him around town. Usually you run into everybody sooner or later at the market – or the doctor's office.

Harold walks to the front of the couch, grabs the TV remote from Anna, and mutes the sound. He bends over the three women, briefly turning his head toward the man in the chair to see if he is listening.

HAROLD (*barely audible*): Milo, the gardener for the senior center, told me that guy talks to him once in a while. He asks a lot of questions about the flowers. Milo says you'd think he'd never seen a petunia before.

OCTAVIA: Maybe that's it. Maybe he grew up where they don't have petunias. Does anybody know where he's from?

HAROLD: He told Milo his name is Meertz, and that he's from Peoria.

Harold drops the remote on a shelf by the TV, walks back to his chair, falls into it, and closes his eyes. Evita, Octavia, and Anna bend forward to dig through a stack of old magazines on the coffee table in front of the couch.

The view pulls back to show the whole room. To the left, the man by the window is examining a vase of flowers on a small table beside his chair. The screen darkens and fades to black.

ROLL THE CREDITS

CAST OF THE INTERCEPTOR PROGRAM

Ponca City, Oklahoma

Leanne Flambeau	KPUT Television news reporter
Durwood Pyle	KPUT Television news cameraman
Orville Pressfit	Aircraft engine mechanic
Harold Versery	Senior citizen
Anna Versery	Senior citizen
Octavia Genarian	Senior citizen
Evita Añejo	Senior citizen
Ray Kathode	Television salesman
Samuel Bigstaff	Mayor
Justin Case	Police Chief
Wendell Ream	City Manager
George King	Commissioner
Dayan Knight	Commissioner
Rene Rook	Commissioner
Elizabeth Queen	Commissioner
Alice Allcaps	Reporter for the Ponca Post

Washington, DC

Thelma Grayfield	First woman President of the USA
Hazel Lazer	President's personal secretary
Lamar Ferret	White House Chief of Staff
Edith Wormbook	Director - White House OSTP

Repulsive Technology, Incorporated

Joyce Plaisant	Public Relations Specialist
Edward Confirme	Manager - Customer Relations
Walter Masterly	President - Repulsive Technology, Inc.
Angelique Del Mundo	Senior Admin to Walter Masterly
John Fulbrane	Chief Engineer
Corey Layt	Engineering specialist
Roy Cordu	Valve designer
Stefan Espacamore	New engineering hire
Anita Guardley	Admin to John Fulbrane
Gregory Korjul	Director - Government Relations
Daniel Brazewell	Vice President – Manufacturing

Repulsive Technology, Incorporated (cont.)

Al Gurithum	Manager - Systems Analysis Group
Leonard Lenz	Staff member - Media Services
Florence Kahdasill	Deputy Dir. - Contract Administration
Sandra Binding	Director - Contract Administration
Bing Chang	Mechanical engineer - recent hire
Chandra Patel	Purchasing agent
Celia Cakpati	Financial Analyst
Kimberly Chi	Manager - Materials Engineering
Susan Shi	Systems Engineering Specialist
Stanley Snappi	Designer - Ground Support Equipment
Michael Headknuckle	Manager - Performance Analysis
Mary Snackmeister	Materials Engineer
Steven Acheever	Manager – Advanced Concepts
Tim Fernway	Cafeteria Manager
Rudy Vault	Manager - Data Classification
Leo Meertz	Deputy Manager - Data Classification
Hap Cawshun	Lead Test Engineer
Bernard Blastof	Senior Technical Fellow
Arthur Gumme	Graphic Artist
Murray Jaysize	Designer
Constance Harmony	Manager - Training
Norman Nevercutt	Test engineer
Polly Propalean	Director - Processes and Materials
Harry Handover	Director - Field Support
Terence Talltree	Director - Financial Services
Clara Closchek	Travel Audit Analyst
Melvin Wholeham	Cafeteria Manager
Warren Neadle	Bing Chang's manager
Lydia Quigley	Chief Librarian
Arnold Trouver	Lotaqual First Article Inspector

White Sands Missile Range

Captain Barry Haggard	Interceptor Project Officer
Major Phillip Ogeny	Captain Haggard's CO
Ralph Rigid	Air Force Inspector
Burton Coyel	KPOW Television News Cameraman

Planet Peoria

Sigmondis Dredcoast   Squadron Flight Commander
Dox Alturi   New RTI employee - PEP program

Supporting Roles

Dr. Clarence Peer   Professor of Cosmology at OU
Hank Keptiks   Staff writer - Cover-up Magazine
Arnold Trouver   Auditor with Lotaqual Consultants
Young Man   Ponca Post lobby clerk
Barber   Owner of shop near RTI
Clipper the Clown   Entertainer at Interceptor launch